A Floating Life 李白

ALSO BY SIMON ELEGANT

A Chinese Wedding

A Floating Life

The Adventures of 李白 Li Po

AN HISTORICAL NOVEL

對酒不覺暝
落花盈我衣
醉起步溪月
鳥還人亦稀

Simon Elegant

THE ECCO PRESS

for Ling

THE ECCO PRESS
100 West Broad Street
Hopewell, New Jersey 08525

Published simultaneously in Canada by
Penguin Books Canada Ltd., Ontario
Printed in the United States of America

Library of Congress Cataloging-in-Publication Data
Elegant, Simon, 1960–
A floating life : the adventures of Li Po : an historical novel / by Simon Elegant.—1st Ecco ed.
p. cm.
ISBN 0-88001-559-4
1. Li, Po, 701–762—Fiction. 2. China—History—T'ang dynasty, 618–907—Fiction. 3. Poets, Chinese—T'ang dynasty, 618–907—Fiction. 4. Civilization, Medieval—Fiction. I. Title.
PS3555.L373F58 1997
813'.54—dc21 97-10202

Designed by Susanna Gilbert, The Typeworks
The text of this book is set in Veljovic

9 8 7 6 5 4 3 2 1

FIRST EDITION 1997

Now the heavens and earth are the hostel's of creation
and time has seen a full hundred generations.
Ah, this floating life, like a dream.
True happiness is so rare!

—LI PO, from *A Banquet with My Cousins on a Spring Night in the Peach Garden*

one 李白

IT IS TWILIGHT. AN ELABORATE RIVER BARGE, FLAT bottomed and equipped with twenty oars on each side as well as a vestigial mast, is rocking on its moorings. The barge is extravagantly lit, bedecked with hundreds of swinging lanterns and torches guttering in the rising wind, the only bright object in the gathering gloom.

From his small sampan Wang Lung wearily contemplates the barge. After a long pause, he rocks the single oar back and forth, sending his little boat skimming up to the barge. He boards unnoticed—there is no one to be seen on deck—and makes his way down to the central cabin, drawn by the sound of loud voices, music, and song. Banks of round, red and white waxpaper lanterns along the walls light up the cabin brilliantly. At one end is a group of musicians sitting cross-legged on a slightly raised dais. At the other end of the room are the low dining tables arranged in a semicircle, crowded with what are obviously the local worthies, mostly middle-aged men sleek with wealth and smug with power.

In the center of the room stands Li Po, a huge man, once muscular, now running to fat in late middle age but still an imposing figure, his full beard bristling out, his head bare, topknot loose and hair wild, sleeves rolled up, the tails of his gown tucked into his belt. As Wang slips into the room, the poet snatches up an enormous brush tipped with a clump of bristles almost the length of the horse's tail from which the hairs came, dips it into a large bowl of black paint, then freezes dramatically, brush poised over the long sheet of pearly silk that is spread out on the low table in front of him. Silence falls in the room and all watch as black paint wells out of the supersaturated brush, a single enormous drop forming with agonizing slowness at the tip, swelling fatter and fatter until finally it detaches itself and falls towards the pristine length of silk.

With a sharp stabbing motion, Li Po plunges the brush downwards, outracing the drop of ink, and in one explosive stroke blazes out a swirling character a foot long on the top half of the silk sheet. Throwing the implement aside impatiently, he selects a small writing brush hanging from a bamboo rack, dips it into the ink without looking, and once again halts, the new brush poised above the gleaming white rectangle. But no drop forms. The violence of its retrieval has sprayed the excess ink onto the table's polished rosewood surface, just missing the silk. A glance upwards at his audience, a small knowing smile, and Li Po begins to write, muttering to himself as the lines form under his flowing hand, never hesitating, twelve lines of characters appearing as if by magic, the only break in the stream the poet's quick dart to the ink bowl to recharge his brush, the only sound his heavy breathing.

The poem completed, Li Po throws the brush down and calls for another jug of wine. He then steps aside to allow the local magistrate, who is the guest of honor, to read the poem out loud.

A stunned silence follows, true appreciation, honest disbelief. Then the hall fills with acclamation, shouts and tables banged, the guests crowding around Li Po, now slumped on a bench behind the rosewood table, calling again for another pot of wine, which he sucks down in two massive draughts. Li Po looks around, clearly bored by the praise, listening only when the magistrate mentions the small honorarium—a mere token of the town's appreciation, perhaps if they could have the privilege of framing the scroll, to be put in the place of honor in the courthouse—the official now tugging surreptitiously at the precious document as Li Po's increasingly wild gestures threaten to knock over the bowl of paint.

And then, without warning, the poet grows peevish, grumbling about the money in his shrill voice, accepting the bags of coin with little grace and no words of thanks, his slurred speech hardly comprehensible. Finally Li Po staggers to his feet and announces he is going to bed, but he doesn't move, propping himself up on the table, his hands resting on the edge of the scroll, the magistrate making small pleading gestures, desperate to get his prize away, tugging ineffectually, pulling the sheet out from under the heavy bronze lions that anchor it onto the table, the poet glowering at him, his eyes shining pinkly as though boiled in his skull, his face an alarming scarlet. But then a look of greenish blankness passes over Li Po's face and he slumps back down onto the bench, the magistrate immediately whipping the still glistening scroll from the table, turning and passing it to a hovering servant, turning back, all oily smiles again, only to find that the poet, at last, has slid off the bench and onto the floor. The magistrate steps carefully over the muddy boots that stick out from under the table and calls for his servants, giving the unconscious poet only a single glance—an unfathomable mixture of awe, envy, and contempt—as he passes through the forward doors and out onto the deck, robes flying behind him, entourage scurrying to keep up, his servants calling for the official barge.

For a moment the room is empty—the musicians and servants have disappeared—and Wang, utterly exhausted but impelled by an uncontrollable curiosity, crosses the polished wood floor, moving noiselessly in his cloth shoes until he is standing over the poet, looking down at the strangely bushy beard, the wide brow, the heavy eyebrows, and the slashing nose. In falling, Li Po has knocked over the wine pot, which now lies on its side rolling to and fro with the motion of the barge, gurgling quietly, the remaining wine soaking into the poet's hair, which has come undone from his topknot and is spread in wispy abundance around his lolling head. Wang bends to pick up the vessel, but as he reaches out, the poet's right eye suddenly pops open and his hand darts out to grasp the boy's wrist.

"Who are you?" he grunts, holding Wang's wrist so hard it hurts.

"Wang Lung," the boy gasps, "Wang Lung. My father sent me."

"Who's your father?"

"Old Wang, sir, Wang Tao, the vintner at Tangchao. Yesterday you were at his shop. You asked him to send me. I can write."

"What?" The eye is beginning to slip closed again.

"I can write, you asked for a secretary, an, an amanuensis, you said, to write your life story, 'to tell those dogsheads at court a thing or two,' you said."

"Yes, yes, I remember now." The bleary pink eye closes again. "Has that fool of a magistrate gone?"

"Yes sir."

"Good. Call my servant to take me to bed. We begin in the morning."

The grip on the boy's wrist relaxes and Li's hand drops to the deck. Within seconds he is snoring. Wang looks up and sees that three men have come into the room. They are dressed in gray servants' robes and, ignoring the boy, they walk over to where Li Po lies. With the ease of long practice, two reach under one of his arms and lift him, still snoring, to his feet. Each then swings one of the unconscious poet's arms over a shoulder while the third picks up his ankles and the procession shuffles out, leaving Wang Lung alone once more.

The boy sighs and begins to make his way towards the exit

at the far end. But he stops as he passes the writing table. The row of brushes has not been cleared, and the coarse hemp paper on which the silk sheet rested is still in place. Glancing around, the boy hesitates, then picks up the brush Li Po used to write his poem and weighs it in his hand. The brush, which is colored in mottled tan and chestnut and made of tortoiseshell, feels heavy between his fingers, pulling his hand down towards the paper. He has hardly ever written with a brush and ink. In the village his father had supplied free wine for a decade to a forlorn—and whenever possible drunk—student who in return drummed the elementary classics into the boy's head. But then it was always with a piece of chalk and a slate, always that impermanence, the ephemerality that could be wiped out with a swipe of a wet cloth. Here, with brush and ink on paper, what's written down stays forever, short of fire or flood.

The boy dips the brush in the pool of ink and carefully writes his name on the hempen sheet, pauses, admires the two characters, then with a secret smile to himself, he bends over the table again and quickly scrawls two characters in front of his own:

宰君王龍

Now the characters read, "His Lordship the Steward, Wang Lung." He nods his head in satisfaction, pleased with the way the simplicity of his family name, *Wang*—king—acts like a fulcrum, balancing the heavier, more complex characters on either side: the elegant dignity of *Tsai Chun*, the two characters comprising a magistrate's honorary designation on the left, and his personal name, *Lung*, or dragon, bristly and proud on the right. Idly he writes his name again, this time preceded by "Prefect," then again, with "Governor," and "Omissioner," "Censor," and finally "Chief Minister." The last looks particularly fine.

A sudden clatter from a hallway outside startles the boy, and he tears off the lower half of the paper on which he has been writing, rolls it into a tube, and slips it into his sleeve, then runs lightly across the floor and is out of the room before the servants appear at the far door with their mops and wooden pails.

In the morning he wakes abruptly, tense, startled. He has slept under the stage in the large main room, squeezing in underneath after the servants finished their cleaning and resting his head on the small cloth sack he has carried with him. He was wakened in the early hours of the morning by the storm which had threatened all night, the boat rocking back and forth as the wind whipped up the river, the rain beating against the wooden shutters that cover the windows, a comforting sound that eventually lulled him back to sleep. Emerging now from his hiding place in the stern and slipping out onto the deck, he finds that all is fresh, the sky pale, washed-out blue in the early morning light, the breeze wafting in from the shore bearing the green dewy smell of plants and trees grateful for the life-giving rain.

Wang Lung hears the sound of clashing steel from the prow and walks over to investigate. The foredeck, normally filled with tables and mats for the disportment of passengers, has been cleared, and Li Po and another man are facing each other. Both are holding swords by their sides, the tips of which have been covered by a small cloth cap, and both are stripped down to cotton pantaloons cinched at the waist by bright red sashes. The poet's opponent, a fit-looking man in his thirties, appears unruffled, but Li Po is breathing heavily, his broad torso and small pot belly covered in a glistening sheen of sweat. As the boy watches, Li Po brings his sword up and advances, stamps his foot once, then lunges. The swords flash and ring in the early morning sunlight as the men move up and down the deck, probing for weakness. After several minutes the poet is clearly tiring, panting harshly, reduced to parrying. The other man, sensing his opponent's weakness, closes in, pushing Li Po backward until he is almost pressed up against the wall of the cabin. His defense grows weaker and slower until, just as all seems lost—the boy is holding his breath, waiting for Li Po to concede—the poet suddenly leaps to the attack, pressing his startled opponent into retreat with a series of slashing lunges and thrusts. The younger man loses his balance for a moment, stumbles, and Li Po is upon him, his blade probing at the base of the other's sword. With an almost invisible flick of the wrist, the younger man is disarmed, stands shaking his arm and staring in surprise at his sword, which has flown loose from his hand and lies on the deck several feet away. Li Po is frozen in front of him, his weapon held high for the death thrust.

The boy lets out a whoop of admiration and Li Po glances around and grins at him, then turns to his opponent.

"The old man still knows a few tricks, eh, Mr. Colonel of the Guards?"

The other man smiles back—a slightly strained smile—and says, "As you very well know, Master Li, I am only a humble Major, but yes, it was a nice little trick."

"Aye, and if our swords didn't have these foolish little caps covering their teeth, you'd have a nice little scar and a good deal of blood to make you remember this little 'trick.' It might save your life sometime when you are fighting someone a little closer to your own age."

Li Po turns and gestures to Wang Lung.

"Run and get us a couple of towels," he commands.

"Sir, I don't know where the towels are."

Li Po turns back towards the boy.

"What?"

"I don't know where the towels are, sir. I am Wang Lung,

the vintner's son, Wang Tao of Tangchao. You spoke to me last night. You said you wanted me to write down your words."

"Last night?" The poet looks baffled. "I said that to you last night? All I remember is that pompous clown of a magistrate."

"No, sir, you told my father, at his shop in Tangchao two days ago."

"Yes, yes," Li Po smiles. "I remember. Your father is the one who makes that delicious "Spring in Autumn" vintage. I had completely forgotten. I told him I needed a clerk to write down the story of my life. I said that I would send it to court to prove my innocence, to show them the kind of man I really am. It seemed like an excellent idea at the time, but. . . . "

He walks over to where the boy is standing and looks intently down at him. Li Po is half again taller, bulky against the other's adolescent slimness. The poet's eyes are clear, his cheeks flushed red with exertion. The only sign of his indulgence the night before—and many, many nights before that—are the heavy pouches under his eyes, the skin of which is dark brown and coarse, the flesh sagging and puffy.

"But you are very young. Can you really write? Do you know enough characters? This won't be some farming manual I will be dictating."

"I am fifteen, sir," the boy says proudly, "and know the four classics as well as any man. When I am older, my father says I must take the imperial exams, become an official."

"Exams, exams, always these cursed exams," Li Po's face darkens for a moment, then clears. "But, why not a vintner's son? Why not?" He stands, staring musingly at the boy for a moment, then smiles and shakes his head.

"I and my friend the Major still need to dry ourselves, however. You will have to vary your duties. For now, go fetch towels from the valet below. And if you are to take the exams, you must know a little more than the four classics. You must understand the later elucidators, the minor classics, Lieh-tzu, Chuang-tzu, and so on, the neo-Confucianists, then the great commentaries, the commentaries on the commentaries, you must have an understanding of the bibliographies, the addenda, the apocrypha; it never ends, boy. It will eat you up. You will disappear into the maw of all that scholarship and never be seen again. Give it up. Go back to your wine shop in the village before it is too late."

The boy looks troubled yet still determined.

"But I promised my father I would study."

"Yes, that is a simple answer the Confucians would love. Confounding the old iconoclast. The disrupter of the natural order of things stunned by simple filial piety. How droll." Li Po sighs. "It's all right. You can ignore my ravings. You shall study, as you wish. Later this morning you can begin work on Chuang-tzu. Once evening comes, the time for revelry and song, then we will begin to tell tales."

He gestures, and the boy turns obediently and disappears down a companionway.

It is early evening when Li Po summons the boy, shortly after the barge has anchored for the night. The tables and mats have all been laid out once again in their horseshoe configuration on the foredeck, and the poet is lolling in state in the place of honor, his lute lying flat on the table in front of him, to one side a pot of wine made of cloudy jade. But this time he is alone; there are no other places set save an area on his right that has been laid with a sheaf of paper, an ink stone, brushes on a rack, a bowl of sand, a mortar and a pestle, and a slab of ink. Li Po waves the boy over.

"Come, come. Grind and mush some ink, then copy me my words faithfully and I'll reward you with a bowl of wine."

While the boy goes about his task of preparing the ink, Li Po strums on the lute, humming something under his breath.

When the ink is barely ready, he snatches up a piece of paper and brush, dips it into the ink, and rapidly scrawls out two ten-line stanzas:

Through the Gorges

Blue sky above
mountains on either side,
the river bending so sharp,
the cliffs so steep
that the waters sometimes appear to
end in front of us,
bubbling and hissing,
the river roaring as the rockwalls squeeze
ever tighter.

For three mornings we have set out to pass
Yellow Ox rapids;
Three evenings we have had to turn back.
Three days and three nights.
I wonder how many more
of my hairs have turned grey
on our little craft
in that time

Li Po passes the finished sheet to the boy, who automatically throws a handful of sand over the wet surface. He reads the poem, then looks up and around. The broad expanse of the river stretches away ahead and to the right, flat and unruffled, its surface speckled with tens of river craft, full-sized junks, their broad russet sails unmoving in the still air, fishing boats awaiting the onset of night, their lamps already lit and swaying over the water, even tiny sampans moving slowly but steadily, propelled with rhythmic ease by their single boatmen standing in the stern and swaying the huge oar back and forth. A cloud of dragonflies hovers overhead. On the near bank, to the left, Wang Lung can see the green of rice paddies and the brown humpback shapes of water buffalo wallowing in mud pools. Here and there is a clump of trees indicating a village, usually hazy with wood smoke, whose pungent odor tangs the air. He looks over at the poet, who catches his quizzical glance and shrugs.

"We'll be at the gorges soon enough. And, anyway, I *feel* becalmed."

The boy looks down to hide his smile.

"Now," Li Po says, not noticing, or at least pretending not to, "pick up your brush and prepare yourself. It is time now you did some work. Let me see, how to begin? I suppose first you ought to have a trial run; then we'll see about starting. Nothing from the classics of course; that would be too easy. Something light would be best. Let me see. Yes, here we go. I thought of something like this the other night but was too drunk to write it down:

A pot of wine amidst the flowers,
I sit alone, no friends to drink with.
I raise my cup to toast the moon;
With my shadow, that makes three of us.
But the moon, of course, has never
Known the joy of drinking,
And as to my shadow, it just
Mimics my tipsy capers.
But for now,
I'll have to make do
With these two
Or waste this Spring evening.

I sing; the moon rocks in time.
I dance; my shadow flickers and tumbles.

While I'm still sober,
We'll make merry together,
Then, drunk, go our separate ways.
But let's pledge eternal friendship
and meet again beyond the Milky Way.

"A little whimsical, you might say, but there's always room for whimsy as far as I am concerned. No more of those turgid, whiny elegies on life's brevity! Now, let me see how you did."

Wang Lung dusts down the paper and hands it to Li Po.

"Not bad," the poet says, scanning the characters. "There are a few strokes missing here and there, and this character is wrong altogether, I am afraid: It's 'flicker,' not 'shake.' Still, not a bad effort at all for a vintner's son. Speaking of which," the poet pours out a cup of wine and hands it to the boy, "here is the reward I promised you. Drink up, drink up!"

He tips back his own cup, but the boy hesitates, cradling the warm cup in his hands. His father—the example of the inebriate student daily before him—had always strictly enjoined him from drinking wine until he passed the baccalaureate exams. But one cup can't do much harm, he thinks, and tips the hot wine into his mouth, the liquid coursing down his throat and pooling in a glowing puddle in his stomach.

It is almost completely dark now and the servants have brought out a pair of long, red paper-covered lampions on wooden stands, which they place on either side of Wang Lung. Overhead the first stars are beginning to twinkle.

"I suppose we should begin," says Li Po, who has already refilled his own cup and is standing on the rail, gazing into the darkness. "That is what I brought you here for. But somehow I am not ready yet. Now I approach it, I find myself strangely reluctant to go ahead, almost as though I was afraid. But of what?"

He falls silent for a time and the boy watches in a flush of slightly dazed appreciation as more and more stars appear in the velvet black sky and the bright disk of the moon peeps out from behind a row of hills on the left bank, then slowly raises itself up into full view to hang over the river, sparkling the waters. Finally Li Po turns back from the rail and sees Wang Lung gazing open-mouthed at the moon. He declaims:

On the bank,
A gentle breeze soughs through the tall grass;
Above, nothing but
That single mast darting into the
Empty, blazing night
Whose stars swell gravid
Over the vast plain,
Whose moon surges in the Great River's rush.

"I suppose you don't know that one. Unfortunately—and you won't hear me quote other people's poetry very often—I didn't write it. It's one of Tu Fu's, poor fellow. A great poet, no doubt about it, probably the only one who can touch me, though he has a few things to learn yet. But he can be so, well, *personal* sometimes. It's almost embarrassing. In this case, for example, you'd think that with such a beginning he'd confine that poem to an exposition on the beauty of the river, perhaps a reflection on the ephemerality of beauty, the usual thing. But no, as always, he has to drag himself into it and moan about the fact that no one appreciates his poetry. The rest of the poem goes like this:

What of my literary labors?
As we all know, they've brought me
Nothing but fame and fortune

('Rank sarcasm,' Li Po interjects, shaking his head. 'That's nothing but bitter sarcasm. Very crude.')

And my official rank?
Simply this:
'Too old and sick; retired.'

So, drifting and drifting,
I float
Between sky and water;
A seagull.

"Terrible stuff. Not worthy of him at all. I always used to tell him to be a bit jollier, stop brooding about life so much, but he couldn't help it, it is in his nature. After I hadn't seen him for many years, I received a batch of his poems, a particularly glum batch, and I wrote a little ditty, just as a joke:

Was that you, Tu Fu,
That I saw on Fanguo
Mountain, wearing a
Broad bamboo hat against
The noonday sun?

How thin you've grown.
Have you been suffering
For your poetry again?

"He took it very well, you understand, wrote me a note saying how funny he thought it was. In fact, he thought I was referring to his method of composition, which is hard, sweating labor, especially compared to me, though that is true of anyone. All the empire knows that I can write a thousand verses in an hour. Even Tu Fu has said so himself; remember his *"Eight Immortals of the Wine Cup"*?

As to Li Po, from each
jug of wine a hundred poems bloom

"But for poor old Tu Fu, he's lucky if he can squeeze out a sonnet in a week. I often wonder if it's worth the trouble when you have to work so hard at it. No fun, no fun at all."

Here, he gestures to the boy, indicating that the wine flask is empty. Another is summoned and, despite the boy's protests, Li Po presses another cup on him.

"Anyway," the poet says as they drain their cups, "I always thought he knew the whole thing was just a joke, but a few years ago, I received from someone else one of his poems about me. Let me see, how did it go?

Autumn comes and
I look upon you,
Still a tumbleweed,
Blowing with the wind.

Ashamed that the immortality pill
Remains elusive,
You drink your fill, sing crazy songs,
Pass your days in vain.

Tell me, all that shouting and gesturing,
The wild bravado:
Who exactly are you trying to impress?

"When I read that, I knew he must have been deeply hurt by my little jest. Otherwise, how to explain that vicious piece of doggerel? Not that it's true, of course. It is sheer invention. What does he know of my alchemical researches? And Tu Fu is hardly one to talk about drinking too much. Fellow has a weak head but loves to drink. The number of times I've seen him pass out, or puking his guts up in some ditch, the sanctimonious wretch.

"In any case I soon came to realize that there was nothing of Tu Fu in that poem. Nothing of the essential man I knew and loved. It must have been someone copying his style, some malicious courtier playing games, or some poetic rival trying to drive a wedge between us. The gods know, I've had to deal with enough of that in my life. And, after all, everyone in China knows that we were very close once, very close. The more I pondered it, the more certain I was that it had been written by an imposter. It's been so long since I saw him, more than ten years, but he couldn't have changed so much, even with all his disappointments and trials. Not the Tu Fu I knew, or the one who still writes me long affectionate letters. He is a sweet man. A sweet, sweet man. I could never stay angry at him for long. . . . "

Li Po trails off, absent-mindedly picks up the flask of wine and drains it, a servant appearing with a new one without being called. He steps over again to the railing, a fresh cup in hand. All is quiet save the whisper of the breeze in the rigging and the ripple of water against the side of the anchored boat. The boy, who has long ago put aside his brush, rests his heavy head in his hands for a moment.

After a while, a long while, Li Po, without turning round, begins to speak again:

"I think I'm ready now, yes, here:

I am the blue lotus man, the banished immortal.
For thirty years I've hid my fame in wineshops.
I am the poet, the Taoist master,
the wandering swordsman and mountain hermit,
full of contempt for the red dust of town,
for cap and gown,
the only free man in a land of Confucian chains.

They say I have eyes of flashing fire,
a voice like a tiger's screech. . . .

Here, noticing a sound like a low, discrete snore, Li Po turns. The boy is fast asleep, his head pillowed in his arms. The poet smiles.

"Well, it was wrong anyway," he murmurs to himself. "It's not poetry I must make now; it's time for talk. Just talk."

Sighing, he walks over to the boy, gently wakes him and sends him below to bed.

two 李白

THE NEXT DAY THERE IS NO SWORDPLAY ON DECK. Wang Lung is called away early from his breakfast of rice gruel in the galley. On the foredeck Li Po sits in the same position as the night before, but this time with a pot of tea in front of him. A canopy has been stretched over the tables to shield them from the sun.

"Come, come," the poet says briskly, "we have much work to do. Sit. Pick up the brush. The ink is prepared. The servants have been overenthusiastic. They have ground enough for a thousand life stories. Are you ready?"

"Yes, Master."

"Just call me by my name, Li Po. Everyone does. And if you must use a title, call me Academician. It's the only one besides 'Poet' to which I am entitled. Now, let us begin. Today I want to start by talking about birds:

"All my life, I have loved birds. When I was a boy we lived in the mountains in Shu, a thousand miles upriver from here, and we kept a house full of songbirds. All women like birds and my mother and sisters were no exception. Most of the time I was the only man in the house, for my father was traveling as a river merchant; some years we would only see him at the end of the season, during winter when the river was too low to travel on easily with a heavily loaded boat; some years not at all. It was a household of women.

My father had four wives, but only my mother, his first lady, had produced a son. I had eight sisters, four older and four younger.

"So, as the only child who was allowed out of the house, I was in charge of trapping the birds. I was young, ten or eleven years old, but went everywhere by myself. My mother and my sisters tried to control me, but they couldn't. I would leave the house before dawn and climb into the hills behind the town, up through the terraced rice fields; I could bound up the mountain in those days like a young goat. The farmers thought I was a cloud-stepping immortal: I used to run up through their fields, slipping in and out of the morning mist, carrying only a little food wrapped in a cloth bag and a special net my sisters had made out of pongee silk for me, so light you could fold it into your sleeve and so cunningly constructed that the stick I carried against snakes could be fixed onto the end of the net. It usually took me until almost lunchtime to get far enough away from the town so that the birds were no longer scared of human beings, just indifferently curious, and angry if they were disturbed. I would eat the wheat cakes and bean curd my mother had prepared, then stand in an open glade for a while listening to the birds. When I found a clearing I liked, I would spread a thick layer of crumbs from my lunch in front of the trees, then wait. Each time I saw a bird I wanted, I stepped forward quietly from behind the tree and caught it in my net. I would hold the mouth of my sack open under the net with one hand, quickly thrust the struggling bird in with the other, then tie the sack shut. After about twenty minutes more, birds would be back for the crumbs and I could take another one. Bang, bang, bang. In an hour I had five birds tweeting and fluttering in my sack.

"I soon discovered that all birds are not the same. Thrushes were the easiest to catch, shy but always feeding on the ground so I could net them easily. But when I brought back a sackful, my mother laughed at me, took them to the door, and opened the mouth of the sack so that a cloud of birds burst out into our courtyard, tumbling through the air in a flurry of twittering, flashing feathers—violet, indigo, scarlet, and white—until they recovered their senses and flew straight upwards and away across the green roof tiles.

"'These little ones are no good for keeping, Hsiao Po,' she said, squatting down and handing the empty sack back to me with a smile. She always called me Hsiao Po, 'Little White,' even though my real name is Tai Po, 'Great White,' after the planet Venus, the warrior's star, the great white shining planet: my star.

"My mother explained to me that some birds will die in captivity, however carefully they are looked after, regardless of which foods they are given or how big and lavishly equipped their cages are. 'These little thrushes have very big hearts. They are proud. A little stupid, but very proud. They will beat themselves to death on the bars of a cage rather than sing for us, so we must let them go.' It is a lesson I have remembered all my life.

"After that I was more careful. I studied the birds before I caught them and came to know each different kind, what their song was like, what they ate, what season of the year they visited our hills. The buntings and finches and robins all could be caught on the ground with the net, though some were much more difficult to trap than others. Finches ate seeds on the ground and had conical beaks, were mostly mute or gave out only harsh squawking sounds. The tree sparrow could always be found around harvest season, clustering around the threshing sheds to pick through the chaff. It lived well in cages and pleased my sisters with its pink, black, white and lavender coat and its bright orange beak. You probably know the bird: it is the common companion of itinerant fortune-tellers who hang the cage on a long stick by the side of the road as a sign of their business. I once sold a few of these in the market, but my mother scolded me when she found out and took the twenty cash I had been paid, saying I should be ashamed of myself, hawking my wares in the market like some common shopkeeper's son.

"I didn't go back to the market until much later. By then I knew what was really valuable, not songbirds, but medicinal birds. Or kingfishers, of course, for their feathers. I never saw a kingfisher in the mountains, but coucals—the hairy chicken we called it, though it bears little resemblance to a chicken, more like a black crow but with chestnut wings, an evil red eye, and a haughty look—those are easy to catch if you know how. The call is very distinctive, 'poom, poom, poom,' like one of those little drums the Sogdians use for their dances, then a strange chuckle that sounds like water emptying out of a flask. They nest on the ground, in heavy undergrowth, so if you are quiet you can trace the call easily and catch them brooding. The beak is ground up and burnt, the ashes mixed in with the bird's blood and taken as a decoction against breathlessness and lung diseases, most often consumption. Usually I could get only the female like this, and just one at a time—their nests are far apart—but it was enough. Doctors would pay two hundred cash each in the market for a coucal, enough for a great many pots of wine.

"The greenfinch was not so brilliant as the coucal, subdued yellow and brown, but best for song, a low trilling call like a flute that sounded so melancholy that my sisters always said it made them cry. They were always talking of lost love and sighing over those pining poems of the time of the partition: the moon shining in on the concubine's moth eyebrows, pearl tresses and kingfisher feathers drooping from her chignon, slim jade fingers tightening the lute stops as she plays softly in the darkest hour of the night, awaiting the call from the palace that never comes. I hardly need repeat those hackneyed phrases for it is, as all know, a commonplace subject, so familiar that all that is needed by any competent poet is suggestion, not explanation. Years afterward I wrote this, called 'Marble Stairs Grievance':

White dew settles on the marble stairs;
The night draws on.
At last, her stockings soaked, she steps inside,
Lets fall the crystal bead curtain,
Gazes through it, swaying and tinkling,
At the autumn moon.

"Robins were impossible to keep. They would not eat seeds, even when starving. Later I read the chapter on perfect happiness in the *Chuang Tzu*, a story about a seagull that landed on the railing of the Marquis of Lu's tower. Exhausted and bedraggled, it had obviously been blown inland by a storm. The marquis put the bird in a cage in his ancestral temple. He played the nine-tone Shao music for the bird and fed it meat and wine from the Tai-Lao sacrifices. But the bird ate nothing, left the wine untouched, and in three days it was dead. 'You should nourish each animal with what is natural to it, not what is natural to you,' the text concludes. Like much else in the *Chuang Tzu*, I think the story is an elaborate joke, or at least ironic. Who would be so stupid as to perform the complex ritual sacrifices to a bird? Personally I much prefer Chuang-tzu's excursions into the fantastic—glorious poetry, glorious. It often doesn't mean a great deal, of course, but what does that matter? The language is unrivaled; that is enough for me. And, on the other hand, it is also full of blunt common sense. In one passage a foolish courtier tries to pin down Chuang-tzu about the exact nature of the Way:

Where is it? the courtier asked, waving his hand
around, can you point it out to me this Way?
It is in the tiles of the roof, Chuang-tzu replied.
So high? the courtier said, sarcastically. Where else?
It is in the ants.
So low? Where else?
It is in your piss and shit.
Charming, this Way of yours. What else?
It is in the emperor's piss and shit, too, Chuang-tzu
said, and the courtier was struck silent, knowing
that any remark he might make could get him
beheaded.

"The warblers made the most beautiful songs, but they are very shy, difficult to catch, always skulking in the bushes. And they are unattractive, the color of mud. Once I even tried to catch sunbirds, all flame and ocher and lime. They were tiny, wings beating a thousand times a minute, hovering over the flowers, hibiscus or peony or poinsettia, then settling on the stems and twisting and turning so that their long beaks, which are curved like the swords of the Turks, could get at the nectar. They, too, usually died when caged.

"Then for a time I gave up on beauty and sought amusement, catching only mynas. The black ones are the best. You can recognize them easily by the band of white across their wings, like soot and snowflakes flashing in the air when they fly from one tree to the next. I liked to teach them to talk, of course. Once after I had begun to study the classics, I spent a long time with two particular birds, keeping them in separate rooms. One I taught the words from the *Analects*: 'Store up knowledge; study without flagging.' I sat with the bird for hours, repeating the words over and over until every time I came into the room it would squawk:

'Store up knowledge, study without flagging, study without flagging, study without flagging.'

"The other bird, my Taoist myna, I taught just as carefully from the *Tao Te Ching* until it too would repeat the words whenever anyone came into the room: 'Banish all learning; exterminate knowledge. Banish all learning, exterminate knowledge.' It was childish, this delight in contradiction, and of course if I had studied harder I could have found passages within each classic that said the opposite to that counseled in other parts. Still it makes me laugh even to this day, the thought of all those pompous Confucians prating day and night about their precious analects. At least the Taoists acknowledge that learning is futile.

"In any case I brought the two birds out together at dinner time and placed their cages on either side of the door leading into the dining room. When my mother and sisters came in to eat, both birds started chanting at the same time.

"'Exterminate knowledge,' one would chime, the other immediately replying:

"'Study without flagging,' then came:

"'Banish all learning,' and the reply:

"'Store up knowledge';

"'Study without flagging';

"'Exterminate knowledge';

"'Store up knowledge,' back and forth and back and forth, with me joining in, running around in circles, shouting the lines again and again, their chants ringing round the courtyard, mixing in with the laughter of my sisters. My mother smiled, I remember, and drew the cloth covers over the cages so the birds fell silent and we could sit down to eat in peace.

"After that, with a child's numbing persistence, I would take the birds out every morning before my lessons and hang the cages in the library so that they would start their chorus the moment my tutor entered the door. His name was Wen, a wispy student with a pockmarked face and trembling hands. He must have been thirty then, but of course he seemed ancient to me, a man who had passed the baccalaureate exams but had no influence in the capital and thus no official appointment. At the time he was waiting for a chance to take his doctorate after six years, hoping that the added qualification would get him the district magistracy he longed for; another fool frittering away his life in the vain hope of getting the cap and gown.

"Each morning when he came in to teach, the birds would start up their chant, with me joining in at the top of my lungs, gleefully shouting the words. Wen—he was a weak man; and his poetry sounded like a farming manual, earnest and didactic, bucolic epics extolling the Confucians' view of the happy peasant: he had no more chance of crafting immortal verses than of becoming an official in the capital—he would just smile that thin smile, put the cages outside, then sit down and open the books, continuing as if nothing had happened.

"Then my father returned home. His boat had grounded at Mochang, nearly a hundred miles downriver. It was very dry that spring, and the river had fallen much faster than usual so he had been forced to ride all the way back. I didn't even know he was home until he came into the rear courtyard where I kept the birds, dusty and still dressed in his high boots and stained traveling robe. He didn't say anything, just walked over and picked up the cages with the mynas. He was in a rage, his normally placid face mottled with livid patches of fury; he must have talked to Wen, I realized with a shock of fear.

"There were three mynas in separate cages, my two classical scholars and one I had caught only a few days before; I was planning to teach it a phrase from the Diamond Sutra that one of the maids, a lay Buddhist nun, had written down for me. My father opened the doors of the cages and set them on the ground. The untrained bird immediately flew out and away, up over the kitchen chimney. But the other two, dulled by their imprisonment, didn't move, simply sat staring at the open door. You can learn a lot by keeping birds about freedom and captivity, and what are the bars and who makes the cage.

"My father picked up one of the cages and shook it, sending the bird squawking madly around until finally it fell out of the opening and flew off. The last cage he shook repeatedly, but the bird remained inside, unable to imagine it was being given its freedom, until my father grasped the bamboo bars on either side of the opening, his big hands hardly fitting inside, and ripped the frail structure in half, tearing off the top and then throwing the cage in the air, bird and all. The crazed myna scrambled out of the twisted wreckage of its prison just as the cage was about to hit the ground, then thrust itself up into the air, flapping desperately. Within a moment, it too had gone, disappearing over the rooftop like the others.

"By this time I was very frightened. I hardly knew my father, had certainly never seen him in such a rage. To me, he was just a big, silent man who kept to his study most of the time he was at home, always very formal, wearing only a simple white or brown cotton robe and a black cap; he never dressed in the silks and embroidered damasks that some of the other merchants in town wore.

"He turned around, still without saying a word, grasped me by my topknot, and pulled me behind him, through the kitchens and out through the back of the house, the servants whispering among themselves, I screaming and struggling. He had picked up a rattan cane somewhere along the way, and when we got to the well, he pointed to the stone bench next to it and said: 'Bend over.'

"I said: 'What? What? What have I done?' weeping by now, but he just pointed again with such an implacable, pitiless look that I quickly bent over the bench, feeling the cool air on my buttocks as he lifted my short child's robe. I remember watching the tears splash onto the ground a few inches from my nose; each drop was immediately covered by dust and turned into a series of little mudballs, a sprinkling of liquid in the cracked soil.

"'Fools mock what they don't understand,' my father said, and hit me, very hard. The end of the cane was frayed and I could feel the ragged edges tear into my flesh. I squeezed my buttocks together and closed my legs as tightly as I could, petrified that he would miss and strike me on my private parts, that I would become a eunuch and be sent to the palace, grow fat and forever have to walk around with my embalmed testicles in my pocket so that when I died I could be buried whole.

"'You will respect learning.'

"Another stroke.

"'You will study without flagging.'

"And another.

"'You will store up knowledge.'

"Again.

"'This family was once great, once a family of scholars and officials.'

"I felt the blood begin to run down between my legs, a strangely shameful feeling, as though I had wet myself.

"'You will take the exams and become an official.'

"He missed and hit me on the back of the legs, the end of the cane curling in and ripping into the soft flesh on the inside of my thighs.

"'Do you want to be a merchant as I am? Condemned to be scorned by men who should be your equals, to counting money every day of your life, all because you were too stubborn to study?'

"He paused for a moment and I thought he had finished.

But then I heard the cane whistling through the air again, felt its burning blow as he shouted:

"'Do you want to waste your whole life?'

"This he expelled in as loud a voice as I had ever heard, a shout of anguish and pain that penetrated even to me in the midst of my self-pity. After that, he fell silent, hitting me slowly and methodically, the blood running all down my legs and over my feet, soaking into the arid earth.

"After a time I must have passed into unconsciousness. The next thing I remember is hearing the sound of my mother's voice. I couldn't understand the words, but hearing her voice was enough: I knew that I was saved. She was angry, I could tell that, but at the same time frightened, even pleading. For a while there was no reply from my father, then at last he said heavily: 'He had to learn this one thing. I am not here to teach him anything else,' then repeating himself, 'he must learn this one thing.' I felt hands grasp my robe, two of the stable boys, and when they turned me around and lifted me up, my father was gone.

"I hated him after that, hated him with a dogged persistence that was deepened by his longer and longer absences. I swore a solemn, childish oath that whatever happened I would never take the exams, even if I studied until I knew each of the classics by heart. I could master them if I wanted to, that I knew, for I was just beginning to understand then that I could easily master things most men struggled for years to attain.

"Gradually, too, I was spending more time on my own, and as I got older and more daring I went higher and higher into the hills, past the rice fields, the orchards of plum and pear, up into the woods of poplar, oak, and beech, the trees as thick as standing grain. You could find much else besides birds on those slopes, of course. Peaches and apricots, tiny wild plums that were pale red and tasted as sharp as the kumquat, white or red cherries, both sweet, or the larger sour ones, and hazelnuts and mountain walnuts to be roasted over an open fire. In summer, when I was older, I would go with a few friends and catch bream and carp from the mountain streams and grill them as soon as they came off the hook, the fish half-cooked before its eviscerated heart had stopped beating, the skin blackened, the flesh melting, a taste almost impossible to describe or reproduce, though my sisters, who of course could never accompany me, complained so much of my endless rhapsodies about fresh-caught fish that I would sometimes relent, smear the bream in mutton fat, then run home, where they would be fried in sesame oil or lard.

"Usually, though, I went by myself. In high summer the sun burnt off the mist, and I would climb to the top of the cleared slopes, where the forest began high above the town and lie there basking in the sun, dreaming of boarding one of the flat-bottomed boats that I could see loading timber or big wooden tubs of the local wine to be carried downriver. Later I wrote this, thinking of those days:

> Too lazy to wave my white feather fan
> I lie naked in the green woods.
> Slipping off my turban, I hang it on a rock
> And let the pine scented breeze
> Sprinkle dew on my bare head

"When I was twelve years old I decided to climb Tripod, the mountain to which our foothills eventually rose. Its three peaks stood sentinel over our town, often cloaked in mist and clouds, veiled by a gauzy covering of haze even on the most perfectly clear day, its broad flanks shouldering above the supplicant waves of foothills, shining with snow in winter, its tips always capped by a white frosting even at the height of summer so that many an envious eye was turned there when the sodden heat lay over the valleys like a blanket.

"I had, you see, decided to trap an eagle. Birds had been my escape and my solace until then, and in my boyish dreams the eagle, the greatest of birds, the freest, most noble, came to represent my means of escaping from the boredom and confinement of family life, from my father, who was home on one of his rare visits, and whose every second of presence was burdensome to me, my mother and sisters completely ignoring me to cater to his every whim. But I wouldn't accept any ordinary eagle. No, I had formed the notion of capturing an imperial eaglet and training it for the hunt. I knew that this magnificent bird, the largest in the realm, so enormous it was used to hunt wolf and gazelle, putting to shame the goshawks and peregrines with their petty kills of quail and duck, was reserved exclusively for the use of the emperor. I also knew that, like most penalties for infringing an imperial prerogative, the penalty for a commoner found keeping one of the eagles was death. But I had somehow conjured up in my childish mind the idea that I would train the bird and then present it to the emperor along with a poem celebrating the occasion. I saw myself marching into the throne room, the bird on my arm staring haughtily at the assembled courtiers forming a lane to the throne. They scurried aside, quavering under the bird's glance. The emperor would be amazed and would ask me to read my poem, then nod his head in appreciation and ask me to come and sit next to him, laughing as he called for the Royal Falconer, saying there was room only for a man, the eagle could wait until later when we could fly him. Strange that when I finally did get to court, my own entrance was something like that scene, though I had no bird on my arm, of course, only a sackful of poems. Dreams are the memories of the gods, but we can never tell if they are remembering the future or the past.

"That was my childish fantasy, in any case, and to pursue it I had to climb Tripod. It was a formidable challenge, far greater than I realized at the time. But I knew, too, that I must go, that the journey was part of my destiny, part of the road mapped out for me, should I choose to take it. Even then, my impetuosity was channeled by an acute, intuitive understanding of the Way.

"My trip was not made entirely without preparation, however. First I collected a set of winter clothes from the red lacquer chests where they had been laid in camphor that spring by my mother: a fleece-lined gown with a heavy hood, double-layered woolen trousers to be worn under the robe, a pongee silk chemise and shorts, my supplest pair of scarlet deerskin boots. I also took an oiled hemp sheet to lie on, two Tibetan blankets woven with odd angular patterns in bright red and green, dried venison, cold wheat cakes, and my silk bird-catching net. On my head I wore a wide-brimmed fisherman's straw hat, and for defense I carried a heavy cherrywood walking stick on to which the blacksmith had forged a crude spearhead. I also had a dagger with a silver inlaid hilt that my mother had given me on my birthday.

"I slipped out of the house in the false light before dawn, and made my way up along the raised dikes between the rice fields, through the fruit orchards, then in among the silent pines, padding over the carpet of fallen needles. This part of the mountain was covered in heavy fog in the early morning, so I could see nothing of the town below. I was cut off, walking through this silent world by myself, dreaming of escape, of meeting an immortal and sailing away with him on the back of a giant crane.

"After climbing steeply at first, the path leveled out, and as the mist thinned and the sun rose higher and higher, I could see that I was walking along the top of a series of low hills covered by scrub, the scattered trees all twisted and coiled over themselves, bent double by the wind. I had started at a searing pace, loping along, the canvas bag bumping reassuringly at my back. But as the day progressed, I had to slow down. I began to sweat heavily, too, even at the much slower pace, and eventually was forced to shed the heavy gown, draping it awkwardly over my shoulders. When I stopped for lunch at noon (it had taken all my willpower not to eat before then), I didn't seem any closer at all to the mountain, which ranged against the sky in front of me, implacable and remote. After eating I lay down under an acacia sapling, watching the green-firred tip sway back and forth in the soughing breeze, a lazy wag like an old dog's tail, the patterned caress of sunlight dappling across my face, the crab grass prickling against my bare arms.

"Later I rose and pressed on, impelled by the spirit of the mountain. For a while I strode along, relishing each upward slope for the sight the next ridge would bring. But I soon tired, slowing to a trudge, falling into a kind of numb trance, my legs moving automatically, my eyes fixed on the trail in front of me, plodding on and on until suddenly I noticed a chill bite in the wind and the long shadows of the trees crisscrossing the path. Light was draining from the great bowl of the sky, the mountain black against the deepening blue of evening, the three peaks grim and foreboding, much closer now, I noticed, towering right above me like the battlements of some inaccessible fortress.

"As the slopes on either side of the path slipped into dimness, they seemed to come alive, and sounds began to emerge. Heavy crashing in the undergrowth followed me for a distance, then would stop abruptly. Strange cries, too, somewhere between a croak and a roar, beginning far off and creeping closer as the darkness thickened. Speeding my pace until I was almost running, I reached a line of oaks stretched along the ridge and, without any conscious thought, scrambled up the nearest one, climbing until I was high up into its comforting tangle of branches. As I sat there chewing miserably on the dried venison, a chill, damp-fingered mist rolled out of the night, enveloping the tree and muffling the sounds on the ground beneath until all was silent and peaceful. Hugging my gown closer, I wedged myself into the fork of two large branches and, sooner than I would have thought possible, was asleep.

"As soon as it was light, I was on my way, stumbling upwards through the mist, which showed no sign of thinning as the morning wore on, a clinging curtain so thick that I could only see a few feet ahead. I had to slow my pace to avoid the tree trunks looming out of the whiteness. Eventually, however, the mist thinned slightly, and I could see I was in the woods that stretched toward near the top of the mountain's flanks. As I climbed higher the trees thinned out and finally disappeared, the path itself also dwindling away, the earthen surface replaced by scattered rocks, then bare slopes of black rock where nothing grew but the blue-green moss and lichen, here and there a few delicate orchids or pitcher plants hungry for a passing insect. From time to time I heard a distant roaring that I couldn't place until once I almost fell into a deep gully. I couldn't see the bottom because of the mist, but I could hear the water far below, crashing through the narrow cleft like a thousand boulders tumbling over one another.

"I pressed on upwards, much more slowly now with no path to follow and the prospect of a swift death in one of the gullies ever before me. At long last the mist seemed to be lifting, and from time to time I caught a tantalizing glimpse of blue sky. This continued for some time, until without warning I simply stepped out of the swirling mist and into a bright blaze of sunshine. I stood there, stunned, gaping around. I had climbed to the base of the three peaks. Though they looked so small from far away, I now saw they were jagged and impossibly steep precipices shooting up from the mountain's broad shoulders, far higher than they seemed from a distance, far beyond my reach. I could see, too, through the pass between the two peaks on either side of me that Tripod was only the first junior sentinel in an army of massive mountains, rank after rank of them, all mantled in snow, marching on and upward. And even as I watched, the mist and clouds began to wrap the mountains in their embrace, blocking them out once again.

"When I turned round I saw that on this side of the mountain the mist was sliding away, burnt off by the sun, revealing the route I had taken upward—a smooth, lichen-covered expanse that ran along the side of the mountain, perhaps fifty feet wide in most places, then dropping precipitately down to the river itself. Looking beyond I saw that the whole river valley was laid out below me, hills on either side rolling away into the hazy distance, the sinuous coils of the river glistening in the sun, a thin border of green fields on either side. It was like the relief maps I was to see later in the military training school in the capital. Directly beneath me was the next port down from us, Hsiwang, and following the river up, I could see that my own town of Lanlian was not so very far away after all: if I could have dropped straight downwards, I recall musing, the journey that had taken two days could be completed in minutes. If it hadn't been for the smoke of kitchen fires, I believe that on the edge of town at the foot of the hills I would have been able to make out my own home.

"For some time I sat on a boulder gazing down at the valley, wishing I had the skill to depict the exquisite scene below, though even then I had recognized that painting was not numbered among my many talents. It would have taken a man with the genius of that pietistic, smug fool Wang Wei to capture something of the majesty I saw that day. But he, complacent slug that he was, always painted mountains from below, gawking foolishly upwards; he never had the courage to climb. The effort might have blistered those dainty white aristocratic feet he was so proud of. Of course his paintings, even with their frog's-eye perspective, far exceeded his feeble, epicene efforts at poetry. 'Court poets,' they called themselves, as though that was a badge of honor, not a mark of shame. Court poets indeed. Caught poets, more like. Prisoners. Poisoners. Pompous poltroons. Shit eaters and asslickers the lot of them."

Li Po splutters to a halt, glaring so fiercely that a servant who has appeared in the hatchway where his gaze is directed blanches and ducks back down the stairs.

"Sir," Wang Lung says hesitantly, "Academician Li, that is, I'm sorry, but I don't know the characters for shit or ass."

"No, no, they're not in the classics, not yet anyway," Li Po says, now smiling again. "Just forget the last sentence, then, I. . . . But no, no, we must have everything in here. This is being written for me as much as anyone else. If it is ever to be seen by anyone else, that is. I'll show you how to write those words."

The poet dips his forefinger in a wine cup and daubs the characters onto the glossy lacquered surface of the table.

"Of course, they do appear from time to time in some of the so-called minor classics. That passage I quoted earlier from the *Chuang Tzu*, for example." He pauses, turns, and regards the boy, who is studiously avoiding his eye, carefully brushing in the missing sentence, complete with the offending characters.

"But what did you do in the earlier passage if you didn't know the characters for piss and shit?"

"I just put 'number one and number two,'" says Wang Lung, still not looking up. "I'll change it later."

Li Po guffaws, swigs down the remaining wine in the pot,

and claps for another. He is beginning to slur, making it difficult for the boy to understand him when he is talking quickly. "Number one and number two, ha ha, from a grown-up boy," he shakes his head. "Anyway, let's get on with it. We're getting to the good part:

"I sat at the base of the peak gazing in awe, lost in a trance of contemplation until something changed in the static scene before me. I shook my head, puzzled, and looked again. Finally I realized that I had unconsciously registered a small black spot where the blue of the sky had previously been unbroken. It grew slowly larger as I watched, and eventually I saw that it was a bird, soaring across and upward from the hills, only once every few minutes aiding its flight with a few flashing thrusts of its wings, the movement that must have caught my attention. As it came nearer I realized with a rush of joy that it was an eagle. But soon I was disappointed, for it seemed very small, far too small to be an imperial eagle. As it came closer, however, I saw that the distance had been playing tricks with my eyes, and I soon was watching in disbelief as it grew larger and larger, impossibly so, beyond the size of any bird I had ever heard tell of.

"When the eagle reached the side of the mountain, it was still several hundred feet below me, and it began a slow spiraling ascent during which I was able to examine it closely. Its wings stretched, as far as I could guess, the length of two men laid end to end. Its feathers were deep black on its body, with only the neck, head, and legs clothed in creamy white, while its breast was emblazoned with a swathe of imperial yellow. Then the eagle disappeared from my view under the overhanging cliff, and when it appeared again it was at the same level as the rock upon which I was sitting, only a hundred yards or so away and gliding directly at me. In its claws it held some animal, I couldn't tell what exactly the mass of bloody fur had once been, and as it passed overhead it seemed to glance down, a distant, pitiless gaze that swept haughtily over me as I crouched there, frozen.

"As soon as the eagle had passed, I whipped around to watch its ascent. The escarpment that faced the valley towered above me—sheer, gray, and unassailable. But in the portion that lay to the side, in the valley between the two peaks, a scree of loose rocks and pebbles ran about a third of the way up the slope before the sheer rock face began. Now, watching the eagle, I saw that instead of soaring to the top as I had expected, the bird had swooped into the cliff face directly above me, only about a quarter of the way up. It seemed to hover for a second, then disappeared. As soon as it had gone, I ran around the side of the cliff to the bottom of the scree and began to climb.

"The climb was impossible. The loose stones were constantly slipping out from under my scrambling feet, and several times I was caught in a mini-avalanche and slid halfway down the slope. Occasionally, too, a larger boulder from higher up would dislodge itself and come tumbling towards me and I would have to throw myself to one side to avoid it, usually sliding a considerable way back downhill in the process.

"My target was a narrow ledge that ran along the rock face at about the same level as where I presumed the eagle's nest was located. When I finally reached it aftcr ncarly an hour—having covered what on a flat surface would have amounted to only a few hundred yards—I was cut and bruised, covered with dust, and utterly exhausted. I sat there resting for a few moments, chewing on a piece of dried venison. The ledge I had spotted from below ran away from me and around a corner that would bring me onto the side of the mountain that faced the river. The black rock lay in the deep shadow of the neighboring peak here, and it was difficult to make out the condition of the ledge. The portion closest to me was a few feet wide, comfortable enough, but it then appeared to dwindle the farther it went, and by the time it reached the corner, it looked to be only inches wide.

"I sat there contemplating for a moment but soon began to shiver: sitting there in the deep shadow, without the sun's warming rays and with a chill wind blowing, the cold had penetrated even my padded garments. I glanced behind me, through the pass, and saw that the advancing wall of cloud had now covered the mountains completely and was plowing inexorably towards Tripod itself. Time was growing short.

"I stood and started to edge my way along the ledge, shuffling my feet sideways. My body was pressed to the rock, with both hands spread out grasping at any projections or fissures that would serve as holds. At first it wasn't all that difficult. The ledge was still wide enough, and the slope I had climbed lay underneath me, a drop of only twenty or so feet. But the farther I progressed, the narrower the ledge became and the greater the drop. To complicate matters, the wind from behind me picked up when I was about halfway along, funneling though the pass, now pushing me sideways, now billowing up from underneath so that I had to press even closer into the cold, dank rock to avoid being plucked off. At one point the wind gusted directly beneath me so that the skirts of my heavy outer robe blew up and wrapped themselves around my head. I was forced to remain in that dangerous and absurd position for some minutes, completely blinded, my teeth chattering uncontrollably, until the wind died down enough for me to risk taking one hand from the cliff and pulling the cloth away from my face.

"I saw then that my surmise had been right: the ledge here was barely wider than my foot, disappearing around the corner to I knew not what. And as I inched forward, I noticed that the soles of my boots were beginning to lose their grip on the wet rock. Several times one foot slipped and I was only prevented from falling by a firm handhold. I remember thinking that, for better grip, I should take my boots off for this stretch, then telling myself that it was too cold, my feet would freeze.

"I had avoided looking directly down until then but now made that foolish error; just one glance was very nearly enough to send me tumbling off the rock. I had passed over the scree slope and out onto the escarpment proper, and there was nothing at all underneath me, just the sheer rock and far, far below, like a child's set of miniatures, the houses of Hsiwang. To this day, nearly fifty years later, I don't think I have ever been more frightened than I was at that moment, all youthful foolishness and fearlessness driven out of me the way the breath is driven from one's body by a hard fall from a horse.

"For a while I was completely frozen with panic. Each time I thought about moving, the image of that emptiness beneath flashed into my mind, then the vivid picture of my body falling through the air, tumbling over and over, my robes flapping, down and down until, after an age, I smashed onto the jagged rocks at the mountain's foot. After some minutes of this, I thought back to something I had been told in my warrior's training: to banish fear you must become one with it. I pressed my forehead to the cold rock and conjured up the sight of myself falling, kept it there in my mind, running the picture time and again until it became commonplace and I was dulled to the thought. Then I gradually replaced that image with another, one of myself standing there on the ledge, gradually animating it so that my visionary self began to move, edged forward inch by inch. After a while, I found myself moving too, almost without thinking, until at last I finally reached the corner and pushed my head cautiously around.

"There was, I saw, a large open space in front of what appeared to be a cave. Almost crying with relief, I scrambled around the corner, pushing so hard on the brittle ledge I had been standing on that a large chunk broke away. But now safely on the other side, I didn't care. I collapsed onto the firm surface and just lay there, panting, bathed in sweat, enjoying the heat of the sun on my face.

"Eventually I rose and walked over to the far side of my haven. Peering over the edge, I saw that there was another outcropping only a little below this one. Almost all of the ledge was taken up by an enormous nest, at the bottom of which I could see two bundles of feathers: eaglets. There was no sign of the eagles themselves, and with a deep breath, I began to clamber down towards the nest. Once, about half way down, a shadow passed overhead, blocking out the sun, and I froze, expecting to feel the impact of those cruel claws ripping into my back. But the shadow passed, and when I glanced around, I saw it was only a cloud.

"The nest was even bigger than I had estimated from above, almost the height of a man, a dense wall of twigs and sticks, even whole saplings uprooted and ferried here in the talons of the mother or father. It would have been almost impossible to scale the side of the nest, but the back of the assemblage rested against the rock, and I was able to climb up the side using the rock face for support.

"Balanced precariously on top, clinging to the cliff with one hand, I threw my leg over the top of the nest, pulled the other after it, and rolled in, almost squashing one astonished eaglet, which had been dozing peacefully in a corner of its home. The bird—it was hardly more than a fluffy bundle of molting feathers—waddled rapidly across to the opposite side of the nest where its sibling lay, emitting loud peeping sounds as it went. Gagging—the smell, a sour vinegary stink of rotting, half-digested meat and unimaginable other things was overpowering—I dashed after it, slipping and stumbling through the piles of dung, mounds of feathers, and the odd bleached bone, from time to time plunging right through the jumble of sticks that made up the floor of the nest, a surface much more suited to scuttling claws than heavy boots.

"Despite the small area of the nest—its interior was no more than fifteen feet across—the chase proved more difficult than I had anticipated. The eaglets were much faster than their clownishly plump appearance seemed to indicate. Each time I had one cornered and was about to grab it, the beast would make a sudden dart across the cluttered, stinking surface, leaving me to turn and stumble after it, usually tripping over a projecting stick and falling, so that after a few minutes I was covered in a slimy mixture of bird shit and feathers.

"Panting, I stood glaring at the two chicks, huddled on the far side of the nest, peeping at me in incessant, exasperating unison. Then I hit upon the idea of using one of my blankets as a makeshift net. But before I could put this plan into action, the bright sunshine was blotted out by a familiar, elongated shadow, and I felt a chill of sheer terror ripple through me. I looked up to see the eagle floating overhead, still some distance away, descending in a leisurely spiral towards the nest. It seemed, too, to be looking away, out towards the valley below. I knew that if I didn't act very quickly, I would soon be dead, ripped into bloody strips by that swordlike beak.

"I still don't know why I chose to act the way I did. Probably some fear-prompted memory swam into my mind of the cuckoo, that ultimate masquerader. Stripping off my woolen outer robe, and clad only in my light cotton trousers and vest, I began to burrow into the floor of the nest, furiously wrenching aside sticks and branches until there was a hole large enough for me to kneel in. I scooped up handfuls of the white, stinking dung and smeared it in my hair and on my shoulders and, lastly, on my cheeks, chin and forehead. I then plucked up handfuls of the fluffy, molted feathers and slapped them onto my face and head. As I climbed down into the hole I had prepared and knelt there, with only my shit-caked befeathered head sticking out, I glanced up and saw that the eagle was still hovering above the nest, now emitting a series of raucous, piercing cries.

"Suddenly there was a monstrous beating of wings, a great rush of air swirling up all the loose debris at the bottom of the nest, blinding me for a moment. The two chicks, meanwhile, appeared to have forgotten about my presence and had rushed out into the center of the nest to stand directly in front of me, redoubling their cries, their heads pointed straight up in the air, their mouths stretched wide open. I followed the direction of their gaze and saw that another eagle, presumably the mate, was perched on the side of the nest, its huge bulk blocking out the sun entirely. Underneath the eagle, pinned down by its great talons, there lay a fawn, panting audibly, its hazel eyes rolling wildly, its brown and white-spotted hide streaked with bright red blood. As I watched, the eagle, which had seemed until this moment almost unaware of the writhing animal beneath it, suddenly bent and plunged its beak into the fawn's exposed belly, with one swift pull ripping the animal open so that its intestines spilled out in a wet rush. With them came a warm gust, the feral stink that is indescribable: the smell of death. I glanced away and my gaze fell on the face of the fawn. A look of offended surprise crossed its features, then its eyes rolled into its skull and its small, wet black nostrils flared in a last gasp, then relaxed.

"The huge bird now bent over the corpse of the deer and, using one leg to hold the body down, ripped off a long strip of flesh with its beak. Then, pulling at the piece until it was divided in two, it picked up a gobbet, leaned forward, and dropped it into one of the waiting mouths. This process was repeated with the second chick. The eagle then plucked out another piece of flesh and bent towards me. Though I had opened my mouth wide in imitation of the eaglets, my eyes were squeezed tightly shut. Still I couldn't help but open them at the last moment to watch with fascination and horror as the eagle dipped its beak to within a few inches of my face, then gently released a slimy length of intestine still coated on one side with half-digested grass.

"I managed to fling most such tidbits aside, all the time making enthusiastic champing motions with my jaws. Probably the worst . . . but no, that's enough, there is little point in my continuing to describe that gruesome meal. Suffice to say that I have never eaten tripe since that day.

"The feeding continued until both chicks had eaten their fill, indeed, had eaten so much that I could almost see them expanding in front of my eyes, becoming more and more rotund, their mottled feathers now smeared with gore, their heads almost completely covered in blood and specks of half-digested meat. At last, their young attended to, the two parent eagles attacked the battered body of the fawn for themselves, swallowing huge chunks of flesh weighing five or more pounds in a single gulp. When both birds had gorged themselves, there followed a period of quiet during which all the residents of the nest save myself seemed to have dozed off into a postprandial nap. I was beginning to despair of ever escaping when both of the adult eagles abruptly swung their heads around, and almost without a pause, launched themselves into the air, disappearing instantly below the walls of the nest.

"Standing cautiously, I walked over to the edge of the nest and peered over the top. Far away, on the other side of the mountain, I could just make out some sort of procession wending its way up the slope towards the pass that ran between the far two peaks. I couldn't tell if they were merchants or monks, but from the distant sound of clanging bells, I guessed that it was a religious expedition of some kind—Buddhists, perhaps, seeking a new site for a monastery. I also noted that the clouds I had seen advancing from the mountain range were now upon us, a solid line of white sliding through the pass nearest me and boiling around the tip of the peak. The two eagles were nowhere in sight.

"I turned, and with the haste of utter fear, swept up one of the eaglets; stunned with food, it could hardly manage more than a feeble waddle to try and escape. Holding it upside down by the feet (as with chickens, this allows the bird the least opportunity to take a painful peck) I frantically emptied the oilskin and the blankets from my bag and stuffed the beast, peeping madly, inside.

"Then, snatching up my woolen robe, I scrambled out of the nest and began to clamber up the slope, all the while the cursed bird bleating out its muffled but still piercing cry. When I reached the first platform, the cloud finally rolled in, swamping everything in white. I could hardly see more than ten feet but hoped that the clouds would confuse the eagles, too, perhaps even smother the plaintive cries of their stolen chick. I stopped for a moment to catch my breath, draw on my robe, and pull the bag around so that it rested against my stomach rather than my back: I needed to have all my weight well forward for the next part of my journey.

"Before I could move towards the ledge, however, there came a great rushing sound out of the mist above me, not wings beating, just the sound of a large object displacing the air, and before I could turn, I was struck violently on the back and thrown to the ground. My head would have been shattered against the rock, but the bag swung forward with the blow and cushioned the impact. Then as quickly as I had been knocked down, I was jerked upward into the air. One of the eagles had hooked its claws into the thick wool of my outer robe and, with a few huge thrusts of its great wings, had hauled me up into the air. The black rock surface below me disappeared, and I was enveloped in the dank white cloud, the only sound the rhythmic flapping of the eagle's wings.

"Instinctively I reached up and grasped the bird's legs as soon as we had left the ground, a move that proved fortuitous, for after only a minute or so, the eagle straightened its claws, intent on releasing me so that I would fall and be killed on the distant rocks. But I clung on with all my might, and once the bird realized this, it began twisting and turning its head, attempting to reach down and slice at my hands with its beak. Each time this happened it would fold its wings momentarily, and we would plunge sickeningly downwards until it gave up and righted itself with a few powerful wing beats. This unequal struggle continued for some minutes, until we abruptly emerged from the smothering mist back into the bright sunlight. We had fallen a thousand feet or more and were well away from the mountain, out of reach of the cloud bank, and continuing to descend rapidly.

"The eagle had stopped attempting to dislodge me, but now I felt a fatal weakening in my arms, which first began to ache with the strain, then run with waves of fire, then tremble violently. In the midst of this agony, I heard the eagle give out its raucous shriek, swiftly followed by an answering call from behind. The second eagle suddenly appeared in front of us, and, flinging out its huge wings, it came to a sudden halt in mid-air, turned with a flurry, then folded its wings and came plummeting down towards me, talons extended, its beak dipping forward to strike. With one last convulsive heave, I hauled myself up and pulled my knees up to my chin so that the bird missed striking me, if only by inches.

"Looking back over my shoulder, I saw that it had turned

again and would pass underneath me, probably preparing to turn and strike once more. My arms were shaking violently, and I knew that I had just a few seconds left. Already my left hand had almost no grip left. As the huge shape of the eagle glided underneath, both hands let go and I plummeted through the air, landing with a thud on the second eagle's back, my legs astride its body, torso laid flat, my hands instinctively reaching forward and clinging on at the base of its wings. The bird tumbled through the air, tipped over by the impact, cawing piercingly, its wings fluttering, twisting its neck in a vain attempt to strike at me.

"For a few moments I thought I was done for, that I was too heavy a burden. But it soon righted itself, and I saw that if I stretched out even more against its back, the distribution of my weight would approximate its own. I tightened my grip on its wings, trying to pull myself upward into a more stable position. The bird immediately began to flap steadily and we rose up in the air. When I relaxed my hold a little, it ceased flapping and we began to glide smoothly along. If I pulled with my left hand only, I discovered, the eagle would wheel right, the same with the left. It was like riding a well-trained horse."

Here Li Po attempts to demonstrate, stumbling about in the bright moonlight on the front of the foredeck, his arms extended, wheeling and dipping, saying: "I pulled thus and thus," pumping his hands up and down and almost tripping over one of the mats. After a few moments he steadies himself at the rail and continues:

"After that discovery it was easy, of course. Lying there, my head at the bird's shoulder, I guided it toward my home village, sweeping in over the river, then down over the red-tiled rooftops, people in the streets pointing up at the huge bird flying so low overhead, until finally we floated down like a dream toward the enormous oak at the rear of the house, in front of the cherry orchard. The eagle settled meekly on a lower branch, one of the few that would support its weight, and closed its wings as though trained from birth for human riders, allowing me to slide off its back and onto the branch. Then with a convulsive heave and a few thrusts of its monstrous wings, it pulled itself up into the air. By the time I had climbed down to the bottom of the tree and begun to walk towards the house, it was only a distant spot in the sky."

three 李白

THE NEXT DAY IT RAINS, GRAY CURTAINS OF WATER sweeping in over the flat farmlands on either side of the river, blotting out the other river craft around Li Po and Wang Lung and drumming on the roof of the main cabin. Li Po, initially ambivalent about a project conceived in a moment of drunken whimsy, now seems consumed by the desire to tell his tale and once again sends for his amanuensis before the boy has finished eating breakfast in the galley.

When Wang Lung arrives, he is waved impatiently to the writing table.

"Come, come. What is all this dawdling over breakfast? We have much to do, places to go and stories to tell before the evening comes. If you are ready? Yes? Good, then let us begin:

"When I returned to the house, my mother was furious, as angry as I had ever seen her, cold and distant in a way that made me quail inside as my own hot fury never had.

"'You are very lucky that your father happened to leave the same morning that you ran away,' she told me. 'If he had been here, you would have received a beating, such a beating that I shudder to think of it. Your father is a quiet man, but he sometimes cannot control himself when he is angry. You know that. In any case, he is gone and you are too big for me to beat now, so my punishment is to ban you from the women's quarters. We all would have liked to allow you the freedom to come and visit for as long as possible, but you have brought this on yourself. You acted, as always, without thinking of anyone but yourself. . . . '

"She continued in this vein for some time, all words and postures familiar to any child and any parent, myself hang-dog, neck bowed in shame, unable to utter a syllable in my own defense (there were none), bursting to tell her of my journey, my adventures, but knowing any hint would only make matters much worse. My mind skittered away as she talked, and I was soon thinking about slipping into the kitchen to see if the cook had made any of his famous apple fritters, deep fried and sugar coated, like a drug to a twelve-year-old.

"But hearing my sentence pronounced—my banishment—was a heavy blow, a very heavy blow. Worst of all was its dreadful finality. Age, the inevitable passage of years, made it irreversible. Once a boy was seen to have made the passage to maturity, to have crossed that invisible line that divided the delightfully innocent child from the sexually preoccupied male, he could no more wander in the women's quarters than he could fly to the moon.

"Until then, you see, the women's quarters were my whole universe, my refuge and playground, a magical world where I could be almost certain my father would never venture (the women would go to his bedchamber, a small bare room off the study that I had only glimpsed once through an open shutter). The area was made up of four interlinked courtyards in the rear of the house blooming with peach and cherry trees and set with small ponds full of goldfish and lotus flowers, in the farthest corner a gazebo shaped like the top of a pagoda. Here were secret corners, resonant of wonder and mystery: a line of stones in the rockery that had often served as battlements for a castle, the pond where I had sailed my crudely constructed rafts, a much-climbed oak that towered over the other trees and from whose upper branches I could gaze over the surrounding country. I spent many an hour alone and untouchable in my bower of leaves, dreaming of life as an official—wise, stern, but fair—summoned to court to solve the empire's most intractable problems with a few well-placed words, leading campaigns far into the endless western desert against the Uighurs and the Hsiung Nu, the Huns, slaughtering them by the thousands, burning their purple felt tents in a huge pile like my ancestor, the Flying General of the Han Dynasty, capturing their leader, the Quagahan, and taking him back in chains to Chang An.

"But the real magic was inside, down those long porticoes that ran around the courtyards, within the cool, perfumed rooms where all the mysteries of womanhood were stored. I was the only boy, of course, and everywhere I went that meant attention and coddling, indulgence to do what I wanted. I was freer then than I will ever be again, free to explore, touch, and taste. I could rummage through drawers, upend baskets and trunks, root through cupboards. All this, and I knew I would receive only a light smack on the wrist and a waggled finger of admonition."

Here the poet falls into a reverie, smiling and stroking his beard. The boy, watching him with brush poised, waiting for the next words to come, reflects that little has changed since those days: here is Li Po, disgraced, banished, a death sentence commuted, being escorted into exile by a troop of guards who are his willing companions in nightly revelry, carried in a barge that a provincial governor would be proud of, attended by fifty obsequious servants (including himself), honored and feasted everywhere the barge anchors for the night. Wang Lung shakes his head, and the older man, noticing the movement, focuses on the boy, nods his head a few times, all the while smiling, then continues:

"I suppose that the fashion in court in those days must have been for much use of powders and creams, for I remember an array of pots and jars on each of my various mothers' tables: blue kohl from India, some of the jars still wrapped in coarse hemp that was covered with the black squiggles of some mysterious language; yellow gamboge made from the thick rind of the mangosteen in the kingdom of Chaam in the far south; long green bottles full of an oily hair tonic, a concoction made from pressed thoroughwort leaves; even a purple-indigo mix, purported to have come from the crushed shells of snails or, some of the women said, from boiled and reduced gibbon's blood. These days the ladies at court concentrate on rich and colorful clothes, and the style is for white skin unadorned, a blessing for the women, who no longer have to smear themselves with creams and powders to achieve a fashionable hue. It is also a boon for their children, I would guess; when I saw one of my mothers dressed in full costume for a formal visit by the magistrate—yellow forehead, red cheeks, blue eyelids, thick black brows, and a purple mouth—I would scream and run and hide, even if it was my true mother, whom I adored above all the others.

"Once I remember gathering three of my sisters and smearing their faces with white cream—they were to be sinners—while I, my face striped with alternate lines of blue, red, and purple, was to be Amalitafo, the avenging demon in the ninth level of hell. I pursued my sisters around the gardens, they dutifully screaming, I leering and roaring as best I could in my high child's voice. But their screams soon became all too real, for the white face cream was made with lead, and even on adults could only be worn for a few hours before it began to burn the skin. For my sisters it happened in minutes. I watched long enough to admire the gruesome scarlet boils flowering on their faces as the cream was wiped away by anxious hands, then hurriedly fled to my oak tree refuge.

"There were many other secrets to discover in that world: cupboards to play in, kitchens and storerooms at the back, even an old ruined watchtower full of bats where I first discovered the differences between my sisters and myself, three of us comparing the way children do, with much shedding of robes, prodding, and puzzled exclamations. And much later, when I was twelve, I made another discovery up in that old tower, with one of the chamber maids: exactly what the differences were used for, this time with a bamboo mat and a gourd full of purloined wine, much desperate fumbling in the dark after the candle blew out, my fingers touching for the first time the hot satiny flesh and cool slim thighs . . . But there's no need for me to go on. You'll find out yourself soon enough, boy.

"In any case, the girl was gone a few weeks later, no one could tell me where. Then my mother called me into her room and questioned me closely: What I had been doing in the tower? Had that little minx lead me there? Instinctively I denied everything, for although what had happened in the tower had seemed perfectly natural to me, I could sense that for my mother, there was much to it beyond just a physical act; that somehow there was danger for me and for the girl, too.

"One of my special joys was the lighting of the braziers when the ladies of the house—my four mothers—fumigated their wardrobes with aromatics. This occurred five or six times a year, usually in the week before a big festival, and was the occasion of much excitement among the children of the house. Servants were marshaled into each of the ladies' clothes cupboards—really small rooms more than cupboards—and all the hidden finery was carried out: net, damask, embroidered silks and taffetas, heavy brocade ceremonial robes, and flimsy undergarments. These were then taken to an empty storeroom at the back of the house. Here the clothes were hung in the air, draped neatly over thick silken cords that had been stretched from one end of the room to the other. Small braziers of stone and metal filled with burning charcoal embers were carried in by the servants and laid in rows underneath the hanging garments. Each child was then given a wooden spoon and a bowl full of hundred-blend aromatic paste and positioned at the end of the room, farthest from the door. When all was ready we would walk down the line of braziers, dumping into each one a full measure of the aromatic mix, the paste flaring into billows of dark smoke as soon as it touched the coals so that each child left behind a thick curtain of fumes, the clouds of smoke gradually enveloping us as we progressed down the line, towards the end coughing and laughing, only dropping a perfunctory dab of paste into the last two or three braziers, running at last towards the light of the half-open door which was slammed shut behind us.

"The paste held only a few aromatics, of course, not one hundred; even my father could not have paid for that. It was probably the usual mix, something like aloeswood, sandalwood, liquidambar, frankincense, and musk, all ground and strained, then mixed with honey. Strange, now I think back, it seems to me that my whole childhood was lived in clouds of scent and smoke and perfume, from incense and aromatics to bath waters sprinkled with citronella and peach blossom oil and clothes impregnated with sweet basil. Even playing hide and seek one had to be careful, for all cupboards, the best places to hide, were hung about with sachets of clove and camphor powder to drive away insects. A wrong movement could pull open a few of the sachets, condemning the perpetrator not only to discovery the instant his pursuer entered the room, but a sharp scolding, too.

"The ladies always carried sachets and small bottles of oil to perfume themselves during the day. Some preparations lasted longer than others. An early popularity for patchouli was soon tarnished by the oil's ability to attract bees and butterflies. It might seem romantic for a lady to be followed by a stream of bobbing butterflies, but the pursuit of a swarm of buzzing bees—though delightful for the watching children—ruined at least one elaborate ceremonial that I recall. There were incense clocks, too, in the garden at evening, burnt in runnels gouged into the stone tables to keep track of time, and rows of candles with impregnated wicks that burnt all night to fill our bedchambers with a pleasing scent.

"Much, too, of this heady delectation of perfume and aroma came from the Buddhist rites that swept through the household when I was six or seven and remained a fixture of the quarters until my father banned their performance seven or eight years later. Everything to do with Buddhism in those days seemed to me to be centered around powders, pastes, and aromatics. Their ritual words attest to it: *gandha*, the Sanskrit word for aromatic, simply means 'pertaining to the Buddha,' while a temple was a *gandhakuti*, 'house of fragrance.' Fragrant King and Fragrant Elephant were epithets of the Bodhisattvas, and Gandhamadana, the incense kingdom, was the fairy land where dwelt the *gandharvas*, the gods of scent. Even the Buddhist holy books, I discovered one day when I crept into the small chapel my mother had ordered constructed in a disused storeroom, were impregnated with camphor and storax so that when their pages were pulled open a wave of heady musk would waft up towards the reader.

"Children were banned from the rites that took place in the little chapel, which naturally increased my curiosity to almost unbearable levels. But when I managed one day to steal in with the servants, I found to my disappointment that the ceremonies consisted mostly of the burning of yet more incense to the accompaniment of chanting of the sutras (or rather, droning, as it seemed to me) by aged bonzes. Even the room was a disappointment—packed earth floor, some wooden benches, a raised dais at the front which was empty save an altar and the usual offerings, though later a large statue of the Buddha and several Bodhisattvas were added.

"There was a good deal of talk, too, among the servants about the practice instituted when I was about seven, of allowing mendicant monks to sleep in the ruined watch-tower. I would see them in the kitchens from time to time, a strange mix—some emaciated, wanderers whose wrinkled and weather-beaten faces reflected a lifetime on the road, others sleek young men who looked as though they would have been happier in the gambling dens of the towns than wandering through the countryside carrying nothing but staff, bowl, and the wooden clapper in the shape of a fish with which they announced their presence. Usually these men would pay for their lodging and food with the recitation of several hours of prayers seeking prosperity and health for the household. Here the devout ladies of the house would cluster into the chapel and sit twittering and gossiping in the pews. My true mother stayed away at first: her upbringing as a Confucian was the proudly preserved legacy of the family's scholarly days, and I knew that she considered such rites to be so much poppycock and mummery. But after some years even she started attending the services, and I would occasionally stumble across some sign of the faith—a rosary, an image of the Buddha—in her rooms. I felt uncomfortable around these strangers, too, and knew from the whispers in the kitchens that something was wrong. Sometimes I found doors locked that should not have been, even in the ladies' quarters themselves, and behind them heard whispering and hushed giggles. It made me feel confused and alone, almost betrayed."

Here Li Po stops for a time, frozen in his seat, oblivious to all around him. Wang Lung is floating, conscious of tingling in his left leg which is folded underneath him on the cushion, the smell of the noon meal wafting down the deck from the galley, the flap of the canopy overhead as it is ruffled by the breeze, the sparkle of sunlight off the water. But on the edge of his idle thoughts, he wonders what Li Po is thinking, on what strange paths these last memories have sent his mind: salacious monks and lonely ladies, a village storyteller's cliché. Real memories or invented? How to distinguish. A mix, like all human stories, a mix of memory and desire . . .

"My father . . . ," the poet is speaking again, and Wang Lung hurriedly dips his brush in the pool of ink.

"My father was almost never at home during this period, and I didn't miss him, for even when he was there, he spent most of his time in his study, presumably poring over his accounts or counting his money. At some point I began to avoid him, even on those rare occasions when he emerged. Sometimes my only glimpse of him was when he first returned, when the whole household would line up to greet him in the main courtyard, all dressed in our formal best, my mother and I at the top of the line, my other mothers behind me, my sisters on the other side with the servants, usually making faces at me from behind their backs. He wouldn't say a word, just climb off the horse, smile and pat its neck, call the groom to brush down the beast and feed and water it, then stride past and on into the house as though we weren't there.

"After that I was free to go: *He* would never notice if I was there or not. Eager to escape I would scurry away the minute he passed through the front gate, setting out for the hills or roaming through the fields with a small band of boys from the town. For long periods my mother would never ask after me, never complain that I spent too long away from the house, sometimes for nights on end. Then suddenly she would turn on someone in the house, one of the lesser wives or a maid, and demand to know where I was, curse the servants when they couldn't tell her, scream and order beatings for everyone around her until I was found. Sometimes, too, she seemed to be swept with fear, to realize that anything could happen to me when I was off roaming by myself or with my village friends. Then she would confine me to the house, ban me from associating with "those revolting little rapscallions." I would smile and nod obediently, knowing that she would forget within a week or two and I would be free again.

"On one occasion she went so far as to beat my tutor with a walking stick when he told her he had no idea where I was. Of course he may have precipitated the beating by telling my mother that I was spoiled and completely uncontrollable. Another time she instructed all the servants not to let me out of the house under any circumstances. That order, which I soon circumvented by finding a way in and out through the roof and the old ruined watchtower, lasted almost six months, the longest of any such ban. I had been playing in town with two of my friends, the miller's son and another merchant's boy. We were fighting for control of a wall that ran alongside the military garrison. It rose about six feet, then sloped inwards in a small step about eight inches wide before rising again. We were able to climb a magnolia tree that grew next to the fort and, edging out onto one of its branches, drop down onto the ledge, pushing and shoving to see who was king of the wall. Usually the loser would land on his feet, the impact broken by the mud of the road. But this time it was high summer, and the earth was dry as bone, packed tight and hard. I had thrown my two friends off and was strutting proudly on the ledge when another group of boys appeared around the corner, among them Lu, the blacksmith's son, muscle-bound and smirking. He quickly scaled the tree to the cheers of his minions and dropped lightly onto the ledge before me, grinning. We were soon flailing at each other, he finally managing to grasp my right arm and fling me outward. Fool that he was, however, Lu did not anticipate the critical maneuver essential to this kind of struggle: ridding yourself of your opponent once he was off balance. As I fell I grabbed onto his left arm and pulled him with me, hoping to use his bulk to cushion my fall. Alas, I miscalculated, and most of his weight fell on my arm when we hit the dusty street. There was an audible sound somewhere between a crack and a crunch as the bone in my forearm snapped. My two friends carried me to the front gate of my father's house, running away after knocking loudly and leaving me there.

"I remember little of the next few days, for my mother immediately dosed me with some concoction that kept me dazed and sleepy. But when I awoke, I was back in her bed, safe again. She was the only one allowed to tend to me, changing my bandage and splints (my entire arm was a wonderful purple-black that faded to an even more deliciously gruesome yellow and green as the bone healed), replacing the herb poultices packed beneath it, feeding me a paste of powdered ginger and licorice root to avoid an interruption in the circulation of the blood.

"A cupboard led off my mother's bedroom, but it had always been closed and strictly barred to me until then. But now I was at last allowed entry. Here she stored her drugs and balms, for she was from a family famous for its medical knowledge, a family that had once supplied the physicians to the court of the Northern Wei before the fall of that house had forced them to flee south and west to Shu. The lore had stayed in the family, though only on the distaff side, for the profession is scorned now, as are all but that single ideal of taking service with the emperor, a last-resort alternative for those whose wit is not enough for the examination halls and who are without the influence or rank to circumvent those tedious tests. Strange how men strive so hard for safety in the imperial system. A kind of little death, a self-emasculation. All my life I have been different, have never wanted the carriage and gown, the hypocritical obsequies that so fill most men's hearts with joy.

"In any case after my arm had healed, my mother banned me from leaving the house and, partly to keep me occupied and partly because she saw my fascination with the way she mixed her medicines, she decided to tutor me in the elementary healing arts.

"'With healing, as with everything under heaven, balance is all,' she told me, though I was too young to understand her fully. 'Too much of either the male or female principle throws the forces in a man or woman out of kilter,' she said; 'men's nature is to slay and wound, to destroy.' With a small flame of the female genius burning in me, with the ability to heal, to repair and build, to nurture, she said, I would bring my life forces closer to balance and live a happier, wiser life. She made me promise, too, not to tell my father that I had been tutored in the lore, a pledge I was more than happy to make, for it bound me closer to her and excluded him, though I don't think he would have cared, so long as it didn't interfere with my studies.

"The storeroom was lined on either wall with hundreds of tiny drawers, each marked with a small red paper circle on which the character specifying the contents had been daubed in gold paint. The first step in the apothecary's education, I soon found, was the same as any other, rote memorization. Before she let me near the mortar and pestle, the grating screens, the decocting tubes, the great copper jaws of the pill-stamper or any of the other apparatus, my mother made me memorize the ancient order in which drugs are stored, a sequence so firmly ingrained, so inviolable, that anywhere the arts of healing have penetrated—from the frozen mountains of Silla on the Korean peninsula to the damp, fetid swamps of Champa in the far south—even there at the fringes of the world, the traveler can visit any pharmacist and know that the storage sequence will begin with those listed in the primal canon of the philosophy, *Basic Herbs of Shen Nung*. First the superior drugs, which lighten the body and lengthen life: azurite, mica, divine fomes fungus, tuckahoe, ginseng, musk, dried and powdered oysters; then the middle drugs: tonics such as orpiment, realgar, sulphur, ginger, rhinoceros horn, deer velvet; then the inferior drugs useful only for healing the sick and purging: ocher, minum, ceruse, wolfsbane, pickled frog meat, peach seeds. Then would come essences listed in the lesser books such as the *Accounts of Famed Physicians of Tao Hung-ching*. And lastly, those more modern resources detailed in the *Basic List of Herbs Compiled Anew*, much in vogue at the capital in later years.

"But despite her honoring of this ancient tradition, my mother's methods were nothing like those of the capital, or indeed of the official pharmacists all over the empire, where deviation from the mixing practices laid down in the canon could mean death. With her ancestral store of knowledge and the freedom to treat our household, unsupervised by the pharmacists' guild and the government's Board of Medicine and Herbalists, she could mix as she wished, taking what was best from the classics and adding what she deemed effective. Thus she had confirmed that purple pulsatilla leaves could cure dysentery, calomel was prescribed for venereal diseases, an infusion of gourd meat in wine for rickets, an ointment made from an amalgam of tin and silver worked to calm anxiety in women, niter was useful for difficult menstruation, shallots to induce labor (many of her remedies, naturally, were directed at women only), mallow and rhubarb was an intestinal demulcent, crushed leeks were useful against the bite of mad dogs and snakes, the pith of an apricot seed stewed in wine and ginseng will aid in palpitations of the heart. These and many more she revealed to me in those years. And though I have lost the art of preparing the drugs now, I remember every word of their recipes, casting my mind back to that narrow room to recall her standing there with the pestle in one hand, with the other waving her willing assistant over towards the row of drawers on the wall to fetch another ingredient.

"There was a darker side to her potions, too, more powerful even than the healing knowledge, though I won't speak of that here. Suffice to say that I gained a basic grasp of this art, too, something I was to regret bitterly later in life, for it led me down paths that to this day I cannot discuss without calling down a new sentence of death on my head.

"No, those matters are better left unsaid. I was speaking of happier things, beautiful things, and so I will continue. I have always loved beauty, whether it be in person or thing. Even as a child, for example, I knew almost every one of the trinkets each mother had, where she stored each one in the lacquered black cases my father had given to each of his wives. I had long ago discovered the secret places where they kept the keys to their jewelry cases and sometimes would lay out the green silk-lined trays from one or another box to admire their contents: the white jade bracelets with their delicate silver clasps in the shape of phoenixes; necklaces of polished rock crystal that shone like spring ice in the sun; a heavy gold brooch in the shape of the simurgh in flight, its eyes picked out in rubies, its horns built of carnelian, girdles made of plaques of yellow jade and tortoiseshell, each depicting a beast such as the unicorn, the roc, the elephant, and the rhinoceros. There were rings, too, rings of the finest jasper jade, or of gold, set with emeralds and amethysts, or earrings made of the shell of the chrysoloclorus beetle, iridescent blue and gold plates hung on tiny gold chains. I remember one piece I particularly liked, a silver brooch that held a lapis lazuli, shining a brilliant blue like the color of the sky on a cloudless evening in midsummer, a stone I only saw once again in all my years of traveling, and then in the Hall of Golden Bells in Chang An. I also coveted one of the headdresses brought in from the western capital. They were stored separately in their own cases, resting on a crudely formed head shaped of balsa wood. They were the height of the jeweler's art in those days, fantastic constructs of lace and mica, crystal and ivory, all built on richly embroidered gold brocade that was layered with hundreds of tiny pearls and hung with brilliant blue-and-green kingfisher and five-colored parrot feathers.

"But little in life comes without a reverse of the coin; a price is always to be paid somewhere. Much later, for example, I found the source of these parrot feathers that had so delighted me as a boy. It was in Lingnan, far, far in the south, near the borders of the empire, in the mountainous country to which our Han people are still only newcomers. There I chanced upon a tribe of men called the Ham barbarians, though they spoke a form of language that was comprehensible and looked much like you or me, as though they had been lost long ago and had forgotten the arts of civilization, living in caves and chasing after wild beasts in the forest for food. These men traded with the border towns in the lowlands, once a month appearing in the market with sacks full of parrot feathers which they sold to local merchants—men like my father—for a fraction of their true worth. I was taken into their country by my host, a banished official, an artist who traveled much into the hills in search of scenery that would inspire his somewhat lackadaisical brush. He showed me the cliffs in which the parrots nest, thousands upon thousands of them. These were sheer rock face, soaring up towards a lofty peak, inaccessible except by climbing. The Ham had erected bamboo scaffolding to get to the lower part of the cliffs, but thereafter they had to crawl up the bare cliffside like flies, trapping the birds in their handheld nets, then stuffing them into sacks they carried tied to their waists. As my host and I stood watching that day, I saw two men fall, to be smashed on the sharp rocks at the base of the cliff—an absurd waste of life in the pursuit of fripperies for the preening ladies of the capital.

"The same holds true for pearls. The ladies in my father's house called them the tears of the shark people and told stories of how they were collected by men who could cease to breathe through magic and walked on the bottom of the sea, traveling in coaches drawn by giant leatherback turtles through the watery realms to collect the tribute to the emperor of the shark people. But, in truth, it is a cruel place where pearls are collected, a place called Ho Pu at the estuary of the Ho River in Lien Province on the south coast. The entire region is under the control of a military official called the Superintendent of the Pearl Fisheries. It is a post much sought after, for the size of the pearl tribute sent to the capital each year depends on the estimate of the superintendent, who naturally pleads disaster and sickness among the oysters, then drives the divers to collect many times the amount he has promised to deliver.

"When I visited Ho Pu fifteen years ago, the superintendent was an evil man who had swept the surrounding villages of their population and pressed them all—men, women, and children, even graybeards of sixty—into service as divers. My ship had been driven into the estuary by a storm. He honored me with a banquet—I was known by then, even in that dark backwater—and the next morning took me to see the fisheries. The countryside through which we passed was empty and desolate, the villages deserted, the houses ramshackle and collapsing, the fields overgrown with weeds. It was barely after dawn when we arrived at the fisheries, boarded his barge, and were carried out to the islands around which the oyster beds lay. In the hard gray light of dawn, I watched as fifteen flat-bottomed craft were lined up, and thirty or so naked men and women were forced over the sides by the guards standing in ranks behind them. Some of the villagers resisted until the soldiers pricked them with their spears so that as they dove into the water you could already see the thin rivulets of blood trailing down their backs. Each diver had a rope tied to his or her waist and carried a basket. They also had a heavy rock tied to one ankle to help them descend quickly. When they were ready, they released their ankle rope and tugged on their waist rope and a companion hauled them up. But when I watched, five of the divers failed to pull on their ropes and were pulled up too late, limp and staring. They were inexperienced, I found out later, had probably panicked on the way down and were unable to untie the rope which secured the rock to their ankles. Later, after the remaining divers had plunged and ascended three times, a great shout erupted from the raft nearest us. I saw a commotion beneath the surface and a cloud of blood boiling up in the water. The divers had been attacked by a tiger shark, I was told. All the villagers at the ropes began to haul frantically, but many pulled up ropes that had been bitten through. One man was pulled up with the shark still hanging onto his leg, its teeth clamped there, its body threshing until it tore the leg away and left him screaming in the water, clutching at the blood-pumping stump.

"A terrible, evil business. And to think that in the first years of his reign, almost fifty years ago when I was a boy, the emperor had had brocade and silk and boxes of pearls burnt in a huge bonfire in front of the Temple of Heaven to show his contempt for luxuries. But a few decades later whole villages were slaughtered at a whim to fetch a few pearls to decorate the palace walls."

Here Li Po, who has left his seat and has been striding up and down the deck in increasing agitation, walks to the railing and stares out at the water, his face grim. After a moment, though, he turns around and looks at the boy with a puzzled frown on his face.

"Ho Pu? Ho Pu? How did I come to be talking of that accursed place?"

Wang Lung shakes his head. "I don't know, Academician. You were describing your house when you were a boy, the ladies' quarters."

"Ah, yes, the ladies' quarters," the poet repeats, a smile now crossing his lips. "I can tell you more about that:

"In my early years, of course, I was kept in the women's quarters all the time. My mother suckled me for as long as she could but—as I found out later—she was forced by my father to wean me after only three or four months: she being the only one of his wives who had conceived a son, he wanted to make her pregnant again as soon as possible, and all know that the seed will not take in a mother still giving milk. However, my mother passed me to Roxana, or Arma as I called her, which means 'second mother.' She had given birth to my youngest sister a few months before my mother had produced me and willingly took me on.

"Arma was my father's second lady. They had been wed while our family was still in exile in the desert, married off to forge an alliance between Chinese and Bactrian trading houses. The alliance was supposed to link the mythical Inland Sea on which Hrum lies in the far west to the Great Eastern Ocean through which the Arabs sail to Canton. But hardly had she entered my father's house and shed her silver bangles and her strange Turkic marriage robes of green and yellow, than the tide of empire retreated and the great garrison at Hsichou—then called by the local peoples Cinackant, City of the Chinese, now simply known as Qoco—was threatened, then overrun. We had already fled from much farther west, deepest Serindia, leaving behind much wealth, first from Tokmak south to Kashgar, then on to Kucha and through the wastes of Turfan, where for a time we stayed at Hsichou. But my father smelled ruin in the air, saw the soldiers shedding their uniforms, disguising themselves so as to join camel caravans heading east, and he uprooted the growing family again, now fleeing all the way past the White Dragon Dunes through the Jade Pass and into borders of Tang proper to find refuge at last in the dusty little town of Tun-huang. After that he had worked his way gradually south, avoiding the capital for fear that despite the lapse of nearly a century, the archives of the bureaucracy would still hold somewhere the banishment order that had driven the family out of court and beyond the bounds of the civilized world.

"Finally deep in the mountains of Shu, my father decided we had fled far enough and, selling a few of his precious stones in the market at the provincial capital Cheng-tu, he retreated another 150 miles upriver to Lanlian, Blue Lotus Village, where he had our house built on the edge of town.

"Arma was a melancholy woman, with green eyes and lustrous braids of silky black hair. She smelled different from my other mothers, a musky odor like that of Indian incense but sweeter. It seems to me that even her milk tasted different, a little bitter, the taste of almonds. Certainly she had enough milk for two, for she was a big woman, almost as tall as my father, and with heavy breasts to match her size. Her nipples, however, were much smaller than those of my other mothers; the others had wide, dark areolas the color of liver, and long thin nipples stretched by nursing babies. Arma's nipples—I remember them because she nursed me until I was three years old and, unlike most others, I can recall everything from that age onwards—were small and rusty brown against the dead white skin of her breasts. My father found her too close to his own size and didn't favor her much with invitations to his bed, perhaps accounting for her sadness.

"Arma would sing us lullabies in Turkic—strange, wailing laments for her lost home that still run through my head in faint refrain sometimes late at night. I had been born in the deep desert, in Tokmak, and she conceived that I should master Turkic, so always spoke to me in that language only, later on teaching me the simple script—only twenty-two characters! I have even written poems in this strange tongue, or rather songs, for they don't distinguish between the two. It was knowledge that was to save my life in later years.

"When Arma weaned her daughter, she tried to wean me at the same time, but I bawled unceasingly for the breast, and she relented, allowing me to continue suckling for a while longer. A few months later my father's third wife, who bore the inauspicious name of Yu Chuo or Jade Bracelet, a name many now cannot pronounce without a curse, a name for a destroyer of empires, had just given birth to a dead child, a son, after a long and troublesome pregnancy that nearly destroyed her will to live. After a few days Arma suggested to her that she take over suckling me, for it would be shameful to let her milk go to waste, hoping that in giving life, sustaining it by her efforts, she would forget her own loss. After much persuasion Yu Chuo reluctantly agreed—I think she would have rather turned her face to the wall, and this was her third miscarriage—and I gained my third mother, my Sanma.

"Sanma was a country girl, the daughter of a trader in Cheng-tu. Her marriage was yet another one of my father's schemes to increase his wealth. My real mother, his first lady, was the only one he married in the normal way, an arrangement among once-noble families that were attempting to maintain their dignity through their bloodlines: if they couldn't marry real aristocracy, at least they could make sure they didn't mingle their blood with some newly rich merchant whose father had squelched pig shit between his toes every day of his life. All the rest were commercial couplings.

"Sanma was a little young when she married—eleven years of age—but was pregnant within a year. For a time after she lost her baby she would hardly talk, but her natural good spirits and the resilience of youth soon reasserted themselves, and she began to sing a little each night to send us to sleep. Much later I realized that just as I am a natural poet, Sanma was a natural singer of outstanding beauty. Without any training her voice was fit for the imperial palace, clear and flawless, delicate but rich with great power and emotion, the words so true when she sang them that if she had set one of my father's cargo manifests to music, she could have made all within hearing weep.

"But Sanma sang only folk songs that she had learned from her mother as a child—she was never educated even in the most elementary characters—simple ballads of love and loss in the fields. She would sing without accompaniment, though sometimes she would play the single-string, an instrument much used by the peasants in Shu, which consists of one string stretched over a small sound box and a long stick. With this she would play a series of notes to accompany her singing. The songs were simple fare, many as old as our race, variations on favorite stories that all know: Lady Lofu picking mulberries outside the city gate, for example, or the story of the weaving girl and the herder boy, star-crossed lovers forever parted. From the first I was transfixed by the power and beauty—above all, the truth—of those peasant songs. Even then, when I was soon to study the lute and zither with a series of ever more foolish teachers earnestly guiding me through the fussy airs popular in the capital, even then I knew how to look through the veil of lies men put up to glorify themselves and see what is really true.

"And, of course, when I finally came to read the *Book of Songs*, which even Confucius himself acknowledges is the true essence and font of all poetry, I recognized much that was there from Sanma's songs, even though the *Book of Songs* was old by Confucius's time more than 1300 years ago. Wondrous that much in there seems as fresh today as a ditty sung by the washerwoman pounding clothes in the river. Who cannot but smile at the passionate urgency of the lady's cry:

That a mere glimpse of plain leggings
Could tie my heart in tangles.
Enough! Let us be one.

"But it is strange, too, how things can change. Look at what were thought to be the ideal attributes of a woman. In the *Book of Songs* you will find this:

Skin like pure lard
Hands white as rush-down
Neck long and white as the tree grub
Teeth like melon seeds
Forehead like a dragonfly
Brows like silk moths

"What are we to make of a forehead like a dragonfly? Or teeth like melon seeds? As for today, we all know what is thought ideal in a woman. Who can forget the list written by Mei Yu, an accomplished poet and the greatest courtesan of her age:

sleek, buttery flesh,
cambric fingers,
cinnabar lips,
sandalwood mouth,
cloudy chignon,
willow brows,
creamy breast,
mare's grape nipples.

"It is an alluring list, though the last is a little improbable. Grape nipples. It puts me in mind of Sanma, who had the opposite—strange, almost ingrown nipples at which one could never quite get proper purchase, a constant frustration. You may wonder at this, my accuracy of recall, but I can remember every detail of suckling at my mothers' breasts: the warmth of nestling against skin; the deep, deep peace, almost a forgetfulness, of that rhythmic sucking; the smell, above all the smell, the special odor of each mother, musky and fragrant, mixed with the smell of milk, the sweet, intoxicating smell of milk that has stayed with me ever since. Even now when I come upon it unexpectedly, it can give me some pale shadow of that sense of calm and safety. And other feelings, too.

"I remember once when I was already half a man, thoughts of nursing far behind me. I was climbing in the orchard, collecting cherries. I was high up in one of the trees when I happened to glance over at the house, into the rear courtyard and through an open window where I saw my father's fourth wife. She had just given birth some months before—a girl, I had been happy to hear, my father never did manage another boy so far as I know—and as I watched, she parted her robe and pulled it down over her shoulders. It was morning and the sun was shining directly on her, picking out the gold stitching that outlined the green-and-red wave design on her robe, her flesh shining a burnished, creamy ocher. I saw her take up a turquoise porcelain bowl with her left hand, kneading her right breast with the other, then plucking at her nipple, squeezing and pulling rhythmically until a thin stream of milk issued forth, almost transparent but seeming to glow in the sunlight. Later I tried numerous times to recreate that feeling with my own wives when they were suckling, often taking their breasts in my mouth and greedily sucking down the milk my children should have had, but it was no use. Some things can never be repeated.

"When I was almost five years old, my true mother took me back to her breast. She had given birth to another of my sisters, her last child, a few months before. The new baby was soon packed off to the nursery along with a servant wet nurse, and one day she swept into Sanma's front room and actually pulled me away from the breast, lifting me into her arms and simply saying: 'I am taking him back now,' then sweeping out of the room and carrying me all the way back to her courtyard and into the dark of her bedroom, where she parted her robe and pulled me sharply toward her, crushing my face between her breasts and almost forcing the nipple into my mouth. I fed there for the next two years, blissfully buried in her flesh. My mother would feed me only once a day by that time, almost always in the late evening before sleep, after she had shed the heavy day robes and removed her powders and creams, untied her chignon, and let her hair down. She would come to me before her bath in a light silk gown and pull me in close. She smelled different; this was no sweet concocted fragrance but her true essence, a heavy mixture of scents, all singly identifiable, but together making up the essence of my mother: sandalwood, yes, that was there, underlying it a taste of vanilla, and overall, the tang of something sharp and slightly sour like the smell of limes.

"Other times she would wait until after washing to feed

me, when her skin was perfumed with bath oils, the scent of rose petals and violets, or magnolia and jasmine, she steaming from the hot water, burning me up as I sat on her lap, enveloped. Falling asleep there, my mouth at her breast, was a sensation that none other in the world has ever matched: a deep calm, a calm beyond all reason, oblivion.

"From the day she took me back from Sanma until I was banished, I slept in her bed when my father was away. About once a month, usually during the full moon, she would wait until I was asleep and slip away. Sometimes I would wake when she returned, feigning sleep when she came to check on me, and I would breathe in another, different odor, a heavy, rank, feral stink that poured over me as she bent down to kiss my cheek. Then she would go over to the window and throw open the shutters, stand there in the bright moonlight in nothing but that transparent silk bed gown, the light outlining her heavy breasts and hips, her slim arms, the smell so strong that I could almost see it coming off her like smoke.

"I remember, too, my fury when she told me that I could no longer feed at her breasts. I was seven years old, and though I knew that other children had stopped drinking their mother's milk years before, I'd imagined that I was different and could nestle there at her breasts forever. I went mad when she told me, screaming and crying and weeping with rage, she all the while looking on unmoved. I could hate her for that implacable gaze sometimes.

"'No more,' she said after a few minutes. 'You are too old now for me to feed you any longer. And besides, your father has finally shown some interest in the oldest of his ladies, shown interest after so long I ought to scorn him.' This I knew by then was no passing threat; from her arts, a scorning meant much more than just some idle form of emotional savagery. 'But I won't,' she said smiling. 'You are too old, and so am I, almost. You must stop so that I may have one last chance. Perhaps we will make another boy, your father and I.' She walked away for a moment, but quickly turned back and lifted my trembling chin with her finger. 'A boy who doesn't cry so much.'

"But it was not to be. My father's interest proved illusory, and his nighttime attentions in particular never shifted away from his younger wives. And then, he was always away on his endless trips in the following years, gone for six or eight months at a time—it might as well have been eternity for a child. So I had my mother to myself.

"Those days were paradise, my time on the isles of Penglai, every day blue skies empty of cloud, a light breeze wafting the scent of the willow catkins in from the garden, and I would awake with a hundred pleasurable possibilities dancing in my head: I could slip down to the river to swim and fish, or take my phoenix and dragon kites onto the open field between our house and the town and battle with the other boys, running here and there, dipping and swaying the kite so that the string, coated along its entire length with a glaze of crushed glass, would cross that of a rival, slice his string, and bring his kite crashing to earth; or I could make my way to the garrison where one of the arms instructors was on retainer to a group of families and would take us through our steps with the crossbow or the long bow or patiently parry and thrust with us on the sandy floors of the exercise arena. Then, too, there were the hills behind our house of which I have spoken, my private kingdom stocked with birds for my amusement, fish and fruit for the eating, the beauty of mountains and streams to please my eye.

"But all idylls must end, and this one ended, as so often, with my father's return. It was four months after my trip to the mountains to catch the eagle, autumn already fading and the harsh mountain winter just beginning to get a grip on the land. This time he didn't surprise me. I knew that he was due back from his trip: he had sent a servant ahead from Cheng-tu with some of his luggage a few weeks earlier. I was apprehensive, of course, for I knew that my disappearance could not be kept from him. But he came, formal and quiet as always, only nodding in acknowledgment as he walked past the assembled household, disappearing almost immediately into his study. I saw almost nothing of him thereafter, and a few days later my mother told me that he was leaving again, to return to Cheng-tu, and I felt a rush of relief, the joy of releasing urine after holding it too long.

"Then, just before he left—the horses neighing and stamping in the front courtyard, long plumes of mist blowing from their nostrils in the chill air before dawn, the ponies loaded with baggage, the servants already mounted, carrying their burning torches—he sent for me. When I arrived fresh from bed, tousled and gummy-eyed, he simply indicated a horse standing next to his. I didn't understand what he had in mind, but climbed aboard obediently. It was only when we had wound through the empty streets of the still-sleeping town and were halfway down the steep slope leading to the jetty that I began to realize he was taking me with him. Strange to think that my reaction was one of excitement: at last I would travel as I had always dreamed—to the delta where the great river emptied into the sea, perhaps to Chang An itself, residence of the emperor and teeming crossroads of the world, the center to which all things eventually flowed.

"It was no more than a few days' journey downriver to Cheng-tu, and I spent the entire trip at the railings of the river barge, waving to the passing boats. There were small fishing vessels trailing nets from their slender booms that stuck out on either side like vestigial wings, and barges like ours being hauled upriver, their decks covered in bales and crates. Sometimes I just stared at the passing countryside, the mountains and hills gradually flattening out into a plain that seemed to stretch on forever but proved only a plateau, the hills rising up around us again.

"Around midday on the second day, I heard a great din from behind, a cacophony of drums and gongs and cymbals, and saw that a line of barges was approaching us from behind, each one bedecked with streaming pennants in the vermilion and cream-yellow livery of the imperial house. Our barge pulled aside to allow the convoy to pass—a paddle wheeler was pulling the convoy downriver much faster than the tide was carrying us—and we saw that it was the month's salt tribute, five flat barges, each one weighed down deep in the water with a mountain of salt shining white as mounds of snow in the sun.

"There were other wonders, too, but sooner than seemed possible, we were in Cheng-tu, the river descending into a ravine, sheer red cliffs towering above us, the buildings of the city just visible, perched on top of the cliff some hundred feet up. When we docked, my father, who had remained in his cabin almost the entire time, allowing me free run of the boat, emerged and gave a few orders concerning the unloading of the cargo. He then beckoned to me and strode down the gangplank. We walked to the side of the cliff where there were a couple of wooden huts without roofs, ropes descending into them from far above. Stepping inside the hut, we seated ourselves in what seemed to be a small sedan chair, complete with curtains that my father pulled tight shut. There was a loud noise, perhaps a horn, from outside and after a sharp jerk, the box began to ascend. I rushed over to open the curtains and gaze out, but my father clamped his hand on my arm.

"'Don't touch the curtains,' he said, his voice grating. I looked back and saw that he had turned away, pressing his face into the padded corner of the box. Despite the chilly weather, I could see a beading of sweat on his forehead, and I realized that he was desperately afraid, afraid to look out, afraid to even move or speak. I felt a hot, exhilarating gush of triumph: He was afraid; I was not. It washed away all the beatings. Somehow this weakness brought me level with him, put him in my power, or so I thought.

"By the time we reached the top, he had recovered his usual grave poise and stepped calmly through the door on the opposite side we had entered, directly out into the crowded noisy streets of Cheng-tu. I remember little of the walk we took, though I must have spent it gawking around at the crowds and the buildings, the chariots and ten-man sedan chairs. After only a few minutes, we stopped in front of a huge red wooden gate and my father rapped for entry with the lion's-head knocker. We were led inside by a cowled monk, plunged into a warren of dark and dank corridors, the sudden change from bright sunlight to a dim illumination from widely spaced torches leaving me almost blind. Eventually we came to a low wooden door—one of many that stretched down the dimly lit corridor as far as the eye could see—and entered what appeared to be a monk's cell. There was a low writing table in one corner, in the other a rolled up sleeping mat, next to it a chamber pot. The only light came from a tiny window high up on the wall. One entire wall was covered with rows of empty shelves. Otherwise the room was bare.

"'If you refuse to study in my house,' my father said, 'you will study here. I shall return in a year to check on your progress.'

"With that, he turned, stepped quickly out the door and pulled it shut. I heard the bar outside fall into place, locking me in.

"I remained there for almost two years. Each day before dawn we were allowed out of the cells to bathe ourselves and empty our chamber pots. On the way back to the cells, we passed by the kitchens and collected our breakfast, a bowl of thick rice porridge—every day for two years the same white, viscous, lumpy porridge, no fragara pepper or shrimp paste to spice it, just a wide bowl of long-cooked rice that had the consistency of boiled glue. We ate this for almost every meal, sometimes with a few flakes of fish thrown in, other times with one or two peanuts, but always the same sickening porridge.

"Our midday and evening rice were brought to us in the cells 'so as not to interrupt our study,' a smirking guard once told me, breaking the rule of silence. He didn't reappear after that comment, the only time one of them ventured to speak. Every other day I was led down the long, dank corridors and released into the main courtyard of the old monastery for two hours of exercise. All these journeys were made alone but for two or three silent guards carrying heavy wooden staves, for guards they were, despite being dressed in monk's cowls. For two years I never saw another human being save those maddeningly silent guards, but I knew they were there in the cells whose doors ran down either side of the corridor, young men like me whose parents were desperate enough for their sons to pass the examinations that they would pay to have them locked away in solitary confinement where there was nothing else to do but study.

"The method was simple: place the inmates in a position where they could either study or go mad out of boredom and loneliness. They gave us copies of the five classics, the various standard collections of poetry, and old questions from the exams. All this came on arrival; along with as much paper and ink as any scholar could wish for. Written requests would produce commentaries, though only one at a time. But nothing else.

"Like many simple ideas ruthlessly pursued, it worked. It was there that I honed my understanding of the classics, though I still knew deep within me that whatever happened, I would never take the examinations, no matter how well I came to understand them. I knew there were more important things prepared for me. I am the only man of my generation to have this unique understanding, the only one with enough courage to reject entirely the whole administrative apparatus, the petty joy of promotion, the allure of power. What can you say about a system to which the greatest minds of the age have failed over and over again to gain entry: Meng Hao-ran, Tu Fu, Chen Tzu-ang, and Lo Pin-wang. They all took the exams and failed. Some of course eventually managed to pass, but at what cost, crammed into those tiny cells for five days every year, the humiliation of appearing in the examination halls when middle-aged, sometimes three times the age of the youngest candidates, year after year of failure. It is enough to drive many men mad, their intellects eaten up by bitterness and disappointment. And even if they do pass after all those attempts, there is no guarantee of office. Look again at Tu Fu, caught three times in political examinations at which the chief minister himself graded the papers (a ludicrous thought, as Li Linfu could hardly read or write and was known to mistake the character 'star' for 'emperor,' which even a half-literate barbarian can tell apart) and failed all the candidates just to prove to the emperor that there were no more men of talent to be discovered in the empire, that his administration was the best it could possibly be.

"Poor old Tu Fu. He never did pass, never recovered from those failures; they ruined his understanding of himself, his assessment of his talents. In any case he was eventually admitted to the service through special dispensation a few years ago, a time of war and special needs. But I am told he has spent the years since waiting for employment, offered nothing but humiliating clerkships, living on favors and loans, reduced to such wretched poverty that one of his sons died of starvation while he was away seeking patronage. Poor old Tu Fu, always unlucky. But what chance did he have? Even Wang Wei, with all his connections and his blue-blood lineage couldn't get a decent position, though he never had to sit the exams, of course. He just slipped in along with all the other inbred poltroons on an aristocrat's waiver. There was never any danger of one of *his* sons dying because he couldn't find employment—he simply retired to his country estate and penned more of those little ditties whose utter vacuity is mistaken by fools for profundity.

"No, I had decided then not to take those accursed exams and didn't pay much attention to the classics beyond what I had to do to keep up appearances, rounding off what I had learned in my studies at home. Much more importantly, it was in those dismal years that I came to take full command of the corpus of poetry. I memorized everything I could—I have always astonished others with my memory—from the *Book of Songs* through to the great Han masters, from Chu Yuan down to greater spirits who wrote the first modern poetry, Tao Yuan Ming being the greatest of these, a true mountain dweller, a shunner of the rewards of office, not unlike me. It was the beginning of my life as a poet, this learning. For nothing of value can be written without a profound knowledge of what has gone before.

"I learned, too, of the horror of being alone, utterly alone. For the first weeks I was like a wild bird in a cage, banging on the doors throughout the day until my hands were bloody and raw, screaming for release until my voice was reduced to a cracked whisper. When the guards came to collect me in the morning, I would attack them as soon as the door was opened a crack, screaming to get out. They beat me, of course. One fat fellow with a walleye took especially great pleasure in it, wrapping the end of his stave in cloth so that I wouldn't be bruised, standing over me as I lay on the ground and administering a few extra blows, often adding a swift kick towards my groin as his parting gift. But eventually even he tired of his sport, and they just left me alone for four long days in the cell, surrounded by the smell of my own shit. Then one night I remembered my mother's treatment of the thrushes, how she had gently taken the bag from me and released the birds, recalled over and over again how the birds had tumbled and flashed into the air, a whirring blaze of colors, how they had righted themselves and sped away over the rooftop. Holding that image of escape before me, I knew I could survive. The next morning I called out to the guards and told them I was willing to cooperate.

"I thought, too, of the myna imprisoned for too long to imagine it was being granted its freedom, and of how we make our own prisons and our own freedom, thence understanding the joys and solace of being alone, the way the mind can concentrate on one thing, a single shining aspect, and find it in the whole world. This is a truth I have sought again and again in the mountains, a glimpse of something that always seems to be just at the corner of our sight, never entirely within grasp, like stars, invisible when gazed at directly even on the darkest night but revealed on the edge of vision when one looks away. Or the way that a single swift darting and weaving in the late afternoon sun, scimitar wings flashing, can be a creature of heaven, a sign and symbol of all that we strive for, in prison and out, the thing that we can never grasp but always want, that shimmering, elusive spirit that will forever remain a mystery.

"After the first few weeks of futile resistance, I became a model student, if student I was, fulfilling all the essay assignments set by the unseen examiners, always smiling and pleasant to the guards, docilely allowing myself to be led back and forth each day like some bemused bull on the way to the slaughter. But all the time I was also building myself up inside, noting the shifts the guards worked, who was attentive and who careless, which men manned the walls of the exercise yard, which ones carried the keys. I made sure to build up my strength, too, pushing myself in the courtyard each time I was allowed out, running endless laps under the high walls, repeating over and over the steps of swordplay and the few Shaolin-style martial moves that the arms instructor at home had taught me, the tiger and the deer, the monkey plucks flowers, and so on.

"Sometime after the first year had passed, I knew my father was not going to come and collect me. Six months after that realization—I think it was that long, I didn't begin keeping a calendar until I had lost track of the days, but I knew it had been near winter when I had entered and it was then late summer—I determined to leave. One morning as we neared my cell after passing the kitchen, I took the bowl of porridge that had been ladled from a boiling pot minutes before and flung it over the head of the guard walking in front of me. Then snatching up the wooden stave he dropped in his agony, I scythed around in a single motion, sweeping the heavy club as hard as I could into the knee of the guard behind. There was a brittle crunch as the wood hit bone and he toppled over like a felled tree. I gazed down at him for a moment as he lay there, opening his mouth to scream in agony, the scream caught in his throat by the shock of it. I felt nothing looking at him. He was the worst of them, he of the walleye and the cloth-covered stave in the early days. I hit him on the head before he could begin to scream, knocking him out, then turned to the other guard who was sitting on the stone floor, struggling frantically to pull off his robe which was soaked in the scalding porridge. I hit him on the head, too, then dragged the two of them into my cell by the cowls of their robes. I tied them both with strips torn from the cover of my quilt, stuffed their mouths with wads of cotton and gagged them, then stripped the robe from the second guard. His knee, I saw, had swollen in a few short minutes to the size of a musk melon. I gave it a kick and he jerked spasmodically, his eyes popping open, goggling at me. I smiled at him and kicked the knee again, turning away from the resulting convulsions. The other guard lay breathing heavily through his nose, giving off a gurgling, snoring sound. His black hair was matted with glutinous liquid and white rice grains, and what I could see of his neck was flushed a bright scarlet, here and there spotted with small darker red boils. Donning the purloined robe, I glanced one last time at the cell that had been my home for two years, stuffed a sheaf of poems in my sleeve, then slipped out the door, dropping the bar into place behind me as I left.

"The rest was easy. I made my way out through the kitchen, the hood of the monk's robe drawn up around my head, then into a grimy rear courtyard full of slop buckets from the kitchens, past a dozing guard who to my horror opened his eyes and called out to me before I was past, but it was only to toss me the key to the outer door, and suddenly I was out into the bustling streets of Cheng-tu. I walked to the cliff's edge, made my way carefully down the 1235 steps cut into the rock face (I counted every one), and used the string of cash the guard had carried in his sleeve to buy passage on a cargo junk heading upstream. In two days I was in Lanlian.

"I arrived in the dark, near midnight, having ridden the last section from Hsiwang. My ship had docked there for the night, and I was too impatient to wait for it to continue its journey the next day. A bright near-full moon blazed its cold light down on the town, and the black sky was charged with a thousand sparkling stars; somewhere a few sleepless ravens cawed, but otherwise all was silent, the town deep in innocent slumber as it had been when I left, all unchanged in the streets as though I had only been gone for a long day's hunting rather than a two-year incarceration. The house, too, was silent and dark when I approached it, not even a glimmer of a lantern where there should have been a watchman in the gate house. There was no noise from anywhere inside, not even the distant barking of a dog in the rear.

"I walked up to the double gates and raised my hand to knock, hesitated, then lowered my arm. It occurred to me to wonder how I would be received, whether my father was at home, whether my mother had missed me, whether she had thought of me over and over each day the way I had thought of her, whether she longed for me the way I had longed for her.

"Instead of knocking I made my way round the side of the compound, back to the ruined watchtower that stood silent against the night sky. I took the old familiar route in, through the top of the tower and over the edge of the roof, dropping down onto the veranda that ran around the second floor of my mother's courtyard. The trees and bushes looked strangely overgrown and the fishpond in the center appeared half dried up, its edges glistening with mud. I walked towards my mother's rooms, my feet kicking up puffs of dust in the bright moonlight. The door to her bedroom was ajar and I pushed it open, made my way over to the windows against which I had watched her silhouette so often, and flung open the shutters with a crash. The moonlight flooded in, revealing an empty room—no bed, no furniture at all, only here and there a few pieces of rubbish, a scattered bundle of rags, a discarded broom, and other objects in the shadows that I couldn't make out. The door to her medicine cupboard was wide open. It was empty, too, the hundreds of drawers hanging out or splintered into pieces on the floor.

"I ran outside, into the corridor, down the stairs and into the courtyard. There I saw a huddle of men coming through the archway, holding torches high. I ran towards them and saw that it was old Fang, my father's estate manager. He was carrying a large woodsman's axe. Behind him were several frightened looking servants carrying torches.

"'Halt,' he quavered, attempting to raise the axe menacingly but barely managing to bring it up to shoulder level.

"'Fang,' I cried, "where is my mother, where has he taken her."

"'Mother? What mother?'

"'My mother, Fang, you old fool. I am Tai Po, come back. Where is my mother?' I was standing in front of him now, the light of the torches on my face.

"'Master Li, is it you? I thought you . . . '

"'Where is she? Where is she? Tell me now!'

"I stepped closer and plucked the axe from his weak grasp, pulled him towards me by the hem of his night robe.

"'She is dead,' he cried, 'dead a year or more, died in childbirth.'

"'No!" I shouted. 'No! No! She is not dead.'

"But Fang just nodded his head insistently.

"'Yes, she is dead. Your father cleared out when she passed away. Hasn't been back since, left no instructions . . . '

"'No! No!' I cried again in anguish, pushing him away from me and running back towards the front gate, screaming and weeping, running until I reached his study. There I burst through the doors with a desperate lunge and brought the axe down on the delicate rosewood writing desk that stood as always in the center of the room, chopping at it over and over until the blade buried itself deep in the wood and wouldn't come free. I kicked the remains of the desk aside and lurched over to the cabinets, scattering the stacked scrolls onto the floor in great heaps, unrolling across each other in a tangle of paper, sweeping row after row of celadon and sancai glaze vases, ewers, and incense burners off the shelves to shatter on the floor, then pulling the cabinets themselves down, one of them crashing onto me as I stood there, ripping a gash in my forehead that began to bleed copiously, I paying no heed to the wound, finally freeing the axe with a huge heave, smashing and smashing at the fallen cabinets until there was nothing left and I stood there panting, Fang and the servants hovering in the doorway with their torches and their frightened faces, the blood trickling down into my right eye, all passion spent, filled with an awful black emptiness, the knowledge that I would never see her again. I threw the axe aside with a clatter, pushed pass the servants, and waited numbly as one of them hurriedly opened the front gate, then walked blindly out, never looking back."

four 李白

"I HAVE NEVER RETURNED," LI PO SAYS.

He stands and gathers his robe about him, gazing out at the water for a moment, then shivers and walks away, across the deck and into the cabin. Although it is early afternoon, the sun shining brightly overhead, Wang Lung notices there is a chill in the air; autumn is coming. His hand—he holds it up in front of him, fire running up his arm—is like a claw, bent and frozen. He twists his neck, links his fingers together, and presses outward, cracking all his knuckles in a single satisfying burst, then begins to stretch gratefully, the bones in his back cracking in succession. But before Wang Lung can stand, Li Po is back, carrying a black lacquer tray set with two flasks of wine, cups, and dishes of sweetmeats and other delicacies: dried oysters—a great favorite of the poet for the way they complement wine; summer garlic; dried, sugared ginger; loquats; and two plump, bright orange persimmons. Popping a couple of oysters into his mouth and pouring himself a measure, Li Po starts to talk and the boy picks up his brush again with a sigh:

"I left there like a quarrel from a crossbow, onto a ship, past Cheng-tu, shooting through the gorges and out in the wide river, thrust into the world like a newborn child. I spent most of my remaining money on a cabin and stayed locked inside for the whole trip, imprisoned as surely as I had been in that tiny cell, weeping day and night, howling out my anguish and confusion. The passengers and the crew didn't know what to make of me and after a while they left me alone. I think I had run mad, screaming abuse at anyone who knocked at my door, pacing endlessly around the cabin. I would run over my brief visit home again and again, then call up a host of happy memories of my mother, always returning to that terrible moment of realization that I was alone in the world, and flinging myself down on the bunk in a storm of tears, venting my shame and grief. Finally after almost a week, I emerged blinking into the light late one sunny morning, my eyes dry at last, purged and clean, older, a little wiser, ready for my new life, whatever that might be.

"The ship was coming into dock at a small river port, a place called Wanhsien. As soon as the gangplank hit the quay, I walked straight off. As I roamed the narrow streets of the town, I took stock: I was frantically hungry after a week in which I had eaten little besides some old rice cakes. I had enough money to pay for one or two meals, but then what? What could I do? How, more to the point, could I earn enough money to eat? I could compose verses, of course, that better than anyone I had met. Sing a little and play the main scholarly instruments, the lute and the twelve-string zither. I knew something of the martial arts, could fight with a sword or quarterstaff, even the pike and long halberd, and feared no man in unarmed combat; my size protected me against most, and the training I had been given by the army drill instructor in Lanlian covered the rest. I could run for an hour without tiring and recite entire books of the classics, could chant most of the *Book of Songs*, to say nothing of the poems of Chu Yuan, Tao Chien, or Tao Yuan Ming. But what did I know of life? Nothing whatsoever. Less than nothing, for I had grown up in a strange, cosseted household of women. Indeed I preferred the company of women; I knew little of the ways of men, men without women.

"Confucius of course said that when he was fifteen he set out to master what had been written: to this day, the characters for fifteen mean 'setting out to study.' But I was far ahead of the old fraud from Shantung: I had already mastered the classics. Now, after those years of confinement, I wanted no more of books and studying, of scrolls and musty library air. I wanted to experience life outside the walls, to meet demons and goblins, dancing girls and courtesans, warriors and immortals, poets like Meng Hao-ran, whose poems had penetrated even to our little town. In short, I wanted to live. First, however, I had to eat.

"It was already late in the morning, the shopkeepers closing up for lunch, so I ducked into a tavern and with the little cash left in my sleeve ordered a few jugs of wine and a plate of wild boar stew, a local specialty, and fell to eating with relish. I was determined that my last meal before complete destitution would be an enjoyable one.

"As I ate I noticed a small raised platform at the front of the tavern. Then I heard a stir and looked up to see an old man carrying a moon guitar come out of a door in the rear and sit down on a cushion on the stage. He had a huge silver beard, a beard such as I had never seen on anyone but a foreigner, covering his cheeks and neck and falling halfway down his chest. By his features he might have been Chinese, but something gave away a desert ancestry, though very diluted, some way of regarding the drinkers in front of him as though they were the servants and he the master. He plucked each of the guitar strings in succession, checking that the tuning was true. Then the door at the back opened again, and there emerged a slim young girl of about my age or perhaps younger by a few years. It was difficult to tell through the heavy makeup. She was dressed in a simple lilac robe, her face like a blossoming rose, flushed slightly in the heat of the tavern. For all the delicacy of her features, however, there was no shyness in her expression, which was determined, even willful, her large eyes full of sharp intelligence, her head held high and proud.

"The old man struck a few deep chords and she began to sing. At once I was enraptured: she had an astonishing voice, not the kind of heartbreaking natural beauty the gods had bestowed on my Arma but the same ability to wring emotion from the music, though this girl did it through the sheer force of will. She was also highly trained, and sang with great power and control, like nothing I had ever heard before, songs from the steppes, from Serindia and beyond, in Turkic and in languages I didn't know, songs of haunting beauty and keening loss that silenced the chatter of the drinkers and even set a few men to weeping.

"But for all her glory, what impressed itself on me most that day was the old man accompanying her on the moon guitar. I had never heard this instrument played except indifferently in just such a tavern. But he was like a god come down from heaven, his fingers flying over the strings and frets so fast that they were invisible at times, producing a range of sounds like an entire orchestra, from frills and ruffles of astonishing speed and delicacy to great reverberating chords that seemed to echo deep in the bones, speaking of the mystery of life, the flawed genius of man, the hopelessness of love, pulling forth primal emotions that cannot be named. As I listened I decided that I would become his student. Oh, to learn to play like him! Like being able to summon a portion of the Absolute out of oneself!

"They performed for perhaps half an hour—I was so absorbed, hardly noticing the time—and when they had finished, she helping the old man to his feet, the two of them turning to leave by the rear door, I jumped up eagerly to follow them. But the fool of a tavern owner, who had been reluctant to serve me and had been eyeing me since—my clothes hardly gave an impression of wealth, after all—now decided that I must be trying to make a quick exit without paying. Without so much as a word, he tackled me as I was fumbling in my sleeve for some coins. In the ensuing ruckus—which lasted for some time, with other customers deciding to take advantage of his preoccupation to try and leave without paying or to help themselves to more wine—the girl and the old man slipped away. When I finally managed to get away, I searched the street for them, but there was no trace to be found: they seemed to have disappeared.

"Keenly disappointed, I spent the rest of the day trudging around that accursed little town inquiring for work, first at the apothecary, though I knew the guild requirements would bar me from working there. I even inquired at the magistrate's compound, hoping for employment as a clerk. But everywhere they were suspicious: where was I from, why did I have no recommendations—petty, quibbling questions of the kind you would expect from shopkeepers. Deflated, I turned to menial labor, but found little there, either. It was far too late in the year for there to be much work for itinerant farm laborers, and most of the shops were bound up so tight by guild rules that they couldn't even hire a sweeper without consultation. At last, late in the afternoon, the shadows long again, I stood before a pork butcher's. The owner was a gross, red-faced individual who stood at the front of his shop with his arms crossed, one moment darting inside to curse and cuff one of the team of choppers and apprentice butchers, the next back at the door, simpering to a new customer. I walked over to where he stood.

"'Excuse me, sir,' I said, as politely as I knew how.

"'What is it, boy?' He didn't even look at me, continuing to scan the busy street for potential customers.

"'I was wondering whether you might have some use for me. Whether I might find some employment at your establishment.'

"Now the butcher swiveled his florid face towards me. His eyes were small and suspicious, lost in the puffy flesh of his cheeks. A sparse moustache sprouted from his upper lip.

"'Employment in my establishment, is it? And what sort of employment might that be?'

"'Well, I can write and also calculate. Perhaps I could help with the accounts.'

"'Accounts I do myself. Do you think I would let someone else get his hands on my books?' He paused and regarded me suspiciously. 'You are not from Wanhsien.'

"'No, sir. I'm from Lanlian, upriver.'

"'Never heard of it. What of your family, your clanmembers?'

"'I am an orphan,' which was near enough the truth. 'Both my parents died last week. My clan home is in the far north, the Li's of Lunghsi. The same as the emperor.'

"The butcher snorted. 'Emperor's clan. And an orphan. Next you'll be telling me about your crippled sister and starving brothers. What else can you do besides add?'

"'Anything. I am strong and hungry. I'll do anything.'

"'Anything, eh?' He stared at me for a moment, stroking his little moustache with his right forefinger. I noticed that the fingernail was long and crusted with what must have been dried blood. Then, suddenly, he smiled, or rather leered, stretching his lips upward to reveal a mouthful of stumpy brown teeth.

"'I think I have just the work for you. Just the thing for a young lordling.'

"He led me through the shop and into a dank corridor at the back. We emerged into a large shed. On one side were piles of pig carcasses, all sliced wide open and eviscerated, the flesh a strange, dead white tinged with blue, their red-washed ribs gaping, the flaccid skin folded over in corrugated rows. On the other side of the room, a team of four men stood at long trestle tables, dismembering the pigs with swift blows of their cleavers, then throwing the severed parts onto heaps in front of them: here a row of heads resting on their ears, snouts pointed skyward; there a pile of trotters and scattered haunches, the sunlight streaming in from the open sides of the shed, picking out the white knob of a hip joint from within the folds of tan flesh. The smell was overwhelming—fetid, ripe, and vinegary—catching in the back of the throat.

"The butcher waddled straight through this shambles without stopping, throwing only the briefest curse at the workers as he passed—*Hurry up you lazy sister-fuckers. It'll soon be dark and you will pay for the oil if I have to bring in lamps so you can finish today's quota.* We passed through a gate at the other end of the shed and entered a long cobbled courtyard filled with hay and a couple of broken-down, two-wheeled carts. Once outside, I inhaled deeply to clear my head and settle my stomach, but another, unmistakable smell hit me with such force that I almost halted in my tracks: shit. Now the butcher was standing by a double-leaved stable door, this one leading into a large barn. He swung the door open and pointed inside.

"'You are lucky I'm offering you this, very lucky. My pigboy is sick, or says he is. You can help him for a while.'

"I hesitated at the door.

"He waved me in impatiently. 'All your meals provided—plenty of meat, too—and forty copper cash a month.'

"'What will my duties be?'

"'Oh, the pigboy will teach all you need to know—your *duties*—no more expert pigboy in all of Wanhsien, I shouldn't think.'

"Still I hesitated. Forty cash was the price of five flagons of wine, not even an evening's drinking.

"'Do you want work or not?' he cried querulously at last. 'There's plenty others would take it if it's too good for the likes of you.'

"Sighing, I stepped inside. The butcher slammed both top and bottom doors shut, cutting off the sunlight and plunging the inside of the barn into a gloomy semidarkness. I took a cautious step forward and my foot sank into what could only be a veritable lake of pig shit, rising up above the ankles of my beautiful red deerskin boots. Squelching forward, I made my way towards a ladder at the rear of the barn that led up to a loft. Strangely there didn't seem to be any pigs, only the evidence that many hundreds of them had passed through on the way to slaughter. I climbed the ladder and scanned the hay-covered loft but saw nothing and was turning to descend when I spotted a dark shape in a corner. Walking over, I saw it was a man, or a sort of man, terribly emaciated, his legs drawn up into a fetal position. He was dressed in rags but almost entirely covered in hay, the patches of exposed skin black with grime. I called out a few times, but he didn't stir, so I bent over and shook his shoulder. At this he groaned and slowly turned his head, muttering something inaudible. He was old, ancient, his face a mass of wrinkles, some of them carved so deep that they had filled with caked dirt, forming sharp black gashes slashed down his cheeks. His hair was long and matted, stuck with hay and burrs and twigs. He gazed at me without speaking, his gummy eyes blank and uncomprehending, breathing in ragged wheezes, a line of dried white spittle ringing his mouth.

"'Are you Pigboy?' I asked, but got no response, just a blank stare. Then he rolled over and curled up again, pulling more of the straw over his body with a claw-like hand. For a long time I stood there, irresolute, then finally leaned over and shook his shoulder once more. This time he seemed to register my presence.

"'I'm here to help you. The butcher has hired me to help you,' I said, pronouncing the words one syllable at a time. 'I'm to be your assistant.'

"The only response was a faster rate of wheezing and a slight shaking of the shoulders. Later I realized he must have been laughing.

"After a moment he stood up, slowly, painfully unfolding himself until at last he was fully erect, a head taller than I was but only half my weight—and I was a slim boy in those days, not my current thickened self. He was the thinnest person I had—or have—ever seen in my life, the ropy muscles of his arms and legs clinging like worms to his bones, of which every corner and joint was visible, his knees as sharp as most men's elbows, his skin stretched taut like the cover of a drum, everywhere jutting bone, all hollows and dark shadow. I gaped at him for a moment, noting with fascination that his Adam's apple, which was just about the level of my eyes, was outlined so clearly under the skin that I could count the number of rings from which it was made, see the sinews that kept it in place. Pigboy ignored me, however, brushing past and levering his long legs onto the ladder. He began to climb down, then paused, looked directly at me, and waved a skeletal hand indicating that I should accompany him.

"Thus began one of the strangest periods in my life.

"The Pigboy initiated me into the ways of his tiny kingdom, which was demarcated as precisely as the degrees of an arc in an astronomer's measuring globe, stretching from the threshold of the door to the butchering room down the alley, encompassing the barn and a walled courtyard in the rear and stopping at the high wooden gates that led into the street. Within the limits of his world, Pigboy was in his element, shuffling confidently from one task to the next on those spindly stick legs that looked as though a gust of wind would snap them. He was terrified of the outside world, that was clear, and in fact I only saw him leave his enclave once, and that was at the very end, when he was forced into it.

"I often wondered where his family was, if he had any, or whether he had spent his entire life in the pigsties. But I soon discovered that Pigboy couldn't—or wouldn't—answer my questions. He seemed to have lost the power of speech, or perhaps given it up, communicating with me mostly by a series of grunts and gestures. Nevertheless we got along well enough; indeed I became quite attached to him. It is astonishing the complexity of emotion that can be conveyed by such simple means. A primitive system of that type also has the advantage of excluding discussion of subjects such as politics or religion, thus at a stroke eliminating much of the basis for disagreement.

"Not surprisingly, though, Pigboy's greatest rapport seemed to be with his charges, the herds of swine that passed through his domain on their way to becoming a mound of shredded pork atop someone's fried noodles. The animals were delivered from the outlying farms two or three times a month, depending on the demand, usually in batches of seventy-five. Packed on top of each other in bamboo crates, they were twisted and crushed by the press, snouts and limbs poking haphazardly out of the bars. When they arrived the noise was something to behold, a storm of oinking, squealing, and snorting protests, something like the sound the damned must make in some deep level of hell while being slowly roasted on the spit or boiled alive. Also, of course, the pigs knew where they were going, could smell the blood of their cousins that was caked inches-deep on the floor of the alley outside the barn. For contrary to what many think, pigs are perceptive and—by animal standards—intelligent creatures, capable of affection as sincere as any dog or horse. They are capable, too, of sensing the emotions of their human masters and understanding the use to which a sharp knife can be put.

"All this Pigboy knew, as well as something more, something of the secret life of pigs that most of us will never know—or care to know. When the beasts were delivered, the cart carrying them rolled through a high set of gates into the courtyard behind the barn. Pigboy would never show himself during the actual unloading, for the gates were wide open to the outside world, and the mere sight of the citizens of Wanhsien passing by on their daily business on the street was enough to send him wailing into the hayloft. The carters, well used to his ways, would dump the crates in the cobbled yard and leave. As soon as they had shut the gates behind them, Pigboy would scurry over and drop the bar into place. Then he would turn to the pigs, passing among the crates like some stork-like Buddhist abbot among a swinish congregation, squatting down and whispering, stroking and consoling, slipping off the catches that held the crates shut and gently easing the animals out one by one, the pigs by now soothed, patiently awaiting their release, then trotting obediently into the barn, all this happening in almost complete silence save for the occasional grunt.

"He loved those animals. Many people would laugh to hear it, but to me it was the saddest thing in the world, this doomed love that saw him pour affection out to a constant parade of creatures he would soon be obliged to slaughter. Even I developed a certain liking for the animals if they stayed with us longer than a week or so, and began to recognize them as individuals. I remember a fat fellow with a torn ear and a black spot just above his right eye who took a shine to me and followed me around like a faithful dog. I kept him out of the knife's way for an entire month, but one day he was the last one left in the sty—a delivery was due—and the butcher was shouting for more meat, so he too took the trip out of the barn and into that gore-caked alley. It was worse for Pigboy, far worse, for as I said, he truly loved the animals. I'm sure he felt much closer to the pigs than he ever had to any human being, and perhaps because of the depth of his emotions, he displayed a bitter ferocity when it came time for the slaughter. Despite his appearance he was immensely strong and would cut a pig's head off with one blow of the cleaver, his face twisted into a grimace of anger and pain.

"The work was as regular as the rising and setting of the sun. The same thing over and over again: feeding the pigs, mucking out the barn, loading the manure onto small two-wheeled carts that were collected by the carters for use in the fields. The butcher was too cheap to let us use water except under his supervision—the water was brought up from the river and cost ten cash for a large tubful—so we were only able to wash the floor and clean up properly once every five or six days.

"And then, of course, there was the business of slaughtering and disemboweling. I am not a squeamish man—I couldn't have done the job if I was—but only the most densely insensitive brute could fail to be affected by the endless extinction of life. I grew expert at dispatching them as swiftly as possible, one very hard rip of the knife in the neck would do it (I didn't have Pigboy's skill with the cleaver), then a few minutes' wait for the animal to bleed to death, though after I had been working for about a month, our job was complicated by an order from the butcher to preserve the animals' blood: he had apparently only just discovered the skill of making black sausage and was quite beside himself over the thousands of buckets of valuable blood that he had lost over the years. This meant holding the heaving pig upside down over a basin while its throat was being cut, a process in which they were not terribly happy to cooperate.

"Once the pigs had stopped struggling, once in fact they

were dead, the procedure was simple: first the long slice from anus to sternum, careful to avoid cutting open any of the intestines, the smell of whose innards was enough to outrage even our deadened nostrils, a few blows with the cleaver to separate the two halves of the rib cage, several swift cuts to loosen the diaphragm and other organs from their anchors and sever the windpipe, then a little manipulation with the hands and the whole steaming, slippery mess would slide out as one. All this I eventually managed to accomplish at a reasonably speedy rate, but I never even remotely approached the skill of Pigboy, who could kill and gut a pig in hardly longer than it would take to describe it being done.

"Once the disemboweling itself was finished, we separated out the intestines and various organs. The intestines we had to clean later—passing our hands along their entire length, squeezing all the time so that the half-digested slops would come out one side and the shit would be squeezed out the other. The liver, kidneys, heart, and so on we placed in separate wooden tubs that were carried into the main butchering room by the butchers working there, a very aloof set of men. They regarded pigboys as beneath contempt, wouldn't even speak to us. Any attempt to cross into their area was met with united resistance, as I found out one day early on when I thoughtlessly carried one of the tubs full of kidneys across the threshold and dropped it on the floor. All three butchers turned and advanced as one, holding their cleavers menacingly in front of them.

"'Get out, you diseased dog's ass,' one of them shouted, 'and if you ever come back we'll cut off one of your hands as a reminder not to come again.'

"Next, we carried the carcasses from the end of the alley where they were killed to the doorway of the butchering room, there to be dropped for collection. It wasn't far, perhaps two hundred yards, but the pigs were very heavy—often they weighed as much as a large man or more—and were slippery and awkward to handle. From Pigboy I learned that the only way to carry the carcasses without dropping them was to sling them onto your back. This was a gruesome process that involved hooking the forelegs over your shoulders (they served as handles to hold onto while walking) and then fitting the gaping cut over your head to prevent the pig from sliding off. Naturally this meant that my hair would become smeared with blood and slick intestinal juices.

"It was this aspect of life as a pigboy—always being smeared in blood and shit—that bothered me the most, not the isolation, the numbing routine, the absurd wages, or the brutal butcher. Perhaps it was because I had grown up in the company of women, but to this day I am uncomfortable if I cannot wash at least once a day, preferably twice. After wine and good food, there is no pleasure more unchanging, more loyal, than a hot bath. In any case, because of the butcher's restrictions, there was nowhere to even splash water on my face and hands in the evenings. If I wanted to wash, I had to walk down to the river, then several miles up the bank to get to an area where the currents were benign enough to allow bathing. It was a long walk in darkness at the end of a weary day, and after attempting to go regularly in the first days, I gave up and resigned myself to making the trip only a few times a month. But these occasions became the highlight of my life, the only real treat I had to look forward to. Until you have spent days and days covered in a thick grime of blood and excrement, your hair caked with it and infested with lice, every part of your body constantly itching, the smell so strong that you gag when waking up in the mornings, until you have experienced that, you can have no real comprehension of the true joy of washing, even at night in frigid river water, the cold mud squelching between your toes.

"In fact it was the cold that eventually brought my time as an apprentice pigboy to an abrupt end. The last time I went down to the river was the third week of the eleventh month, when the hoarfrost was so heavy on the ground in the mornings that I was grateful to step down into the floor of the barn and plunge my bare feet into the steaming piles of newly deposited shit. I had been forced to stop wearing my beautiful red leather boots some time before; they simply couldn't stand up to the daily wear and tear, had begun to rot, so I washed and dried them, then stuffed them with straw and buried them under a pile of hay in the farthest corner of the loft.

"That evening I had made my way down to the river for the first time in nearly a month. But when I arrived at my usual spot, shed my clothes, and stepped in, an icy vise clamped itself around my feet: the mountains which fed the mighty river were already in the grip of winter; soon it would be the turn of the lowlands.

"Standing there irresolute, naked and shivering, I told myself that, having come all this way, I would be a fool to waste the trip. So I blundered out to where the water came up to my hips. There I quickly splashed some onto my chest, plunged my torso and head once into the river, and then retreated. I didn't even consider attempting to rinse my clothes, simply dressed as quickly as I could with my limbs shivering uncontrollably and stumbled back through the dark, the sharp stones piercing even my calloused soles, promising myself I would buy a warm woolen robe and a pair of cloth shoes.

"Despite the brisk walk, my teeth were still chattering as I made my way through the town towards the night market. There, mingling with the crowds, the narrow streets brightly lit by huge lanterns proclaiming good luck for the mid-autumn moon festival, I suddenly felt an immense loneliness; for the first time since my solitary confinement on the boat, I allowed myself to think of my dead mother and felt a rush of bittersweet tenderness, memories of festivals past, I as a child running through the courtyards of the womens' quarters, a lantern in the shape of a goldfish bobbing in front of me, running towards the waiting arms of my mother.

"'Hey you stinking dog's head, get out of it. Do you want to ruin my business?'

"I was jerked out of my reverie to find that I had stopped in front of an open-air wine shop, a cart equipped with a charcoal stove from which the owner, a squat, surly looking individual, dispensed pots of heated wine to his customers who sat under an awning. I had forgotten that though I had bathed myself, the clothes I wore were still impregnated with half a month's worth of pig excrement and viscera.

"'Listen, prickface,' I snapped back, 'I'll stand where I want. And if you don't show a little more respect I might decide to come and sit down and have a chat with a few of your customers. A little hot wine would do wonders to keep out the cold, however,' I added more amicably, 'and if you were to give me a couple of flasks, I might consider drinking somewhere else.'

"He hesitated, then from the corner of his eye saw several of the drinkers who had been regarding me with disgusted grimaces begin to shift back their stools from the low wooden tables he had placed under the awning. 'Sit down, sirs, sit down, the boy is leaving,' he called over his shoulder, thrusting a couple of flasks at me. 'Take them and begone, you shit-ridden bumpkin, and if you ever come back again I'll take my knife to you.'

"Well pleased, I tucked the bottles into my sleeve and wandered further down the street to a clothing stall where I purchased a robe and a pair of shoes, also at a remarkable discount, for the merchant had seen the crowds magically melt away as I approached. Walking back, humming a song, I drank most of the first flask in a few long gulps. Indeed, by the time I returned to the barn and lay down in the hayloft, I felt surprisingly dizzy. And despite the wine and my new robe, I had started to shiver again. Pigboy was there, huddled in his usual spot, wheezing like a creaky old bellows. I was concerned, for in recent days, I had noticed that his breathing had grown more labored and his movements slower and slower. In his weakened state he had even begun to forgo his normal method of dispatching the pigs, now forced to slit their throats and watch them bleed to death, his expression more anguished than usual.

"Taking another long swallow of wine, I stumbled over, shook him by the shoulder, and thrust the wine at him. Pigboy looked up blearily at me, grabbed the flask from my hand, and swallowed the contents in a series of long gulps, his Adam's apple bobbing madly, then rolled over and curled up in the straw again. Shrugging, I lay down and almost immediately passed into a sleep that was rent with gruesome dreams, pigs with the face of the butcher presenting their throats for the knife, stacks of disemboweled human carcasses, liquid demons made of blood hovering round me, red eyes burning.

"When I woke I knew that I was sick, sicker than I had ever been before. My skin was burning, my throat on fire, my bones ached, and when I stood a wave of dizziness forced me to lie down again. I didn't move—couldn't—when Pigboy rose a few moments later, and I fell back into a feverish doze after he left. When I woke again I could see by the angle of the sunbeams penetrating through chinks in the barn's wooden walls that it was late afternoon. I had been awakened by shouting outside in the alley, shouting that grew louder as it came nearer, the hoarse voice of the butcher unmistakable in the ruckus. He was shouting for me, that I soon determined, breaking off now and then to berate Pigboy:

'Malingering shit-caked dog, sleep on the job will you? Sleep away the day when there are hungry customers in the store? Get up, you spindle-shanked sod; and where is your friend, that good-for-nothing boy? Asleep too, snug in his bed of hay. Where are you, you lazy little turtle turd?'

"I scrambled to my feet and made my way to the ladder. On the floor below, the butcher was standing over the prostrate form of Pigboy, cleaver in hand, kicking at the curled up body.

"'Stop,' I called out hoarsely, climbing down. 'He's sick.'

"'Sick, is it? Sick of working more like, though it's not something he'll have to worry about any longer.'

"With that he grasped the back of Pigboy's short hempen robe as though he was picking up a cat by the scruff of its neck and dragged his spindly form towards the far door that opened into the rear courtyard. By the time I had clambered carefully down—though I was feeling much better, I still had not recovered my sense of balance—the butcher had crossed the courtyard and was standing at the side door next to the high wooden gates leading out into the street. As I watched, he flung open the door and, lifting a dazed-looking Pigboy to his feet, bundled him out the door.

"'And don't come back, you useless old fool,' the butcher shouted, slamming the door and dropping the bar into place. From the other side of the gate came a plaintive squeal, then a thrumming of fists on the wood. The butcher ignored Pigboy's anguished entreaties and strode over to where I was leaning weakly against the door frame.

"'As for you,' he said, glaring at me, 'if you don't want the same treatment you'd better get back to work right this minute.'

"Of course I went with him—I didn't have much choice—but the desperate wailings of Pigboy echoed in my ears for a long time afterwards. And though I soon recovered my strength, I decided within a few days that my time at the butcher's was over. There had been something strangely comforting about the place when Pigboy was there, the isolation, the contempt others had held us in, the endless work: all these things had helped me to forget my own grief. But now, with Pigboy's mute companionship gone and a scab forming over the wound of my sadness, there was little to keep me. There were only a few days to go before month's end when the butcher would grudgingly hand me my forty cash. After that I would go.

"The evening before I was to leave, I sought to retrieve my boots from their hiding place under the straw. But when I had burrowed down through the hay, I discovered they were gone. In their place was a small oblong-shaped object wrapped in cloth. I unrolled the cloth and found to my disbelief that I was holding a gold ingot which gleamed dully in the darkness. Pigboy, the only other person to have been in the loft since I had come, must have found the boots, taken a liking to them, and paid with his only possession, a chunk of gold worth more than he could make in ten lifetimes. Where could it have come from, I wondered. What did it say about his past, his family? Had they been rich once and overtaken by some devastating misfortune? Or perhaps he had committed some terrible crime and been ejected from his family home out of shame. Perhaps, too, he had stolen it in the distant past, then buried himself in the sty out of remorse or fear. Whatever the case, he would be sorely missing it now. Nor did he even have the boots, for after a short search, I found them hidden under another pile of hay. The poor fool had probably forgotten the use of the gold in his years of isolation, I thought to myself as I drifted off to sleep. Why else would he trade the whole bar for a pair of boots. He could have had a hundred pairs of boots for that weight of gold. A thousand even.

"In the morning I was awakened by a cacophony of squealing from below. Looking down from the loft, I saw that Pigboy was standing in the middle of the barn, surrounded by a mob of pigs nuzzling against his legs and wallowing happily in the muck around him. He wasn't moving, just standing there, ignoring the beasts, staring around helplessly. I climbed down and walked over to him, groping in my sleeve for the gold ingot.

"'Here. Have you come back for this?' I thrust forward the bar, but he pushed my hand away.

"'Pigboy, don't you understand? You are free. With this you can leave here forever. You can live in a house of your own. You can even afford to rent a little shop.'

"But Pigboy just grunted and shook his head, violently flinging it back and forth as if to rid himself of the image.

"'You don't have any choice,' I told him as gently as I could. 'You must leave here.'

"At this he flung his head up and let out a plangent wail.

"'What do you want then?' I asked, puzzled.

"Pigboy wailed again and threw up his sticklike arms, waving them in the air, his gesture encompassing the barn around us, the courtyard outside, the alleyway: he wanted to come home. I shook my head, wondering how to explain. I was about to try and give him the gold again when I saw a movement behind Pigboy and heard the voice of the butcher roaring out.

"'They said you'd been creeping about outside. I told you to get out, and I meant it. This time I'll make sure of it.'

"Pigboy ran past me towards the rear doors, then stopped. There was nowhere for him to go. Before I could move, the butcher was on him, dragging him towards the courtyard gates once again. But this time Pigboy wrapped his hands around the door frame as he was pulled towards the gate, wailing all the while, hanging on grimly so that his long body rose perpendicular to the ground. The butcher dropped the leg he had been pulling on and advanced towards Pigboy, his cleaver raised.

"'This'll teach you what your hands are for,' he shouted, bringing the cleaver down in a flashing arc. As the blade hit the wood with a thunk, I saw three of Pigboy's long bony fingers fly off and land in front of an inquisitive pig. The pig bent over, gave a perfunctory sniff, then slurped up the fingers, swallowing them in a single gulp.

"I ran forward and wrapped my arms around the butcher, pinning his arms to his side, then put my leg across his ankles and flung him sideways so that he lost his balance and toppled over, his head hitting the cobbles with an audible crack. Then I turned to Pigboy, who was standing there, his wounded hand at his side, blood pouring from the finger stumps. I bent his arm up so that it lay across his chest, then turned and ripped a length of cloth from the prostrate butcher's robe, which I used to try and staunch the flow of blood from Pigboy's hand. As I was wrapping the cloth around the wound, I glanced up at Pigboy's face. He was silent now, staring in utter desolation across the courtyard at the gate, tears trickling down his leathery cheeks.

"I bent over the wound again and had just finished wrapping it and tying the ends when I heard the only word Pigboy ever spoke to me: 'Beware!' he croaked. I ducked instinctively and stumbled to one side so that the blade of the cleaver that had been intended for my head passed over me and buried itself in Pigboy's neck with a squelching thunk. Pigboy's scrawny neck was half severed by the impact, but his body remained upright, pinned to the door by the cleaver, twitching spasmodically, great gouts of blood pumping from the severed arteries. The butcher was struggling with both hands to release the cleaver, which had buried itself in the soft wood of the door frame.

"With a roar of rage, I picked up the butcher by his robe and flung him to the ground, jumping onto him before he could move, my knee in his back holding him down. He had fallen partly into a pothole filled with urine and pigshit, and I pressed his face down until his mouth and nose were submerged. I held him there until he stopped struggling. Then I rose and walked out the small side door leading to the street, closing it quietly behind me."

There is a long silence as Wang Lung carefully strokes out the last characters, then looks up at Li Po, who is staring down at him expectantly. The boy can't think of what to say, just gapes at the poet, the image of him kneeling on the butcher's back, pressing his face into a pool of excrement burning in his mind.

"So," Li Po says finally, slightly exasperated at the other's silence, "what do you think? Quite a story, eh? And I was no more than the age you are now. Do you think you could do those things?"

Wang Lung shakes his head silently.

"No, I don't think so either, though you never know what you can do until the time comes."

He calls for another pot of wine, well pleased with himself, and Wang Lung puts his pen down gratefully. But the poet still has not finished. Standing at the rail, wine cup in hand, he begins to talk again:

"Naturally I was quick to make myself scarce. The easiest way to leave, of course, was by river, and I managed to find a boat heading downriver that afternoon, using up most of the money I had been paid by the butcher on the fare. Several hungry weeks followed, for I couldn't afford to have the gold bar broken down too close to Wanhsien; once I was away from the district, there was no chance that anyone would come looking for me. But until then I had to survive on the few pennies' change left from the boat fare. Even though no one at the butcher's had known my name—or even seen my face more than a few times—there was no point in taking chances.

"Later, though, after I'd had the bar broken down at a goldsmith's in some anonymous trading town further down the river, I proceeded to make up for my time as a pigboy, lashing out with a shower of gold everywhere I went, staying at the best inns, sampling foods I had never before dreamed of: whole sea turtle baked in its shell, Venus clams from Shantung, sugar crabs from the Great River delta, white carp marinated in wine lees, musk melon pickled in rice mash, tiger prawns cooked alive in millet spirits. In short, I conducted my voyage of discovery in grand style, a state to which I quickly became accustomed.

"Those wandering years after Wanhsien were my true education, the gold my talisman, a magical key that showed me for a time how the world of money and privilege worked. I roamed as free as an immortal, staying for a day or a week or a month, then leaving without warning when the mood took me, sliding downriver in the soft light before daybreak, silent but for the clanking of oars and the creak of the rigging, the dawn revealing gibbons bending to drink from the river or an otter swimming along with a fish still flapping in its mouth, head held high above the swirling waters, the first rays of sunlight sparkling the drops of moisture that trembled on the ends of its long whiskers.

"Down I traveled to Hangchou, fabled pleasure city on the West Lake, a city of canals and ecstatic evenings on mahogany and spice-wood lotus boats, then south and away from the Great River, into Lingnan. I was aiming to see Canton, the city of Five Rams, but halted in the Mist Mountains at the Spirit Pass, which leads into the pestilent south, where so many exiles have wasted away their days in the humid miasmas dreaming of the bright clear desert skies of Chang An. There they told me that the rainy season had started early and the roads into the valleys below were impassable. Before turning back I roamed the mountains in the company of a young aborigine called Ngoc, a member of the Lao tribe. He was only half my height but could walk forever over the mountaintops. The birds that I saw made me swear I would return: great flapping hornbills, plump pittas banded with the colors of the rainbow, scuttling away across the forest floor, calling out shrilly in indignant alarm, or bee-eaters, sunbirds, and flowerpeckers in incandescent blurs around a hibiscus bush; and there were legions of others: shrikes, bulbuls, babblers, white-throated partridges, the astonishing Java sparrow and, of course, the vermilion Bird of the South itself—the shrieking peacock, with its flashing bronze-and-metallic-green tail. Ngoc showed me the birds, where they nested, how to catch and cook them. Peacock smeared with wild honey and roasted over an open fire—it may be the sweetest dish I have ever eaten. I was lucky, the little man told me, for I had come in the rainy season, when the peacock was easy to catch: his great tail became sodden with water and he couldn't fly. Killed by his own beauty, there is a lesson there. Ngoc gave me a present of three full tails when I left, and I carried them north with me, selling them in Hangchou for a truly exorbitant sum, for the plumage of the peacock is even rarer than that of the kingfisher and more highly prized by sophisticated ladies as adornment for their headdresses. Of course now the peacock feathers are taboo, to be used only by the imperial family.

"Then I made my way north and east again, back to the Great River and the stone grottoes of Lai Lake, such weird and beautiful cave formations, though these days many of the caves have been mined and the rocks carried to the capital so that courtiers can put them in their gardens and boast to each other about how much they spent transporting the stones to Chang An. One of the poems I wrote was after I had seen the boatmen hauling a barge full of the stones upriver. It doesn't really bear rereading—even I put a foot wrong now and then, especially when fired by youthful outrage—but there were a few good lines. Hmm . . . the water they drank was half mud . . . hearts weeping tears like rain, dum dum . . . mute stones crying out in sympathy for their plight. . . .

"Farther and farther down the river I traveled until at last I reached the great delta where brown river water mingles with the blue ocean, the banks growing more and more distant until they vanish altogether, leaving only a great silver-gray expanse of sky and azure water, and birds wheeling and diving in their hundreds—petrels, herons, storks, an arrowhead formation of geese, even web-footed cormorants in thrall to boatmen, diving into the water for fish, then hauled back to the little skiffs by a length of bamboo twine attached to their legs and, squawking madly with anger, forced to regurgitate their prey.

"From the delta I journeyed up the coast by land, eventually happening on the town of Mingchou, famous for its tidal bore. It was a grim little place, a mere collection of huts clustered round the magistrate's compound, the streets narrow and cluttered with mangy dogs and dirty children, and worst of all not a single fluttering blue flag signifying a wine shop. The town stood on a range of bluff, dun-colored cliffs dropping some one hundred feet to the shore. The tide was out when I arrived at midday, revealing a long expanse of stinking mudflat speckled with stooping figures collecting oysters. A few hours later, however, the ocean had risen to cover the exposed land and was only a hundred paces from the base of the cliffs. I clambered down to explore the beach, crossing in front of a narrow canyon that I guessed must be the course of the tidal bore, now dry and empty. I strolled a few miles down the shore, enjoying the ocean breeze, but when I turned to go back I saw that the waves were only ten paces from the cliff base and rising fast. I walked briskly at first, then broke into a jog, then a run, arriving at the mouth of the canyon just as the first wave broke against the rock. There was now a fast-flowing stream flooding into the canyon and no question of crossing over to the other side, where I could climb back up to the town. Happily, I did find a set of narrow steps carved into the cliff face. I struggled to the top, where I was gratified to find a small tavern called The Water's Return perched at the edge of the cliff.

"A considerable crowd had gathered a few hundred paces away on the other side of the canyon, all of them peering down, presumably in anticipation of the famous tidal bore. There were also ten or so travelers gathered outside the tavern on my side, similarly preoccupied. I hesitated, torn between darting in to secure a flask of wine and not wanting to miss the spectacle. Just as I had decided to nip in for the wine, however, there was a resounding rumble from below—far louder than anything I had ever heard except thunder, which it resembled, though much more hollow, like the beating of some drum built for giants, a thrumming bass reverberation that rattled the teeth in my head. Naturally I hurried over to the edge of the cliff and peered down. The water was now about a quarter of the way up the canyon walls, black and shining, flowing very fast indeed.

"I glanced over at the crowd on the other side, some townspeople, but mostly visitors it was clear, some of them women, their silk robes rippling and shining in the late afternoon sun. One woman, or girl really, was sitting on a pony, slightly separate from the rest. Her head was bent as she leaned over to watch. She wore earrings of beaten silver set with chunks of crystal that flashed in the sun and a robe of silk shot through with gold thread, the iridescent material a shimmering young green, the color of thirty-day rice stalks, the color of life. When she straightened, raising her eyes from the canyon and looking across, I saw that it was the singer from the tavern in Wanhsien. Her luminous eyes fixed directly on me across the narrow divide, and we stared at each other until I made to lift my hand in greeting and call to her.

"But before I could move or speak, there was a sound like the earth splitting open between us, a rumbling roar, then a great detonation that made me reel backward a few steps as an explosion of white water blew out of the canyon, rising fifty feet in the air, drenching all within a hundred paces, then settling, revealing a boiling torrent coursing through the narrow defile, its surface only a few feet from the rim. I gaped at the rushing water like a dazed fool, then finally looked up. The spectators on the opposite side were equally stunned, most of them just staring down, amazed by the awful power of the water. Several of the ladies were shrieking, some attempting to wring out the sleeves of their sopping robes. But of the girl and her pony, there was no sign.

"Naturally, I set out after her, but at every turn I was frustrated. First there was no way to get across the canyon short of trekking fifteen miles upstream and fording it at a shallow reach. This would have taken so much time that I decided to wait, and very early in the morning when the water had subsided with the tide, I hurried across to the town, walking straight down to the docks. There I asked after a beautiful girl, perhaps traveling with a white-bearded old man. But I got no response save from a surly fool mending his nets on the stone dock, who grunted a curse and told me grudgingly that two junks had sailed with the tide, though no pretty misses to be seen, worse luck, just a few painted rich men's whores dripping with gold. I inquired at the two taverns in town, and spent a full day walking the narrow streets. But all to no avail: she was nowhere to be found.

"And so, I continued my wandering, strangely troubled for a long time thereafter by that chance meeting, the lost opportunity. But as the months went by, her image faded, as it must. And I had other worries, too. All too soon I was down to my last few thousand cash, having thrown to the winds wealth enough to feed and clothe a whole generation of farmers, most of it gone to fill the coffers of the gambling houses of Hangchou and in silks and jewels for the ladies there and in other such towns along the way. Soon, indeed, I began to wonder vaguely how I might feed myself when the last of my cash finally disappeared. I was not unduly worried, though, for a few years of high living and youthful arrogance—or should I say the ignorance, they are near enough—had made me confident that something would come along. And in a way, I suppose, I was right, for I never went hungry and often I possessed, through one means or another, enough cash to spend on sables and silks and wine at ten thousand a flask, or even to buy freedom for some indentured bond servant, if I wished. Perhaps, too, through those tumultuous years of wandering there was a pattern, a destination. You see, like most shiftless citizens of the empire I had been drifting slowly towards the capital . . . but I see that you are yawning, my boy. Perhaps we shall save this tale for tomorrow. Run to the kitchen now and tell the cook that I want you to be fed the biggest bowl of congee on the boat. Then to bed."

five 李白

BUT THE NEXT DAY THERE IS NO TALE.

Instead, when Wang Lung arrives on the foredeck, Li Po as usual waving him over impatiently, the poet says: "Today I have an important task for you. You are to take down a very important document, a memorial to the emperor on my behalf. It will go in the name of my good friend, Sung, the assistant director of the censorate. I'm seeing him tonight and I want to have this ready. Don't worry about the salutations and so on, the clerks at the censorate can fill in all that formal nonsense. But it will have to be written in draft, then copied over again fair. Now, are you ready?"

Brush poised over paper, the boy nods.

"Good. Let me see, 'Greetings, humble servant,' and so on, just mark in a line saying something like, 'Insert formal opening salutations here,' then, let's see, yes, here we go:

"With all deference, I have heard that when heaven and earth are closed, the sage goes into hiding, and that when clouds and thunder burst, the superior man is employed. I respectfully submit that I have met the former Han Lin Academician Li Po, who is fifty-five years of age. When your majesty's father was still in the early part of his illustrious Tien Pao reign, the five grand officers of state, one after another, called him to office, but he did not seek fame. Like Tzu-chen of Ku-k'ou, his name rocked the capital. The emperor heard this and, pleased with Li Po, called him to the re-

stricted wings of the palace. Thus, he lent color to the grand enterprise of imperial state craft. Growing bored of court life, he left the red dust of the capital and returned to the mountains. There he dwelt in obscurity and engaged in creative literary activity. His writings amounted to several tens of thousands of scrolls.

Like all your subjects, Li Po has suffered during the rebellion of the Sogdian-Turk usurper. He took refuge on Lu Mountain and . . .

"No, no, no. Stop writing for a moment."

Li Po stands and stares unseeing at the passing riverbank. Finally he sighs and turns back to the table.

"No, that is wrong: one should never remind people, one should never apologize; remember that, young man, one should never apologize."

Wang Lung, staring up at the standing poet, nods obediently.

"No, let's return to the part about Rohkshan."

"Sir?" The boy looks at Li Po questioningly, his brush poised once more.

"Our Sogdian friend, lad, An Lu Shan. The sentence I think began: 'Like all your subjects . . .'"

"Like all your subjects, Li Po has suffered during the rebellion of the Sogdian-Turk usurper."

"Yes, from there. Start a new sentence:

"But his name has now been cleared of guilt by both the chief pacification commissioner and your humble servant.

"Your servant has heard that, in ancient times, when feudal lords recommended worthy persons to the court, they received gifts from the emperor. If they kept worthy persons in obscurity, they were executed in public. If they thrice praised someone's admirable qualities, they would certainly be granted the nine marks of imperial favor: chariot and horses, state robes, musical instru-

ments, the right to have vermilion doors, right of audience, the right to armed attendants, bows and arrows, battle axes, and sacrificial wines. That glorious precedent comes down to all later ages as a lesson.

"This Li Po in your servant's charge has according to the facts been adjudged free of guilt. He is possessed of considerable administrative talent and his moral integrity could be pitted against that of Chao Fu and Hsu Yu. His writing can alter habit and custom; his learning can penetrate heaven and man. If he is not granted official rank, the four seas will cry out against the injustice.

"It is my humble opinion that your majesty's perspicacity is of far-reaching influence. Your superior, royal precepts are without bias. You gather about you those whose eminence is rare in the world and make them the jewels of your unimpeachable court. How can this man whose name has spread through the universe be allowed to languish in obscurity? It is my humble opinion that your highness can bend the rays of the lofty sun and throw light on an overcast day. I make a special request to your honor that you release Li Po for appointment to a post in the capital. He will present you with what is acceptable and eradicate what is not permissible and thus brighten the ranks of your court. Then all of the outstanding men in the land will crane their necks in recognition of their fealty to you.

"Then the usual close: 'with utmost circumspection I am so bold as to memorialize the throne, in fear and trembling, dust under your shoes, unworthy piece of dung, et cetera, et cetera, et cetera.'"

There is a pause as Li Po calls for a pot of tea, and the boy dusts down the draft memorial. When it is dry, he hands it to the poet who scans the lines of characters rapidly, makes a dozen or so emendations, and hands the paper back.

"I think it should do the trick. You can copy it out once

more, incorporating the changes and corrections. Don't rush: make sure you use your best hand. Now, off you go."

And so for the rest of the day, Wang Lung sits on the deck, carefully copying out the memorial in his best calligraphy, very conscious that the clerks at the censorate will be reading it, imagining them laughing at his boyish hand, imagining that they will recognize his humble origins from some flaw in the way he writes his characters. In his preoccupation he makes numerous mistakes and is forced to begin a new page many times, finally finishing the document as dusk is falling.

Li Po soon appears on deck, dressed in what passes for his formal wear: red leather boots, a snowy white gown cinched at the waist with a black leather belt hung with intricate carved jade plaques, and a stiff black cap, octagonal in shape. Apart from the jade at his belt, the only sign that he is on his way to a formal dinner that will be attended by the most powerful men in the province are the gold hairpins that keep the cap in place atop his coiled hair, a discreet twinkling of gold against the shiny black silk of the hat. He also has an earring in his left ear, a simple hoop of gold, and has put a little rouge on his cheeks, rather unnecessarily, Wang Lung thinks, considering his ruddy complexion. The poet scans the pages, then grunts his thanks and sweeps out.

Later, much much later, Wang Lung hears Li Po return. The boy is sitting on a stool in the kitchen, topping and tailing beans for the cook. Just as he is about to finish and seek his reward—a portion of sugared rhubarb—there is a hubbub of voices from the shore, gradually drawing closer and sharpening into snatches of song mixed with shouting, then a stumbling, banging progress up the side of the boat and onto the deck, Li Po's shrill tones rising above the others momentarily before disappearing altogether. There is more muffled thumping, then silence, and a few minutes later the poet's valet appears wearing the smile of a man who has completed his work for the day.

"Come now Cookie, you old dog," he calls cheerfully on entering the kitchen, "you have a bottle or two hidden somewhere in here, that I know for sure."

The cook demurs, but the valet, a burly ex-sergeant, persists and he is eventually rewarded when the cook sighs deeply and produces a stone flask from the back of a cupboard. The stopper is still sealed in by wax, and as the cook cuts off the seal, the valet, a garrulous man named Chiang, watches expectantly and says:

"You must admit, old slubberypots, that I deserve a little of the warming spirit. After all, while your lot has been sitting comfortably on your asses, I've been standing in a drafty hall, listening to a crew of fools parading and posturing, every one of them trying to get the sole attention of our friend upstairs. How many of these occasions have I attended, I wonder? A hundred? Two hundred? They're always exactly the same; the only change is the company. Tonight we had the deputy governor, but we've had censors, the president of the metropolitan court, even a prime minister once. But as I say, it makes no difference who is there, it's always the same: each one of these fellows fancies himself a poet and has to try and prove it to the others, and most of all, of course, to the Grand Panjandrum of Poetry himself, the incredible Li Po. That means a lot of idiotic games, usually, capping each others' couplets, compositions on a set subject, that kind of thing. Dull, dull, dull. Oh, you may say that it's because I am ignorant, that it's all too sophisticated for a simple soldier like me. But I know all about the rules and regulations, about old verse and new verse, regulated and loose, sonnets and sestets, odes, epodes, and palinodes, distich, tercet, and sestina. You don't hang around with the greatest versemaker in the empire for ten years without picking up the nuts and bolts, not unless you're a complete bloody fool. No, I know my way around the poetry business, but that only makes it worse, having to listen to these ponces mouthing their doggerel: life is short, a moth fluttering around a flame, falling peony flowers, crumbling tombs of once-great kings. . . . Always the same hackneyed images and themes. Don't they have any imagination? Whatever else you say about our boy—and there's plenty to be said; I could tell you tales that would curl your hair—at least he writes a bit of verse now and then that a man can understand. Did you ever hear the one he wrote for his wife?

Three hundred and sixty-five days
I'm drunk as mud.
Poor old Mrs. Li Po;
They should have called you
Mrs. Wine Bottle

"Ha, ha, ha. Now that really speaks to the human condition. Or here's another one that will put a bit of ginger in your cucumber, if you follow my line of thinking:

Grape wine, gold goblets
and a pretty maid of Wu.
She comes on ponyback
Fifteen years old,
Eyes painted with blue kohl,
Slippers of pink brocade
On her dainty feet.
She can hardly speak a word
But sings bewitchingly in her own tongue.
Feasting at tortoiseshell inlaid table
She in my lap, tipsy;
Ah, child, what caresses to come
Behind the lily-embroidered curtains!

"Now that's what I call poetry a man can sink his teeth into. I . . . thank you, very much. Ahhh, that warms the cockles of the heart, and I will take another. What was I saying? Oh, yes, these bloody banquets. By the end of the evening he's usually so stinking that he's ready to get up on the table and take a piss on the assembled company. And even if he isn't actually up there with his willy out, he's doing it anyway, if you know what I mean, usually telling all those beards what a bunch of pampered fools they are. Great fun that is, all of us servants roaring behind the screens. And they lap it up, absolutely lap it up, as long as it is coming from him. But it's not just the worthies that like his stuff either, you know. Go to any bawdy house in the land, there'll be some little missy crooning one of his songs to herself. Once I was with him and Tu Fu and someone else, another poet, a famous one, Kao Shi, I think it was. They wanted to go to the upstairs room in a tavern in Chang An—the room looks down on the main road leading to the bridge; you can see all the traffic coming in and out of town. Anyway, when they climbed the stairs they found there was a party up there already, complete with Mei Yu, the most famous courtesan in the city. The three of them hid behind a screen and made a bet; whosoever's poem she sang first, the other two would have to buy dinner and wine for him. They'd hardly been there for a minute before she launched right into "The Girls of Yueh," so Li Po had a very good evening at the others' expense. Of course, I found out later that he was slipping it to her on the sly, so it's not surprising that his was the first song to come to her mind. Though, as I say, it's not just your rich rakes and high-priced ladies who go mad for his stuff. Anywhere you go in the empire, I guarantee it, there'll be someone singing something he's written. Why, once, I was walking through the fields, I can't even remember where it was, some shithole miles and miles from anywhere, and a little number comes past me on the back of a water buffalo, gives me the eye as she goes by, then starts singing one of his ditties about lotus pickers on the West Lake. That's the difference between him and most of them: they're all pouring out this high-sounding guff, all of it copied out of books. But our Li Po, he's out every night in the wineshops, talking and singing to real people: that's the difference. Of course that means there's a lot of stuff about drinking and dancing girls. Me, personally, I prefer the poems with a story in them, especially the ones about the frontier. What's the poem he wrote to the tune of *We Fought South of the Ramparts*? Umm, 'We washed our swords in the Caspian's waves/And grazed our mounts in Himalayas' snows.' Dum dee dum dee dum. I can't remember it after that. Something about trailing guts and blood-smeared grass. It reminds me of when I was in the service. We never made it to the Caspian, of course, that's just for the poem, but our brigade spent five years on the frontier at Kokonor. Terrible place. Sandstorms lasting four days. Men would go mad with the boredom of it, the constant noise of the wind whining away. Once we were on patrol and . . . "

Wang Lung, the sugared rhubarb hot in his belly, has retired to his cot in the pantry and can hear Chiang droning on through the open door. It is a comforting sound, and he drifts off to sleep happily, images of blood-red skies and sand dunes whirling in his head.

Li Po doesn't appear the next morning, and Wang Lung waits in his accustomed spot, reading a tattered copy of *Chuang Tzu,* puzzling out the harder passages with the aid of a commentary recommended by the poet. When Li Po finally does appear, the boy has just returned from the galley for noon rice and is contentedly full, nodding off over his scrolls. The poet doesn't say anything, simply nods brusquely towards the brush stand, then walks over to his place at the low table, drops down on a cushion, and begins to talk:

"I arrived in the Loyang, our second capital city, on a beautiful spring day, and decided to have a few cups of wine to celebrate reaching one of the two pivots of the empire at last. At that time Loyang had the reputation of being more purely Chinese than its western counterpart, Chang An. Farther from the desert and the nomads, deep in the Han heartland, it was supposed to be the place where our art and culture was best preserved. Chang An, of course, was the main capital, the site of the court for most of the year, and thus the crossroads of the world. Persians and Greeks, Arabs and Malays, Sogdians and Indians all could be found walking its dusty streets. And if you listened to the old aristocratic families of the East of the Mountains clans in Loyang—the people who had run things before the Tang had established itself and still looked on the Lunghsi Li's of the royal family (my own clan, I might add) as half-barbarian usurpers—if you listened to them, everything in Chang An was debased and vulgar, a place where the flashy taste of the steppes had debased pure Chinese blood and true Chinese aesthetics. Alas, only too soon we would all wake from our dreams to find the stink of camels hanging over the city and their brutal masters from the deep desert lording it over Chang An and Loyang, too.

"In any case such things were far from my mind in those days. I was simply curious to see what all this meant for poetry, to see what was meant by 'pure Chinese,' for of course, I had been born in the steppes myself, was raised hearing Turkic songs, had even written some of my first pieces in Turkic because the rules of versification were so much simpler: no rigidly prescribed strictures, just a rhyme scheme and a tune to which words were set. Child's play by comparison to the new-style regulated octets, where everything is laid down like squares on a chessboard. It could have only been invented by a Confucian: two lines of introduction five or seven words long, the tone pattern cast in bronze—

oblique, even, oblique, high, even even, high—no variations. You can of course use only one of a few permissible rhyme schemes. And for the exposition, four lines in two parallel couplets, each of the lines within the couplets setting each other off, just as the two couplets themselves must contain parallel thoughts; then finally the two closing lines, also rigidly prescribed, always with some uplifting thought to conclude the verse. I've never liked it myself, find it as tight as a dowager's corset; no room to maneuver. But others took to it like an otter after a carp. Tu Fu, for one. To this day most of his poems are in the form of octets. I tell you all this, boy, because you will have to start studying composition soon if you are to pass those wretched exams. Ever since they made poetic composition a compulsory—and high-scoring—part of the exams thirty years ago, every flap-eared fool who has passed for an official fancies himself a poet.

"So I arrived in Loyang eager to talk over these matters—pure versus adulterated poetry, which verse forms best suited which subjects, and so on—with other poets in the city. I headed straight for the Bridge of the Ford of Heaven on the edge of the palace grounds. There were taverns on either side, and I knew that somewhere inside there would be a group of poets arguing minutely about versification. I had come north using the Grand Canal but forsaken water for the roads in Pienchou, acquiring a frisky, silver-maned Tartar horse with sharp little ears like sliced bamboo shoots at an auction of goods belonging to a merchant executed for smuggling salt. I dubbed him Confucius. I rode down the Imperial Way taking in the sights of the city: the red-roofed houses stretching away on either side of the road, the stream of carriages passing by, affording the occasional glimpse of a pretty face inside, the rainbow banners flying from the ramparts to indicate that the court was in residence, the young bucks cantering arrogantly through the crowds, the call of itinerant hawkers and the song of sedan-chair coolies; in short, the whole buzzing turmoil that distinguishes a great city.

"I dismounted when I got to the bridge and called out for the groom at a large double-story tavern that stood in the left-hand side. No one came, however, and I led my horse round the back, looking for the stables. It was evening, the light fast fading from the sky, and the alley running beside the tavern was in semidarkness. As I entered I could just make out a couple talking intently next to a side door—a short, squat man with his back to me standing very close to a slim girl or woman whose face was hidden in the shadow. As I passed, someone swung open the door, and light from the tavern flooded out, illuminating them. I caught a glimpse of the girl before the door shut. It was an achingly familiar face, a face that had haunted my dreams, still in the first flush of youth, perhaps eighteen or twenty, not beautiful in any dainty, retiring way, but strong and striking, the face of one of the women singing out lustily for her man in the *Book of Songs*, I remember thinking. Before I had a chance to speak, however, the man raised his hand threateningly, as though he was about to hit her.

"I let go of the reins and took a few paces forward. He was very short, didn't come up to the middle of my chest, I simply grasped the collar of his short clerk's gown and lifted him up so that his feet dangled in the air. Despite his size, he was surprisingly heavy.

"'You weren't about to hit a lady, were you shortass?' I said, swinging him around so that I could see his face and immediately regretting it, for he was as ugly a specimen as I had ever seen, his skin mottled with smallpox scars, two beady eyes glaring out at me. He didn't reply, instead pulling back one of his legs and directing a vicious kick at me. Normally this wouldn't have mattered much—someone as short as he was couldn't reach very high—but the way I was holding him gave him a perfect target, and his foot drove straight into my groin, causing me to drop him and fall to the ground myself. There is nothing that reminds us more quickly of our essential vulnerability than a swift blow to the groin, a lesson that large men like myself occasionally have to relearn.

"'I'll teach you to interfere,' I heard him hiss. He pulled a dagger of some kind from his girdle, the long curved blade glinting wickedly in the semidarkness. I rolled away from him, fumbling for my own dagger, then remembered that it was in one of my saddle bags, placed there at the order of the guards at the city gate who insisted that the privilege of carrying weapons openly was reserved for nobles and officials. Obviously this little fellow hadn't heard about that rule.

"He leaned over to take a swipe at me and I rolled again, this time banging into the wall. He scuttled forward, the knife held low, an evil grin splitting his face. I scrabbled about in the dust of the alley for a weapon, but found none. Just as he was about to slash at my upraised hands, there was a sharp crash and an expression of comical surprise crossed his face. Then his eyes rolled back into his skull and he toppled over. Behind him, panting and flushed, the gleam of battle in her eye, stood the girl. She was holding up the remains of the pot of poinsettias she had smashed over his head.

"'Now you are my benefactor when I thought to be yours,' I gasped, gingerly rising to my feet.

"'That means we are equal then,' she replied, 'we owe each other nothing.'

"'No talk of owing, please. This runt was about to strike you. Have you done something very terrible to anger him so?'

"'No,' she said, turning and walking over to my horse, which was still standing placidly at the end of the alley, and picking up his reins. 'It is more what he wants to do to me but cannot that bothers him.'

"As she walked towards me leading Confucius, I thought of mentioning our previous encounters, then dismissed the idea. Best to start afresh.

"'Come,' I said, taking the reins from her, 'if every man who wanted to have his way with a woman were to hit her, where would the world be then?' I prodded the prone figure with the toe of my boot. 'There must be more here than just lust.'

"'There is more, as you say, but it needn't concern you. You have done enough.'

"'I have done very little except behave foolishly, and have the bruises to remind me. Tell me what your trouble is.'

"I looked down at her. She was only a few inches shorter than I, very tall for a woman. Her skin seemed to glow like moonlight on snow in the half-light. Her eyes were wide and set far apart, shining now with a wary intelligence that sought to assess me: threat or ally? I noticed, too, that there seemed to be streaks of green in the hazel of her irises, though it was difficult to tell in the dimness.

"'I cannot stay here,' she said at last, regarding me neutrally, the examination over. 'I must return to my inn.'

"'Fair enough. We'll both walk that way.'

"Though it was now fully dark, she pulled the hood of the long cape she wore up over her face. As we walked over the bridge and into the Drum Tower quarter, she spoke:

"'It is a common enough tale. I am a singer. We work mostly in taverns, though sometimes we are hired for private parties, too. I have been traveling with my mother and father—he accompanies me in my singing. Last week we stopped here in Loyang on the way home to Chang An from the south. I hate this city, have always disliked it, a false, self-regarding, brittle place, full of thieves who call themselves aristocrats, a place where the tide of our people's history has receded, leaving only scum. It is accursed for my family now, too, for three days ago my mother contracted the bloody flux and was dead within a day, dead in agony, vomiting blood, fighting hard to the bitter end. We were still two weeks travel from Chang An and had little money and no friends or relatives to supply it, so were forced to borrow for her funeral. We knew that repayment would be onerous, but if we hadn't buried her ourselves, her body would have been tossed into a pauper's grave and we would have been fined by the city for not being able to cover the cost. I thought we could perform for a few weeks and recoup the loan. It isn't much, only 500 cash, but the audiences here are penny-pinching dolts and the money has been slow coming in. And then, yesterday, the evil man who lent us the money suddenly changed the terms. He now wants repayment within two days or I must enter his household as a concubine.'

"There was no hint of self-pity or tears in her account, just cold anger.

"'And who is this evil man, the one who lent you the money?'

"'He is called Liang. Butcher Liang. He runs the pork stalls at the Drum Tower market. That man we left in the alley was one of his apprentices. He was trying to persuade me to give his boss an *appetizer* as he put it.'

"Another butcher, I thought. What was it about them?

"'Where is your father?'

"'He . . . he's not well this evening. He is in bed.'

"'I see.'

"There was something strange in her tone, but I let it pass.

"'How far are we from your inn?' I asked.

"'It is just around the corner.'

"'Good. Now listen to me,' I said, handing her two strings of cash. 'Take this and go back to your father. Tomorrow you can continue on to Chang An. The money should take care of your travel expenses. I will see to the butcher.'

"She stopped walking and gazed at me levelly, weighing the money in her hand. I noticed she didn't try to count it.

"'What will you do?'

"'I have some knowledge of such men. I know how to deal with them.'

"'This has nothing to do with you.'

"'No. No, it doesn't. As I said, I've had some unpleasant experiences with this type of bully before.'

"Once again she regarded me without speaking. Her face was hidden in the shadow of her cowl and I could read nothing of her expression. After awhile, she said:

"'All right. Thank you. Come to Chang An and I will repay you.'

"She stood in silence for a moment longer, as if about to say something more, but then turned to go without speaking.

"'Wait,' I called after her. 'Where can I find you in Chang An?'

"'Goldfish Street, next to the Water Gate,' she called over her shoulder. 'Ask for Peony.'

"Peony, I repeated to myself as I watched her disappear in a flash of white skirts and black shadow. Peony . . .

"Shaking my head, I climbed onto Confucius and made my way towards the Drum Tower. Once there I saw that the market was still bustling despite the hour, the square illuminated by four-foot-high red lanterns hanging from the eaves of each of the shops. I tied Confucius to a bridle post and strolled into the square. All around the voices of hawkers resonated in the clear evening air: salted-fish sellers, pie makers, vegetable sellers, rice wine brewers, poultry vendors with their geese, chicken, and quail, all clamored for my attention. But my eyes sought only the pork stalls, and finding them within a few moments, they drew me straight to a brawny man standing on the pavement outside the biggest stall. He was surveying the crowds, occasionally shouting encouragement to the apprentices inside. For a moment the sense I had been there before was so strong that a wave of dizziness swept over me. The same piggy features, the same close-set, calculating eyes that roamed through the crowds, the same bullying manner with his workers and unctuousness with his customers. This time, though, I was not a mendicant seeking employment.

"I shook my head to clear it, straightened my robe, and strode over to where he stood, assuming the arrogant air of servant from a large household.

"'Are you the butcher, Liang?' I demanded, standing over him, a string of cash dangling conspicuously from my right hand.

"'Yes, young master,' he replied, simultaneously fingering a large mole on his cheek from which a four-inch tuft of hair sprouted and leering at the money. 'What can I do for you?'

"'I need a large order for a banquet my master is holding tomorrow. First, five catties of your best loin meat, minced as fine as you can. There mustn't be a speck of fat in it.'

"'Certainly, sir,' he replied, smirking at me, then turning his head to shout out the order.

"'No, no,' I interrupted him. 'I don't want those clumsy clowns to do the chopping.'

"A flash of irritation crossed his face, but then his eyes fell again on the string of cash and his smile returned.

"'Of course, young sir, of course. I will attend to it myself.'

"He levered his bulky frame up and made his way to one of the chopping boards, pushing aside a young boy who had been working there. For the next twenty minutes he stood there, mincing meat with the blade of a cleaver, a prickle of sweat appearing on his brow as he worked. Finally, when the mound of minced pork was a foot-and-a-half high, he laid down the chopper, called for waxed paper, and wrapped the mincemeat in two packets, which he brought over to where I was standing.

"'Let me see,' he said, handing me the packages, 'that comes to . . . '

"'I also want five catties of fat, also minced very close.'

"'Just fat?' he said, puzzled. 'But why would you want . . .' then he shrugged and smiled again. 'Whatever you say, young master. Five catties of minced fat it is.'

"Once again he labored diligently for twenty minutes, carefully slicing off greasy lengths of white fat from the tea-colored meat, then dicing it until a mound of creamy lard was ready. By the time he had finished, his thinning hair was soaked with sweat and he was breathing heavily. Liang, it was clear, was no longer used to working in his own shop.

"'Now, sir,' he said, bringing out two more wrapped packages, 'here is your second order. The total comes to . . . '

"Again, I interrupted him.

"'I also want two catties of minced tendon, not a speck of meat in it, mind.'

"'Minced tendon?' he goggled at me, his face turning a deeper shade of puce. 'Minced tendon! Who could want minced tendon?'

"'Do you want my order or not, you insolent dog?' I shouted.

"'Are you playing the fool with me, boy?' he roared. In reply I threw the packets of mince at his head, the wrapping breaking open and spraying the meat onto the dusty pavement.

"'If you don't want my business you fat pig fucker, you can keep your poxy meat.'

"With this I turned and sauntered away. The butcher gave out another roar and began to chase after me. At the last moment I spun around and swung my fist in a wide arc, smashing it into his nose, which produced a crackling sound and immediately began to gush blood. Liang gaped at me for a moment, clutching his nose, then turned and began to waddle back towards the stall.

"'I'll teach you, insolent puppy,' I heard him mutter. 'I'll teach you to make a fool of butcher Liang.'

"He swept up the cleaver from the chopping block, then turned and advanced on me. But fortune seemed to be with me. Liang stumbled on the stairs leading down to the street, and before he had recovered, I was upon him, tripping him up and giving him a blow to the side of the head as he fell. Once down, he remained prostrate, blood and snot coating his face, his mouth agape. I gave him a few kicks, but this failed to revive him, and I noticed that his eyes had rolled into the back of his head, only the whites showing.

"'Get up and fight, you great fat cheat,' I said, now a little alarmed. A crowd had gathered round. Could I have killed him with one blow? Granted I am large and exceptionally strong, but to die after such a light tap on the head seemed most unreasonable.

"'He tried to cheat me, the bastard,' I shouted out, 'and now he won't even fight. He is playing dead and that after coming after me with his cleaver.'

"There were a few murmurs of 'serves him right,' but most of the onlookers just stood there, alternately gaping at me and the butcher's prostrate form. Then I saw several men coming from the back of the butcher's shop. They were carrying cleavers, so rather than discover whether they intended to use them on me—there seemed a certain porcine family resemblance to Liang—I began to move sideways, muttering all the while: cheating butcher, overcharged all his customers, his meat rancid, his scale notoriously overweight, just like him, the fat bastard. I continued in this vein until I managed to slide into the crowd, down the side alley to where Confucius was tethered, and then away.

"It was an absurd thing to do, of course. I was very young then, though. I thought of myself as a kind of wandering knight, righting wrongs, saving damsels in distress, the usual thing. Some such gestures came out of generosity or compassion, I suppose. But others I did out of sheer foolishness and ignorance, things that are enough to freeze my blood just thinking about them; so close to death, so often, I all unknowing.

"I fled the city, leaving by the west gate—I could hardly take the Drum Tower Gate on the east side, though I knew that someday I would head for Chang An to find Peony and collect my debt. Once outside I abruptly decided to head for the Honan mountains in Shantung, where I planned to seek out Master Ku, a famous Taoist sage and teacher who was supposed to live in the vicinity of Mount Tai, most sacred of the five marchmonts. For some time I had been feeling a kind of spiritual restlessness, a dissatisfaction with simply roaming from place to place. However pleasant such a life was, I felt there was still something missing, something that could not be found in scrolls or in the city streets and mountain dawns. I wanted instruction in the greater mysteries, I wanted to understand the way that magic worked, who the immortals really were, where my name was written in the book of the dead and if I could expunge it from those awful rolls. Master Ku understood the ties that bind the numinous with the banal. Men said he could walk upon the clouds and speak the secret language of dragons and phoenixes. So I set out that day, with a few strings of cash and only a little yellow millet in my saddle bags. I didn't even own a heavy robe, and yet off I went into the frigid mountains—the vain foolishness of youth. And yet how often it is proved right, showing up the trembling caution of age.

"After four days I fell in with a group of travelers going in the same direction, as is common on the road. They seemed a commonplace set of men to me—not wealthy, that was easy to see by their clothes, which were old, patched, and made of the roughest hemp—but otherwise undistinguished except that all of them were mounted, which argued a wealth that contradicted their shabby attire. They had a certain studied vagueness about their destination, their homes, their professions, in fact a disinclination to answer questions at all. But I was oblivious, eager to talk about myself and to tell them of my exploits.

"On the first night we made camp in the lee of a rocky overhang and huddled around a large fire, for though it was late spring, the mist that rolled in at night was cold and dank. They shared their food with me, a little rice sprinkled with small pieces of salted fish, and questioned me in detail about my family, where I was going, and so on, questioned me in fact with such insistence that had I not been tired from the long day's ride—I had come that morning all the way from Chingchou, the last town on the post road before the pilgrim trail leads off into the mountains—even I would have taken note. However, I babbled happily away, saying I was an orphan from a poor cloth merchant's family in faraway Shu, which seemed to satisfy them. They were particularly impressed by the fact that I could read and write and by my knowledge of medicine and the apothecary's art, of which I boasted volubly, averring that from the bushes around us I could cure a fever or stanch the flow of blood from a wound, then close it up with thread made from the bark of the white mulberry, puffing myself up as I talked so that when they asked how I lived, I told them with a smirk that it was as easy to come by money as it was to pluck a millet stalk, if one knew how. I meant, I suppose, for I can hardly think across the gap of so many years what posturing bravado prompted this remark, that opportunities like the peacock feathers given to me by Ngoc in the Mist Mountains always seemed to fall in my lap and that, if need be, I could always work as a clerk for a magistrate. But they took this piece of braggadocio another way, I was soon to realize, and there was a round of grunted agreement and a few significant nods.

"The next morning when I returned with water from a nearby stream, they were huddled together listening as Huang, a ratlike fellow who appeared to be their leader—small with darting eyes, sharp nose, and a silky little moustache—talked intensely. The group dispersed as I walked towards the horses, most of them regarding me with such open speculation that I finally became uneasy. Still, there was little I could do short of jumping on my horse and riding away, and as they appeared to know the trails intimately, there wasn't much point in trying that. After we set off at a measured walk—the paths were still deep in mud from the spring rains and progress was very slow—my fears dissipated and I was soon chatting amiably about horses (a subject on which every man has an opinion) with a gaunt individual named Liu who reminded me vaguely of Pigboy. The sun soon burnt off the remaining mist and a glorious clear day dawned, the sky a single sheet of cobalt stretching above the mountains, a light breeze blowing up the scent of wet earth from the valley into which we were descending, while orange, crimson, and yellow trails of wildflowers blazed through the purple bracken that covered the slopes on either side of us and orioles fluttered like a cloud of golden butterflies through a stand of tall pines on a distant ridge, their cheerful call—*wei-wei-weiliao*—floating down to us.

"As we neared the mouth of the valley, a small party of travelers on foot appeared around a corner. When they were a hundred paces or so away, Huang gave a sign of some sort and all fifteen men suddenly swarmed forward. For a few confused moments, with the horses milling and rearing and a few muffled cries emerging from the melee, I couldn't see what was happening. Then a lane opened and I saw that there were four bodies lying in the mud. Several of their cloth bundles had broken open and bits of clothing and a few cooking pots were scattered about. I watched in disbelief as three of my companions dismounted and began to search the bodies and baggage for valuables, tearing rings off the fingers of one middle-aged woman, ripping open the blouse of a young girl to reveal budding breasts, now smeared with blood from the gaping wound in her throat.

"'Definitely fuckable,' one of the searchers called out. 'This one you should have kept alive for a few days at least.'

"Huang was squatting next to one of the bodies, a man who had died from a massive blow to the side of his head and a swordthrust under the ribs. Pushing the corpse round so that the wound gaped open, Huang dabbled his fingers in the cut, then turned and walked towards me, holding out his bloody hands in front of him. At this, finally dazed and slow as in a dream, I pulled my horse's head round with the thought of making some escape, but Huang simply nodded behind him and two of the men on horseback produced crossbows. He gestured for me to dismount, then said, 'Don't move' and took my face in his hands, imprinting two bloody handprints on either cheek, then drew a symbol of some kind on my forehead.

"'Now,' he said, leaning down to wipe off his hands on a patch of grass, 'you are one of us. The next time you will make your first kill. Until then, do not wash off the blood.'

"With that he turned and walked back to his horse, all of us remounted, and the whole party rode away, leaving the sprawled bodies in the middle of the road, their exposed flesh gleaming a terrible, naked alabaster in the bright sunlight.

"During the following days I moved as in a trance, watching as if from a great distance as the gang went about its bloody business. Much of that time I have tried to forget, though for years after, I would wake in the pit of the night, sweating and shaking, my heart pounding, having been back there around one of the fires they built, huddled under my cloak, off by myself, the rest of them roaring and joking and drinking purloined wine, some unspeakable horror usually being perpetrated on a female prisoner in a nearby bush or even out in the open, they taking turns then cutting her throat after the last man had finished. They were beasts, nothing human left in them, criminals who knew that if they were apprehended the only question would be how they would die, the probability being one of the most severe forms the law prescribes—flaying alive or gradual dismemberment over a period of days.

"I was a strange addition to their band. It seemed they had inferred from my boasting remarks that I would be amenable to their life, but to guard against treachery they also wished to see me commit the acts that would bring me down to the bestial level to which they had fallen. So I was half-trusted, or not even that, for I refused to kill or rape. The first time I was ordered to do so, I told them that it made no difference. To outsiders, I was one of them and would die with the rest of them if we were taken. I offered, too, to fight any man who doubted me and after some argument, Huang accepted my reasoning—he was the most intelligent of them and saw the need for someone who could tend their wounds and sickness, not to mention read and write, for once a month or so they would descend singly on a large town like Pingchou and send letters and drafts on the gold merchants' guild off to their families, to whom they were uniformly models of devotion. Looking back, I think it likely that he also didn't believe my story about being from a poorish cloth merchant's family, had looked at my rich silk robes, the jade rings, and the gold earrings and seen a rich man's son out on an adventure. I would guess now that on top of my immediate utility as a physician, Huang had it in his mind to wait until we were settled somewhere for a few days, then extract the truth of my parentage from me, hoping to secure a fat ransom.

"But despite his acquiescence, some of the others resented my exclusion from the law of murder by which they bound themselves to each other. Liu—the gaunt man I had been chatting with on that first morning—seemed to take it the worst, taunting me, shouting that I should be forced to kill or die myself. Finally on the third night the issue came to a head and the two of us fought with daggers, the others just watching, evidently having decided that this was a personal matter. We crouched low, feinting and slashing, crabbing to and fro in the light of the flickering bonfire until I tripped him and plunged my dagger into his scrawny neck to put an end to it. Liu's death, as well as a number of impressively bloody wounds I suffered in the fight, seemed to take the pressure off me for a time. I settled into their bizarre life, still not accepted—two of them rode behind me and slept close to me at night—at least I was no longer the focus of their resentment.

"In any case, resentment and thoughts of ransom were soon driven from all of our minds. I had been with them about ten days, and we were riding through a thin screen of trees that ran along the top of a ridge when Huang suddenly brought the group to a halt and gestured urgently for silence. Below us was a village and peering down I could see what had so alarmed him: the rainbow banners of a troop of imperial soldiers fluttering in the morning breeze. Without a word he waved for us to dismount and retreat through the trees to the other side of the ridge. This accomplished, we waited (I noted that my two guards had drawn their daggers and stood ready to silence me should I be so foolish as to cry out). It was well into afternoon by the time Huang signaled that the troop was gone. He called me over.

"'Go down into the village,' he said, peering suspiciously at me. 'Find out what the army wanted, what the bastards are doing here. And don't try to play any fucking games. At the first sign of trouble, we'll come in and gouge out your eyes.'

"I don't remember what thought ran through my mind

that afternoon as my little horse picked its way carefully down the stony slope: plans of escape, probably, although I knew that Huang was right: even in the unlikely event I could persuade every one of the villagers to pick up their scythes and hoes on my behalf, they would be no match for fifteen heavily armed, experienced fighters.

"In fact, the village was almost entirely deserted when I arrived; most of them must have been out in the fields, I supposed. A few graybeards were dozing in the sun next to the village shrine, which stood at the foot of a dark old cypress tree. A proclamation had been pinned to the tree trunk. It spoke of the coming visit by the emperor to Tai Marchmont to perform sacrifices, a solemn and numen-charged ceremony usually held only once in a monarch's reign. In anticipation of the event, it continued, imperial forces were sweeping the hills and mountain of bandits and criminals. In this region, the foothills under the north slope of Mount Tai, one band of renegades had been terrorizing the populace, I read. A force of several hundred troops was now searching out these marauders and, with numerous reports of their whereabouts and identities pouring in from responsible citizens, their capture was only a matter of time.

"It was signed by Liang, Colonel of the Leopard Banner Guards of the Left. Below his signature was a list of fifteen names, complete with aliases and previous employment. (Huang had apparently once been a tanner's assistant, and I reflected that the stink and filth of that job was enough to account for his bitterness and cruelty, if not excuse it.) Under the last name, I was chilled to see, was a space in which had been written: 'Unknown new accomplice; believed responsible for several murders.'

"I retraced my steps even more cast down that I had been on the way down to the village: Every man's hand seemed against me.

"On being informed of what I had discovered, Huang ordered us all to mount, and we set off on what proved to be a nightmarish week of almost constant travel, moving ever higher, stopping only for a few hours of snatched sleep, each night colder than the last and more sodden, for the rains began again and even in the shelter of the trees we became completely soaked, my broad bamboo-skin hat at least keeping my head dry, but my robes and cloak always damp, the cold rain trickling down the back of my neck, my feet rotting in my boots. Occasionally we would glimpse an army patrol across a valley or on a ridge, very conspicuous with their bright banners and shining armor. I don't think they saw us, or at least not knowingly, but we never could seem to be rid of them. I guessed at the time that the villagers we encountered must have been guiding the soldiers, and on the fourth day we were woken by one of the sentries posted during our short slumber with the whispered news that a patrol was passing along the ridge above us some fifty paces away. It was deep in the night and we were well hidden by the trees and the mist, but Huang nevertheless changed his tactics after that encounter, hugging the woods but moving steadily in one direction: whereas before his object had simply been to evade the army, now he appeared to have some definite goal in mind.

"By the fifth day I was too exhausted to care any longer whether we were caught or not. I only wanted to sleep. Barring that, I would have settled for a quick execution. Saddle sores plagued us all, the raw wounds on our thighs and buttocks bleeding slowly but steadily, soaking our robes. The horses too were near exhaustion, for without the luxury of time to forage, they had hardly eaten more than green grain for days and were reduced to plodding at a bare walk, their heads drooping, some of them dribbling a bright yellow mucus when pressed into a canter.

"When we hadn't seen a patrol for two days, it finally seemed we might be rid of our pursuers. By then we had left the forested slopes behind and were riding—or, rather, often walking, for the horses could barely find their own way, much less carry us while doing so—over a long sweep of rocky ground that led to the base of a cliff. As we neared the rock face, however, I saw there was a small cleft near the base, only visible from very close. We passed through this opening and rode for half an hour along the bottom of a gully barely wide enough for two men on horseback, the sheer sides rising up hundreds of feet, the sky a ribbon of gray above our heads. We halted where the canyon made a sharp turn to the right and Huang beckoned to me.

"'Around this corner is a Taoist temple. Ride up to the entrance and give them some claptrap about being a pilgrim, I'm sure you can dream up something convincing, eh?'

"I nodded my head.

"'Old Pang,' he said to a fat jovial-looking fellow who in fact was one of the cruelest in the group, delighting in violence. 'You go with him. If he tries anything, kill him.'

"When we rounded the corner, it dawned on me that this must be the Stone Lotus Temple, a reclusive Taoist retreat on Mount Tai. The temple was built into the living rock face, several tiers of courtyards and other buildings ascending up a long slope behind the entrance, the flat face of the mountain towering straight up on all sides. There was a large open space in front of the temple, leading on one side to the canyon mouth, on the other descending to a series of increasingly steep fields planted with wheat and vegetables. The fields ended in a precipice that fell hundreds of feet to the stony lower slopes of the mountain. The only way in—or out, I thought gloomily—was along the path we had just navigated. Old Pang and I made our way wearily to the high wooden gates and I called out:

"'Open please for followers of the Way. Pilgrims seeking to worship at the temple.'

"Short of the threat of imminent violence or death, the temple priests were compelled by their beliefs to open the gates to such a request, and sure enough a rotund face with a shaven pate popped out of an embrasure, regarded us for a few moments, then disappeared. The sounds of bolts being drawn back and a crossbar being removed soon penetrated to us, and within moments the gates were creaking open. We ambled in as the doors swung wide and as soon as we had passed the threshold, there came a thunderous clattering of hooves from the canyon as the rest of our group pushed their tired horses into a final gallop. This prompted the two monks at the gate to begin pushing the heavy doors shut again, but Old Fang skewered one of them without a word, while I simply brandished my sword at the other and he turned and fled, calling out shrilly in alarm. Once the rest of the bandits were inside, the gates swung shut behind us. There followed a confused period during which they roamed throughout the temple, slaughtering all the monks they could find, I simply wandering through the courtyards and passageways, the idea of finding another exit beating in my tired brain. I stopped for a while in the kitchen and wolfed down some boiled millet cake and cold chicken, then made my way to one of the monk's cells and, barring the door behind me, curled up in a corner and went to sleep.

"Minutes later, or so it seemed, there was a hubbub outside the cell door, running feet and shouts of alarm echoing down the hallway. 'Imperial troops are at the gates,' I heard someone cry. When I emerged from the cell, the passageway was empty. I could hear shouts and the clang of metal from the front of the complex and turned and ran in the other direction, through several courtyards and cavernous kitchens into another tiny alley leading to a winding staircase. I climbed up and up and up, slipping on the dank stone of the narrow stairs, slamming into the cold, moss-covered walls, always scrabbling for purchase, on and on and on, my breath coming harsh and labored, my lungs and throat burning, until finally I burst out of a low stone lintel onto a long gravelly field, bigger than the other courtyards, the size of two polo pitches, completely sealed off by a high wall that ran around it in a semicircle. The entrance I had come through was the only access, and the remainder of the field was bounded by sheer rock walls. There was nothing above but rock and wind, immensely strong swirling currents that whistled and moaned across the face of the cliff and along the surface of the field. Struggling against the river of air cascading down the mountain, I staggered over to the wall, panting heavily, and pulled myself onto the wide rampart.

"Below me, laid out as though on a map, I could see the several courtyards I had passed through, the front gates, and the field outside, now filled with several hundred imperial troops and their brilliant rainbow banners. As I watched, the gates swung open and the massed soldiers poured in, swamping the little group of bandits. I watched with some satisfaction as they were swiftly dispatched, Huang's head cloven in half by a tremendous blow from a double-handed saber wielded by an officer dressed in brilliant red, green, and blue armor. It was all over in a matter of minutes and the tide of soldiers now began to flow into the other courtyards, swelling up toward my refuge.

"I raced up and down the wall, seeking a means of escape, but the only way down was the way I had come. On the other side was a cliff that dropped down to the open area in front of the temple where the fields began, far too steep and long a fall to even contemplate for long before being overtaken by dizziness. There was no way out. I peered over the rampart once again and saw that a knot of soldiers was swarming into the tiny alley that led to the winding staircase. I turned and surveyed the long field again, looking desperately for a rope, anything. Then my eyes fell upon a small shed I had overlooked, tucked under the ramparts. I wrenched open the flimsy wooden door and pulled at the dark shape inside, a long, box-like construct of cloth and wood, brilliantly painted. For a moment I gaped at the thing in puzzlement, then my heart sank as I realized what it was: a kite. I threw it to one side and pulled at the other objects inside: more kites. Flat kites, triangular kites, kites with two wings and four and six wings, more box-shaped kites, ten, twenty, thirty of the things, all gorgeously painted with lions and dragons, unicorns and simurghs; all useless. This must be the recreation the monks of Stone Lotus Temple allowed themselves; when not meditating on the Way, they were at play in the high-thrusting mountain winds, 'riding the ether' as the Taoist books spoke of it. *Riding the ether*. . . .

"I could hear the pounding of heavy boots echoing up the stairwell; death approaching. With a grunt of effort, I pulled out the sturdiest looking and largest box kite, scrambled with it to the part of the ramparts overlooking the fields, slipped it over my head and, with a single thrust of my legs and no thought between action and execution, I launched myself out into the turbid air.

"I fell, the kite twirling around and around, spinning end over end, the blows and buffeting of the wind knocking the breath out of my chest so that for the first few moments my only thought was the struggle to suck in air. Down and down I plunged, tumbling over and over, the kite finding no support. Then my descent was suddenly checked by a stunning impact from below. The kite jumped upward, then was plucked this way and that by successive blasts, now sideways, now upwards until there were two blows from either side simultaneously and the kite seemed to come to a complete halt in the air, then slip out of the fray, settling onto a steady stream of air that bore it gently forward. It was the most extraordinary sensation, more astonishing even than riding on the back of the eagle, for here there was no visible means of support, no powerful wings to hold me up, just a few bits of canvas cloth and flimsy struts of green maple to which I was clinging with all my might.

"After a while, my dazed eyes focused on the scene below. I was drifting over the troops remaining outside the temple, a group of officers on horseback cantering towards the gates, behind them a platoon of archers who fortunately remained oblivious to the sight above them. I gazed down in wonder, then realized with a start that the sustaining current seemed to be dying, that I was drifting slowly lower, down towards the troop of archers who, all oblivious, were watching the front of the temple. Beyond them were the wheat fields, which might offer some refuge. But if they discovered me, I would soon resemble one of those delicate silk-covered pincushions that my mothers had always kept on their dressing tables. Lower and lower I sank until I thought the wind had died completely, and I was about to plunge straight down onto the heads of the soldiers.

"Just as I thought I was bound to smash into them from above, a gust suddenly punched the kite into a staggering heave upward. I gasped at this, a sound that seemed loud enough to cause some fool to turn his head upward. Another buffet and I felt my intestines rumble and a great gout of gas bubble up inside me. I clenched my muscles with all my strength, but it was no use, the pressure was unrelenting, finally bursting out in a thunderous fart like the heavens being rent. I could feel another one building up inside and closed my eyes and squeezed, squeezed for my life. It was as though someone had stuck a bellows into my stomach and was pumping madly. I opened my eyes and glanced downwards.

The soldiers were still staring at the front gates of the temple, but as the pressure in my bowels became unbearable, I was obliged to relax my hold, letting loose a string of small eruptions, louder and louder until a last huge detonation like a giant firecracker caused several of the men to gaze around in puzzlement. Any moment I knew they would look up. I squeezed my eyes shut expecting within seconds to feel the impact of those steel arrowheads tearing into my stomach. Instead of cries of alarm, though, I heard laughter from below. Opening my eyes, I saw that the archers had focused their attention on one of their colleagues, a fat specimen overflowing from his armor. They shouted something at him—I couldn't catch it exactly, though obviously some form of abuse; the words 'fatty farter' floating upwards along with a gale of laughter. The unfortunate object of ridicule reacted angrily, waving his arms and shouting in denial but only succeeding in provoking more laughter.

"All this I watched but hardly saw, so intensely was I concentrating on controlling myself, my fists clenched, arms rigid, every muscle in my legs and lower back tensed as tight as steel, sweat beading on my forehead. And yet the contraction seemed to make it worse, pressing more of the gas outward towards release. At last when I had nearly cleared the archers, was on the verge of the fields, a series of sputtering pops emerged, despite my efforts, gradually growing louder; then I was halfway over the fields, one hundred and fifty, two hundred paces away, drifting downwards again towards the lip of the precipice which led down to freedom. As the cliff approached, the pressure inside me was so strong that my stomach seemed to be bulging out, tight as a drum. Once again I could control it no longer and just as we sank below the edge of the cliff, I let go—blissful, glorious release—a long burbling roll swelling to a single, final thunderclap.

"But by then the kite had slid beneath the cliff, out of sight of the soldiers, and a soft sustaining breeze cradled it like the flying cloud-platform of the Western Mother, easing me down to the shining pastures of grass that stretched from the base of the cliff to the treeline like vast fields of green silk, the slopes rising gently towards me until the last moment when all became a tumbling blur and I hit the ground very hard, rolling, rolling onto the sweet, thick grass, over and over, the kite disintegrating until I was spinning unencumbered, rolling the way I did as a child on the slopes outside my father's house, turning slower and slower until at last I came to a halt, lying on my back, face up to the sun, caressed by the breeze, the companionable sound of orioles wafting down towards me from some distant stand of pines, *wei-wei-weiliao, wei-wei-weiliao.*"

six 李白

THE NEXT DAY THE BOAT DOCKS AT A SMALL TOWN nestling in a bend of the Great River. The poet appears late in the morning and disembarks without a word to Wang Lung who, used to his erratic ways by now, is sitting in his customary place, still struggling with the equally eccentric Chuang-tzu. Early in the evening a flushed Li Po climbs the gangplank, walks over to the foredeck, and drops heavily into his seat.

"Now then," he says, "where was I?"

"Somewhere on Mount Tai," Wang Lung replies, putting aside his scroll.

Li Po turns and looks sharply at the boy. Wang's head is bowed over the table, his brush poised over a blank sheet of paper.

"Somewhere on Mount Tai, indeed," the poet sniffs. "I was on my way to find Master Ku and had become sidetracked. I suppose that you are wondering where all this is leading. 'He's not like the village storytellers,' you're saying to yourself, 'no beginning, middle, and end.' And being the age you are, young man, the one thing you would really like to know is what happens to the girl, eh?"

Here Li Po fixes the boy with a knowing eye. But Wang Lung remains bent over his scroll, silent, brush poised.

"And well you may keep quiet," Li Po says with a smirk, then closes his eyes, leaning back and sinking into the silk cushions piled around him. "I'll wager you are blushing under that bowed head. Well, never fear, we'll get to her eventually. Consider that perhaps there is a reason for these side excursions of mine. And even if there isn't, you must admit that they are tales worth hearing. One day I may even tell you about the third time in my life that I flew. But that must certainly be kept for another place than this. Now we are back, somewhere on Mount Tai, as you put it, I searching for Master Ku:

"I picked myself up and began running as fast as I could down the mountain, away from the Stone Lotus Temple, away from the imperial soldiers, away from the memory of those terrible days with Huang and his gang of beasts in human garb. I ran until I reached the tree line, plunging into the thick forest of pine from which the orioles had beckoned me, gradually slowing to a trot and then a walk, my footsteps muffled by the thick bed of needles covering the forest floor, calmed by the peaceful silence, disturbed only by my ragged panting. Here and there a golden shaft of late afternoon sunlight pierced through the thick canopy of trees, my passage stirring up dust motes that danced in the blaze of light, the only movement in that empty world. After awhile the urge to sleep overwhelmed me. I lay down in the fragrant bed of needles and passed into unconsciousness.

"When I awoke it was late afternoon. Refreshed but ravenously hungry, I jumped up and began to blunder my way through the woods. The trees soon thinned out, then disappeared, and I was back out in the open again. I had circled around the side of the mountain to an area of rolling foothills, a sea of round crests and valleys that lapped away from me like waves on a vast brown sea tinged with purple. Hitching up my robe and sighing a little, I set forth, stiff and slow at first after so long in the saddle, but my youthful legs soon found their rhythm. If necessary, I told myself, I would walk all night.

"And so indeed I did, a long, long night of stumbling into streams and tripping over roots and branches, a night that at times seemed as though it would never end, a night of utter exhaustion but no chance of rest, for the night air was frigid enough to prevent sleep, even if I had been so inclined. When the sun finally rose, though, it brought with it warmth and its usual glorious renewal of hope and strength, a feeling that my stumbling journey through the darkness had been little more than a bad dream. Soon, I was striding along energetically, ignoring the grinding in my belly, sometimes walking easily through patches of dense forest, other times out in the open, the whole glorious mountain panorama soaring around me. Twice I met woodsmen carrying bundles of faggots on their shoulders and asked about Master Ku, but they just shook their heads and continued on their way without a word. Later, I wrote this:

A dog barks amid the sound of rushing water;
Peach blossoms, stained dark with dew.
In these deep woods, a deer appears, then vanishes,
and beside the mountain stream
the tolling of the noon bell cannot be heard.
The green mist slides behind a screen of wild
    bamboo;
cascading streams hang from blue peaks.
No one knows where the master has gone.
Suddenly melancholy, I lean against a pine tree,
waiting.

"This was the first poem that I submitted to the scrutiny of others; before I had written mostly for myself, but as I came to understand the ways of the world, I sent copies of this piece and a few others to a few friends, scholars, and poets I had met in Loyang and Yangchou. They in turn circulated the poem so that eventually it reached the capital. A few months on, the judgment of Wang Wei and his fellow court poets reached me. The poem was 'adequate' they said, showing a good grasp of the rules of tonal balance, though striving somewhat for conventional poetic effects and overcrowding the lines with too many things: too many trees and too many streams (*too many streams!*). What's more, they said my provincial background showed when I used the word 'hang' instead of the more elegant 'suspended.' And the opening couplet should set the scene, they said, not contain any action; any capital poet would know that the abrupt 'barks' unbalance the piece and focus too much attention on the first line.

"Shit! Shit! Shit! That was my reply to those self-appointed arbiters of poetry. By binding everything within a tight corset, according to rules they alone determined, they sought to bring real immortals down to their level of mediocrity. If anything, the way the literary establishment in Chang An had reacted to that first poem made me even more determined to write just as I liked. I knew whose poems would be read in a hundred years, or a thousand, when no one would remember their carping quibbles. I swore a great oath then that I would shun the capital until they begged me to come, implored me to shine my brilliance upon them.

"Ah, but it's not worth wasting my breath on such petty fools. Back to my tale. As the poem says, I was waiting, waiting for the Master. It was early afternoon and I had come to a clearing in the woods that remains one of the most beautiful spots I have ever seen, waterfalls hanging (yes, 'hanging') in the distance, the sun beaming benevolently down, the air full of birdsong, a light breeze wafting up the springscent of pine. I sat down on a fallen log, thinking vaguely that I might eat, and was soon lost in contemplation.

"After a time I looked up to see a small boy dressed in a

bright robe of yellow and green standing on the other side of the clearing. He gestured for me to follow him, turning without a word and plunging back into the trees. I rose hurriedly and pursued him—somehow, he always stayed a few hundred paces in front of me however fast I walked—until we came to a cave entrance into which he disappeared. Entering, I found myself walking down a long corridor half-lit by some unseen source that cast a greenish glow over the rough walls. Eventually the way ahead became brighter and brighter and I turned a last corner to emerge into a long hall. Half the roof overhead was made of some micalike substance, cloudy but transparent so that sunlight poured into the room. At the far end three men sat on mats on the floor listening to another who stood in front of them, lecturing. He looked up as I came in and waved me over. 'Ah, Li Po,' he said, 'here at last. Come. Come join the others. We have just begun.'

"I walked over, dropped my bag on the floor, and sat on a mat that seemed to have been laid out for me. Then he began to talk, if that is the word for the blazing brilliance of his speech that held us all transfixed, he soaring and dipping, now flying to the myriad stars, now burrowing in the earth with the meanest worm, illuminating the heavens with his words, sowing together the disparate elements of man's life into a grand cosmic tapestry. He sketched the alignment of the five elements—wood, fire, water, air, and metal—with the five planets, the five musical tones, and the five colors, always returning to this theme, that matter is balanced, always balanced, sun and moon, dark and light, yin and yang.

"He explicated the ancients, too, the Weft books of the Han, now banned on sentence of death, and the great alchemical treatise of Ko Hung, his words like a light shone in a dark corner we pass every day to reveal untold riches. For it is not enough simply to read such books and follow their instructions: they are not cooking manuals, after all. In Ko Hung many have found the recipe for cinnabar elixir:

"Take Quicksilver and roast it until it changes color to red-gold, it is then Returned Cinnabar; prepare one pound of the Returned Cinnabar and insert into a bamboo tube, adding two ounces of Saltpeter and Malachite. Close the openings and seal with hard lacquer. Place the tube in strong vinegar and bury it three feet under the ground; after thirty days it will have transformed into true Cinnabar; a pinch taken each week for a month will extend the life by thirty years; a spoonful each day for a hundred.

"But how many have tried this and failed, some dying from ingesting too much of their own mismade mess, ha, ha! No, a man must have more than mere words on a page. He must know the exact timing for incubation, the hour of the day and the season in which to conduct the transformation; he must fortify himself for three hours each day with breathing exercises, by abstaining from flesh or grains, sustaining his body on dew, nuts, and honey; but, more than these, the Master taught us that all such practices are useless if he is not a Superior Man who understands the warp and weft of the universe and his own place in it. Otherwise he might as well be eating dirt.

"Ah, what glory it was to rise each day and feel the power of the place, its fundamental mystery, charging through the blood anew. Nowhere in the wide world could have been better for acquiring the secrets of the heavens and the depths of the earth than Mount Tai; the soaring peaks and valleys; the waterfalls and long sweeps of green, russet, and red forest; the mist that would descend without warning, cutting off the outside world completely: all were at once belittling and exalting. And best of all was when night descended, the 'stars so close I could pluck them with my hand and I dare not speak aloud in the vast silence for fear of disturbing the dwellers of heaven,' as I later described it. Late in the night the master would lead us up a rocky path behind the entrance to the cave, a hard half-hour scramble to the platform where he made his observations of the skies. There, we seated cross-legged in front of him, the great spangling firmament his backdrop, he would name the stars and their relations, creating order out of the chaotic mass of asterisms before our startled eyes, sketching the great star concatenations that weave together to form the core of the cosmos: the Grand Tenuity, the Forest of Feathers, the Threading Garland, Azure Thunderbolt, Curling Tongue, the Heavenly Barrier, all of them hanging on the Great Pivot of Heaven, the Northern Culmen asterism, which is the nexus at which the twelve mainstays of the sky are tied together in hooked array: the Pivot itself, Great Polaris, Radiant Moonsoul, Illustrious Theocrat, Northern Chronogram, Knot, Heirgiver's Palace, Grand Monad, Grand Heir, and the Five Princes. Then it was on to the Dipper, the source and object of cosmic power. We learned the standard and hidden names of that most magical of star chains, though of course I can only repeat the superjacent callings, not the true secret appellations: the Jade Cog, Armil, Jade Transverse, Disclosed Yang, Gemmy Light, and Occult Tenebreity. The Dipper is more potent even than the Pivot, the gateway through which a man can project his secret self and become a Transcendent. Or the means by which the Superior Man can grow immortality from the inside out, sprouting dragon bones and skin of jade if he can master the incorporation of the Dipper within his anatomical chambers by correctly pacing the void, dancing the star-patterns laid out in rivulets of quicksilver on the marble floor, the five-color banners representing the cosmic clouds hung from the rafters, chanting all the time from the *Book of*. . . . But what a fool I am, talking on and on."

Li Po suddenly leans over a little unsteadily and whispers in a hoarse, wine-stinking voice to Wang Lung: "I must stop myself there. In my enthusiasm I reveal what cannot be spoken. You must learn of these matters yourself, my boy, for I am bound not to disclose the rites to any except an initiate. And besides, any more from me and some nosy servant will inform the charming Major, and my life will be forfeit again. No, let us stay firmly on the ground today and talk of ordinary, earthbound miracles."

Li Po pats the boy on the shoulder, settles himself back down, pours the last drop out of the wine flask in front of him, calls for another, then starts talking again:

"Each day as part of the physical and mental conditioning that accompanied our studies, we were required to spend three hours in meditation, breathing exercises, and the precise, languorous movements of tai chi. Naturally these sessions were conducted alone, and my chosen spot was the glade in which I had sat dreaming on the day of my arrival. It was a place charged with calm as well as beauty, and during that summer I made my way eagerly there each day in the early morning.

"Over the course of the summer months though, I noticed something odd: each time I visited the clearing there seemed to be more birds, more and more each week until the branches of the encircling trees were filled with them from trunk to tip, often jostling politely for space, but otherwise well behaved. And I found, too, that with each passing day my sense of their presence swelled and grew inside me so that by the eighth month of the year I could call them down to me with a whistle, they descending in ones and twos, birds of every size and shape, from tiny robins and flycatchers to geese and storks, strangely out of place on the high mountain slopes, even huge, brutish black crows and kites and once an eagle owl, cat-faced and usually very fierce but then quite docile, landing on my outstretched arm as meek as a little girl. Later still I found that at a command they would flock down in tens and scores, lining my arms and shoulders in close-packed ranks, the smaller birds perching on my head, the ground dwellers—quail, pheasants, and the like—nestling happily in the grass around my feet. Perhaps it sprung from the magic of that great mountain, the spiritual center of our race, a numinous magnet drawing all that is transcendent from the creatures around it. I pondered little on this sudden empathy I had acquired, however. Surrounded by the awe-inspiring beauty of the mountain and being taken up entirely with self-cultivation and the study of the mysteries, everything that happened seemed perfectly normal. And, as you must have guessed by now, I have always had a special admiration, even reverence, for birds, my avatars—strong, graceful, often startlingly beautiful but most of all fiercely, even foolishly, free, like those thrushes of my youth that would rather die than live in cages.

"By early autumn my strange powers had been remarked on by woodsmen in the area, who would sometimes come into the clearing when the birds were gathered round me in their hundreds. Once, one of them threw a new over a couple of pied kingfishers hovering at the edge of the glade, but I chased after them and took the net away, disentangling the birds from its folds and releasing them—a task made extremely difficult by their absurdly long, daggerlike beaks, nearly half the length of their own bodies, which always seemed to catch on some corner of the net. And then one day in early autumn, the Master informed us that the provincial governor was to pay a visit to a nearby temple and having heard about my 'abilities' wished to witness them himself.

"A week later, he duly appeared. He was spotted many hours before his arrival, a strange sight in the quiet calm of the mountain, a long, lone line of men and beasts winding up towards us, the six gilded palanquins of the governor and his most senior assistants (the road was too steep for carriages), a cloud of lesser officials and military men following on horses, then the squadrons of foot soldiers with their lances and pennants, and behind them scores and scores of servants all dressed in motley livery, robes of deep blue, green, gray, and red, all patterned with the circular chrysanthemum design that was the governor's personal symbol, some carrying red lacquer food containers and chests slung on poles, others pushing single-wheel carts loaded with casks of wine and flying yellow and pink flags stamped with the chrysanthemum roundel, others still bearing enormous embroidered fans and triple-decked silken umbrellas should his eminence suffer from the unseasonable heat. At the rear came a full orchestra mounted on horses, ready to play at the performance of rites—kettle drums that hung at the waist, clapping boards and cymbals, flutes and bamboo reed pipes, trumpets, horns, and cloud gongs, a popular court instrument. You probably haven't seen one, eh boy? Ten brass gongs, each sounding a separate note, all suspended from a wooden frame, played with a small metal hammer.

"Watching all this, and hearing even at a distance the enormous noise such a group of men could generate, I wondered what birds would remain for him to see. But the expedition turned at the fork in the road and proceeded to the Summit Temple about five miles away, and that evening the governor, evidently not as foolish a man as I had assumed, sent a messenger saying that he would come with a only few close aides the next day at dawn.

"In the morning I went straight to the clearing and started my exercises, paying no attention whatever when the governor arrived and stood with the Master at the edge of the glade. He and his vast retinue symbolized everything about the outside world I had come to the mountain to escape: the preoccupation with office and its trappings, with pomp and ceremony, with the self. Deep in the grip of the hermetic ideal, I would have nothing to do with such nonsense, or so I told myself. Indeed when the time came for me to summon the birds, I hesitated for a moment, pondering whether to forgo such a vulgar display altogether rather than perform on demand for this incarnation of worldly power. Then on reflection I told myself that the best course was to act as though he wasn't present at all, simply not to acknowledge him in even the smallest way.

"And so, having spent an hour on my breathing and another on the underwater dancing of tai chi, I turned at last and slowly extended a hand, pointing toward the far end of the clearing where I could see a mating pair of amur falcons, the male magnificent in a coat of silver-gray, his breast ivory, his undersides and legs heavy with rufous orange fur; the female much the same except that her breast and legs were covered in a sweep of creamy white down interrupted by regular black bars, for all the world like ermine. They were both staring down with arrogant indifference, their weird red eyes glowing in the morning sunlight. I gave a single tremolo whistle, pulling them towards me, and without a moment's hesitation they were off the branch, a single wing beat carrying them across the two hundred paces separating us and onto my outstretched arm. Next I called a line of tiny lime-and-yellow warblers and a brace of red turtle doves, both the common prey of the falcon, but here happy to settle next to their enemy on my shoulder. Then I gave the signal for a general assembly, and there was a deafening whirring and beating of wings as clouds of birds descended from each tree or came scurrying across the grass: pigeons and cuckoos, woodpeckers and wrynecks, swifts, swallows, and sparrows. Lastly, when all other movement had stopped, an enormous shadow like that of a temple door unhinged and thrown into the air by some cataclysmic wind appeared on the far side of the clearing and drifted slowly across the grass towards me—a black vulture landed without a sound a few paces away, folding its great wings and gazing levelly at me with its empty black eyes.

"After a time they began to drift away, at first in ones and twos, then tens and scores, the smaller birds darting into the trees, the falcons flapping laboriously for height, then catching an updraft and racing away. Last to go was the black vulture, which was obliged to run clumsily down the entire length of the field before it lifted heavily into the air with a series of whooshing flaps of its huge wings, just clearing the treetops, then a few more great thrusts and a sudden gust of wind from underneath and it was in its element, great wings spread, soaring higher and higher, straight up until it disappeared from sight in the clouds.

"The governor came hurrying across the glade, his aides trailing behind him, the Master—who had never witnessed my bird show—following at a slower pace. The governor—who was dressed as magnificently as any of the birds, scarlet robes embroidered in yellow and blue with his badge of office, a crane—waved the other officials away and stood in front of me, his round face beaming with pleasure.

"'Wonderful, young man, a wonderful display. Like nothing I have ever seen. It surpassed even the Indian snake charmer of last year who cut his little son into small pieces and then reassembled them. We found blood on the sand afterwards and the pieces in a straw basket. Very lucky for the second boy; he would have been chopped up the next time around.'

"I said nothing, gazing down at his elaborate court shoes peeping out from under his robes like small river barges, heavy three-inch heels at the stern, the tips curling at the prow. I noted too that their silk sides were now smeared with bird shit, one of the hazards of my little display.

"'What is your name?' he asked. 'Is this your home province?'

"'My name is Li Po,' I replied. 'I am an orphan from Shu studying with Master Ku here on Mount Tai.'

"The governor turned his plump face to the Master.

"'This is something you taught him?'

"'No, he has accomplished everything by himself. That is all I teach.'

"'Well, I think it's marvelous however you came to it,' he said, turning back to me. 'Li Po, Li Po. You write poetry, don't you?'

"'Yes, sir, I do.'

"'Then I have seen some of your writings, passed on to me by Liang, the deputy censor in Hunan. You're the Li Po of *barks* in the first line of the octet, aren't you?'

"I nodded, surprised that the poem had reached him. But the governor was famous for his literary tastes.

"'You have a great talent,' he burbled on. 'If you nurture it, one day you could sit among the greats.'

"Then he turned back to the Master. 'Perhaps you weren't aware that the young man can conjure with his pen as well as his hands?'

"The Master merely nodded and smiled, not replying.

"'Well, it only confirms my conviction that you must go to the capital as soon as ever you can. At first I thought of sending you to the emperor's Pear Garden School, where his entertainers are trained, but if you are the Li Po of those poems, it is a different matter altogether. I shall send you up as one of my Recommended Scholars; we governors are only allowed two a year, you know. You can skip the baccalaureate exams altogether and have the right to sit for your doctorate whenever you choose, receiving a stipend in the meantime for your studies. Not a huge amount, but enough so that you won't starve. As I said, you must nurture that talent through study, then bend it to the task of administering the empire. We can't afford to let men like you slip through our fingers. The emperor himself sent out a memorial on the subject only last month.'

"He turned to the Master once more. 'It will take him from you, of course, but you must concede, it would be a waste for a man of his talents to hide himself away on a mountain.'

"Again the Master smiled without replying.

"'So, my boy, what do you say? You can come down the mountain with me now, take a few days rest in the provincial capital, and then be on your way to Chang An within a few months, just in time for the winter exam cycle.'

"I opened my mouth to speak, to say yes, in fact, that I would be happy to follow him off the mountain, visions of Chang An, of the robes of office forming in my mind. But then I looked at him again, that plump, shining face, the air of benevolent condescension that radiated from him, the bright ruby, gold, and jade rings on his plump fingers, the certainty that no one could refuse such an offer—I saw all this and felt an enormous, physical pressure well up inside me that shouted 'No! No! No!' and I gave way to it, saying, as in a dream, 'I am very grateful, your excellency, but I cannot accept. To travel to the capital would be to destroy everything that I have done here. What I am seeking can't be found in worldly glory, exams, and robes of office.'

"The governor—clearly unaccustomed to refusal—frowned and looked intently at me.

"'I remind you that the emperor himself has sent out an edict recently ordering us to redouble our search for responsible men of talent. Your duty lies in service; such talent leaves you no choice. Come, now, you will soon forget this anchorite will o' the wisp. The life of the hermit is all very well for mystics and dreamers, but it is not for practical men. Think again.'

"'No sir,' I replied, stung by his assumption that my life on Mount Tai was just a velleity, a passing fancy that would disappear once I was back in the world of men. 'No, sir, I think not. The *Tao Te Ching* says *favor and disgrace are a goad to madness; high rank hurts keenly as our bodies hurt,* does it not? I will stay here and pursue this will o' the wisp; the world outside will always be there, but the chance to voyage in the inner world is rare.'

"This was enough for the governor. 'Very well,' he said, frowning with anger, 'but this chance will never come your way again, I can promise you that.'

"'So be it,' I replied pompously, but he was already striding away, his aides scurrying behind him in a flurry of robes. I looked at the Master, who gave me one of his enigmatic smiles, then turned to walk back to the cave. I followed him, triumphant on the surface, but under it numb, aware that my life had just taken a great swing on the pivot of fate, a single thought repeating over and over: 'What a waste. What a waste.'

seven 李白

"AND, INDEED," THE POET CONTINUES THE NEXT morning, as always picking up without a pause from the previous day's narrative, "I soon came to realize that you can't build a life on words spoken in pride. For a time, life went on as before. At least on the surface it was the same. For after the governor's visit, I was overtaken by a growing restlessness that would see my attention wandering as the Master spoke, intense flashes of memory exploding in my head when I least expected it: the poems left on the bamboo walls of a famous tavern in Hangchou, or a lady's magical walled garden with a hidden door beneath a wisteria tree in Yangchou. Sometimes, I simply nodded off, for I often woke in the middle of the night and, unable to go back to sleep, walked about under the friendly beams of the moon, my faithful companion on many a night, returning to the chamber where the four of us disciples slept, lying awake on my mat and trying to concentrate on the Absolute while listening to the others snore; there is nothing to take your mind off the ineffable like someone snoring.

"The other three disciples were quiet fellows taking the first steps in a long, long journey of contemplation and lonely self-cultivation, all too ready to confuse seriousness with wisdom—not very good company, in short. I had thought at one point that I might be on the same path—and I think the Master believed that was the way my future lay, too, one of the few times I remember him failing utterly in his judgment, which was usually exquisite.

"I had come to learn, and learn I had. But finally I realized that the solitary life in the mountains could only be temporary for me. Such a life was, in any case, meaningless in and of itself: to appreciate the virtues and rewards of an anchorite's existence, one had to know the worries and joys of the outside world. Otherwise, where was the balance? Night after night such thoughts ran through my head, as though there had been a landslide inside me, changing the terrain beyond recognition.

"Then one day when I was walking about in the late watches of the night, all others asleep, I was suddenly struck by the idea of leaving and did, rolling up my mat and a few other things and simply walking away without a word to anyone.

"It was yet another journey begun with almost nothing. I strode down the mountain slope, carefree, humming a tavern song about Tartar maids under my breath, my way guided by a brilliant full moon. Then the cheerful thought occurred to me that there was 500 cash waiting for me at Goldfish Lane next to the Water Gate in Chang An. That would keep me fed and housed for a few weeks, a month if husbanded. And I would be able to see Peony once again, too, perhaps even persuade her father to teach me to master the moon guitar.

"That was the plan I carried down the mountain—much faster descending than coming up—meaning to make for Chingchou, where I had begun my journey into the mountains nearly a year before. But circumstances were against me; a heavy fog dropped over Mount Tai on my second day out, soon followed by a lashing rain, very cold. I lost all sense of direction in the storm, and when the skies cleared I found that I had long ago taken a wrong turning. I was at the foot of the mountain, but on the south side rather than the north where the road to Loyang and Chang An began.

"There was little to recommend the southern coast of Shantung Province that lay before me, a narrow swathe of land between the sea and the mountains, blasted by the ocean winds, cut off from the rest of the empire by Mount Tai and its minions so that most travelers go in and out by boat. There was one major town, Michou, famous for its seafood and not much else. From there, however, it was only a two day sea voyage to Hai Ling farther down the coast. A branch of the Imperial Canal started there, and I could travel all the way to Chang An itself.

"I didn't linger, taking passage to Hai Ling, which was hardly any better than Michou, most of the place given over to a huge Korean quarter from which the smell of burnt meat, garlic, and fermenting cabbage emanated like an evil miasma. They were merchants, controlling the trade from the client kingdom of Silla on the peninsula, channelling it to the barges that plied the spur of the Grand Canal leading to Hai Ling. Many of them were pirates, too, smuggling ginseng and kidnapping young Korean girls, who were much prized as servants and concubines. I stayed there for just a few days, shaking the stink of the place out of my coat as I left, having joined the crew of a barge hauling trade goods to Chang An, a two-month journey away.

"The first month was a pleasant dream, the work minimal, the food tasteless but regular, the sun shining down each day in a last gasp before autumn set like an icy hand seizing the heart. I spent much time leaning on a railing at the rear of the barge, or at the tiller, dreaming the dreams of the young, visions of fame in the capital, the emperor himself praising my poems, appointing me to some high office, perhaps the generalship of an army that was to drive into the west or south and chastise the barbarians. But I pondered, too, on the nature of my verses, for I was writing more and more, had emerged from my hibernation on the mountain during which I had not written a single character. Once again the poems flowed like water, spring flowers blooming from my brush.

"After that first month of easy living, however, the weather turned blustery and cold and such thoughts were driven from my head. One dirty evening, a freezing rain dappling the teak decks with dancing explosions of slush, then changing to tiny balls of hail, we pulled into Pienchou, still a week out of Loyang and another three from the capital itself. The crew, myself, and three other young deckhands disembarked in good spirits despite the weather, for Pienchou was the first real town we had come to in two weeks and all of us were ready for a little song and laughter. We were walking through the center of the town, seeking out a wineshop in the eastern quarter, joking among ourselves like children, when above the shouting and horseplay I caught the faint sound of someone singing, so high and clear and pure that it almost hurt to listen. I stopped and bade them be silent, which they did for a moment, puzzled, then thinking it was another joke of some kind, cursing me loudly, I straining but unable to catch the voice again. 'Go on then you noisy bastards, get away to the wineshop,' I said and, seeing that I was serious, they went on, a little hurt.

"Standing in the middle of the street, listening, I heard the rain dripping from the eaves all around, the strong flow of water in the gutter, a rippling gurgle, the splash of someone hurrying home through the puddles in the next alley, a dog barking; then, faintly at first but growing stronger, the voice that could only be hers, singing a song I recognized, a keening desert lament that usually closed a performance, the finale a single note held for as long as the breath lasted while the accompanying guitarist skated and whorled around it, the voice going on and on, the guitar weaving a mad arabesque until at last a series of three strong chords gave the singer the cue to finish. This time, though, the improvisation was cloddish and the ending bumbled, the guitar faltering at the last, the final chords muddy and uncertain, followed by silence.

"All this I registered as I hurried towards the source of the sound, within minutes finding a huge house set in a large garden, a gloomy line of cypresses blocking the front from view, the building constructed of some dark mahogany, a high stone wall and a heavy gate surrounding it. I walked round to the servant's entrance and stood in the shadows next to the back gate. Before long I heard them coming across the rear courtyard, her shoes clacking angrily, her voice now shrill:

"'Don't think I didn't see you slip away at the intermission. How many jars did you manage to swill down? Three? Four? The whole of the second half, you were on the edge of passing out instead of just playing like a drunken gibbon, the way you usually do. Why couldn't you have waited until after the performance. This Mr. Chan could have been a very powerful patron. He has friends in Chang An who could . . . '

"At this point they emerged through the gate, the old man first, stumbling slightly as he negotiated the high step, his head bowed against her tirade, his eyes bleary in the light of the single lantern swinging from the lintel. She followed, eyes blazing, her cheeks flushed with anger, struggling to pull on a heavy robe against the cold, underneath wearing only her diaphanous performance robe. He passed by without seeing me, but Peony noticed some reflection from the corner of her eye before I could step forward.

"'Who's there!' she shouted, whirling around and brandishing her umbrella in a way that made my heart turn to water. I stepped forward and she regarded me for a moment, then said:

"'The perfect ending to the night. It is Mr. 500 Cash, Father, come to dun us for what he is owed. Here,' she flung down a cloth bag that rang as it hit the pavement. 'Take this, there's 500 cash and more for the interest, our evening's fee, not that we earned it.'

"'I didn't come for my money,' I said softly, trying to calm her. 'I happened to be in the same town. I heard your voice from the next street.'

"'Well, now I've paid you back,' she nodded down at the bag that lay on the slick cobblestones between us. 'I owe you nothing more.'

"'I didn't come seeking you, young lady,' I replied coldly, 'nor the return of the money. I came seeking your father.'

"The old man, who until now had been leaning against the stone wall wheezing gently, looked up.

"'My father?' She frowned, puzzled.

"'Yes, your father, his playing. When I first heard him play I promised myself I would study with him.'

"My answer silenced her for a moment, so I continued. 'I am already a more than competent lute player and have some knowledge of the moon guitar, but there is still much I could learn. I would even be willing to sit in as your accompanist when he isn't well.'

"'Isn't well' she repeated sarcastically, tossing her heavy mane of hair. 'We don't need any help,' she said flatly, turning away and attempting to pull her father upright.

"'Why not?' the old man quavered, throwing her hand off with surprising strength and standing on his own. He wasn't really all that old, perhaps in his early fifties, but with that beard and the wine weakening his limbs, he seemed ancient. Still, at that moment he had recovered his wits somewhat.

"'He can take over as your accompanist,' he said, giving her a hard glance. 'Then you won't have to worry about being embarrassed.'

"'Don't be foolish. I'm not worried about embarrassment. I'm worried about not being asked back to play again. Anyway, how do you know he can play? He's probably some dilettante merchant's son.'

"'If he can't play, then we'll send him on his way. He only has to have a small talent; I can train him. We can both accompany you at first, then as he becomes familiar with the songs, he can take over from time to time.'

"Throughout this exchange I was silent, watching them talk about me as though I wasn't present, both of them eyeing me assessingly like farmers at a market sizing up an unpredictable bull.

"'My dear girl, don't you see, he is a godsend,' the old man said, placing his hand on her shoulder. 'Someone will have to take over sooner or later, especially if you are to achieve your ambition of playing at the capital's great houses. You need some fresh young blood. I am getting too old for these nightly performances. They take more out of me than you think. My joints won't take sitting in the same position for hour after hour while those drunken fools ask for yet another rendition of *Watching the Brahman Moon.*'

"'Those drunken fools pay for our food and your wine,' she replied, but not altogether unkindly.

"'Come now, girl,' her father said. 'Don't be stubborn like your mother. You must see that we could do with his help.'

"'We don't need anyone's help!' she flared. 'We've come this far on our own. Why do we suddenly need help now?'

"'Because I am getting old. Because I won't live forever. Because sometimes, sometimes, yes, I do take a few too many.'

"Still, she shook her head, turning away from both of us.

"'He can carry the bags and the instruments, too.'

"She cocked her head slightly to see my reaction to this sally. I smiled and nodded to the old man.

"'I would be honored to help with your luggage,' I said.

"'You see,' he crowed, 'a true disciple.'

"Peony shrugged and began to walk briskly away.

"I stayed where I was and the old man raised his eyebrows at me. 'Go on, then, what are you waiting for?' He gestured towards the bags.

"I picked up the moon guitar in its cloth case, a set of small lacquered Sogdian drums, and a canvas bag. She stopped and watched me for a moment. The sack of coins she had flung down lay on the ground between us. I gazed down at it, then at her, stepped over it carefully, and walked on. Peony spun around again and strode away. The old man, who had been watching us, gave a curse and bent down to pick up the bag, shaking his head as he stuffed it into his sleeve and muttering about 'a stubborn young minx and a bullheaded fool.'

"And so, off we went, a strange threesome, a little uncomfortable at first, I being a stranger and they very used to their own ways, but easier after a few days, for Peony was by nature a spirited woman, not one to sulk. She could be very cold indeed and hard as granite when it was required, but a cheerful surge of spirits was her natural state—she was, after all, not yet twenty, still in some ways a girl—and she was soon treating me quite civilly, though still with much reserve.

"They were heading south, running from the onset of winter, planning to trace a huge circle around the heart of the empire, first making their way down to the cities strung along the Grand Canal to Yangchou, at the confluence of the canal and the Great River, where they would linger for several months, then moving upriver with the spring tide to Cheng-tu, where they would again rest for a while, thence north over the mountains back to Chang An just before winter, a year after setting off.

"We headed back the way I had just come, traveling in comfort aboard a commodious river junk that plied the canal (the pay from private parties was much better than gleanings from the taverns, I gathered). Each morning Peony would rise and stand at the stern, practicing her scales or trying out a new version of a familiar song, her voice wafting out over the mist that clung to the water in the hour after dawn, dipping and echoing along the banks and fields like a magic spell weaving awake the world. On the third day out, I sat behind the cabin entrance, hidden from her view, and listened. Her last song was the famous lament composed for the Lady Chao Kun, who was sent out by the emperor to marry a barbarian chieftain deep in the desert. You probably remember the story: her lover was the court painter charged with composing the likenesses of the royal seraglio. He deliberately marred her picture for fear that she might be selected to serve as the pawn of the empire in some stinking yurt on the frozen sands. But the emperor chose her picture because he thought she would be the easiest to spare, and she was sent off in a golden palanquin to her new husband. Her lover stood in front of her portrait in the palace and watched as its eyes shed real tears, smearing the paint. It was one of my Arma's favorite pieces, a haunting melody and words that spoke of the grief of unending exile. I wept, too, as she sang out into the glowing morning, wept for all that I had lost, all, I suppose, that I had never had, and when she finished, Peony came upon me sitting there, the tears streaming down my cheeks. She placed her hand on my shoulder, not saying anything, passing me one of her long silk handkerchiefs to mop my eyes. Later she told me that it was the sight of me weeping that first opened her heart to me, that made her understand what the music meant to me.

"As for the old man, he proved to be a patient and dedicated teacher—it was how he made his living before he had realized the potential of his daughter's voice. He was always a little alight with wine; the trick was to get him before the midday meal. Ironically it was their very success that was wreaking its ruin on him, for when they had been touring the wineshops, there wasn't enough money for him to drink at will. But now that his playing (and her singing, of course) was bringing in a steady income and invitations to sing in the houses of the great, he could drink to his heart's content, and did, hence his fumbling fingers and bleary eyes.

"But at my morning sessions, he was in fine form, more than happy to be training a replacement. And once he understood that I knew what I was doing, and more importantly that I not only loved the music but also had the talent to express that love, he opened up to me, showing me sheaf after sheaf of songs he had collected over the years, most of them recorded in faraway taverns and inns. You see, he had originally been trained in the capital as a clerk for the Yueh Fu-fu, the Music Bureau, which is charged with the collection and preservation of folk music, the bureaucrats having decided that if the *Book of Songs* was the true source of all music, as Confucius said, then popular songs needed to be corrected so as to accord with the written record. Corrected indeed! Like chastising the sea for its impetuous tides. Ever since their precious Confucius, these fools have been trying to 'correct' the world so that it fits their image of the way things should be. They have a particular hatred for popular music—'the lewd songs of Cheng and Wei'—all because their master was once driven out of the state of Lu by a bevy of singing girls. Confucius couldn't bear to be in the same palace as such women, the prissy old fool, and retired in a huff 'to compose Wu-chang music to criticize the trend of the times and lead the people on the right path, but none heeded his counsel.' Mark those final words: none heeded his counsel. There was a streak of common sense in people even then that made them ignore a pietistic old prater like Confucius.

"Unfortunately, of course, they go on trying to 'correct'

music to this day. Which is why I had never received any formal instruction in the moon guitar, only the lute and the zither. What I knew of the guitar I had picked up on my own. For the guitar, you see, is a 'lewd' instrument, much disdained by the so-called literati. The lute on the other hand. . . . But once again, I digress, the besetting sin of old men. I was speaking of my lessons with Maestro Ma, wasn't I?

"The old man called me into his cabin on the first morning, handed me the guitar, and said: 'Play.' After an hour, he nodded and passed over a couple of sheets of cheap banana hemp paper on which were scrawled the notations for some of the songs Peony performed. I could start practicing with her in the afternoons, he said; he would continue to train me in the mornings, and the rest of the day the two of us could spend going over the simpler pieces.

"During this portion of the voyage there were only a few towns of any size along the route that led down to Yangchou, and they had only two performances booked, giving me plenty of time to learn my new trade. The weather remained gray and overcast, too, with sleet and freezing rain lashing the junk almost every day, so each afternoon Peony and I would gather in her little cabin, sitting cross-legged on woven sea-grass mats opposite each other. For the first few days, she was still quite formal, insisting that we keep to the business at hand, that we go over each song three times in succession, even the simplest ones that I had already memorized. But then the music began to weave something between us, and she being a naturally garrulous creature like myself, we began to talk, hesitantly at first, then more naturally as some essential compatibility emerged, gradually falling into an easy companionship that was deepened over our long, long conversations. She was lonely, for though she didn't say so, I gathered that she had spent much time with her mother as they traveled around. With her death, Peony had lost the one person to whom she could unburden herself. Indeed, it seemed that her mother's death had been a terrible blow to both Peony and her father, whose wine consumption, already heroic, became legendary.

"But most of the time we talked of less serious matters, joking and giggling over the most absurd things like a couple of twelve-year-old girls. One of the first tales I told her was that of the fate of Liang the Butcher, at which she clapped her hands in appreciation and laughed at the thought of him finally getting his comeuppance, then thanking me most graciously, even apologizing, for her behavior in Pienchou: 'I was very angry with my father,' she said, 'so angry and afraid that word would get around, the invitations would stop coming, and we would have to return to the taverns. I will never go back,' she said, her jaw thrusting forward and a familiar hard glint coming into her eyes. 'I would rather die than go back to singing in the taverns.'

"Day after day we were ensconced together from noon until deep in the night, talking, talking, always talking, as though we only had a limited time to tell each other everything we knew, everything we cared about. And indeed, looking back, I wonder what it was that we spent so long discussing. Music, of course, and later other scholarly subjects, for I was amazed to find that she was deeply knowledgeable about literature and history. Her father had educated her as well as he could, tutoring her in the classics, the Taoist texts, the great poets, and of course in music. I asked her once why he had lavished so much time on educating a girl, and she replied that he had longed for a son, longed to see him triumph in the exams, and when denied more than one child, he had determined to educate his daughter as he would have a boy. So, I asked her, why had he never taken the exams himself? But he had, she said, he had taken the exams each year for fifteen years in weary succession, until he had started to appear at the examination halls drunk and the examiners had barred him from returning.

"There was a pause as I digested this, then she said to me: 'And you, why have you never taken the exams?' 'Oh,' I answered airily, 'why should I put myself in competition with a pack of idiots, men whose fixed and only dream is to become a petty official, a drudge-in-office? And besides,' I added, 'if a man distinguished himself enough he was usually recognized without the need to take any tedious exams.' At this, Peony gave me a sharp look: 'If I were a man,' she said, those amazing eyes sparking, 'you can be sure that I would take the exams and come in first, too.'

"Another time she said that she wrote poetry, and I asked her to recite a few pieces for me, which she did, without embarrassment, no simpering pretenses that they were unworthy of hearing. One I remember well, part of a series that only a woman could have written called *Trying on New-made Clothes.* The last one went like this:

This skirt's in the style
worn in paradise.

It once trailed heavenly
courtiers grasping
magic-mushroom scepters.

Each time they meet at the palace,
to sing and dance,
they bow from the waist
and sing, 'Step through the Sky,'
a star walker's song.

"It was delightful, a perfect little piece, I told her, and she recited a few more, all equally charming. When she had finished, she asked me if I wrote poetry myself, and I smiled and said, yes, a little, reciting a couple of mine in return, after which she told me: 'You have a very great talent.' I smiled my thanks and then she said: 'But I'm not sure about using *jasper* in the third line of the second piece; it sounds very pretentious; why not *emerald* instead? Also, I don't think your bird imagery is consistent throughout . . . ' continuing in the same vein, calmly pointing out an awkward phrase, a word that didn't ring true, finally closing with the observation that, in her opinion, I made too many classical allusions, always striving to dazzle with my erudition. But, she said, didn't it say in the *Chuang Tzu* that he who strives shall never succeed? Similarly, if I tried so hard, made it so obvious how much I cared, who was going to be impressed?

"There was a long silence and perhaps she thought I was offended, for she said to me, 'Here is a poem I have made for you,' and she recited:

Your grand thoughts have the gloss
and coolness
of Blue Mountain's marbled jade

or a bag of ice
smashed to shards
on a golden plate from the south.

When the master poets hone
their tools, their fame lives on.

Why bother to check
the passing list posted
on Exam Hall Gate?

"She must write it down before it disappeared from her mind, I said, quite touched, and she produced a long sheet of scarlet paper that was to become her trademark in later years, scrawling her composition down one side. Now, I told her, give it to me, and I took the paper and filled in the empty space with a poem of my own:

Clear autumn wind
Bright autumn moon.
Fallen leaves swirl, then settle;
Cold ravens flutter, then perch.
This day, our verses run in tandem
By next autumn, will they be parted?

"'Oh,' she exclaimed, blushing a little, for I had made my poem too strong, a little too much like wooing—'oh, you have used a new verse form, I've never seen this before. How ignorant I am.'

"And I, too, fumbling to make the moment pass, babbling: 'No, no, you couldn't have seen it before, I invented it myself. It's called three, five, seven words; three couplets as you can see, the lines in each matching, so *clear* pairs with *bright, moon* with *wind, ravens* with *leaves,* and so on, though I'm not very happy with the final couplet, which doesn't quite scan, for though *day* and *autumn* are more or less a match, I don't think that *tandem* and *parting* quite fit together.'

"'Such strict parallel couplets,' she said musingly when I had finally run out of words, her composure restored. 'I would never have expected something you invented to be so, well, rigid.'

"'No, no,' I assured her, 'it's just a kind of exercise, a means of honing one's skills, as you say in your poem. For myself, I abhor the constrictions of such form, why . . . '

"But she was laughing, a clear sound like two pieces of jade coming together, and saying: 'It's all right, really, I don't think you so hidebound. I was just teasing you.'

"At this, a silence fell between us, we staring at each other, her eyes shining, my heart thumping loudly in my ears, the creaking of the rigging and the sailors padding about on deck quite clear above us. But then there was a heavy thud against the door as someone passing lost his balance—probably her father returning from the storeroom where he kept his wine barrel—and that tiny silken thread snapped, and we looked to one side, then both spoke at once, she fiddling with the hem of her sleeve, exclaiming that she had dipped it in soy sauce at lunch and never noticed, I picking up a sheaf of poems and asking her what we should play next.

"Despite those meandering talks, we did also spend much of the time working, Peony instructing me in the cues I should take, when to come in, how she would indicate that she wanted a song extended by a verse or two, the various programs she had designed for different occasions. For a formal banquet hosted by a governor, for example, she would limit herself to the more traditional Chinese songs, with only one "foreign" tune thrown in for a taste of the exotic. For a small group of scholars seeing one of their number off to a new posting—a very common gathering for which her services were in demand—she would lean much more heavily on Indian, Sogdian, and other tunes from the west that were all the rage in the capital. Peony took great pleasure in making these fine judgments about the nature of the party, the tastes of the guests, the tone at which she was to aim. Indeed, one day as we sat with thirty song sheets spread out on the floor in front of us, sorting through them to find the perfect song to cap a recital in Lian Hua, our second stop, she confided in me that her ambition was not just to make a name for herself in the capital as a singer but as a fully-fledged courtesan.

"'It is the only life for a woman of spirit,' she told me earnestly, 'the only life I could bear to live. At least then I can do what I am good at, singing, composing verses, discussing the issues of the day in the company of men. Chattering with women about the latest embroidered pattern from India or similar matters leaves me ready to scream. As a courtesan of some repute, I would be able to choose my lovers rather than be chosen,' this said with never a blush or pursed lip, a simple statement of fact, 'and I could even exercise a little influence, perhaps on literary matters if my poetry continues to improve.'

"I nodded my head: her writing was certainly superior to that of most men, and with time and attention she might produce some really first-class pieces.

"'There's no alternative, you know,' she said, 'I mean, what else is there? Marriage to some dullard who would leave me cold in bed, either for his other wives or for some concubine, would keep me shut up in the women's quarters amidst all that bickering and petty hatred, unable even to venture out the door. Go become a nun, you are about to say, that's an alternative. Perhaps, perhaps. And there are a number of women who have chosen that life and can move in the company of men, writing as they wish, attending banquets, moving freely about the country. But even now when little is expected in the way of sanctimony from a nun, it would be difficult for me to sustain even the minimum necessary piety. The hypocrisy of it would make me want to laugh, make some display, take off my clothes in public.'

"I am ashamed to say that I ceased to listen for a moment, for the image of her stripping off her robes was burning painfully in my mind. I had seen her emerging from the bathing room a few days back, only caught a glimpse from the rear, her shift wet against her body, clinging, the soft sweep of her shoulders, the tapering back, even the line of delicate knobs that was her spine; it was enough to send me away in a daze so that I thwacked my forehead against a low beam hard enough to bring out blood. I bent over and tried once again to concentrate on collating the song sheets.

"'Anyway,' she continued, not having noticed my discomfort, 'you need to have plenty of money if you want to be independent as a nun. They are usually the daughters of very rich men who endow a convent somewhere, then make themselves prioress. No, let me be the greatest courtesan the court has ever seen.'

"'Is marriage such a bad thing that you could never bear it, not even if you found the right man?' I asked, perhaps a little plaintively.

"'The right man doesn't exist because no man can allow me to come to his banquets, to roam freely in the way that I want. Why, even if he did, he would be the laughingstock of his friends and would lose his position, for you know the adage that he who cannot control his household can hardly be trusted with affairs of state.'

"I made no reply to this and we continued to sort through the songs, she eventually deciding that in such a small town, it would be best to stick to the old favorites and so end with 'Breaking the Withies,' a song expressing the sorrow of lovers parting that had been sung for as long as there had been Han people living on the banks of the Yellow River.

"Finally, on the day of the concert in Lian Hua, I carried the instruments and case containing her costumes, but the old man seemed to have taken her admonitions to heart and remained quiet and to all appearances sober throughout, his playing again astonishing me with its virtuosity. This was only a minor affair for Peony, but she couldn't eat for most of the day preceding, quite a common occurrence, I was to discover; sometimes she had to run from the banquet hall into the garden after she had finished, retching and gagging. This time, however, the performance passed off smoothly.

"A week later we arrived in Yangchou, never a favorite of

mine, a drab place reeking of commercialism, its fine river vistas spoiled by hordes of coolies baling or loading the long lines of cargo ships and barges. It was a town where everything in life was submitted to an economic judgment and as a consequence could boast of no poets or calligraphers of any consequence. But surprisingly there was a lively appreciation of singing, and Peony was booked almost every night for a month, her first banquet a feast given by the governor for the regional prefect, a man called Huang, a very eminent personage indeed, ruler of three provinces, a sort of semi-demi-viceroy, responsible only to the emperor himself. Huang was a well-known connoisseur of poetry and the arts and had a considerable reputation as an eccentric, often dismissing his attendants and walking about in the streets in the dress of a clerk. He was also known for his weakness for a pretty face, this despite his four wives and numerous concubines. Peony was well aware of this, not to mention the fact that he had excellent connections in Chang An, both in the palace and society, and if he liked her might give a great boost to her chances of becoming known in the capital.

"The evening of that performance, just when we were due to leave for the banqueting hall, Peony informed me that her father had disappeared: his room at the inn was empty and his guitar gone. Peony remained composed, calmly reshuffled her song list to accommodate my lesser talents, and managed to borrow an ancient guitar from the inn's landlord by promising to sing there. Despite all this—the assemblage of great men, my inferior skills as an accompanist, the old guitar's weird booming tone—or perhaps because of it—she gave the performance of her life that evening, lifting herself a notch higher, the singing purer, more charged with emotion than I had ever heard it, a remote expression on her face as she sang that scared me a little, for I knew that wherever she was it was very far away from me. It made me feel that in some essential way she was unknowable, that a small but important part of her would forever be hidden from me, burning hard and bright inside her.

"When she had finished, Huang himself, sitting in the guest of honor's position on the host's left, stood up from his cushion and called out his praise, beckoning her to join him. I, as a lowly musician, remained where I was; as far as they were concerned, I had been a piece of furniture. This was quite agreeable to me, however, for I had noticed early on that one of the guests was none other than the governor of Shantung and though I hardly expected him to recognize me after only that one encounter on Mount Tai, and that one very brief, I tucked my head down and was happy to be ignored. I had, after all, rejected his invitation to go to the capital—a signal honor—on the grounds that I was set on the life of a hermit, something that couldn't easily be reconciled with playing the moon guitar for a budding courtesan.

"I watched discreetly as a space was cleared for Peony and she sat with those sleek men, talking quite as naturally as if she and I had been in her cabin, drinking several swift cups of wine, a flush appearing in her cheeks, joking and capping their lines of poetry with her own. Three times I saw Huang lean close to her and whisper in her ear, an action that made my own face flush and the blood pound in my head. After an hour or so, Peony stood and made her excuses—another performance the next day, needed her sleep—but allowed herself to be persuaded to give them a few more songs, both of which I hardly knew, she having run through my entire repertoire, so I was obliged to sit strumming quietly, doing my best not to get in her way. At last we left, the calls of the banqueting governors—by then mostly fairly tipsy; losers in the capping game had to drink a cup of wine as default—echoing behind us. We ran down the long, dark front hallway of the governor's mansion hand in hand, gasping and laughing, I saying that if they had asked for another song she would have had to sing without accompaniment, she saying that Huang had offered her a silver ingot—a whole silver ingot!—to stay with him that night. 'But I told him you were my fiancé and he apologized very prettily.'

"In the corridor of the inn, we stood outside her door, listening to her father snoring in the next room, a snuffling rasp.

"'Wait here,' she mouthed and slipped into his room, emerging triumphantly a minute later with a large jug of wine which she carried into her own room, the two of us chattering in whispers like a couple of children, even through the first cups of wine, urgently recounting to each other the details of the evening, laughing again at the near disasters, Peony's eyes shining so bright, her cheeks so scarlet with emotion and wine that eventually I reached over and stroked her face, saying she must be burning up. She grasped my hand, held it for a moment, then pulled me toward her. I leaned forward and stroked her shoulder through the thin performance gown, my fingers shaking just slightly as they pulled the robe open and down her shoulder, she shrugging out of it so that her shoulder was bare and her silk chemise exposed. I touched the bare skin of her upper arm, drawing my fingers over her shoulder to the shadowed hollow of her throat. Her skin did indeed seem to be burning, fiery to the touch, so unnaturally hot that at first I almost jerked back. Then I saw a line of goose-pimples spreading like a wave in front of my trailing fingers, the nipple popping up under the soft swell of her breast against the silk. She pulled me to her once more, and we fell over onto the matting that covered the floor, suddenly desperate, fumbling with sashes and encumbering robes until we had shed them and at last we were flesh to flesh, her skin burning, everything I touched flushed pink, swollen with rushing blood. When I kissed her I thought I could taste strawberries. Her hair smelled of incense and lime.

"'How could we have waited so long?' she asked, but I could only groan in reply, the urgency almost unendurable now, stroking her so that she opened up like a rose for me and I sinking in, burying myself deep within her, clenching every fiber of my body to hold back, she moving slowly beneath me and then the sensation, the heat, always the burning heat, the tight heat, too much, and I speeding now, gasping, hoping she was with me and at last both of us crying out at once, together.

"After that night we were together every minute of the day and often much of the night, either talking intensely or locked together on the floor of some inn, straining to be quiet so as not to wake her father, rocking gently for long minutes, hardly moving at all until neither one could stand it any longer and we would race to the end, always finishing together. And by day, the music flowed out of me with as little effort as writing poems; even Peony's father was astonished at the speed with which I learned his most complicated flourishes. And Peony, too, seemed to blossom, her skin glowing, her eyes shining, incomparable when singing, the diners stunned. Our feelings seemed to grow more and more intense in the confined atmosphere until sometimes when I looked at her studying a sheet of music or brushing her hair, I thought my chest would burst. On and on that journey went through the mild days of autumn and early winter, the sun shining benevolently down on us each perfect day, the sky bluer than cobalt, the air so clear that when a great white egret launched itself from a tree on the far bank of the river two miles away, I could see the yellow of its feet, the two plumes tipped with gold growing from its head, could tell that the wiggling silver fish it carried was a bream.

"All too soon, of course, the idyll came to end, as all idylls must, six weeks out of Yangchou, when I asked her to marry me. There ensued a bitter argument, full of recrimination and taunts that were almost unbearable to me. We made up, of course, and things went on as before, but I wasn't able to leave the subject alone, raised it again and again until finally she wearily agreed and I, elated, began to talk of taking work, perhaps with a magistrate at first, even taking the exams if that was what she wanted for me. A week later, I rode inland from the river to the provincial capital, Langchou, where there was a vacancy in the governor's office for a clerk. It was a two-day journey either way, but I rode back in a daze of joy, for they had offered me the post and I could think of nothing but our life together, the house we would take, a small garden in which to grow cherries and peaches. But when I reached the river inn, Peony and her father had gone, leaving only a note scrawled on a length of scarlet paper and left with the grinning landlord: 'We have returned to the capital where I have been offered the protection of Prefect Huang. I am sorry.' There was no signature."

eight 李白

"NO. NO MORE STORIES, MY BOY, YOU CAN PUT YOUR brush down," Li Po says when he comes out onto deck the next day. "Enough sad tales for awhile. Let us have some music today. What about you, young man? What do you know of music? Have you been trained to play an instrument?"

"No, sir, I have never studied music. Just books."

The poet looks taken aback.

"And how do you expect to become an official if you don't know the lute, the touchstone of the scholar's world? To gain office you must have the appearance of a scholar as well as the learning. If mere scholarship determined appointments then eighty out of a hundred of today's apes-in-office would be out of a job. For all the talk of exams, most of them gained their positions through birth. I can't make you an aristocrat, but I can at least help you pretend to be a scholar. Go fetch the lute."

And so Wang Lung hurries down the companionway and into the poet's cabin, where the lute is hanging on a peg on the wall, secure in its soft brown pigskin case. He lifts it carefully down and maneuvers it out the door with some difficulty, for it is an awkward shape, nearly as long as he is high, like a wooden chest for storing scrolls, though much narrower, of course, and thinner. On deck he slips off the cover and sets it on a high table that is kept specially for lute playing, then pulls up a stool for the poet to sit on.

"Now," Li Po says, sitting down and pulling the instrument closer, then drawing back his sleeves so they won't hamper his motion in playing, "though all profess to revere this object, the fact is most officials can't play a note. They have these beautiful lutes hanging on the walls—it is practically a required part of their study, along with the ink stone, the brushes, the scrolls, the chessboard, and so on—and will often spend vast sums for a famous instrument, some of which are a thousand years old. They talk in hushed tones about finger technique, timbre and pitch, and the color of the note, but it is all pretense, the usual hypocrisy. You'll find those capped and robed charlatans whose company you so earnestly seek to join are very fond of assembling in a bower somewhere and spending a few minutes making a pretense of playing the lute, thereafter passing the rest of the day in drunken debauch, usually leering at some courtesan strumming the moon guitar. Some particularly brazen fools I have met don't even have instruments with strings or pegs. The unheard note is the most beautiful, they say, and cite Tao Chien as boldly as you like: 'I have understood the deeper significance of the Lute; why should I strive after the sound of the strings?' Utter nonsense!

"Enough talk. Let us get down to the actual playing. I'll play a couple of famous compositions for you—'Treading the Cloud Ladder' perhaps, and 'The Barbarian Pipes'—then over the next few weeks you can practice by yourself so that you can pull them out if social circumstances demand it. With the lute, the aim is to build one note on another in a succession of individual sounds that make up a constant flow of music, something like a waterfall. This is 'Treading the Cloud Ladder.' Listen."

The poet takes a breath, hitches up his sleeves a little more, then plucks a single string with his right hand, waiting until it has almost completely died away before plucking another, then another slightly faster, the time between the notes diminishing until he is throwing forth a racing cascade of notes tumbling over one another so that the very air seems alive and shimmering with their flowing vibration; then, suddenly, he strikes a single chord, very heavy, and as quickly as he began, Li Po stops playing.

"You see how slowly the adept starts to climb the cloud ladder, then realizing he has acquired the magical powers he sought for so long, he climbs faster and faster towards the heavens. At the end of the piece, he comes to an abrupt halt when he arrives at the top of the ladder and sees the Plain of the Skies laid out before him. There are another five parts to the tale, exploring the cloud gardens, feasting in the sky pavilion, cutting the cinnabar, dancing in rainbow garments with the blue phoenix, and so on.

"The music for the lute is supposed to induce contemplation of the Absolute, the suppression of gross passions, and the perfection of the spirit. That is the idea, anyway. Which is why the moon guitar is so reviled, for it is exactly the opposite: played in taverns, relatively simple to master, the tunes easy to remember and, above all, aimed at inflaming the emotions. That's why it is so popular among the performers of the floating world. And that in turn is why your Mandarins hate it so much. The music of the floating world is something they can't control or correct, so they just pretend it doesn't exist. Though it is a simpler instrument, only four uniform strings, I realized when I heard Peony's father playing the guitar that it is the player not the instrument that makes the music. I would rather listen to old man Ma than a thousand idiots displaying their perfect technique on the lute. What those fools in Chang An don't realize of course is that the guitar is less concerned with the intellect and more with emotions, and thus could be much more suited to the composition of verses, if only we could escape from the imprisoning forms, the court prescribed odes and octets. Why I remember . . . "

But Wang Lung never hears this particular story, for a servant who has been hovering at the edge of the foredeck for some time now comes forward and stands directly in front of the poet, who glares up at him angrily.

"Well, what is it, man? I told you not to disturb me."

"Academician Li, a skiff is approaching that carries the flag of an imperial messenger."

"Where? Where is it?" The poet jumps to his feet and rushes to the railing. Following him, Wang Lung sees that a small vessel is indeed racing downstream towards them, the rainbow banner fluttering at its prow signifying that it is on imperial business.

"This must be the reply to Sung's memorial," Li Po says excitedly. "Heaven grant that this is deliverance." He pauses for a moment, then says more soberly: "But no, it was only sent off a few days ago . . . " He trails off and stands in quivering silence as the boat is pulled alongside. The messenger pulls himself over the rail and produces his burden from a cloth sack he is carrying. Li Po practically rips the scroll from his hands. He walks over to a far corner of the deck, all watching him as he unties the bind and unrolls the scroll. Holding it stretched out with both his hands, it only takes him a minute to scan what is evidently a short communication. Then the poet stares unseeingly at the river, releasing his hold on one end of the scroll and dropping his arm to his side so that the wind blows the long piece of silk this way and that, twisting it around his ankle. He stands immobile for a moment, then suddenly flings the scroll overboard, raises his face to the sky, and lets out a shriek of pain, a howl of anguish so shocking that it causes the messenger, Wang Lung, and the two curious servants on the foredeck to start backward. Li Po stops in midcry and whirls, running over to the low table where Wang Lung is sitting. He snatches up the multileaved scroll in front of the boy and hurls that over the side as well, its pages fluttering open and partly unrolling as it tumbles through the air end over end like a goose pierced by a hunter's arrow.

"Wasted, wasted!" he shouts, turning back to pick up the heavy inkstone from the table and throwing it after the scroll. "All wasted time. What is the point of all this talking?"

Now the brush stand, the brushes swinging wildly back and forth on their hooks, follows the inkstone. Then the bowl of ink, a trail of black liquid frozen in the air behind it for a moment before it splatters on the deck in a long gash like a trail of blood.

"A waste of breath and spirit, talking and writing. They are beasts, not men, beasts dressed in gowns and caps. 'No possibility of reprieve . . . a dangerous and unreliable man . . . should be grateful to have had his death sentence reprieved rather than pestering busy officials with his constant importuning letters.' Importuning letters! The blackhearted bastards, pompous and oily in office, no feeling, no feeling at all."

The table is bare and Li Po stares wildly about him, his topknot loose, hair flying about in wispy confusion. The servants back away alarmed, the messenger scurries over the side and back to his boat, thinking it safe to assume that no reply will be called for. Wang Lung sits at the table, frozen. In a bag at his side is the manuscript of Li Po's tale; it was the *Chuang Tzu* commentary that lay before him when the messenger arrived. He had indeed been at the point of asking the poet about a particularly difficult passage. Surreptitiously, he slides the bag under the table.

But Li Po is in no condition to notice such subterfuges. He is striding up and down the deck, shaking his head, and occasionally bringing forth a shouted curse or some fragment of a thought, mostly incoherent, an expression of such desolation on his face that Wang Lung wants to jump up and comfort him. He stands silent and unmoving for perhaps five minutes, staring intently at the deck, his hands clasped in front of him. Then, at last, he raises his head and looks around him, seeming suddenly very old, his eyes full of pain, turns around and passes through the door leading down to his cabin.

It is four days before the poet reappears. The trays of food outside his cabin lie untouched, but a constant stream of wine disappears inside. The noise of singing or muffled chanting penetrates occasionally through the closed door, and sometimes deep in the night Wang Lung, whose little alcove is directly beneath the poet's cabin, seems to hear a low groaning, a sound so desolate that he covers up his ears with a heavy woolen blanket to block it out. Finally, Li Po emerges, his eyes streaked with blood, his skin an unhealthy yellow, his face drawn and gray, his hair loose like a senile old man's, wearing only a sagging cotton sleeping gown, stained and rumpled. He calls for the captain to pull over to the bank and anchor, then strips off his robe and plunges straight off the side into the dark waters. For a while he swims against the fast flowing current, barely making headway, his heavy arms flashing white, his unfettered black-and-silver mane streaming out behind him, then calls hoarsely for a rope, to which he ties himself and lies on his back in the water, the river rushing over him, his face to the sky.

After fifteen minutes in the frigid water, he boards again, shivering, tying on a fresh robe brought by a blushing maid, then walks over to Wang Lung and sits in his usual place, calling for food, "some carp, I am on fire for some grass carp, bring it here alive, I want to see it sliced fresh for me here at the table, 'flakes of snow-white flesh falling from the sparkling knife,' and some bread, enough of this endless rice, bring me wheatcakes, and dumplings, too." Then he turns to the boy and says:

"I have neglected you sadly, I am afraid. You have kept your side of the bargain, taking down my ramblings. That is finished now, so in all honor to your father, I must keep mine and turn you into a proper little official. Come, let us review what you have done. First start with the odious Confucius: you must memorize all of the Analects save only the sections in Chapter Ten that deal with clothes: no one cares any more about whether you have purple or maroon cuffs or if you wear lambswool or fox furs. And don't bother with all that guff afterwards about refraining from meat and drink. They never ask for a recital of that section. Ah, the fish has arrived. Don't mind me, I'll eat while you recite. Now begin at the first book: 'The Master said . . . '

"The Master said," Wang Lung chants obediently, "is it not a pleasure, having learned something to practice it? Is it not a joy to have friends come from afar? Is it not gentlemanly not to take offense when others do not appreciate your abilities? Yu Tzu said . . . " On and on he continues as the poet sits eating and nodding his head approvingly, occasionally stopping him to correct a miswording or explain an obscure usage, of which there are many.

That day set the pattern for the next month, Li Po's own story apparently forgotten and the confirmation of his exile never mentioned, each day the two of them sitting out on the deck, running over the texts endlessly. Otherwise life continued as usual, the barge leisurely making its way upstream, the poet feasting with friends or admirers in each town along the way, though often also sitting by himself on the foredeck with his wine and his music, composing verses and singing them quietly to himself, scrawling them down with a new set of brushes.

It is the tenth month by now, and the nights grow colder, the days shorter, the land changing too, the flat fields disappearing behind them and hills rising up on either side of the river, the banks drawing in as they approach the gorges, the water around them losing its muddy tinge and turning a deep, cold black, sometimes swirling in whirlpools and eddies that presage the turbulence to come.

Then late one afternoon as the sun is disappearing behind the hills, Li Po says: "Tomorrow you can leave your books for a day. We will visit Lai Lake as I promised you." And so the next day, Wang Lung finds himself sharing a lotus boat with the poet, a long and narrow vessel specially built for pleasure expeditions, the gunwales wrought of magnolia and the inner planks on which they sit of a beautiful mahogany, from time to time enveloped in the fragrance of incense wafting from a burner sitting in the prow, the smoke drifting back to where the boy is paddling. They glide over the placid lake, the prow nosing aside the enormous, flat leaves of water lilies floating like green elephant's ears on the surface, the heavy pink flowers that stand clear of the water on stalks occasionally thumping against the side with surprising weight. A second boat accompanies them, and from time to time the boy turns to steal a glance at its occupants, two girls the poet has hired for company on this expedition, a little shiver running through him each time he hears their tinkling laughter or catches a coquettish look.

"Stop gawking boy. Haven't you ever seen a woman before?" Li Po calls, his shrill voice raised higher than usual by the wine he has drunk with lunch, a seasonal local brew made of pine resin. Several miles away over the water is their destination, a series of black gashes in the limestone cliffs that rear up on the far side of the lake. Presently the poet falls asleep in the prow, and when he wakes he calls over to the following boat for more wine from the flasks that have been hanging over the side to cool them.

At last they reach the cave mouths, Li Po mumbling to himself—"fourth from the left, or was it the fifth?"—and calling the other boat over, securing it by rope to a cleat on their stern, then kneeling in the front with a paddle and stroking them gently into the blackness, the hazy white of the day fading until it is a distant blur behind them, no sound but the swish of water against the side and, from far away, the dripping of water. The cave smells black, too, not unpleasant, though, colorless and dank but strangely clean—water washing constantly over stone. For awhile there is only the sound of Li Po's paddle swirling in and out of the water and the odd, far-off squeak, barely audible. Bats perhaps, or some restless spirit.

When the darkness surrounding them is almost complete, there is a bump from the front, then another behind them as the following boat knocks into theirs. It is very cold and Wang Lung shivers in the darkness.

"Now," says Li Po in what for him is a muted screech, his voice rising up and disappearing into the darkness, "let me just tie up." There is a clanking noise and a good deal of fumbling, then the boat rocks again as the poet settles back down in the prow. Behind them, there are a few stifled squeals from the boat behind, rocking in its turn.

"Don't worry girls, light coming soon," Li Po says and indeed a small flame flickers at the front of the boat, then grows as the poet lights a candle, then another and another.

"No one move," he whispers, dripping wax from the candles onto a series of saucers he has dug up from a cloth bag. The flickering flames cast his shadow huge onto the dim ceiling above, and Wang Lung can just make out that the boat's painter is anchored to a large rock protruding from the water. He dips his hand into the darkness over the side. The water is icy and, he is surprised to find, flowing steadily farther into the tunnel. It will be a hard row back.

Now the poet is leaning over the side, carefully settling one of the saucers into the water, then freeing it. For a moment nothing happens, then the saucer begins to move with the current, now spinning, now dipping, but despite the speed of the flow, the water is flat and unruffled by wind, and the candle remains upright, soon to be followed by its mates so that a procession of light begins to play along the walls and ceilings of the cave, bringing gasps from Wang Lung and the two girls as row after row of stalactites are revealed, some hanging down straight and alone, other twisted and curled over and around each other like animals' tails. Their surfaces are shot with streaks of yellow-ocher, cobalt blue, and the bright green of spring, all strangely out of place in this dead world. The glassy stone is sparkling with embedded quartz so that the colors blaze out in glittering profusion and the water is speckled with ten thousand diamonds that tremble in the wake of the passing candles. Li Po has lit more candles and sent them out, and though several are swamped only a few yards from the boat, the remainder form a bobbing line that sends long shadows from the hanging rocks chasing around the cavern and makes the chemical colors flash and glow with a weird luminescence unlike anything to be seen outside in the world of daylight.

But at last the flames of even the rearmost candles grow dimmer and dimmer, then finally are snuffed out in the black recesses of the cavern. Darkness envelops them again. There is a long pause and then Li Po says: "You can light the lanterns now. We have used all the candles. The show is over."

Wang Lung and his counterpart on the other boat busy themselves with the lighting of the lanterns, three suspended from poles at each end of the boats, and they and the water around them are soon bathed in a familiar soft glow. Part of the roof and its hanging spires are also illuminated, but they now seem rather tame, the steady, diffuse light muting the mad colors and smoothing out the shadows. The two boats are pulled alongside each other and the poet pours wine all around and calls for a song. One of the girls produces a moon guitar and strums it softly, while the other sings a popular ballad of lost love. Despite himself, Wang Lung feels a strong melancholy creep over him and he turns in his seat to gaze fully at the singing girl, whose pert features are set in an expression of sadness she deems appropriate for the song. The song ends and the girl giggles and turns to whisper something to her friend, all the while staring at Wang Lung, who blushes and doesn't hear Li Po fumbling around among the bags that are sitting on the floor of the boat. But a cry from the poet soon snaps him out of his reverie.

"What is this?" Li Po says, brandishing Wang Lung's bag. "Brushes, ink, ink already ground and carried in a lacquer container. And here is a scroll, why I do believe it is the collection of little tales I told you. I thought that had gone overboard long ago. What a sneaky little man you are!" This is said without malice, however, for it is clear Li Po is happy to see his record preserved. "What a sneaky little fellow indeed. And what possessed you to bring it with you, may I ask. Did you hope to hear the rest of the tale? A stirring ending, a devoted marriage, hordes of children, and a respected dotage?"

He tosses the bag to Wang Lung, who catches it and grasps it close to his chest, one hand on the gunwale, bracing himself against the rocking: he will not lose it now, not after keeping it safe for so long, even carrying it with him on this little boat for fear that some inquisitive crew member might discover its hiding place under his mattress.

Li Po meanwhile leans into the bottom of the boat, lifts out a cloth sack, and in a single flourish pulls out a cape and swings it round his shoulders. Even in the half-light, Wang Lung can see that the cape is made entirely of feathers, a thick row of iridescent red-and-blue kingfisher feathers around the collar, the hem trimmed with the peacock's whorls of bronze and green, and the remainder a snowy white that can only be a crane's plumage.

"Perhaps you'd like to know how I came by this, for example? How it was conferred on me by the emperor, though mine by right as the supreme poet in the land and a master of the Taoist mysteries?"

Here Li Po stands abruptly, too abruptly, and the boat rocks violently from side to side, throwing him down in a tumbled heap and leaving several white feathers floating in the air. On the other boat both girls burst into peals of laughter, joined by a high-pitched cackle from the boat boy. Even Wang Lung cannot help smiling. Li Po, cursing, pulls himself upright and sits heavily in the prow. He calls for another flask of wine and continues talking, apparently oblivious of their laughter.

"Oh, I've had my share of children, and marriages of course, for after she left—you know who I mean, boy—after she left, I had to go on with life and lived fully, married for three years to poor tiny Ching Yu, who bore me a son but died in the effort. Lei Gen he is called, a game little lad but sickly for so many years. And then there was that sow from Kueichou with a tongue that could flay a man alive. She gave me a boy and a girl, both as beautiful as the dawn, but was always harping over money and her 'position'—her father had some absurd title—Subprefect of the Royal Wardrobe, something like that—and she thought she had married below her station. She left me and none too soon, though she took the children with her and has poisoned their minds against me. No, I lived a full life in those years in between, a life filled with passion, the only kind worth living, a life most of all filled with poetry, for I was like a whale swimming among minnows then, spouting forth great gouts of verse from my pen to astonish and amaze. I wrote and wrote and wrote, couldn't be stopped, a rising tide of words that I knew deep inside would eventually wash over the petty men standing in my way and bring the recognition I deserved. For you see, I didn't just write, I created poetry of a kind that no one had seen before. At first I moved cautiously, not sure whether my talents had an end, exploring, seeing the nature and subjects of the poems changing as I grew, becoming more complex, the imagery deeper and sometimes very difficult, changing from the simple odes to a new temple or the sonnet of thanks to the assistant magistrate, growing far beyond the stock topics of court poetry: the lady in her bower, the ruin of ages, the briefness of youth, the black wings of death beating always at our backs, so on and on, a dozen at most. Instead of the neglected concubine in her cold room, stiff fingers flying over the loom, the lonely rattle of the shuttle sounding in her ears and so on, I wrote this:

While my hair was cut straight across my forehead
I played at the front gate, pulling flowers.
You came out on bamboo stilts, playing horse,
You walked about my seat, throwing blue plums.
And we went on living in the village of Chang An:
Two small people without dislike or suspicion.

At fourteen I married my lord you.
I never laughed, being bashful.
Lowering my head, I looked to the wall.
Called a thousand times, I never looked back.

At fifteen, I stopped scowling,
Desired my dust to be mingled with yours
Forever and forever and forever.

At sixteen, you departed,
You went to far Ku Tao by the river of swirling eddies,

And you have been gone five months.
The monkeys make a sorrowful noise overhead.
You dragged your feet when you went out.
By the gate now, the moss is grown, the different
    mosses,
Too deep to clear them away!
The leaves fall early this Autumn, in wind.
I grow older.

If you are coming down through the narrows
Please let me know beforehand
And I will come out as far as
Long Sand Beach to meet you.

"None of those court dandies would think of writing about a river merchant's wife, but isn't her loneliness just as poignant as that of a court lady? Later I moved out of the bounds of those topics altogether, burst out into a universe of my own, new verse forms, new dreams, passages like this:

I flew across the Mirror Lake one night and
The moon in the lake followed my flight
To the foot of Mount Heng where the
Monkeys cry and the green waters curl upward.

I climbed, shod in the sky stepping shoes of Prince
    Hsieh
Up the cloud ladder, where, halfway up,
I saw the morning sun and heard heaven's cock crow.
Along a thousand endless precipices, down flower-
    choked paths
I strode
Until there came a peal of thunder and
The mountains crumbled

The stone gates of hollow heaven opened wide,
Revealing a vast realm of bottomless azure
Sun and moon shining together on gold and silver
palaces.

Clad in rainbow and riding the wind,
The ladies of the upper air descended like flower-
flakes
Followed by their immortal masters riding in winged
chariots.
Phoenix birds circled their cars and panthers played
on lutes. . . .

"There is much more, a long dream poem that left Wang Wei and his minions speechless. They didn't know what to make of such poems—the broken meter, the celestial imagery. 'Strangeness piled on strangeness,' they called it among themselves, though I knew it was really strength upon strength. They tried but couldn't stop me, no more than they could halt the changing of the tides or the advance of a sandstorm blowing out of the desert. I swore I wouldn't set foot in the capital until called by the emperor himself, and I didn't. No, I waited and waited, many long years, with only my conviction and my verses to comfort me, turned away by every hand, scorned by the fashionable, until, at last, came that glorious day in Henan when an imperial messenger arrived at our little thatched hut. My wife—that awful Kueichou woman—was shrieking at me about something when I saw him come over the hill and ride down toward us, the familiar rainbow banner strapped to his back fluttering in the breeze. I said to her: 'Hush now woman, for I am summoned to the capital,' though she didn't of course, just kept harping on as usual until I got up and walked away, out the door, took the scroll from the messenger, scrawled a respectful reply, and went round to the rear where I kept my horse, a dun mare called Lady, near-lame, but game for all that. I saddled her up without another word and was away and on the road to Chang An at last."

Li Po smiles at the memory and takes a great gulp of wine.

"Perhaps, my boy, I will tell you more tales to fill the blank pages of your scroll, tales of Chang An and the court, of the Lady Yang, of eunuchs and soldiers, poets and priests, empires crumbling, sacrificed for love—stories you can tell your children and they theirs."

He gestures to the two girls, who are watching like round-eyed eleven-year-olds at bedtime.

"You see, even Ling-ling and Mei-lan are eager to hear my account. What about you, my boy?"

Wang Lung nods his head, fumbling hastily in his bag for the brushes and his manuscript.

"But," the poet suddenly says, "what is the point? You ought to be able to guess how the story turns out."

Wang Lung shakes his head, but the sad truth is that he can indeed guess the fate Li Po made for himself.

"Besides," the poet continues, "no one will ever read it. If they do it will mean another death sentence for me. And in any case, it is poor stuff. Let us sit here and drink wine and sing songs of ancient heroes instead."

"Oh, please sir," cries Wang Lung. "I would, I really would like to hear about the court and the emperor."

The poet demurs, but Wang Lung senses that he is ready to tell his story once more and, after more pleading—at his encouragement the two girls both chime in with childish cries for a tale—Li Po allows himself to be persuaded.

"Very well, then," he says, settling back into the cushioned prow, "I will tell you what happened at court. But first we must row out into the sunlight. For this is not a story to be told in the dark."

nine 李白

"THERE, PULL OVER AND MAKE US FAST UNDER THE weeping willow," Li Po says when they emerge at last into the bright sunshine. He waves toward a huge tree whose drooping branches trail slender leaf-covered vines into the water at the lake's edge. Several yellow and purple butterflies chase each other over the grassy bank, and as they watch, a golden oriole swoops out of the tree, catches one in its beak, and bears it off. It is late afternoon now, the heat heavy over the land, little else moving, an oppressive stillness hanging in the air. Underneath the canopy formed by the curtain of willows, however, it is pleasantly cool. Wang Lung ties the two boats together side by side, while the other boy secures them to the trunk of the tree.

"I must start if I am to finish this story before we return to the barge," Li Po says, beckoning for more wine. "So:

"So, so, so. But it is difficult to know where to start in trying to describe Chang An to you who were barely born then, who in recent years have known nothing but war and chaos, who will never see its like again, however long you live. The city then was overflowing with the riches of the world after forty years of peace under our Bright Emperor, Hsuan Tsung, forty years of prosperity and stable prices, when it seemed that Chang An was a whirlpool into which was sucked everything within a radius of ten thousand miles:

the most prized goods, the most skilled artisans, musicians, and dancers, the most rapacious criminals, the holiest men. Sometimes I would spend hours just wandering through the great Western Market where the tide of trade from Serindia and beyond washed up, past shops staffed by hook-nosed Arabs in woolen robes and purple shawls standing guard over their trays of rubies and emeralds from the far south, chunks of crystal worked into bracelets of jade and rings of silver, dragons and phoenixes wrought of gold and studded with carnelian and obsidian, necklaces woven from a thousand strands of white gold. The stalls of the Uighurs sold everything from hawks and falcons to felt hats and capes, the men wild-eyed and stinking of rancid butter. Row upon row of great carpets for the halls of the rich, as well as prayer rugs and dancing mats, all brought from the myriad Iranian city-states of the Trans-Oxus—Bukhara, Khwarizim, Farghana, Samarkand, Chach, Maimargh, and more—ablaze with red and gold and green patterns, or sometimes scenes of a hunt in far-off mountains, the clothes, the buildings, and people so utterly strange that at first sight the eye could not make sense of what was depicted. There were stacks of aromatic woods at 5000 cash a cubit and tubs full of myrrh and cloves and frankincense, storax and camphor. Sharkskins and leopard skins lay side by side, sealskin and horse hide, mounds of sable and ermine pelts, glossy and sleek. There were live animals, too—five-colored parrots and peacocks, elephants and, of course, camels, 'the desert argosy,' swaying and smirking and pissing noisily, their urine thick and viscous and dark as mud, throwing off a wild, gamy reek that sent the horses mad. And there were other strange beasts, some with no name. I once saw a kind of bird, or at least the man who was selling it called it a bird, a camel-bird, and indeed, in size it was closer to a camel than to any bird I have ever seen, standing as high as a horse and able to knock over a cow with a kick from one of its long leathery legs. It had a plump body and a sleek plumage of white and black, a long scrawny neck and a tiny head in which rolled two small, bright-red eyes. I was in money then, and bought the bird to keep in an enclosure in my garden, along with the little black boy who was its keeper. But it died soon after of the cold and we ate it, one of those enormous thighs providing enough meat for seven—tough but tasty, not unlike beef, though leaner.

"And everywhere there were men who had brought the goods. Green-eyed Sogdians, some with hair like bronze, long and flowing over their shoulders unbound, shining a metallic red in the sun. They were quite monstrous, like weird beings from another world; children would run screaming to their mothers when they appeared in the street, and while I was in the capital, it was decreed that they must cover up their heads and tie up their hair when walking about. There were also short brown men from the isles of the south, Srivijaya and Kalzzinga, and from the five Indian states, usually Buddhist clergy of one kind or another, especially saffron-robed and shaven-pated monks hawking their religious wares—copies of the Mahaprajnaparamita Sutra inscribed on palmyra in looping Sanskrit for the greater glory of the Mahayana, or the Diamond Sutra translated into characters and woodblock printed upon cheap hemp paper and sold for a few cash to propagate the faith. There were flat-faced, suspicious Mongols, gape mouthed Japanese pilgrims, brass-skinned Tibetans in furred caps and orange-and-red cloaks, even tiny, nap-headed aboriginal slaves running naked behind the carriage of some fashionable lady, ready to hold her robes and abase themselves for her pride.

"And, of course, there were women—dusky Annamese swaying past in their tight sheath dresses; Korean girls with high, clear voices and skin like peaches; even the girls of the west with whom I spent much time singing and laughing in their shops, where they served nothing but grape wine. As I wrote in one poem:

The western houri with the face like a flower
She stands by the wine warmer and
laughs with the breath of spring,
Laughs with the breath of spring and says:
'Will you be going somewhere *now*, my lord, before
you are drunk?'

"Those were glorious days, the tide of our people at full flood and I swimming strongly in it, buoyed up by the knowledge of my powers, the knowledge that when I sat down to write the verses would flow out like milk from a pitcher, the poems would be like nets of wonderfully intricate mesh set out to capture my meaning. I knew that when the emperor called, day or night, drunk or sober, I would be able to please him, to make his lady give out that gurgling laugh that made all around her smile. Why once he asked me . . . but again I get ahead of myself. We must do this the right way, for my amanuensis is village-trained."

Li Po sits up from his pile of cushions and addresses the two girls who smile back uncertainly.

"For your information, ladies, that means he likes a story to march from one episode to the next, strictly according to the events as they happened, each piece fitting smoothly into the next, no exaggerations, no skittering back and forth in time, no side excursions on interesting topics; probably not too much poetry either, for he wants to know what happens in the end, don't you Wang Lung?"

"It is your tale, Master Li," Wang Lung says without looking up.

"Yes, it is, but now it is yours, also. The listener is as important as the teller, my boy, you'll realize that when you get older. There's no having one without the other. And besides, you saved the scroll when I was ready to fling it into the river. You have a debt to the story now that you can't escape."

Smiling at this remark, Li Po leans back onto the cushions and resumes:

"Let us go back then, and I will tell you of how I finally came to be invited to Chang An and how, once there, I received my first lesson that in the capital, nothing is as it seems. What happened was this: for a long time I was acquainted with a certain Wu Yun, a Taoist adept and teacher. This fellow was a good drinking companion, very sharp and amusing in conversation. He could compose couplets at the drop of a wine cup, though oddly enough he never had the patience to write longer works, or perhaps his talent only extended to extempore verses. At any rate he and I shared a good deal, a love of wine, of poetry (for though he couldn't write, he was keenly appreciative of others who could), and an interest in mystical Taoism, a pool in which I had swum several times myself. Now Wu Yun was a clever man, a very clever talker, as I have said, and he chanced to meet a Taoist nun in the Pure Light Monastery on Mount Heng one day, a lady of some bearing whom he recognized as one of the emperor's nieces. He didn't let on that he knew who she was, just began to talk passionately of the Cavern Mystery Transformations, of which he was an initiate. It soon transpired that the princess her Taoist name was Jade Perfection—was seeking to become an initiate into the mysteries herself. Naturally Wu Yun volunteered to be her sponsor, and naturally she was very grateful. After the ceremonies he followed her back to the capital and was installed in a sumptuous suite in one of the wings of the Ladies' Palace. Being a glib talker, he quickly wiggled his way into the presence of the emperor himself. There he found that the son of heaven, while under some personal or perhaps political obligation to show interest in matters spiritual, reserved his true love for poetry. Seeing a chance to impress, Wu Yun told our ruler that while he had no talent himself, he was a very close friend of the greatest poet of the age, that is, me. The emperor, it seemed, had never heard my name—this despite years of submissions by my friends in the provinces, all buried in some file in the imperial library by Wang Wei and his claque, no doubt—but expressed an interest in meeting me and seeing some of my compositions. He then turned to other things, but as is often the case at court, one word from on high was enough, and the order went out to summon me, albeit penned by a eunuch whom Wu Yun had spent time cultivating.

"I was only vaguely aware of all this when I crossed the Wei River on the outskirts of Chang An after an arduous two-month passage through the mountains. For me the imperial summons lying in a leather bag next to my skin—much folded and a little greasy with use, but still recognizably the product of the chancery—was all that I needed. Ah, such ignorance. It seems almost endearing when I look back on it now.

"When I presented my letter to the clerk at the Audience Hall Gate of the Ta Ming Palace, I soon found that my summons meant very little indeed without someone to take responsibility for it. I also discovered that while I was traveling, my friend Wu Yun had been a little too clever for his own good. When I mentioned his name, the clerk, a very fat man with a huge belly and a gaunt face, started back and an expression of fear and anger crossed his pinched features.

"'He is known to you?' he whispered sharply. 'You are a friend of his?'

"Alerted by his tone, I merely said that an abbot of my acquaintance had asked me to carry some religious books to him, averred that I had never met Wu Yun myself, wouldn't know him to run into in the street, and so on. This seemed to satisfy the clerk, who nodded, made some remark indicating that it would be to my advantage never to mention that name again, then took my precious document, placed it in a folded paper file, and told me to come back in a week, when my case would be attended to.

"There followed one of the most miserable months I have ever passed, shuttling back and forth between my lodgings and the Audience Hall Gate, sitting for hours on the hard wooden benches, waiting to see yet another minor functionary, the little cash I had brought soon dwindling so that I was forced to move out of my comfortable rooms near the Ta Ming Palace complex and into a grimy little hole in the middle of the foreign quarter where the chatter of the desert—drunken songs in Turkic, whores screaming at each other in Uighur—rose up along with the stink of clogged sewers and the smell of frying mutton fat to pierce my sleep. All the time, too, I was oppressed by the knowledge that I couldn't go home. I wouldn't go back and live off a stipend from that Kueichou sow's father. It was too humiliating for a man of forty, a poet renowned throughout the empire.

"And worst of all, I made no progress at the palace. The original clerk I talked to had disappeared, the file couldn't be found, the docket was lost, on and on and on endless excuses until one day after the ninth time I had been told to come back in four days' time, I tipped over a whey-faced clerk's desk and stormed out. So much for the royal summons.

"I did, however, find out by other methods that Wu Yun had been exiled for some unspecified transgression, something to do with one of the princes of the blood, of whom he should have known to be wary. Even I had heard that the emperor kept the princes—all forty-two of them—under a tight rein, and that any appearance of plotting would bring swift and terrible retribution. The suicide five years earlier of the crown prince at the emperor's orders, the turbulent years before the emperor's own enthronement when four of his predecessors had come and gone in rapid succession, and, even farther back, the wholesale massacre of imperial relatives under the Empress Wu—all these should have served as a grim warning. Eventually, too, I discovered that the eunuch who had set my summons in motion had been executed. That piece of information, gleaned with my last hundred cash, was the final straw, and I resolved to leave Chang An. I didn't care where I went, I just wanted to get out, stopping only to pay my respects in the great Temple of Lao-tzu.

I stood in contemplation before the enormous statue of Taoism's founder, holding the bag of poems I had brought to submit to the emperor. But the peace I sought wouldn't come, just a black boiling bitterness at the failure of my long-nourished hopes. In a spasm of rage, I flung the bag of scrolls into a huge bronze cauldron in which a coal fire was kept burning all year round and turned to leave. But I had barely gone two steps before I felt a tug at my sleeve and turned to find that a very short man of sixty or so dressed in a simple brown robe had plucked the sack out of the flames and was proffering it to me.

"'Never destroy,' he said. 'Any fool can destroy.'

"I wanted to snatch the scrolls from him and hurl them back into the cauldron, but the moment passed: he was right, after all. Sheepishly, I took the bag from him and we fell to talking, he listening sympathetically as I poured out my tale of woe, his lined features set in an expression of concern. When I had finished he suggested that we repair to a tavern ('life always looks better on a full stomach'), where he asked to read some of the poems. He read them all, turned to me and said: 'If you penned these, you are no ordinary man.'

"He then called for platters of pickled vegetables, salted

peanuts, roast suckling pig, and soyed goose, as well as more wine, the best the house had to offer, an aged brew called Spring Blossom, flavored with fragara pepper and chrysanthemums. When the dishes came, however, he proved to have even less cash than I.

"'Never fear,' he said. Jumping up and fumbling in his sleeve he produced a jade turtle embossed with gold that I recognized as the badge of office for first level officials of the highest grade. He hurried across the street to a pawn shop and returned a few minutes later, grinning, two strings of a hundred cash clutched in one hand.

"'They didn't want to take it at first, asked where I had stolen it. But when I told them I was the president of the metropolitan court and said that if they didn't accept my offer I would set the bailiffs on them, they soon changed their minds.'

"That was my introduction to Ho Chih Chang: poet, scholar, statesman, the emperor's sometime confidant; he was all those things, but also a man like no other, genuinely contemptuous of rank, completely unafraid of men or gods, generous to the point that every month his wives complained there was no food in the larder because he had given away his entire rice ration. We spent the money from the pawn shop that night and much more over the following weeks, drinking and singing in the cavernous banqueting hall of his mansion or in the meanest wineshops, talking and laughing until the candles guttered, the twinkling stars dimmed, and the first light of dawn crept across the sky.

"It was, of course, Ho who arranged my first audience with the emperor. Characteristically though, the exact time of the meeting—dusk—slipped his mind and he was still at the imperial library—another of his responsibilities—at the appointed hour. He had arranged all the correct passes, however, and I was ushered through a succession of gates and doors until I found myself walking with a guard along the rampart of the towering wall that encircled Palace City. Enclosed within were the myriad imperial palaces—the Hall of Princes, the sprawling complex in which the princes of blood and their families were housed, the Cinnamon Palace, home of the Crown Prince, the Ladies' Palace where the royal widows and unmarried relatives lived, tier upon tier of double-leaved, forest-green roofs rising out of the evening mist, hundreds of buildings in the center of the city but surrounded by a park so big that they were as cut off from Chang An's two million residents as a country estate.

"We soon passed into a separate complex housing the emperor's own palace, the Ta Ming. Following the guard's steady tread, I saw that we were approaching the Pear Gardens, a vast open space dotted with gazebos and pavilions set amidst clumps of pine, poplar, wisteria, and of course pear trees. There was also a huge stand of bamboo covering three acres into which the emperor would sometimes retreat to sit by himself, away from the cares of court, hearing only the clink and rustle of the hollow bamboos swaying in the breeze. Dotted among the trees were numerous lakes, ranging from ornamental duck ponds to wide stretches of water in which the court bucks took their ladies rowing in small skiffs. Around many of the lakes were rows of peach and cherry blossoms, pink and white buds just peeping forth from the branches, soon to burst forth into their full spring glory. I saw, too, that there were long lines of willows along the banks of the Serpentine—the stream that wound through the scene glistening silver in the moonlight—and that a blanket of silky-white catkins covered the ground beneath the trees like a layer of freshly fallen snow.

"We did not go down into the gardens but continued to follow the curving wall round until, after twenty minutes or so, we came to the rear of the palace grounds. Here we descended and passed by a field dotted with the mounds of icepits where ice was buried during the summer, then past the stables, with a special wing for the ill-fated dancing horses, bigger than most villages and housing seven hundred horses. After the stables, came a long double line of mews for the hunting birds, followed by the kennels where the hounds could be heard baying, then at last we arrived at our destination—the cock walk—where the fighting cocks lived in pampered splendor. This was a large field featuring row upon row of knee-high wooden structures like little huts, each one a home for one of the cocks. On the right-hand side of the field, there was a splendid, deep cockpit and several fenced-off runs where the birds could be exercised singly; always singly, of course, for had they been put together they would have tried to rip one another to shreds, even without the aid of the steel spurs that are strapped onto their legs for the fights.

"A crowd had gathered round the far end of the field, an odd mixture of grave Mandarins in full official robes standing together at the rear, then perhaps twenty gaudy young bucks, flushed with wine and excitement, jostling each other for position at the front. As we came closer, I saw that all eyes were focused on a tall, lanky man wearing a brilliant 'sunrise coat' of yellow, orange, and red over his robes. He was standing apart from the rest in front of one of the little huts, closely inspecting a cock being held up for him by a short, broad-shouldered man with a pleasant, open face. It was, of course, the Emperor Hsuan Tsung himself, putting several sharp questions to the bird handler in a high-pitched voice: When had the bird last been fed and exercised? Had he been kept on a diet of wheat bread soaked in rice wine for the last two days as instructed? Had he been kept away from the hens? The handler replied in a much softer tone, which I couldn't catch, then handed the bird to the emperor, who turned it over so that he could inspect its legs. A fighting cock's fate depends on the strength and rapidity of the blows he can administer to his opponent, and the condition of its legs is crucial. Like human combat, the fighter who can get in the largest number of blows in the shortest space of time is almost invariably the victor.

"The crowd hung back at a respectful distance of some fifty paces or so, only a few eunuchs standing with Hsuan Tsung. But as far as I knew, I was supposed to meet the emperor at this time and place, so I strode past the small crowd toward him. Before I had covered ten paces, however, two guards sprang forth, one grabbing me by the right arm. I have always disliked being manhandled and reacted quite instinctively, grasping both of the guard's arms and twisting them violently sideways and outwards, at the same time placing my foot between his legs so that he tumbled to the ground. The second guard fumbled with his sword, but fortunately he proved as clumsy as his companion had been eager and managed to trip over his scabbard, also falling to the ground in front of me.

"More guards appeared from the edge of the crowd and ran in my direction, several succeeding in drawing their swords without tripping. I stood my ground, not moving at all, for it would have been the height of foolishness to be skewered by some overenthusiastic young idiot intent on proving his devotion to the imperial house. Evidently the emperor's attention had been attracted by the commotion, and he glanced over at the two guards sprawled on the ground and the others rushing towards me. Our eyes met. I didn't look away, held his stare, and he regarded me with a puzzled frown for a moment before turning and saying something to one of the eunuchs hovering at his side. The eunuch was a plump middle-aged man (they were all plump, especially those who were cut when very young; it seemed to be one result of their loss, the other of course being those odd whispery voices) with a set expression of haughty arrogance. That was my first sight of Chief Eunuch Kao Li Shih, as slimy a creature as has ever walked the earth. He stared at me for a few moments as though trying to recall whether he knew my face. I noticed he had a twitch that pulled the left side of his cheek and mouth sideways and upwards in a comical fashion. Then he shook his head and spoke to another, much younger eunuch who immediately broke away from the imperial train and rushed over towards me, arriving at the same moment as the little knot of guards, whom he waved away impatiently as one would pesky flies. He didn't speak, just beckoned, and I followed him over to where the emperor stood. The eunuch whispered something to his master, who in turn spoke softly to Hsuan Tsung. To my surprise the emperor whipped around and examined me with the same intensity he had been bestowing on the cock.

"'You are Ho's find, aren't you?' he said, passing the bird back to its handler and wiping his hands on the side of his gown, smearing a large patch of bird shit all along an absurdly intricate piece of embroidery featuring phoenixes and dragons gamboling in the heavens at dawn, easily 1000 cash an inch when ordered and the cause of early blindness in many a seamstress. The buttons on the coat, I saw, were emeralds the size of quail's eggs.

"'He told me that you were impulsive, but that you wrote poetry like *a banished immortal*. Even so, is it really necessary to abuse my guards? We can't have you barging in, knocking down people at will, can we?'

"'Sire, I am called Li Po,' I replied, a little alarmed. 'I am a friend of Ho Chih Chang, as you say. As to the guards, I'm afraid they were very clumsy. One fellow tripped on his sword scabbard, and for no reason that I could see, the other simply flung himself on the ground in front of me.'

"The emperor laughed, a welcome sight, for his natural expression was grave, his deep-set eyes full of sadness, and when he chided me over the guards, I had feared he was truly angry.

"'I see that you do have spirit. I like that in a man. And you have a very great talent for composition. He gave me some samples of your verses. Can't think why I haven't seen your writing before.'

"I opened my mouth to reply, but he continued:

"'Come to eat tonight, and we shall hear more.'

"With that he turned back to the cock handler, leaving me standing there foolishly with my mouth agape. The crowd swirled in his wake as Hsuan Tsung moved down the line of hutches. Presently I felt a familiar tug at my sleeve and turned to find a red-faced, breathless Ho Chih Chang sweating and mumbling apologies between breaths—he had lost track of time, most sorry, could lead to me to the emperor now.

"'I have already seen him,' I said, still a little dazed by the briefness of my long-anticipated interview. 'He has asked me to eat with him this evening.'

"'Excellent, excellent,' Ho said, mopping his brow absently with a length of white silk. 'That will be in the Hall of Golden Bells. Hsuan Tsung dearly loves a feast and best of all he likes to watch poets compete against each other. He has a genuine appreciation of poetry, even writes very competent verse himself—but most of all he likes the drama of competition. I told him of your powers, how when we were already nine parts drunk you had thrown down an octet that was as perfect as ice in a jade bowl.'

"Indeed, as Ho had predicted, the banquet that evening was punctuated by numerous displays, some of the type popular in the streets during festival days—contortionists, a team of child acrobats, an Indian juggler who did complicated things with cobras (fortunately I was seated far away), and so on. As to the competitions for poetry—and singing—these didn't come until after the food had been served. Perhaps I should describe the scene to you (here the two girls and Wang Lung wag their heads in unison, but Li Po, leaning back, his eyes closed, lost in his tale, doesn't notice), for although I later had so many such meals that they blended into each other indistinguishably, I shall always remember that first banquet in the Hall of Golden Bells. It really did have golden bells in it, too, row upon row of them hung from the rafters, tiny things with tongues that were so small they were beaten almost to the thickness of an eggshell. There were thousands of them twinkling in the light of the lanterns that hung below them so that when you looked up, the entire ceiling seemed to be made of sparkling gold. They were designed as wind bells, but there was of course no breeze inside the hall. I was told by my neighbor, an ancient, bewhiskered general, there were great swathes of cloth stiffened with starch and wooden battens hanging above the bells. Each piece of cloth had two ropes attached to it and a little boy on the other end charged with keeping it swinging back and forth so that the bells gave off constant high, tinkling rustles like a field of golden reeds. Though drowned out much of the time by the high buzz of conversation, it was a charming effect, especially as a background to the poetry and singing that came later.

"There were other wonders, too: walls made out of solid mother-of-pearl, spoons and chopsticks of jade and silver (the emperor's utensils were all made from rhinoceros horn, which turns black in the presence of poison), tortoiseshell mats, gold weave tablecloths, a great many such things, most of which I had seen before in the houses of great officials and rich merchants, though never on such a scale. But while such opulence caught the eye (and wearied it after a time, if truth be told), I was truly stunned by the wave upon wave of food and wine, a vast outflowing of plenty from every corner of the empire—rice wines from the Great River, peach wine from Shantung, the fiery "burnt" wine brewed in my native Shu, wine made from cherries and from lychees, grape wine imported in casks on camelback from the far-off groves beside the Caspian, even the lowly spirit distilled from glutinous millet that is the daily comfort of the town dweller, though this was very different from the common fare of Chang An's taverns, made with the choicest grain and flavored with licorice.

"As to the food, well, I can hardly recall even a tenth of the dishes. A stream of eunuch attendants flew back and forth from the kitchens carrying an endless array of steaming silver and jade dishes to the emperor's table. After Hsuan Tsung had tasted or rejected each offering, the rest of us, perhaps one hundred fifty guests seated in six long double lines, would be served. There was whole saddle of venison cooked with vinegar and ginger; camel hump sliced down the middle, its purple flesh steaming; goose baked with apricots; whole baby soft-shelled turtles fried in mustard seeds and dill; striped white mullet stuffed with garlic, peppers, and fermented beans; swan eggs boiled in sulfur springs, the shells a dark yellow, the taste ripped from the bowels of the earth; tiny sea horses from Lingnan fried with ginger and spring onions; deer tongues in aspic from Kansu, dried pit viper flesh from Hupei soaked in wine lees; a pie in which tiny songbirds had been stewed with dates; lamb chunks baked in saffron rice in the style of the Turks; shrimp dumplings made with cardamom and coriander; and lastly, a whole calf, taken from the womb a month before birth and boiled in milk, the sweetest, most delicate flesh you can imagine, melting in the mouth. Then the soups—water mallow and crab, fat gobs of yellow roe floating on the surface—and sweet dishes—heart of the sago palm swimming in coconut milk and 'silver cakes' made from sugar and flour and milk, even tiny newborn white mice stuffed with honey, then released onto the tables where they sat peeping feebly until snatched up by a flashing pair of chopsticks and consumed whole.

"As to the guests, the men were an ordinary looking set for all their finery. Without their brocade robes, their gold earrings and rouged lips, their elaborate gauze hats twinkling with gold and silver hairpins, they were just a paunchy group of nondescript middle-aged men, the flesh of their lined faces sagging. The only difference between them and their counterparts in the city wineshops a few miles away was the puffy arrogance of their expressions and a certain wary coldness in their eyes. The women, however, were astonishing, courtesans of the highest class, not one over twenty, the result of years of sweeping the countryside for the most beautiful children, their every movement—pouring wine for their companions or tucking a stray hair back into their chignons—as graceful as a dancer's, the result of long hours of strict training. Perhaps, too, now that I reflect on it, they seemed all the more glorious because of the age and dissipation of the men.

"And, of course, there was the emperor's favorite, the concubine Yang Gwei-fei, a being on another plane altogether. When I first glimpsed her, I wondered that she had achieved such a reputation for beauty. In truth she had none of the doll-like perfection of feature that marked every other female at the feast; indeed I noted that she was inclined to plumpness and that her nose was somewhat large. But when she threw back her head a few minutes later and gave out that gurgling laugh, the sound cutting through the talking and the clash of dishes like a temple bell on a mountain hillside, then I saw her true beauty. It was something from within, an extraordinary, brilliant animation that seemed to make her glow, that set all that were with her smiling, raised their spirits to a fever pitch. I have met others within whom the essential numen, the vital spirits, seemed to burn with the power of several ordinary mortals, but never someone with as much power as Yang Gwei-fei; she was like a bonfire, her blazing spirit inflaming everything around her.

"There was no doubting that Hsuan Tsung was utterly consumed by her, either. That night when he entered the hall with Gwei-fei at his side, I was astonished at the contrast to his demeanor earlier in the day. He trailed along slightly behind her, his eyes never leaving her face, his tall frame bent so that he was down to her level (she was rather short, too), his face—previously so full of authority that I had feared his displeasure—now set in an expression of vacuous devotion, the desire to please emanating so strongly from him that one was reminded of a faithful but foolish dog. I noticed also as he shuffled along and his robes swung forward that he was barefoot. At first I thought this some peculiar court custom, though a quick glance around confirmed that everyone else in the hall was wearing boots or shoes. Then I wondered whether the emperor wasn't going a little senile, whether he had simply forgotten his shoes and none of his attendants had dared to tell him. But then I saw that Gwei-fei, too, had discarded her shoes, her dainty feet, white as frost, peeping out from under the hem of her robe as she walked. She was giggling and whispering to him as they entered, and it soon became apparent that the idea of going unshod was hers. All of us rose from our seats and bowed low as they passed. There was a long moment of silence after they had seated themselves, she looking expectantly around to see what reaction her little trick would prompt. Within a few moments, the hall was filled with an odd shuffling sound and there was much wiggling among the guests. After a moment of puzzlement, I realized that every person in the room barring the prime minister and a few grizzled generals was removing his shoes and socks, most attempting to do so discreetly, others openly leaning down and pulling their footwear off, but all maintaining an embarrassed silence. At this Gwei-fei laughed out loud, a great chuckle that rolled out across the silence and sparked sympathetic smiles from many of the guests. Her laugh, the acknowledgement that her joke was over, broke the silence, and the hum of conversation rose up again.

"Now as I said before, there were numerous small performances during the banquet, most of a fairly commonplace type. But once the seemingly endless flow of dishes had stopped and the diners were settling down to their wine, a gong was rung at the emperor's Table of Seven Jewels, and an enormously fat butler dressed in a magnificent robe sporting the imperial rainbow colors called for silence, then announced the names of the four contestants in the verse-writing bout. Mine was the last. The others were all fairly well known to me, extremely competent court poets all, but locked in the tight technical corset that description implies. The topic was 'The Hardships of Travel,' the butler said, the winner to be chosen by acclamation. He called for the first contestant, a certain Liao Cheng, a very smooth individual who strolled to the front of the hall, bowed low to the emperor, took up the writing brush, and within about ten minutes (during which time conversation rose to its former pitch and drinking resumed) he had finished, handing over the poem to the major domo, who read it out loud to the assembled company. It was a conventional octet: a trip to the ruin of the King of Yueh's palace in Shaohsing, the sight of the scattered stones and crumbling towers once filled with song and intrigue, the beautiful women who had danced through its halls now all bones and dust, his feelings of life's ephemerality. You know the sort of thing. Still, it was a creditable effort, and he received a murmur of approval from the crowd, with Hsuan Tsung nodding his head in appreciation.

"The next two, I forget their names, didn't venture very far outside the court conventions either, one taking almost half an hour to produce a long-winded account in the old style meter of a trip during deepest winter to the hot springs at Hua Ching; it soon became embarrassingly obvious that the poem was an elaborate attempt at flattering the emperor and Gwei-fei, who were known to frequent the area. The next stayed within the octet form; I have no recollection of his poem, only of the inordinate time it took him to compose it and the yawns that greeted its reading. By then most of the guests were in a state of near coma, as far as I could tell, the only activity coming from behind a pair of gauzy curtains that covered a small alcove at the back of the hall. When the curtains billowed, I could see the indistinct shapes of a number of women milling about. I nudged my neighbor the old general awake—he had dozed off after the first poem—and asked him what was going on.

"'Eh? What? The gels in the back? Singers and dancers, I expect, getting themselves gussied up for the competition.'

"He settled back, his eyes slipping shut once more. Just then the butler called out my name. I rose, my heart full of joy, for I knew that whatever I produced, it would be far better than anything that had come before. I strode to the front, bowed to the emperor, and then walked to the butler.

"'I'm going to do this a little differently,' I told him in an undertone. 'I'll read my poem out as I write it.'

"He looked skeptical. 'What, no revisions? Straight from the brush?'

'That's right.'

"He shrugged his shoulders. 'As you wish, sir,' he said, then called out in his booming voice, 'Silence for the gentleman who wishes to read out his poem as it flows from his brush.'

"He stepped aside, and I saw that I had piqued the interest of the jaded crowd. Their faces were turned toward me expectantly. The only sounds were a few curious whisperers and the far-off clash of dishes being returned to the kitchens. I stood there in silence for almost a minute until a few of the guests began to shift and mutter. Then I opened my mouth as wide as I could and let out a shriek:

Yeeeee-Yaaaaah!
Yeeeee-Yaaaaah!
Sheer danger!
High struggle!
The road to Shu is hard,
Harder than scaling
The blue sky.

"Here I stopped for a moment and looked up from the scroll on which I was scrawling the poem. The faces near me looked stunned, some gaping at me like fish, a few of the nearest rubbing their ears. The hall was dead silent, not a grumble to be heard. I grinned out at them and continued:

Above us,
Cliff-cut tracks and swaying plank-bridges
Wind up to peaks so high
That each day they turn back the sun's nine-dragon
chariot.

Below,
Endless chasms, a chaos of boiling water
Roaring through them,
battling waves that smash the racing torrents into
foam.

Here,
Yellow cranes beat their wings

vainly in the thin air and
gibbons wail, apes lie gasping, unable to climb any
further.

Greenmud Way winds
Round
And round
Forever.
Nine turns for every hundred steps.

Trembling,
I grasp at taunting Pleiades.
So close!
Then,
hand on chest,
heaving a great sigh,
I collapse.
Can go no further.

"But that day in the Hall of the Golden Bells, I did go on, chanting like a madman, like one possessed, four more stanzas, pausing between each one to make sure the crowd was still with me. I'd give you the whole thing, but to be honest the meter is so irregular that even I who wrote it cannot recall the exact words. As I came to the last stanza, I stopped for the last time and scanned the hall, my eyes passing over the ranks of seated guests, then on to the back where a line of servants was leaning against the wall and a single female figure stood in front of the gauze curtains, head bowed, hands clasped together. I looked down to begin writing the next stanza, opened my mouth to speak, but my voice dried up, and I slowly raised my head again without speaking. The woman lifted her gaze and looked directly at me. We stared at each other until I became aware that there was a restless shuffling among the crowd, and I forced my hand down to give them the last stanza:

'Tiger! Ware, tiger!'
Is the shout.
'Snake! Beware snakes!'
at dusk.

Every animal is against us,
teeth bared ready to suck blood
and mow down men like a sickle
slicing through hemp.

Of old, I've heard tell of Cheng-tu's charms,
But the lure of the Brocade City
Isn't enough: Best homeward quickly.
So, I sigh and turn back,
Singing:
Yeeeee-Yaaaaah!!!!
Yeeeee-Yaaaaah!!!!
Sheer danger!
High struggle!
The road to Shu is hard,
Harder than scaling
The blue sky.

"For a moment after I finished there was a profound, shocked silence, and I feared it had been too much, too soon. But then a great roar rose from the middle of the hall where I had been sitting—my old general had finally woken up—and the rest of the crowd immediately joined in, some shouting out their approval, others banging on the wooden tables, a wave of sound washing over me, a first repayment on all those years in obscurity. I turned to bow to the emperor and saw that he was thumping the table as hard as the rest, his face flushed. I made my obeisance and turned to go, but Hsuan Tsung was beckoning me, so I walked towards the head table. I saw why it was named the Table of Seven Jewels: the top was inlaid with thick bands of emerald, ruby, red coral, pearl, ivory, jade, and lapis lazuli. Strangely, as I made my way round the table, the emperor motioning me to his side, calling for a chair, the sound of acclamation still washing over me from the crowd behind, my only thought was that it must be very difficult to balance cups and plates on such an uneven surface, though looking closely, I saw that each place was set with a special silver platter in which there was a depression to fit a cup's base.

"'Well done, Li, well done indeed,' Hsuan Tsung said, clapping me on the back, for all the world like my archery instructor when I had made a bull's-eye as a boy. 'You've really woken the place up,' he continued, pointing to a chair that had been wedged between his seat and Gwei-fei's. She was smiling politely—poetry never really excited her much unless it was about herself—and Hsuan Tsung turned to her and said: 'My dear, this is Li Po. Ho calls him a *banished immortal* and says he's the greatest poet in the land. I had my doubts, but after that performance I am much more inclined to agree. At first I thought it was a joke of some kind: those two screams at the beginning; what a shock, ha, ha! Then the wildly irregular meter, why it was as though . . .'

"He went on, praising my effort extravagantly. Gwei-fei turned away to speak to her neighbor, a grossly corpulent general, a Sogdian or Turk of some kind from his features, though speaking quite intelligible Chinese from what I could hear, albeit with a kind of lisping insincerity that made my flesh creep. I beamed at the emperor, who was telling me about a new academy he had set up, the Han Lin Academy, or Academy of the Forest of Writing Brushes. It was a way of circumventing the tiresome bureaucrats, he said, and ensuring that men of talent could serve in government even if they didn't have an official title or hadn't passed the examinations: I must certainly become a member.

"Hsuan Tsung talked on happily, I nodding and smiling at the right moments, occasionally murmuring my agreement or briefly answering a query, hardly aware of what he was saying, oblivious to all else except my happiness. Presently, though, I realized that all eyes were on the two of us. Hsuan Tsung had picked up a little silver wine cup and poured me a measure from a bottle that stood on the table in front of him.

"'Here,' he said, pouring himself some too, the wine a beautiful amber color but with tiny specks of green rice floating on top. 'It is my own little supply. There are so many kinds of wine, but I still prefer this, the best rice wine, unfiltered, of course, that's why you'll see the *green ants* floating on top.'

"We toasted each other—it was a signal honor, the emperor himself serving me wine! No wonder the rest of the diners had watched in amazement—and I sipped. It was like nectar—though to be honest, I think at that moment a cup of horse piss would have tasted the same, so high were my spirits—the half-grains of rice tickling at the back of my throat as I swallowed, the taste as clean and pure as liquid jade. I opened my mouth to express my appreciation, but a eunuch had sidled up to the emperor and was whispering something in his ear.

"'Very well, very well. Let the singing competition begin,' he said, turning to me and speaking over the sound of the gong. 'It's Gwei-fei's favorite part of the evening. She is quite a singer herself.'

"The butler announced the name of the first contestant—Hsueh Tao, he called out, though I knew who it was already and also knew her true name. She came up the center aisle between the rows of seated diners, her head held high the way she had carried herself in that Wanhsien tavern so many years before. Scurrying behind came two young men, both westerners of some kind, all big nose and bulging eyes, one carrying a set of drums, the other, I was pleased to note, a moon guitar. When they were seated cross-legged behind her, she signaled to the butler, who rang the gong again and called for silence. Without any preamble she opened her mouth, threw back her head, and gave out a single high note, holding it steady as it rose clear and pure to the rafters and hushed the rustling bells. Then the drummer came in with a light thrumming beat and the guitar gave a few chords, she still singing the same note until at last she cut it off, breathed in almost imperceptibly, and began the song.

"After the first line I realized with a start that she was singing one of my own compositions, put to music I knew not by whom, a haunting tune full of melancholy, perfectly suited to the poem, which was a mother's lament for her son who had been taken by the army conscripters and was headed for the desert. Her voice, once so technically perfect, its passion arising from her own will to succeed, now was colored and deepened by emotion and experience. Her range and power were undiminished, but there was a profound conviction in the lament that brought a prickle of tears even to my eyes.

"She finished and an immediate storm of acclamation roared out, almost as loud as that which had greeted my effort, I joining in, thumping the table, then recalling where I was and limiting myself to shouts of approbation. When the sound died down she bowed to the head table. She was not twenty paces from me, her face radiant, eyes sparkling, a huge smile breaking through the solemn performance mask. Then she walked slowly to the rear of the hall.

"The other three contestants came and went, but on such an evening as that, there was never any doubt that she would triumph as I had, and my mind wandered as they sang (quite creditably all of them); I was in a daze of joy, being at the emperor's table, her presence in the hall, all buzzing about in my head quite unassimilated, one minute buoyed up on a great wave of euphoria, the next pondering on the fickleness of fame and other similar topics that spring to mind at such moments.

"I also wondered a little anxiously whether Hsuan Tsung would enquire as to who had penned the verses that she had put to music, for although my poem was nominally set in the time of the Han Dynasty and castigated that house's great fifth emperor for his bloodthirsty martial fervor, any fool could see that it spoke directly of Hsuan Tsung's own campaigns. In the thirty years he had been on the throne—thirty years of unprecedented peace and prosperity in the core empire—the campaigns on the borders had never stopped, campaigns to chastise the Koreans and our uneasy client kingdom of Silla, or those driving into the deep south, always pushing the borders of the Annamese protectorate further and further south, others probing into the great Nan-chao kingdom that bordered Burma, others still fruitlessly pursuing the Tibetans across the arid plateaus and precipices they call home.

"The common people paid for it all, of course, as they always have. Both in the endlessly rising taxes levied to fund the vast armies that we were obliged to maintain on the borders and in the regular decimation of their menfolk, each new set of doomed recruits whipped along the road west, new fodder for the dusty killing grounds where they struggled against the desert tribes, Turks and Uighurs, Khitan and Hsiung Nu, and a thousand others. Hsuan Tsung had harnessed the vast wealth of the core empire to the military machine and taken war to the Tartars' very homes, and now our forces had driven so deep into barbarian territory that the distance between Chang An and Canton, our principal city in the south, was only half that from the capital to our westernmost outpost, beyond Samarkand at the edge of the Mountains of Heaven. But at what cost? The human cost I had written about in many a poem including that which Peony—or Hsueh Tao as I must now think of her—had sung that evening. But more important might be the cost to the empire itself. Even then, traveling almost constantly as I did, I had a unique perspective; I knew more of what was really going on than all the high officials in the capital put together. I knew that the cost in manpower and treasure was becoming unbearable. I had seen the empty villages with my own eyes while crisscrossing the northeast, the mud shacks collapsed, the fields overgrown with weeds. Sickened by the loss of their sons and fathers and brothers, by the taxes that meant borrowing to pay, selling children to pay, the peasants had fled south, far, far south where the tax collector and the conscripter couldn't reach them. Such disappearances, of course, only served to worsen the burden on those who stayed.

"I knew too, having visited their camps that the arrogance and power-lust of the generals who commanded these huge armies—hundreds upon hundreds of thousands of men, territories half the size of China—were swelling day by day, along with their resentment, which was deepened each time they visited the capital and came to banquets like this, scorned as an unpleasant necessity by the Confucians and the aristocrats ('You don't make good steel into nails or good men into soldiers.' Who hasn't heard that old saw?), lavishly rewarded by the emperor for their loyalty, paid off, and then sent back to the desert where all the silks and gold cups would avail them nothing.

"Sometimes in my dreams the burden of this knowledge would press down upon me and I would wake sweating and screaming from some terrible vision of what was to come. I saw a horizon obscured by smoke, the fields burnt, stack upon stack of gaunt gray corpses by the side of the road. But who could I tell? I could only write about those terrible dreams. Anything else would have been suicidal. Even so, blood-drenched visions forced themselves into my verses, even my most whimsical flights of fancy. Take the poem I wrote after a year in Chang An. It is a dream poem telling of a journey to Lotus Blossom Peak and a meeting with the star maiden and Wei the immortal on the Cloud Terrace. This is how it ends:

We feasted,
Then, in a blur they were gone,
Riding their swans over the purple darkness.

Left alone, I looked back and down to the earth,
At Loyang, and behold!
Far and wide Tartar troops were speeding
And rivers of blood flooded the scrub-grass plains,
Jackals and wolves were riding about,
Dressed in officials' robes and caps.

"Perhaps it is from looking back, from knowing now what was to come, but over all my memories of Chang An in those years, all those bright summer days in the Pear Gardens, the polo matches and cockfights, the vast hunting expeditions, the banquets and concerts, over all that hangs the dark shadow of the rebellion, the cataclysm that Rohkshan, sitting only a few feet away from me on that night, was to release, decades of chaos, famine, and war, all let loose because that fat Sogdian felt unappreciated. Of such absurdities are our lives—and deaths—made.

"Of course, no such thoughts crossed my mind that evening. There was little time for brooding, anyway, for the singing soon came to an end and, as I knew it must, the prize went to Hsueh Tao. The emperor sent a eunuch to fetch her, and she emerged from behind the gauze curtain once more and walked up the central aisle, walking directly towards me, her every movement still as achingly familiar as if we had parted the day before. Before she reached us, however, the emperor asked her to give us another song, which she did, a piece called 'Astrakhan Coat' that was very popular in the capital at the time. This was greeted with equal acclaim and Hsuan Tsung called her over to the Seven Jewels table, just as he had called me over earlier.

"She came and bowed low to him, but he quickly raised her up, smiling with open pleasure, his mood very bubbly.

"'Excellent, excellent. A wonderful rendition, quite fresh, though the entire time I was asking myself: *Why is this the first time I am hearing her sing?* I think that there must be a conspiracy afoot to keep me from hearing the most talented performers in the empire, what with Li Po here suddenly appearing out of nowhere and then Miss. . . . What is your name again, my dear?'

"'I am called Hsueh Tao, Your Highness,' her voice very mild and low. Hearing her speak again sent a jet of pleasure and melancholy through me so strong that I almost cried out.

"'Hsueh Tao, eh, *Snow Peach,* a lovely name, I . . . '

"Suddenly, Gwei-fei, still sitting on one side, pulled him around, almost roughly, pulled his ear down to her mouth and whispered something that brought a flush to Hsuan Tsung's pallid cheeks. Without a word they rose, the two of us forgotten, and walked rapidly out into the main hallway, a dozen assorted eunuchs and other flunkies jumping from their seats and scurrying after them.

"Bemused, I looked at Hsueh Tao. A servant had brought her one of the low banqueting seats and she settled gracefully into it, adjusting her purple damask gown before turning to regard me.

"'Did you hear what she said to him?' I asked her.

"'No.'

"'She said, *I want to fuck you, my big bull. Now.*'

"Hsueh Tao—Peony as I still thought of her—threw back her head and laughed, not a giggle, no coquettish covering of the mouth with her hand, but an outright guffaw. She and Gwei-fei had that in common at least. For me, just saying those words, even in jest, was almost too much, sent my thoughts reeling back to those nights on the boat, her hot flesh, her little whimpers.

"'It's sad though,' I said, 'isn't it?'

"At this, she frowned and glanced around quickly. Many of the guests were drifting away in ones and twos—apparently the emperor's abrupt departure was nothing new and had signaled the end of the feast. We were alone at the Seven Jewels table.

"'Sad or not, you must watch what you say,' she said, leaning forward and speaking in a low voice. 'You could be executed for a remark like that.'

"I shrugged my shoulders, but she was very insistent, reaching forward and grasping my arm and speaking with great conviction.

"'It has been a very long time since we were together, Li Po, but let me say that if you are still the same impulsive, contrary man you once were, you'd best leave Chang An now, before you do yourself some terrible damage.'

"I smiled but said nothing. There seemed nothing for me to say. After a while, she shook her head.

"'Come with me,' she said briskly, rising from her seat and shaking out her skirts. She had all the decisiveness of old, but now a new authority to go with it. She was used to commanding, to getting what she wanted, and who was I to argue with that?

"'All right,' I said and stood up.

"She had a palanquin waiting outside the hall, one of many along with sedan chairs and carriages that clogged the outer courtyard.

"'Time to go home,' she said and the eight bearers, who had been squatting in a circle playing dice, jumped up and took their places under the shafts. We climbed in—there was just enough room for two people to sit opposite each other and she drew the curtains. In the darkness she reached forward and took my hand in hers.

"'I'm sorry,' she said, squeezing my hand briefly, then letting go.

"Once again, I remained silent. We swayed along for a few minutes and then she said: 'And are you the same man?'

"'I am,' I replied, 'But you have changed.'

"'Yes, I suppose I have. I . . . but let's not talk now. I must see your face when I talk to you.'

"She didn't live far from the palace complex. Within minutes, I heard a gate swing open and we were deposited in the front courtyard of a small house. A high wall surrounded the house, and fruit trees—cherries, peaches, and apricots—grew in abundance around the courtyard. There were two huge jasmine bushes on either side of the front door, both covered in a profusion of tiny yellow-white buds, and we were enveloped in a cloud of fragrance as a servant ushered us in. Once inside, she led me to a small room off the main hall. The floor was covered in sea-grass matting and a low red lacquer table sat in the middle, atop it a glass vase holding a single yellow carnation. She called for wine to be warmed, and I saw that there were two scrolls facing each other on the side walls, both featuring calligraphy by the same hand—muscular black lines slashing across and down. The signature was hers.

"When the wine had been served and the servant dismissed, we sat opposite each other sipping the warm liquid.

"'I'm not sure what to say, now that you are here,' she said matter-of-factly. 'Perhaps it was a mistake.'

"But it wasn't a mistake, for after a few awkward minutes

we fell to talking easily as we had in the old days, as though there had been no gap, no years of pain and joy, of travel and growth in between, as though we were back in the cabin of that boat once again, breathlessly recounting our hopes and dreams. Now of course we were telling tales of the past, but the essential harmony, the way we fitted together so smoothly, was the same. The candles burnt low, the servant brought more wine, then was sent to bed. Outside a nightjar called incessantly for hours, then finally was silenced by the coming dawn.

"She told me of her years under the protection of Prefect Huang, how at last she had broken free of him. A kindly man, but limiting, he would not let her sing outside his home. In that time she had devoted much effort to the study of poetry and even circulated a few pieces which had been well received. She had left Huang on good terms, however, and he had given her this house and a small sum in gold, enough to set herself up as a courtesan. That had been eight years ago and since then she had prospered, her reputation growing slowly, her poems gaining circulation, slowly establishing herself, taking the position she had talked about on the boat as an independent courtesan, the greatest courtesan in the city.

"For my part I told her of my travels, my wives and children, of Wu Yun and the Princess Jade Perfection and my summons. But all the time I was marveling at her, at this smooth coming together after so long. Only a few times in our lives are we privileged to come across our completing halves, our other selves from whom we seem to have been separated at birth, so complete is the mutual understanding. She was such a one. The only one.

"We talked and talked until my voice was dry and the wine gone, that deep understanding swelling again despite the chasm of years, the words weaving us closer and closer until a silence fell and I said to her:

"'I wrote a poem for you after you had gone:

Fair one, when you were here I filled the house
with flowers.
Fair one, now you are gone—
only an empty bed left behind.
On the bed, the embroidered quilt is rolled up;
I cannot sleep.
It is three years since you went
but the perfume of your body still
clings to the quilt.
That's all I have, a fading scent.

Yellow leaves fall from the branch;
Dew twinkles white on the green moss.
Where are you, my beloved?

"She said nothing, merely closed her eyes and looked away for a time, then turned back.

"'And I wrote many poems for you my dear Li Po, mostly trying to explain, mostly very bad. I have kept only a few. This one is called *Falcon Parted from the Gauntlet*:

Vision keen as bell-ring,
talons, sword-tip sharp:

she seized hares, out on the plains,
and pleased his
high-flying will.

Then,
she bolted, by chance, beyond
that noble,
lofty cloud.

Now she no longer perches
on the forearm of her lord."

Here Li Po, still lying back in the prow, his left hand trailing in the water, his eyes closed, falls silent. Wang Lung and the girls watch expectantly for some minutes, but he doesn't stir. Presently the boat boy, who has been wading in the shallows collecting water lilies, having no interest in fantastic tales, returns dripping wet and carrying on his back a straw basket filled with the bulbous pink flowers. The others don't see him and he climbs quietly onto the boat and carefully unstraps the basket. But in depositing it, the boy knocks a wine pot off one of the gunwales, and it smashes to pieces on the floor of the boat. At this, Li Po's eyes spring open and he sits up.

"That's all. The tale's over. It's time to go home. Like all the best stories it ends in joy, for there is already enough sorrow in our lives. So just be content to know that all the lovers in the story were joined in sweet bliss, all evil men were thrown down, and the children grew up strong and healthy and knew the dream of cap and robe of high office, siring generations of their own, on and on, nothing but rank, riches, and progeny down the ages. What more could anyone ask for?"

He stands up a little unsteadily and shrugs off the feather cape, rolls it up carefully, and returns it to the bag.

"And besides," the poet says, yawning hugely, "I must get the girls back to their house. The proprietress was most insistent that they return before sunset."

ten 李白

BUT OF COURSE, THAT ISN'T THE END OF THE STORY. The next day when Wang Lung walks out onto the foredeck, he finds the poet is there already, breakfasting austerely on dried seaweed, rice, and pickles. His mouth full, cheeks bulging, the bowl held up in one hand, chopsticks in the other, Li Po waves him over and points his chopsticks at the low table, where for the first time in a month, brushes, inkstone, and an inkstick have been laid out.

"Come, sit. Sit," he says through a mouthful of rice.

And when he is ready, the last of the rice dispatched, a cup of thick Oolong tea in his hand, he begins again:

"The day after I had won the poetry competition, I received another summons to the palace, this time to the office of one of the senior eunuchs—all blackwood furniture and racks of scrolls, more like a scholar's study than a petty administrator's den. He told me with a smirk that one of his men would escort me to my new lodgings. I knew nothing of any new lodgings but had no desire to ask anything of this unctuous functionary, so simply nodded my head and climbed into the gilded palanquin that awaited me. After ten minutes or so, we passed through a gate and then along a winding drive, which I could see by twitching aside the brocade curtains was lined with rows of poplars standing in lines as neat as soldiers on parade. The palanquin swayed on for another few minutes, I craning my head out of the little window to see ahead, without much success. When we finally stopped, I jumped out almost before the bearers had lowered the shafts to the ground.

"Before me was a splendid mansion set on a little hill with a view of the red-tiled roofs of the city and the gardens that surrounded it. At the rear I could see what must be stables and the kitchens, perhaps servants' quarters, too. There was no sign of the escort I had been promised, and before I could say anything, the bearers lined up in their places alongside the palanquin's shafts, heaved it up and around, and trotted off, disappearing behind the screen of trees that hid the drive.

"That was my first introduction to Hsuan Tsung's extravagant generosity. When I thanked him effusively a few days later, he said it was no less than I deserved for my triumph in the poetry competition, and that, anyway, it was nothing much, just a place to sleep, though in truth it was one of the finest houses in the city, worthy of a duke.

"That extraordinary gift left me in a strange position, however, for I had barely enough money to eat fried wheat cakes at the nearest street stall (a long trudge down from the house it was, too, through a wealthy residential neighborhood where the servants gave me some very strange looks indeed, knowing I was not one of them, but also knowing that if I was rich enough to live there, I was rich enough not to walk). I certainly had nothing to spare for the horde of servants needed to run such a place, and for the first few weeks slept on a mat in one of the front rooms, leaving the rest of the place shuttered and sealed.

"But I spent little time there at first, being either at the palace or in the company of Hsueh Tao, as she insisted I call her. 'Peony,' she said, stretching her eyes wide in disbelief, 'how could I ever have been called Peony? Every farm girl from Canton to Loyang is called Peony.' This was said to me in bed, the early morning spring sunshine pouring in through the open windows, a cool breeze bringing the intoxicating scent of jasmine from the bushes outside. In those first months, we spent much of our time together in bed. Like a couple of children, we seemed to be discovering the joys of the flesh anew, and in a way, I suppose we were, for it was as though the intervening years of sorrow and joy had rolled back, leaving us innocent again. Just as it had been when we began to talk that first night—the deep familiarity, the bond renewed with greater strength—so it was when I reached out at last for her: the same glowing heat, the same sensation of almost unbearable urgency, those same cries wrenched from us both. Her skin seemed softer, creamier, more luscious with age, more forgiving perhaps than the taut flesh of youth, flesh to bury oneself in forever, snuffing up the scent of her, almost unbearably familiar and yet changed, a smell of peaches and passion, a smell of home.

"Quite apart from the burning pleasures of the bedchamber, however, she was once again my friend, someone who could guide me through the intricacies of the court, the matters of manner and form whose omission would seem foolish or, worse, provincial. It is rarely good to be regarded as a fool (except by one's enemies, of course), but at the imperial court it is crippling. Of more immediate practical use, Hsueh Tao also insisted that I take a loan from her; naturally, I couldn't have asked her myself, but was happy—indeed relieved—to accept when offered. The money proved most useful, too, for that day I was invited to the palace for a celebration to mark the spring festival of Cold Food, a time when a series of grand cockfights are always held.

"The emperor, you see, was obsessed by cockfighting. Oh, he undertook the other diversions well enough, hunting, hawking, polo, and so on. But for much of the time I was at court, he was completely taken up by fighting birds. For myself I have never liked the creatures, which aren't really like true birds at all, lacking all the qualities that make, say, a migrating goose or a proud fish-owl admirable. Apart from anything else, their pinion feathers, the key flying feathers, are clipped so they become utterly earthbound, capable only of a few awkward flapping leaps in the cockpit. Cocks are completely domesticated and profoundly stupid because of it, resistant to any communication, lacking some wild understanding that their free cousins retain. And when trained to fight they are even more unattractive, full of rage and arrogance, constantly pampered and stroked, entirely unnatural.

"Nevertheless I enjoyed the thrill of watching them fight as much as any man, the glinting slash of steel spurs, the roaring crowd, and the rancid smell of greed and sweat mixed with that of cheap millet spirit and the ammonia reek of bird shit, feathers flying in the air and blood on the sand, the bravery and pathos of watching a blinded bird flail out vainly, its opponent circling behind for the death blow. And though I didn't much like the cocks, I know birds deep in my bones, even such emasculated specimens, and I had an excellent sense of which to back, a talent that stood me in good stead, for my spending habits were prodigious even by Chang An standards. My acumen—that I could spot a really game beast instantly and knew at once whether it had the brute determination to fight to the finish—also served to bring me into the emperor's inner circle in a way that poetry might never have done.

"I can confess now that, though I was renowned for my judgment of birds, in fact I paid as much mind to trainer as to cock, for a sharp trainer who really understands his charges is almost more important than the appearance of the bird itself. I don't mean the kind of man who went in for gimcrack, underhanded tricks like smearing the bird's feathers with raccoon-dog grease, the smell of which cocks hate, or dusting mustard powder under its wings. (The mustard, if you are wondering, my boy, is used because when birds fight they often thrust their heads under each others' wings to try and unbalance their opponent. The powder makes the bird's eyes run; it can't see properly and your fight is over.) No, a really good trainer knows instinctively which birds have the strength and stamina to be winners and just as importantly when to fight a bird and when to let him rest.

"These men—the most talented trainers—were much beloved by Hsuan Tsung. He showered gifts on them: country estates, bolts of silk and brocade, the finest horses, jewelry, golden cups and spoons and chopsticks, all of which excited the envy of other courtiers. But it was the Confucianists who reserved their most bitter spite for such men. To the Mandarins they represented everything that had changed for the worse in their ruler. There was nothing unusual in this, of course: remember what happened to Tai Tsung, first emperor of the Tang. He was much enamored of hawking but was so intimidated by his chief minister—an old tutor—that when out riding one day and seeing the old man approach, he tucked his goshawk into the breast of his heavy robe. The chief minister, who must have spotted the emperor's guilty expression, contrived to launch into a long, rambling diatribe on the state of political affairs, during the course of which the goshawk suffocated. Presumably a lesson was supposed to be imparted to the young emperor, but it was a typical Confucian action, fueled by a brutish self-righteousness.

"For the Mandarins of Hsuan Tsung's court, matters were much different, however; they could not expect such deference, something that was all the more galling because until a few years before they had been held in high honor. For the first twenty-five years of his reign, Hsuan Tsung had heeded their counsel scrupulously and lavished rewards of rank and title on them. Then suddenly, five years before, he had seemed to lose interest in the business of governing the empire (perhaps it had come too easily; year after year of prosperity and military triumph), and turned to pleasure and luxury for diversion. Like little children who have had their toys taken away, the Mandarins were by turns puzzled, disbelieving, and enraged that the imperial countenance had been so abruptly withdrawn. They wrote endless memorials excoriating the waste of state resources on everything from the pearl-inlaid walls of the Ta Ming Palace to the hunts that swept across huge swaths of the countryside, leaving them bare of life. More practically, perhaps, they turned their craftiest wiles into smearing Hsuan Tsung's new objects of admiration and companionship: the bird trainers, the falconers, the polo players, the eunuchs, Yang Gwei-fei and her relatives; in short, anyone who seemed to be feeding the emperor's sybaritic tendencies, a category into which they eventually placed me, too.

"In those days, though, I thought nothing of such matters as palace intrigue. My greatest concern was that Hsueh Tao couldn't share the pleasure of such gaudy and raucous festivals at the palace, for she was not invited to the Cold Food cockfights or to anything else for that matter. As we had both seen, Gwei-fei was a possessive woman (she had much reason to be so, too, considering the emperor's history of discarded wives and concubines), who tried her best to keep her charge out of temptation's way and knew a potential rival when she saw one. That evening in the Hall of Golden Bells, Hsueh Tao had been invited to perform only because the emperor and Gwei-fei had just made up from a month-long spat the day before, so that Gwei-fei for once had no control over the guest list.

"This situation—being effectively barred from the palace—actually suited Hsueh Tao very well. She was freed from the usual worries about palace intrigues and jealousies, instead continuing with her round of poetry and banquets among the very large set of officials who shunned the more frivolous side of court life. She was much respected in this world, I soon found, and with good reason, for her verse-making skills had flowered along with her singing to the point that I would sit and smile to myself, watching her hold back her richest lines so as not to show up the poverty of talent that afflicted the other guests. Her shining qualities—her beauty, wit, grace, and poetic and musical skills—made her much in demand as a society hostess, often at official functions, for the wives of the various governors and ministers who were her chief employers could not, of course, be seen at public occasions. And when it became generally known that she had taken me as her lover, her life was further improved, she told me, free of the constant plague of middle-aged men making moon-eyes at her or sending round their servants with lavish gifts: 'It is enough to make me think of becoming a nun after all, if I ever do collect enough money to be really independent. At least then I wouldn't have to put up with the constant pawing and sighing. Absurd! And particularly so from men who usually have three or four wives at home and a mistress or two in another quarter, all of them left to burn in their lonely beds because he is too drunk, too tired, or has dallied with some flower girl and spent what little pneuma he has, his watery reserves of passion, on her. What pathetic creatures you men are! Like greedy little boys eating honey.'

"All this said with those lustrous great eyes flashing fire and indignation and a contemptuous toss of the head that would have left the subjects of her scorn limp as boiled noodles. Peony—Hsueh Tao—had not lost her own ardor with age; if anything it had grown stronger, both in bed and out.

"So despite her absence (she never liked cockfighting anyway: 'Why should I want to watch a couple of chickens squabble?'), I happily took my borrowed stake of 500 cash to the cockpit that Hsuan Tsung had recently constructed between the Ta Ming and the neighboring Palace City, where the rest of the royal family was housed. He had done this principally to please Gwei-fei, who was a great fan of the fights but found the arena at the cockwalk uncomfortable and smelly. The new pit was built entirely of aloeswood, an extravagance aimed at protecting her delicate nose from the rank odors of battle. Not the true resin-dripping 'sinks-in-water' aloe, that dark and diseased wood best for medical use, for burning in a thurible or decoction in wine. This was the younger, healthy wood that gave off the same lush scent when cut. But the scent soon faded, so that each time she visited, the planks had to be shaved deep. After her fifth visit, they were so reduced that the structure collapsed in a violent summer thunderstorm.

"On that day, though, the new cockpit had just been completed, and everywhere the sweet, heady aroma of aloe filled the air, mixing with the pungent smoke from scattered pots of hundred-blend aromatic paste burning under the stands. It was a strange atmosphere for a cockfight, particularly with the ladies of the court standing in a squealing mass, waving their sachets of camphor under their noses with one hand and pointing to the desperate birds in the pit with the other. Naturally Gwei-fei was the most brilliant among them, shining like a blazing torch in the darkness, clinging to the emperor's arm, giving out her deep chuckle to his passing comments, but all the time keeping her eyes firmly fixed on the bloody contest, licking her lips, and shivering with excitement.

"She looked up as I approached the royal pair, raising her head from the spectacle of the defeated rooster lying in the dust, cawing feebly, its lifeblood pumping out from a great slash in its throat. Her lips were drawn back slightly, baring her pearly teeth. Then, as her eyes caught mine, I glimpsed a glow of animal lust, a fierce hunger that sent a violent shock rippling through me. She was usually so like a little child—plump and girlish, full of high spirits, always giggling—and the contrast, that look of profound knowledge and feral desire, a look that spoke of boreal twilight and frenzied rutting, halted me in my tracks.

"But then her gaze refocused, she recognized me and smiled, the animal fire in her eyes dimmed, and she pulled coquettishly on Hsuan Tsung's sleeve for attention, pointing at me. He called me over, asked very cordially how I was, then more urgently whether I knew anything of cocks: his picks from the imperial cock walk had lost four times in a row, and he was beginning to doubt his own judgment. I averred that I had some knowledge of the birds, and we walked over to the run on one side of the stands where his charges were kept. I saw at once that the proximity of the pit with its sounds and smells of battle had brought the birds to a state of near prostration, so excited had they become.

"They were in no condition to fight, I told Hsuan Tsung. If he wished to fight them today, he must move the cocks to a covered area, well provided with water and preferably darkened, for at least an hour. Then one of them, perhaps the fellow with the outsize comb and the glossy green-and-blue primaries, might be in a condition to conduct himself with honor. Hsuan Tsung gazed at me uncertainly, but I had spoken with such assurance that eventually he nodded and instructed one of his handlers to do as I said. Then he strolled away, saying he would return in a few hours.

"I passed some anxious moments alone with those accursed birds, knowing that in the way of courts, if I failed now I might never have the chance to shine before his eyes again, however many accursed poems I wrote. The handler and I moved five of the most likely looking cocks to a small room under the stands, and there I tried to calm the birds, speaking to them in the fashion I had learned on Mount Tai. And gradually, with agonizing slowness, some responded, I willing the rapid beating of their hearts to slow, their darting eyes to shut for a few moments. At last, after the allotted time had nearly passed, I was confident of the bird I had picked earlier, he of the long drooping scarlet comb. I picked him up, strapped the wicked steel blades to his legs, and carried him carefully out.

"Hsuan Tsung was sitting in the royal stand with Gwei-fei. She was giggling and dropping candied mango slices into his open mouth. When he saw me carrying the bird, he smiled and waved encouragingly. Within minutes, it became known that the emperor wished his bird to fight, and a match was arranged with a cock belonging to the Duke of Hsieh. I shall not describe the battle itself—who has not seen a cockfight or read a breathless account of the maneuvers, the hackneyed comparisons to famous duels, in some second-rate poem? I will say, however, that it was a very close-run thing, my bird strutting confidently out, his comb standing straight up, attacking so ferociously that the other side called their break first. He was hardly touched then, but when they were put back in the pit, I could see that I might have mistaken his stamina, that he was fading.

"Sure enough, he was soon moving more and more slowly until, suddenly, his opponent sensed an opening and surged into the air, landing on his back with a crash and throwing him to the ground where he lay, stunned. I immediately called our break and rushed over to his side. I saw with a sinking heart that his wing was broken. Still, his eye was as fierce as ever, if a little confused, so I blew some water down his throat, wiped off a deep cut in his leg, held the quivering body close to my chest for a few moments, speaking softly to calm him, then carried him back to the pit just in time for the gong.

"My bird stood perfectly still as the other circled him, his useless wing trailing on the ground, bright eyes following his opponent. There was a great flurry of feathers and he staggered back, blood dripping from another cut on his leg, now listing to one side like a holed ship. The other bird, sensing victory, gathered itself and scurried in for the final charge. But just as he was about to strike, my long-combed wonder gave a convulsive heave of his good wing. That desperate effort was enough to push him a few inches into the air. His leg shot out and he slashed the other across the top of its beak, slicing open one eye and causing a gaping wound above the other so that blood began to pour down, blinding his opponent, who gave out an agonized squawk and began to stumble about in circles. At this, an umpire stepped in and declared the emperor's bird the victor.

"I looked up, completely wrung out, a sheen of sweat covering my forehead. Hsuan Tsung was beaming at me with appreciation. I beamed back awash in relief and warm with the knowledge that I had bet my entire 500 cash on my bird—Hsuan Tsung's bird—at odds of ten to one.

"Thereafter, I was at the palace almost every day, either touring the cock walk with the emperor, endlessly running over the merits and weaknesses of the various birds, methods of feeding and training (fighting with dummy spurs and so on), or lounging in some beautifully appointed hall or perfectly manicured garden, drinking and singing and composing verses for Hsuan Tsung or his lady. Once, on the Festival of the Peonies, in the midst of their revels, surrounded by the glory of the Pear Gardens, the exquisite music of Lu wafting into the clear air, they were both struck with melancholy and I was called in to capture for them the beauty of the passing moment. I was half-drunk, having been taken from a tavern where a group of poets and officials who called themselves the Eight Immortals of the Wine Cup had been doing their best to live up to the name. But I dashed some water on my face and hurried to the Ta Ming Palace.

"It was a spring evening, the shadows lengthening but the light still so pure and magical that it turned the park into a perfect wonderland, every leaf picked out on every tree, and the hundreds of peonies that had been gathered for the festival aglow with a soft scarlet fire. I found Hsuan Tsung and Gwei-fei sitting in a little pavilion overlooking the lotus pond, watching the swans glide through the still waters, parting the long strands of duckweed that lay like ribbons of jade between the clumps of pink flowers. A cloud of iridescent blue-and-red dragonflies hovered over the lake, darting to and fro. Above the palace walls, spring clouds gathered and a cool breeze ruffled the trailing willow vines that hung in the water.

"After I had made a rather clumsy obeisance, I saw that Gwei-fei's usually sparkling eyes were red with weeping, her face cast down, and that Hsuan Tsung too looked glum. Whatever the reason for their sadness, most probably an excess of pleasure, I knew that if I made her happy, so in turn would the emperor's spirits revive, just as the sunrise follows the night. I set about to do so by the simplest of methods, singing extravagant praises of her beauty in three songs. The first one went like this:

> The glory of the trailing clouds in her garments
> And the radiance of a flower in her face.
> Oh heavenly apparition, found only far above
> On the Mountain of Myriad Jewels, or
> The Crystal Palace of the moon fairy.
> Yet I see her in an earthly garden. . . .

"And so on. Fairly standard stuff, you may say, but true when I wrote it and right for the moment, for Gwei-fei looked up, chin trembling at my first effort, gave a small smile at the second in which I swore that her beauty outdid every other royal companion, even the legendary Lady Flying Swallow of Han, and lit up with her customary radiance in the last, chuckling with pleasure at the lines in which her beauty outshone the massed ranks of peonies, rendering them limp and deathly pale. They both clapped in delight when I had finished, Hsuan Tsung called for wine and musicians, and we stayed in the pavilion until late that night, laughing and singing under the light of a gibbous moon.

"They were a strange pair, at least by mortal standards, though, of course, mortal standards didn't apply to them. Even after spending many such evenings with them, I can't say I understood the reasoning of either one's heart. They seemed entirely mismatched for one thing, she garrulous, frothy, full of energy, but also a shrewd judge of others, not a schemer—she had no love of power for its own sake—but a natural manipulator, fiercely protective of his love, or infatuation, or fixation, call it what you will. Hsuan Tsung, on the other hand, was a man who had changed his habits so completely that he was hardly recognizable—formerly ascetic, abstemious, and urgent in persuading others to follow his example, serious, even dull, preoccupied with matters such as raising tax revenue without increasing taxes and the funding of canal construction, an avid procreator (witness his seventy-five offspring) but known to be somewhat perfunctory in matters of the bedchamber, as though he was consciously performing a dynastic duty rather than pursuing his own pleasure.

"So it had been until five years before. Now he was utterly changed, seeking only amusement, brought to the council chamber barely a few times a month, reluctant to rise for the dawn audiences at which barbarian ambassadors were greeted and much of the day's administrative business done.

And, of course, a slave to his lust for Gwei-fei. Yet there were still some traces of his old self to be seen. His eyes were full of a knowledge of coming tragedy, and he still rarely smiled, except for when in the presence of his beloved. With her, he became animated in a babbling, foolish way, his eyes then empty of all but a goatish carnality infused with a desperate longing.

"I came to regard him with some affection, at least the man I knew when we were away from Gwei-fei, a man deeply steeped in literature, a fair poet, an excellent huntsman, and a good companion in the field or at the banqueting table. But I never honestly came to like her. She was too false at the core, a quality most obvious in his absence, when she would shed her girlish airs and coquettish pout and allow her inner self to peep out for awhile—a wild, almost insane spirit that could hardly be contained by the palace walls and that rebelled at the court's endless pomp and formality. I remember one time, when Hsuan Tsung was away on one of his extravagantly large hunting expeditions in the frozen north, I accompanying him, along with a few hundred others, she conducted a mock adoption of Rohkshan. I heard only the most sketchy rumors on my return (even in that intrigue-ridden atmosphere, most people were too frightened to repeat such things) but it appeared that he had been naked except for a huge white woolen diaper and had waddled about after her as she walked through the Pear Gardens, sucking his thumb, her ladies shrieking with laughter and pelting him with plums. What the purpose of this show had been, what events had followed, I could hardly guess. But I did know that little good could come of it, even after I found out that not only had Hsuan Tsungn known about the 'adoption,' he had encouraged it.

"The true, secret life a man and woman lead together, we can never understand. Perhaps we can never even understand the man or woman alone. As emperor Hsuan Tsung was far more alone than most men, and it often seemed to me that he had been playing at roles for so long —wise emperor, martial lord, pleasure-sated dilettante, infatuated lover—that there was nothing left of the true man inside, just a hollowed-out shell.

"I remember once on a very cold spring morning we were riding on the great northern plain, very far west, on the edge of the true steppe. It was soon after dawn, the ocher earth stretching away on either side to a far purple horizon in the east, the vast bowl of the sky arching overhead, beginning to lighten, a handful of stars twinkling in the still-black west.

"I was watching Hsuan Tsung as he released a snow-white gerfalcon, deliberately loosening her jesses, then slipping off the hood and, after a moment to allow her to take in her surroundings, to understand that she was back in her native place, no longer chained to a perch in the gloom of the royal mews, throwing her in the air. The first rays of sun glowed around us, bathing Hsuan Tsung in a soft orange light as the bird launched itself into the frigid air with a few wingbeats of flashing white. His face was set and expressionless, untouched by the glory of the new day or the aching beauty of the hawk in flight, quite dead and unfeeling. It was eerie, as though he was a body animated by some mere mechanical force, as if some malevolent spirit had burrowed into him and eaten away at his essential self until all that remained were the external motions.

"I looked away from him and thanked the gods that I was alive and feeling the cold air around me, the icy wind cutting through my sable pelisse. I sucked in a deep breath and felt the sheer joy of living another day burst upwards in me, racing through my veins and pulsing so strongly that I could hardly sit still in the saddle. An austringer rode up behind us and handed the emperor another falcon, this one mottled gray and black. Hsuan Tsung released the bird, then turned automatically to receive another, a crested goshawk. On and on this continued for the whole morning, each bird returning with the limp body of a bird or rabbit clutched in its claws to be received by one of the attendants. At the end of the day, Hsuan Tsung had taken nineteen quail, ten green pigeons, and five rabbits.

"A few weeks later we were hawking in the forest and had become separated from the bulk of the party—only myself, the emperor, Kao Li Shih (the chief eunuch, who was always at his side), and a few guards, riding in silence through a thick stand of pine. The quiet was broken by a loud shrieking above our heads, and I looked up to see a sparrowhawk drop from a branch and disappear into the heavy undergrowth. Just above where it had been perching, there was a nest, a circle of broken branches stuck into the rim forming a miniature fence. I called out to Hsuan Tsung, and he pulled round and ambled his horse over to where I had stopped.

"I pointed up to the nest. 'Did you every climb for chicks in your youth, sire?'

"He followed my gaze, then turned and smiled at me sadly.

"'You forget that I had a rather unusual upbringing.'

"Indeed, I had forgotten. He had been a boy in the time of the Empress Wu, surviving her wholesale slaughter of the imperial family only because of his youth. He and his brother had nevertheless spent ten years confined to a house in the palace grounds, barred from venturing farther than the small garden. An unusual upbringing indeed.

"'I thought you might want to take a sparrowhawk chick. You see, the branches ringing the nest are dry and the leaves yellow. That means the chicks are at least ten days old and can be taken from the nest without harm.'

"'What are the branches for?'

"'The mother puts them there to prevent the chicks from falling out of the nest.'

"'Oh.'

"He considered for a moment, then said, slightly puzzled: 'But why would I want another sparrowhawk? I have fifty in the mews already.'

"'But none is your own.'

"'They are all mine.'

"'They are yours, but only in the sense that a man can claim that every grain in a handful of sand is his. You don't know their names. You didn't find them and raise them up and train them. You don't *know* them.'

"Unspoken but hanging in the air was the thought that his cocks didn't win for the same reasons. Hsuan Tsung frowned, looking perplexed and slightly irritated. He wasn't used to even implied criticism or suggestions that his life was less than perfect.

"'So what do you suggest?'

"'I suggest that we climb up—there is a row of branches almost like a ladder—and take a chick each.'

"For a moment he continued to frown, and I feared I had gone too far. Then his brow cleared and he grinned, just as he must have grinned as a little boy, before the constant fear of sudden death and then the years of crushing responsibility had robbed him of his joy.

"'Very well. I haven't climbed a tree in . . . well, I can't remember when the last time was.'

"There was a great deal of fuss from the fat eunuch and, less volubly though still with grave conviction, from the captain of the guards. Hsuan Tsung listened patiently, then silenced them with a wave of his hand.

"'If it worries you all so much, you needn't stay. Captain, take your guards and find the other party. Kao, you accompany them.'

"This inevitably caused an even greater uproar, but when they saw he was serious, they had little choice but to go, Kao shooting venomous glances at me over his shoulder. We dismounted, tucked the hems of our robes into our belts, and Hsuan Tsung unbuckled his sword and dropped his elaborate gilded headpiece on the ground next to it.

"'Right, your majesty,' I said, squatting slightly and interlocking my fingers, 'put your foot in here and up you go.'

"Hsuan Tsung stepped into my clasped hands, then pulled himself up.

"'I'm going to have to go round a bit to get to the next branch,' he called down in a slightly strangled voice, staring upward, his head craned back.

"'Sire,' I called.

"'Yes?'

"'You have forgotten to pull me up.'

"'Oh, Li, I'm sorry. Do you think the branch will bear us?'

"'Certainly.'

"He leaned down and pulled mightily, hauling me up until I could reach out with my other hand and scramble onto the branch. We stood there side by side, he panting heavily, his eyes sparkling. Somewhere far off in another part of the forest we could hear the horns and cymbals of the others.

"'It'll be a long time before they find us.'

"'Yes,' he said, smiling. 'What a pleasant thought. Like escaping from lessons for a day.'

"We clambered up to the nest, the smooth soles of our riding boots slipping on the branches. There were four chicks in the nest, which made me happy—I always prefer to leave some behind—and they were peeping lustily, their gaping beaks pointed upwards, their eyes still sealed shut. Hsuan Tsung and I each slipped one of the tiny, warm bundles of down into our sleeves, then began to descend. Inside our sleeves the little birds redoubled their surprisingly loud peeping, reminding me of another time I had stolen chicks from a nest. Sure enough, when we were again standing on the lowest branch, preparing to lower ourselves to the ground, there was a frenzied beating of wings from the branches above us, and the mother bird appeared with some unrecognizable forest rodent clutched in her claws. Seeing us, she immediately dropped the length of bloody fur and plunged into an attack, heading straight for the emperor. Before I could do anything, he had flung up an arm to protect himself, overbalanced, and toppled backwards off the branch. I watched in horror as he fell, flailing his arms comically, the chick flying out of his sleeve. He came down with a soft thump on the thick carpet of pine needles, sat there for a moment, stunned but obviously uninjured, then frowned, leaned to one side, lifted up his buttock, and examined the ground beneath him. The chick had landed squarely under the royal posterior and was now a flat circle of tiny feathers.

"He looked up at me with such an expression of bewilderment that I began to laugh, leaning on the trunk to support myself, bowing my head, and bellowing with unrestrainable mirth. No man likes to be laughed at, least of all an emperor, but I couldn't help myself, and after a time he was laughing too, leaning back on the bed of pine needles and quaking.

"'Never mind, sire,' I said, dropping to the forest floor and fumbling in my sleeve for the chick. 'Take mine. I was never much of a hand at raising birds anyway, only at catching them.'

"He rose, brushed off the pine needles clinging to his robe, then came over and took the bird from me, holding it gently in his cupped palms. He opened his mouth to speak but was interrupted by the sound of the gongs and cymbals, much closer now, almost upon us. Evidently Kao Li Shih had lost no time in returning. At this, Hsuan Tsung's smile vanished and he quickly set about adjusting his dress and remounting, so that when Kao and a numerous body of courtiers and palace guards appeared a few moments later he was astride his horse, impassive, his usual dignified, regal self. The crowd quickly surrounded him, all calling questions and solicitations in high voices. Watching, I wondered at the confusion of beings in a man, until at last I heard him exclaim my name amidst the babble around him. A lane opened in the crowd and he beckoned to me with another of those rare smiles, then turned and rode away. I had seen him smile more in the last half-hour than for the six previous months, and that was something, at least. And with that thought, I dug my heels into the horse's flanks and set off to catch up.

"The months that followed were as near perfection as a man can ask for, like sailing a well-found craft downriver, with the wind behind and the current bearing you swiftly to your destination. Then one day I was playing chess with the emperor at the hot springs palace. I had surrounded most of his remaining pieces and the remaining moves were more or less a formality. Gwei-fei, who was an excellent player, stood watching over my shoulder, holding in her arms her little Tibetan terrier, a hairy but amiable creature that was much caressed by all. Just as I was about to make a decisive move, the dog gave an uncharacteristic yelp and bounded out of Gwei-fei's arms, landing on the chessboard and scattering all the pieces, then jumping to the floor and trotting away without a look backward.

"'Well,' Hsuan Tsung said, leaning back, 'I must thank the animal for my rescue, I find. It was a nasty position, though I might have surprised you yet, Li.'

"I made no reply to this but turned to glare at Gwei-fei, who smiled sweetly, then flounced off to catch the dog.

"'My mind is in a state of sad confusion, in any case, with my ministers all pressing for decisions on a great many tedious matters. The most vexing of all is the shifty fellows we employ to interpret for us. I have been obliged to order four of them executed after they were found conniving with the caravan-masters. They will pay enormous sums for information about the state of our relations with the Turks, whose territory they must of course pass by on their way west.'

"'Is it Turkic translators you need?' I asked casually.

"'Yes, above all.'

"'I have the tongue myself, your highness, was raised to it, one of my father's wives being from Bactria. Perhaps I could help.'

"So began my time assisting the emperor and his highest officials in the direction of imperial policy. My first task was to draft a letter to the Quaghahan himself, offering a minor princess in marriage in exchange for solemn promises of peace and five thousand prime horses, no less than three thousand of which must be mares. This last item was perhaps even more important than the promise of peace, for thanks to the endless levies, the empire was well equipped with soldiers but chronically short of horses, animals so vital to its defense. Even then the vast imperial pastures of Lung-yu in the southwest were suffering from almost constant harassment by the nearby Tibetans, tying down huge numbers of troops. Now, of course, the Tibetans have taken Lung-yu and much else besides, and we must rely entirely on the Turks for horses, a sorry predicament.

"I soon became a regular adviser to the emperor on Turkic policy, giving him my views on such matters as what terms the Quaghahan was likely to accept, interpreting the sincerity of his reply to our proposal, outlining what our response should be, and so on. At last I was involved in the great decisions of state and exercising my true talents. Only my lack of official position barred me from entrance to the formal state councils, and I often pressed Hsuan Tsung to give me some office, however minor. Quite apart from the official recognition and respect this would have given me, the steady official stipend and the annual rice ration would have been very welcome, too. He seemed strangely reluctant, however, even uneasy, making vague excuses and telling me that I had no need for some trumpery title, for I was to be honored with induction into the Han Lin Academy, his own private repository of genius. It was an odd institution, with far more musicians and poets among its members (and not a few conjurers and sword swallowers, if truth be known) than true statesmen. But Hsuan Tsung insisted it was the only way to bring me into his service without infuriating the rank-obsessed bureaucrats. He waved away my protests and said that if he brought in outsiders above the heads of those who had strived for their posts over several decades, he feared they might all resign in protest (thus losing precisely what they had for so long sought; an unlikely prospect!). Perhaps later, he said, when I had served him in the academy for awhile, then he could grant me an official title.

"And so, on the fifth day of the fifth month, I was inducted into the Han Lin Academy, a ceremony full of drums and gongs and much public honor which allowed me to shed my commoner's robes at last, though not for the uniform of the mandarinate, with its badges and seals of rank, but instead for an efflorescent yellow gown that Gwei-fei herself had designed for the new institution. Though it didn't carry official status, by joining the academy I became a member of the imperial household and thus could attend meetings of the state council and acknowledge openly my role in drafting documents and drawing up policy regarding the Turks. Because of my speed and facility with the formal language required in edicts, imperial circulars, and the like, it wasn't long before the emperor came to rely on me for drafting most of his documents, calling me to his side at all hours of the day and night.

"Once I was at a banquet given by my mentor Ho Chih Chang when I was summoned away to the palace. I found Hsuan Tsung closeted with Li Lin-fu, the chief minister, and several senior generals. Li, as always, gave me a black glare. He was a very commonplace man himself—no talent in writing, could hardly distinguish one character from another—and he was bitterly suspicious of anyone who had the gift, and particularly those who had poetic talent. But I ignored him, made my obeisance, and sat slightly to one side, waiting. They were discussing an incursion by the forces of the kingdom of Parhae into territory controlled by Silla, our client state. I knew nothing about the Korean peninsula and the northeast, so could contribute little. Indeed I must have dozed off for a while and woke to find a servant shaking me by the shoulder and the emperor and the others gazing at me with a variety of expressions, amusement from Hsuan Tsung, more than the usual contempt from the chief minister, and astonishment mixed with outrage from the generals.

"'Well, Li,' the emperor said smiling, 'you have chastised us with your snoring, and quite rightly, too, for we have been talking this over for far too long. There are few things more useless than a discussion that cannot come to a conclusion. Now, Li, if you will take up a brush, I want you to draft me an edict ordering Wang Liao, the commander of the Yuchou military district, to raise a punitive expedition to aid our friends in Silla. If we allow these provocations to go unpunished, they will only grow bolder. We will also need a letter for the chieftain of the Magal tribes to the north of Parhae seeking a concurrent attack, and another to the Quaghahan of the Turks to make sure he remains a neutral in all this. He might otherwise take the opportunity while we are preoccupied with Parhae to attack the Khitan and gain sway over Manchuria, which would never do.'

"Despite having consumed a great many cups of Ho's excellent wine, I was able to dash off the various documents to the emperor's satisfaction on my first attempt, and returned to the banquet before the singing was over. When I reentered the dining hall, a babble of questions rose up from the guests: What had I been doing at the palace? Was it a new campaign, a new tax, a rebellion?

"'Please, please,' I said, returning to my seat and beckoning to the servant for wine. 'I am bound to secrecy by the emperor himself.'

"'Oh come now, Li, don't be so mysterious, you can at least tell us what it was you were called to do.' This was from Hsieh, the son of the secretary of the Board of Rites and one of Chang An's most notorious rakes.

"'Well,' I said, pouring a large measure into a clean rice bowl—on some occasions, our tiny cups are just too small—and drinking it off in one draught, 'I can tell you that the emperor asked me to draw up some orders for one of our military regions.'

"'Not more trouble from the Khitan?' cried one of the guests at the far end of the table.

"'Not exactly.'

"I filled the bowl again and began to sip from it.

"'If *not exactly* the Khitan, then it must be the Koreans,' said Hsieh. 'Are those fools in Silla in trouble again?'

"I smiled back at him noncommittally. He then launched into a diatribe aimed at the King of Silla and his generals, at one point averring that 'not one Chinese life should be spent to preserve a barbarian king.' I was forced to correct him on several points (my knowledge of the situation on the peninsula had improved out of all recognition by what I had heard and written at the palace), and the conversation grew very lively, with strong views expressed about the wisdom of supporting the kingdom, the cost of an expedition in blood and treasure, the follies of the first emperor of the Sui Dynasty, and the emperor's own great-grandfather Tai Tsung, who had very nearly emptied the imperial coffers and decimated the farms of the northwest in three disastrous expeditions aimed at conquering the entire peninsula. Whenever I spoke, all present were silent, for they knew that I was privy to the thoughts of the emperor and his top officials. I later heard that a few fools complained I had been indiscreet, that I had revealed the emperor's plans, that Korean spies would send news of the expedition back to their homeland, but this was just jealous vaporing.

"Many would say that I had everything a man could ask for in those days: the honor of my peers. (Oh, yes, they were all happy to praise me now that I was in imperial favor. Don't forget the five-color cape—the one I wore the other day on the lake, boy. It is awarded at the recommendation of the Board of Rites in recognition of the poet held by the community of scholars to be preeminent among them; it is not granted at imperial whim. Of course, most of their praise was outright hypocrisy fueled by fear and awash with envy. Not that I cared a hoot for the lot of them, for there were only two—Tu Fu and Wang Wei—who could be considered on my level in verse making. I never did meet Wang Wei in the years I was at court; he had been given some official position in the provinces by Hsuan Tsung, who I think may have wanted to get rid of him, for he was a somber, serious fellow by all accounts, not much given to ribaldry and song. It always nagged at me that we never met, for I had been convinced for so long that he was the source of my failure to be called to court that I felt I owed him—and myself—the challenge of a direct confrontation. But alas, it was never to be. I left, then came the rebellion and the downfall of all our hopes. He was forced into taking some kind of official position in the rebel administration, and now that our troops have retaken the capital, he will face trial for treason. Unhappy fellow! It is punishment enough for all those years of bad verse. We will never meet now, even if he escapes execution. . . .)"

Li Po, who is staring out at the river blankly, pauses and frowns.

"Where was I?"

"I had everything a man could ask for, the honor of my peers . . . " Wang Lung automatically reads back to him, quite accustomed by now to this sort of thing.

"Ah, yes, the honor of my peers, the praise of my sovereign—sometimes even his affection, though not friendship, for there can be no true friendship between an emperor and one of his subjects; their standing is too violently unequal—along with some gratifying monetary recognition. Above all, I had the love of such a woman as most men can only dream of knowing, my lover, my friend, my companion in versification: all that friendship is supposed to give, and love, too. All this I had, and yet . . . and yet it wasn't enough. It never is, it seems. There is always some canker gnawing away at the heart of our happiness. Even then, foolish pride was rising inside me like a cockerel's bravado, destined to come between me and all I loved, to destroy everything. . . . "

Here Li Po falls silent and stares out at the river musingly. The boy puts down his brush and waits, almost as reluctant to hear the end of this tale as Li Po evidently is to tell it. After some minutes, Li Po looks around with a start, then nods his head as though affirming some inner decision and begins to speak again:

"You see, I had long studied the manuals of war and peace, the histories of our ancestors' attempts to control the barbarians and keep peace within the empire. I knew that was where my true talents lay, knew that if I was given an opportunity I could dazzle the world with my victories, could make them forget that I had ever put a pen to paper and written a single line of verse. So the day after being summoned to the conference on Korea and Silla, I sat down in my study (a lovely, airy room in the house Hsuan Tsung had given me) and began a memorial to the throne, a long, long essay, twenty thousand characters or more, plotting out the precarious strategic situation of the empire and detailing my plans for its rectification. It took me—me!—three weeks to write.

"I poured everything into that memorial, the fears and dreams that plagued me, all my hard-won learning, all my years of travel: all my genius. It was a call of warning, a voice crying that in the midst of our revels there were dangers on every side; each one was containable individually, but together they could overwhelm us.

"I set down the parlous state of the border regions in the north and west, the great military commands of Shuo-Fang, Ho-Tung, and Yuchou, the bulwarks of the empire against the desert hordes, how once there had been ten or twelve commanders reporting to the capital, but now time and expediency were gradually whittling down their numbers so that soon all three huge regions, with their armies of three hundred thousand men each, would be in the hands of a single man, all foreigners, men like the gross Rohkshan, Ko-shu Han, a brilliant Korean who was coming to the end of his career, and a few others. Far in the west, too, there were signs of trouble from the Arabs, who were pressing us at the Talas River, a lonely outpost deep in the desert, a full year's travel from Chang An. I ranged to the south as well, warning of trouble to come from the Tibetans, of our overcommitment in the swampy kingdom of Nan-chao, even the danger from pirates, the folly of allowing more and more Arab merchants, tens of thousands of them, to settle in Canton and Yangchou without proper supervision. This last warning was thought particularly laughable, but no one was laughing last year when Arab pirates based on Hainan Island took advantage of our weakness to revenge a hundred years of gouging, brutally rapacious governors and sacked Canton, burning the entire city to the ground. And that only a few years after our ignominious defeat at Talas River by those same merchants' cousins of the Abbassid Caliphate.

"Above all I railed against the greedy expansionism that had pushed our frontiers so far out of their natural bounds that in the name of protecting the borders of the empire we had actually weakened them. We had sucked the lifeblood out of the peasantry by taking away all men under forty and never returning them; only one in fifty ever returned from those expeditions to the far west, dying either of disease or in battle or forced to man the veterans' colonies that were seeded in the newly conquered lands. I cited the example of the fifth emperor of the Han dynasty, of the first emperor of the Sui, of Hsuan Tsung's great-grandfather, all men who became obsessed with the idea of conquest and nearly destroyed their realms in so doing.

"But all those warnings were for naught, although everything I wrote has come true since. It was my greatest work and every word was ignored, scorned. It fills my heart with bitterness still and makes a sour bile rise in my throat at the injustice of it, the sheer waste. I . . . "

Here Li Po jumps up from his seat and begins to pace up and down the deck, scowling, fists clenched. Perhaps he won't be able to finish his tale after all, Wang Lung thinks.

But after a few minutes, the poet takes several deep breaths, shakes his head, and looks over to the boy quizzically.

"Ummm," Wang Lung says, his finger tracing down the

line of characters. "Yes, here it is: 'And that only a few years after our ignominious defeat . . .'"

" . . . at the Talas River," Li Po completes the sentence. "Let's go on or we'll never finish:

"As soon as I had finished writing the memorial, I hurried to the chancellery to make an official request for an audience with the emperor, my right as an academician. The clerks there looked at me a little oddly, for they knew who I was, knew that I saw the emperor almost daily; why should I need to ask for a formal audience? Of course, I was all too aware that the emperor would ask me the same question, so I stayed away from the palace for several days before the appointment, pleading illness, although it is notoriously bad luck to do so and often brings sickness onto the liar. Many hours before dawn on the appointed day, I paced outside the Grand Audience Hall with the others, mostly provincial governors or very senior capital officials, they carrying their tablets of office under one arm, their papers under the other, all of us dressed in formal court robes, the jade plaques hanging from our belts tinkling against each other as we walked. An envoy and several companions from the Iranian city-states stood in one corner talking quietly in their rasping language. The envoy's features were startling even for a barbarian, an enormous black beard that fell halfway down his chest, bushy eyebrows, an improbably large hooked nose, and bulging eyes that were a weird, unnatural pale green, the color of branching coral.

"When at last I was admitted into the audience chamber, I made the complex prostration and obeisances (they alone had taken me days to learn; here in the most formal of settings the easy formality of the Pear Gardens or the hunting camps was eschewed and court etiquette ruled), then looked up. Hsuan Tsung was at the far end of the long room, sitting on a magnificent throne wrought of ivory and jade. His voluminous robes were so richly woven with gold that he shimmered like an apparition amid the clouds of smoke from the numerous censers lining the hall. He was surrounded by the high officers of state: Li Linfu, the chief minister; Niu Hsien-ko, his partner in that office; the grand secretary; the chancellor; and the ubiquitous chief eunuch, Kao Li Shih. The emperor's face, normally impassive in any case, was like a death mask. He might have been a bronze statue.

"I hardly noticed any of these details, however. I was concentrating on completing the ritual obeisances so that I could hand my memorial to an attendant. Once that was accomplished, I knew that there was no reason for me to linger. No reply would be forthcoming, nor was it really possible until he had read my essay; I backed out, my head bowed as was prescribed. It was all over very quickly.

"I saw Hsuan Tsung again the next day. I was summoned to give advice about the care of the sparrowhawk chick, which he had been keeping in his bedchamber in a small stick-lined box; the bird was not eating and he feared for its life. But I found that the chick was merely malingering, and soon persuaded it to swallow a mashed earthworm; Hsuan Tsung had been attempting to feed it a whole, live worm, almost as big as the chick itself. He was very congenial, completely different from the remote figure of the previous day, cordially asking how I was and fussing over the bird like a mother hen. But never a word about the memorial.

"Nothing was said in the succeeding weeks, either, though I was summoned to the palace on numerous occasions, most of the time by Gwei-fei to compose for her little parties. In truth I was growing weary of her endless bubbly energy and coquettish ways. She treated me more and more like one of her pet puppies. Each time I appeared she would say the same thing: 'Oh, it is our banished immortal. Come, make me live forever.' And then she would laugh and laugh, Hsuan Tsung joining in with a weak chuckle, even after the twentieth repetition.

"I had also begun developing a new verse form and regretted intensely the hours spent at the palace making idle chatter and eating lychees (Gwei-fei's obsession). Often these occasions were sheer torture, for Gwei-fei didn't care for wine like most women, and when Hsuan Tsung wasn't present, would invariably forget to order it for others, however broad the hints. The new verse vehicle was to be based on the ballads sung in taverns, an idea first suggested to me by Hsueh Tao. She had done some experimenting herself but didn't wish to show the results to anyone else for fear of developing a reputation as an eccentric (she moved in very conservative circles, remember). I, however, was happy to try out the new form; it could only add to my reputation. After all, there were only two conventional forms available—the old style, a freer vehicle which I favored, and the confining new style, with its rigid rules on tone patterns, length, and rhyming, which was used by the court poets and others such as Tu Fu. But I reasoned that there should be a third way, one that had the virtues of both, the discipline and structure of the new style combined with the freedom and openness of the old. To me the solution lay in the myriad ballads of the taverns, just as much the true poetry of the people as those so praised by Confucius in the *Book of Songs.* Here there was the structure of a song, the meter and rhyme scheme laid out, but the tone pattern was much more flexible, allowing even lines of *irregular* length—sacrilege! Most importantly there was a huge range of songs, thousands available, all with differing structure, stanza lengths and number, rhyme scheme, meter, and so on—a song to fit every occasion that a poet might encounter.

"But in order to use this new form, I knew I had to record

a very large number of songs and their structures—in other words write down as many of the tavern ballads as I could. Naturally this required a good deal of time spent listening to singing girls in wineshops, which wasn't entirely a burden. Indeed it was often a relief to escape the cloying, hothouse atmosphere of the palace for the tavern's bawdy spontaneity. Sometimes I would repair to the dirtiest, most ramshackle wineshop that I could find in the hope of foiling the imperial messengers. But they always found me.

"A few times I arrived at the palace after a very long session, a whole day almost of singing and drinking and writing down songs. But as you know my boy, though I may be too far gone to walk, my eyes may be crossed and balance unsteady, my hand can always hold a brush and my tongue can speak the verses I write. But even in this Gwei-fei made a game of me. She would order flagon after flagon—I of course never refusing—until even that capacity was at the utter limit. Then she would cock her head to one side and sweetly ask for a poem, 'just something simple, one of your little ditties.'

"Nor did she have any compunction about summoning me for the most trivial reasons. I recall dozing in front of a blazing fire with Hsueh Tao one day in midwinter when a servant came in to say that an imperial messenger was waiting in the front courtyard. I was surprised, for the emperor and Gwei-fei had traveled to the hot springs palace at Hua Qing a few days before, and it had snowed almost nonstop since then, a powerful, bitterly cold wind blowing out of the desert, piling the snow into great drifts against the walls and hillsides. The snow had stopped that morning, but the steely gray sky promised more to come.

"My heart sank when I saw the messenger, for it was evident that he had just ridden a considerable distance through the cold. Icicles hung from his fox-fur cap and his saddle cloth, his exhausted horse was giving off clouds of steam, and his own face was pinched and blue. He proffered a cloth-wrapped scroll in a gloved hand and watched impassively as I read the usual terse summons, ending with the standard 'Tremble and obey!' In this case I would certainly be trembling as I obeyed. I sighed and told him to go into the kitchen and get some hot soup while I changed into riding clothes and ordered two fresh horses.

"It was only a matter of twenty miles or so from Chang An to Hua Qing, but in such weather the ride could be very unpleasant indeed, even dangerous if conditions worsened unexpectedly. I resented being taken away from Hsueh Tao, too, for we had both been much preoccupied in recent months, she always out at one banquet or another, her services in almost constant demand, and I at the palace, though for some reason the emperor had more or less ceased to use me as a translator (he said it was a waste of my talents to force me through the drudgery of composing bureaucratic documents). I spent most of my time as Hsuan Tsung's companion at the cockpit or while he was dancing attendance to Gwei-fei.

"Hsueh Tao and I were apart so much and had come together so forcefully after so long that sometimes I would wake up deep in the night and gaze at her as she slept, the features as familiar, as close to me as my own but at the same time utterly unknown and unknowable, the face of an intimate stranger. Sometimes I would catch her watching me pensively and wondered whether the same thoughts weren't passing through her mind.

"Oh, oh, how I wish that she had told me those thoughts, had made me see what a fool I was being, that I would never be suited for the life at court, that I was hastening my own destruction with every day's antics, grasping in vain for military glory and high office. A few times, she tried to give me some sense of what others were saying, that the enemies I was making were busy scheming for my downfall. But each time I dismissed her warnings, dismissed them harshly as feminine vaporings, and soon heard no more. For she was proud, too, the gods know, proud and strong and very unwilling to seem foolish or ask for help or forgive an insult. And in the heady madness of those times, when months seemed to pass in the blink of an eye, there was never time enough for such talk anyway, we were hardly seeing each other more than once or twice in ten days.

"So it was that I was particularly unhappy to see the imperial messenger that day, when we had been sitting in the kind of companionable laziness we almost never enjoyed, she strumming on the lute, I singing along, improvising with her. But I went, as I always had, wrapped up like a corpse and plunging into the cold, even my unfortunate horse whinnying its wonderment that we were to venture forth in such inclement weather.

"It was a hard ride, our feet and hands numb, eyes watering in the knifing wind, the horses struggling through snowdrifts that lay several feet thick on the road, the countryside silent and empty around us under its white blanket. The messenger's horse was lame by the time we limped through the palace gates in late afternoon, the darkness coming on fast, and the snow beginning again—huge, wet flakes drifting out of the sky, billowing in languorous eddies at the stable door. I handed my horse to a shivering groom and hurried straight to the springs, not bothering to stop and change out of my riding clothes.

"After riding through the frozen countryside all day, the grottoes were like a mystical fairyland. The waters of the hot springs were run into pipes and collected into pools carved out of the living stone so that the caverns were filled with the tinkling and dripping of running water. Everything was cloaked in the steamy mist that rose from the numerous pools, massive tendrils wrapping around the rough-hewn stone pillars and hanging in the thick air. I walked for some minutes, soon sweating heavily, then heard the unmistakable sound of Gwei-fei's chuckle emanating from somewhere in the steam. I found them a few minutes later, completely alone, not a servant or courtier in sight, lolling in one of the pools that had been lined with blue-veined white marble. Their robes were draped over a chair, and some cups and a silver flagon of wine shaped like a goose's head sat beside the pool, next to them a bucket filled with snow and a tray of candied fruit. When she saw me materialize out of the mist, Gwei-fei gave a little false squeal of alarm.

"'Oh my, who is that dressed in a fur hat and heavy cloak. Is it some rough barbarian come to ravish me?'

"Then she stood up—the pool was only a few feet deep—quite unself-conscious as though I was a servant, squinting and holding her hand over her eyes as though to shade them from the sun. She was a magnificent creature, her breasts heavy (Rohkshan had once famously compared them to the cheeses the Huns make from mare's milk), pink nipples standing out from the milky white skin, then the soft swell of her belly, and below it her hairless pudendum, swelling like a ripe fruit from between her heavy thighs.

"'Oh, it is only our banished immortal, all dressed in dirty clothes,' she said, affecting relief, pretending to be unaware of the effect her naked body must be having on me. 'How is it you are dressed so when we are wearing nothing?'

"'You summoned me, Lady Yang.'

"'Perhaps I did,' she said, settling back into the water next to the emperor. 'But you can go away and change immediately, summons or not. We can't have you wandering around in here dressed like a Tartar. He'll scare the bath maidens, won't he, my dear?'

"'Certainly he will,' said the emperor, nodding his head.

"It took a surprisingly long time to find a cooperative servant who could secure a light robe for me, and by the time I returned to the grottoes, Gwei-fei and the emperor were nowhere to be found. Eventually I tracked down a eunuch who informed me rather haughtily that his highness had retired with the Lady Yang, and they were not to be disturbed. For two days I chased them around the palace, but they always seemed to be busy with each other, unwilling to receive visitors, and on the third day I learned that the court was moving back to Chang An, the snow having stopped and the way now clear for wagons and coaches.

"I rode wearily home and went straight to my favorite tavern, the Persian Girl, right by the palace gates. I stayed there for much of the afternoon, talking and drinking with the Persian proprietress. She was no longer a girl by any means, though still pretty in a big-nosed, foreign sort of way, and was possessed of a low, musical voice that whispered intimacy to her patrons, singing as though she was lying in bed alone with each man in the room. She was also one of the few tavern singers to my knowledge who actually wrote many of the songs she performed. Her singing wasn't particularly accomplished, she lacked the training, but her understanding of the music and the popular mood was profound, and she was of great help to me in noting down the rhythm and structure of many wineshop ballads.

"But I was not to be left alone that day either, and soon found myself trailing along glumly behind yet another imperial messenger. This time it was Gwei-fei alone who received me in one of the empty reception halls, quite brisk, all her coquetry and girlish airs put aside.

"'Come, come,' she said, waving me to accompany her, then turning and walking briskly away, speaking over her shoulder. 'The emperor's youngest children are putting on a show for him and they need someone to play the lion and sing a little song. Well, I thought to myself, what about Li Po? He is a big strong fellow who could roar quite convincingly. And you could certainly write the little song the lion is supposed to sing after the hunters—that is, the children—catch it.'

"I won't even attempt to describe my feelings at being dressed up in a moldy lion skin, my beard colored yellow with gamboge and long whiskers painted on my cheeks. Nor will I recite the song I composed for the mortally wounded lion to sing in between roars of quite genuine pain as a horde of children pranced around, poking at me with sharpened sticks. In fact it was a poignant little piece, but between the squeals of the children, my growling, and the brittle laughter of the courtiers, no one heard a word.

"The late winter and spring of that year, the thirty-second of Hsuan Tsung's reign, was a wearisome time, a time when I often wondered why I had come to that golden city, the crossroads of the world. I had achieved everything I ever dreamed of only to find myself numb, enchained as a peasant pulling a plow on a barren field in deepest Shu. I even thought of hinting at my dissatisfaction to the emperor but could think of no way of doing so that wouldn't have been interpreted as a slight to Gwei-fei, which would have been fatal to his affection for me, or even just fatal. I told myself, too, that if I waited a little longer, he might give some indication of having read my memorial, might even still act on it.

"Finally, one glorious spring day I suddenly had enough. I was sitting on a bench outside a little riverside inn a few miles from the city walls, cup of wine in hand, watching the peach blossoms falling around me like a miniature snowstorm, when I saw the rainbow coat of an imperial messenger. Once the sight had made my heart bound with joy, now it produced only gloom. After he had delivered his message—a command to attend the Lady Yang Gwei-fei—I said the following, quite unplanned: 'My regrets and apologies, but I must decline. Say this is my message: *I am the god-king of wine and am busy tending my subjects.*' With that I tucked a small cask of wine under my arm, climbed aboard a skiff, and rowed away, leaving behind the stunned messenger, mouth agape. No one had ever refused an imperial summons until then, and I believe no one has since.

"That evening I was already in bed, the curtains pulled round, the servant asleep outside the door, when Hsueh Tao swept into the bedchamber. She had been at a banquet hosted by the secretary of the chancellery and was still dressed in her evening finery. I awoke to find her standing next to the bed, the lamp held high in one hand, illuminating her blazing eyes.

"'Have you gone mad?' she demanded.

"I didn't have a chance to reply before she plunged on.

"'Is it true that you refused the imperial summons today, that you gave some answer about being the god of wine?'

"'Something along those lines, yes.'

"'Then I repeat my question: have you taken leave of your senses?'

"'Of course I haven't. Listen,' I said, sitting up in bed and shielding my eyes from the light, 'I don't enjoy being interrogated as though you were one of Li Linfu's torturers. Put down the lamp, come to bed, and we can talk all you want.'

"She put the lamp down on a side table, but made no move to disrobe. 'Is it possible that after all this time here in Chang An, at court, you still don't realize what you have done? I'll put it simply. All your friends—every single person who knows you, even those who just nod to you in the street—we could all be executed tonight. Is that clear enough?'

"'Come now, my dear, all I did was refuse one summons, it isn't as though I told Gwei-fei the truth, that she is a tiresome, vulgar woman who is too fat to boot.'

"'You don't need to tell her those things. She already hears voices whispering that you mock her, that you are trying to turn the emperor against her. Don't you know how many enemies you have out there, those who are jealous of your intimacy with the emperor, those whom you have insulted when you were drunk? Think of the eunuch Kao Li Shih. He might never have been a friend, but he needn't have been an enemy, and he was not an enemy until you humiliated him in front of the entire court.'

"For a moment, I didn't know what she was talking about. Then I remembered the incident. Six months earlier, I had been called from the hunt to a banquet in Gwei-fei's private rooms and was still dressed for riding. When they asked me for a poem I said that I would comply, but only if I could remove my boots. No man should compose poetry in his muddy boots I said, and called to Kao, who was hovering behind the emperor as usual, his cheek twitching in an irritating manner, to help me take them off. Hsuan Tsung had laughed and nodded his head, and Kao had waddled over to my couch, most unwilling, seething with rage, and pulled off one boot. The whole party of diners was watching in amusement as he knelt in front of me to pull off the second. I bent my foot inside the boot so that he pulled and pulled but couldn't remove it, the laughter rising all around, his face growing red with the unaccustomed exertion and rage. Finally, I straightened my toes abruptly and the boot slipped off. Kao, who by then had stood up and was desperately pulling to get the damned boot off, reeled back and crashed into the wall, knocking over a stand that held a large pot of flowers, he sitting there stunned, the floor around him covered in water and shards of pottery and flowers, the whole room roaring with laughter.

"'Now,' Hsueh Tao was saying, 'he is your implacable foe and has spent the last six months poisoning Gwei-fei against you, most recently saying that the poem of praise you wrote for her in the Lotus Pond Pavilion was really a hidden insult. Apparently you compared her to the Lady Flying Swallow, a very small woman, famously slim. Kao has convinced Gwei-fei that you meant to point out her plumpness.'

"'But that's absurd, I . . . '

"'I'm sure it is. I'm just trying to tell you of the danger you are in.'

"'Why didn't you tell me this before?'

"'Much of it I didn't know until tonight. Most of my friends were too embarrassed to speak of it. Then this evening they heard you had refused an imperial summons and began to fear that by knowing me they might be in danger, too.'

"She fell silent, then turned to go, picking up her lamp. At the door she turned back. 'When you first came to Chang An, I told you that it was a mistake, a dangerous mistake for a man like you.' She shook her head. 'You should never have come.'

"'Hsueh Tao, you worry too much,' I said, trying to reassure her, though her words had sent a chill into my heart. 'Tomorrow I shall go and see the emperor and he will laugh and chide me for being impossible, and then we will go hunting or to the cock walk and he will forget what happened.'

"'I hope so. I hope you are right. Even so, you must never do something like this again. How could you, that is what really puzzles me. I had always assumed the person you act out in public—the untameable poet, the outsider always ready to speak his mind, even to the emperor—was a role, a shrewd artifice.'

"'Are you telling me that you thought I was lying? That I was just acting a part like some creeping courtier, like every other hypocritical backstabber in this contemptible city, like . . .' I paused, aware even in my rage that what I was about to say was foolish, irrevocable, disastrous, but my vain pride carried me on. "Like the marquises and dukes and judges for whom you perform every day, lying about their poetry to keep the gold flowing into your coffers? Do you think that is what I am? Just another whore like . . . '

"'Like me?' she flared. 'A whore like me? If I am a whore, what does that make you? And if you despise Chang An so much, then what has kept you here for two years? What has sent you to the palace every day to play the buffoon for the Lady Yang, to write those oily songs of praise and dress up like a street performer in animal costumes and debase your genius composing children's ditties?'

"I was so choked with rage at this, that after all this time she could know so little of me, that I couldn't speak, just glared at her.

"'In a few years, I will leave here,' she continued more calmly, her voice cold. 'By then I will be known as the Lady Poet, not as Hsueh Tao the courtesan. I will have the money and the freedom to do as I wish. But you,' she made a gesture of dismissal with her left hand, 'you must know that you will stay here as the Lady's performing bear until she decides to release you. Tell me now, who is the whore? Who is the slave, and who is free?'

"She turned and walked through the door, taking the lamp with her so that the room was plunged into darkness. For a few moments I lay there stunned like a man who has been thrown from a horse at full gallop. Then I jumped out of bed, ran out after her, naked, throwing open the front doors to see her stepping into her palanquin. The bearers gaped at me, but she didn't even turn to look, merely rapped out an order and they set off at a trot, craning their heads to look back until they disappeared round the bend in the drive, I shouting something after them, I don't know what, shouting for a long time before I grew hoarse and stormed back into the house, calling for wine.

"All the next day I was beset by a barely suppressed fury that pounded in my head and left me almost incapable of civil discourse. I smashed a bowl of breakfast rice in a vent of spleen, then sent the maid-servant away in tears. I strode out to the stable, kicked a groom, mounted and rode into the street, heading for the palace. Every ten days I was charged to come and assist (that is, *educate*) Hsuan Tsung in his training of 'Marshal' as he had dubbed his sparrowhawk. Marshal was more than a year old now and had already molted once. The streets were even more packed and slow-moving than usual that day, full of gawking oafs up from the country, innumerable coolies carrying bales of cotton or baskets of fruit on poles slung across their shoulders, tea vendors pushing their two-wheeled carts, old ladies hawking a few muddy turnips from straw baskets, streams of little boys pursuing each other through the crowds like fish darting through water, Nestorians in black robes preaching on street corners in fractured Chinese, all jostling for space with contortionists, acrobats, and Indian snake charmers, all seemingly determined to bar my path and delay my progress, so that by the time I arrived at the palace gates my temper had grown even fouler.

"The emperor made no mention of my refusal of Gweifei's summons the day before. He and I spent two hours with the bird, attempting to train it to return to the lure, but the sparrowhawk—usually sweetly cooperative and a quick learner—was in a pigheaded mood and could do nothing right, finally giving me a sharp nip that sliced clean through the heavy leather of my hawking glove and opened a deep gash in the soft flesh at the base of my thumb. The bird was sent away in disgrace, doctors were called for, and a poultice of white mulberry bark was strapped over the wound to stanch the bleeding. Then, when the fuss had died down and we were alone again, Hsuan Tsung was searching through a pile of scrolls to show me a manual on hawking that he had discovered in the imperial library, I found my mouth opening of its own accord and my tongue abruptly asking him whether he had read my memorial, 'the memorial,' I said, 'that I submitted to you in the audience hall six months ago.'

"Hsuan Tsung didn't even stop leafing through the scrolls, merely nodded his head and said, 'Oh, yes, excellent, I remember it well, very interesting.' But it was said distractedly, his mind clearly fixed on finding the scroll. So I said, 'In that case, if you thought the memorial had virtues, what is barring you from giving me office as you said you would? I have served in the academy for some time now.'

"A shadow of irritation fleeted across his face and he said, 'No, I am sorry Li, it is impossible.' The subject clearly closed, he turned back to the scrolls and began to talk of the author of the hawking manual. But I interrupted, something that probably hadn't happened to him in twenty years, cut him off in midsentence and said, 'Why not? Why is it impossible?'

"At this, Hsuan Tsung dropped the papers he had been holding and turned to me with a frown, saying, 'You persist, Li, even though I have already spoken. Very well, you shall know. When Ho Chih Chang first recommended I see you, he said you were a *banished immortal,* capable of writing verses that would make the heavens weep. And he was right. You are the great poet of this age and have been so honored and humored in my court, allowed indulgences that others have suffered gravely for, as you well know. But he also said to me that you drank immoderately, and he was right in that, too. Yes, I did consider at one time giving you a post in the secretariat or even the governorship of one of the western provinces, but happily I was dissuaded by wiser heads, and when I saw that you couldn't even stay silent about the drafting of the few edicts, well, Li, what was I to think?'

"Here the emperor gazed at me with a quizzical expression, as though he really expected a reply. I stood stiffly, the stream of half-truths reverberating in my mind, bitterness filling my heart almost to bursting. And it came to me in a flash that he *had* read my memorial and had resented so intensely my criticism of his expansionist policies that he was willing to believe the slander spread by my enemies. That explained a great deal.

"Then Hsuan Tsung smiled and said with a kindly air, as though speaking to a child, 'Why do you want one of these mundane bureaucrats' jobs so badly, anyway, Li? You should be content with what you have, a talent that really *will* make you immortal.'

"I smiled, too, and made some conciliatory reply, though my mouth was dry and my tongue stiff and thick as I said it. Somehow we began talking of hawking again, and then Hsuan Tsung's eye fell on a scroll lying under the table and he bent with a cry of triumph, his face clearing, calling me over to the table where he spread the scroll out and turned eagerly to the section dealing with training young birds, his irritation completely forgotten.

"Later we went down to the Hall of Golden Bells. Hsuan Tsung was holding a feast to honor a past chief minister who was returning to his native province in the south for retirement. I was seated at a side table and sat silently for the long meal, ignoring the chatter of my neighbors, full of a heavy, venomous anger, drinking with sullen doggedness, ignoring an urgent voice that called on me to leave, plead sickness, to get out before something irrevocable came to pass. And then I noticed that the cackling of the other guests had died down to a hush and the eyes of the whole hall were upon me. A neighbor nudged me and said, as though from a great distance, 'They are calling your name, Academician Li, for the competition.' I rose slowly, the sour bile rising inside me, my steps slow and plodding as though I was walking through water. When I reached that little lectern I looked around and saw that the hall was silent, Gwei-fei and Hsuan Tsung in their familiar places at the Table of Seven Jewels, the emperor looking at me with a slightly amused expectation, Kao Li Shih, Li Linfu, and the others all watching me impassively. I thought of the lies Hsuan Tsung had told me, of how they had cheated me of my destiny, ignored my warnings, scorned all criticism of his insane policy of neverending conquest, and then my mouth opened:

Last year, we fought at the Kashgar's source,
This year at the Pamir River roads.
We washed our swords in the Caspian's waves
And grazed our mounts in Himalayas' snows.
On and on we march and fight,
Straying ten thousand miles from home
Until the three armies are aged and worn.

The Huns look upon slaughter like tilling,
Sowing their yellow-sand fields with alabaster bones.
House of Chin built a Great Wall to keep them out
And still the House of Han must keep beacons
burning;
The fighting never ends!

We struggle and die on the battlefield where
Maimed horses howl their pain to heaven and
Ravens and kites peck at the entrails of the fallen,
Flying up with intestines trailing from their beaks
To drape them over withered tree branches.

A whole generation has been snuffed out
In the desert sands. And for all our sacrifice,
The generals have accomplished nothing;

The Huns still mass at the desert's edge.
Surely you know that warfare is an accursed tool
The wise ruler rarely picks up.

"The hall resounded with a deadly, fearful silence when I finished, a silence that swelled into a screaming crescendo as I walked back to my place and sat down. I drank three cups of wine in rapid succession, and gradually a low buzz of conversation resumed, though most of the talk stopped again when I rose and made my way to the front of the hall, pausing to make a low obeisance to the emperor's table, then out through the great double gates with leaden steps and a head ringing with the closing of another one of destiny's doors."

eleven 李白

THAT NIGHT THEY MOOR AT YI CHANG, A DRAB collection of huts on a large island in the middle of the river. The town's only distinction is its position at the entrance to the famed gorges. In the morning Wang Lung and Li Po watch from the deck as hundreds of men assemble silently on the dock and the captain passes among them, dismissing those he deems unfit. The men are dressed in little more than loincloths and dirty turbans, all strongly muscled, their bodies those of young men but their faces those of ravaged ancients, eyes sunken, cheeks hollow, skin gray. About three hundred are herded onto a bamboo raft, ferried across the river, and unloaded on a broad sandy reach on the southern bank. A rattan rope as thick as a man's thigh has been secured to the boat's prow, and is carried across the river with the crowd of men. The remaining hundred or so feet of rope is laid out on the sand on the far bank. Smaller side strands about ten feet long have been plaited into the end of the rope, radiating out from the main body so that it resembles the bedraggled tail of some huge bird. The men gather on either side of the rope in two roughly equal groups, then divide into smaller groups of about ten men, each then picking up one of the side ropes, two teams lining up opposite each other, row after row of them standing in silent lines, files of men radiating from the rope like branches on a tree.

The crew unmoors the boat and it swings out into midstream, the racing current quickly pulling the vessel down and away so that the rope, which has been lying slack in the water, tautens and whips up into the air, dripping, now stretched almost to its full length of nearly a third of a mile. At this the captain gives a signal of assent to the chief of the haulers and with a cry of "Running!" they bend their backs in unison, taking the strain as the current pulls the boat downstream, the rope hard as an iron bar. Their chief, who stands at the head of the mass of men, a small hand-drum buckled to his waist, now cries "Ready!" and starts to beat out a funereally slow rhythm. At his cry of "Go!" the men strain forward in time with the drumbeat, digging the heels of their left feet into the ground and bringing their right legs forward in an agonizingly slow step. There is a pause followed by another thump of the drum, and now the right heels dig in and the left feet swing forward, then a pause, another drumbeat, another step, with each step the haulers grunting "ayah" together, a low exhalation of immense effort that carries across the water like the groan of a dying man. Once the team of men swings into a rhythm, however, their progress is surprisingly fast, a slow walking pace, and Wang Lung soon loses interest, returning to his place on the foredeck.

By late afternoon they have passed the entrance to the Yellow Cat Gorge and the boy gets up, stretches, and walks over to the railing again. The river has narrowed dramatically to perhaps a third of its previous width, and the compressed waters bubble and surge around the boat, throwing it about with terrible strength so that it sways and bucks like an unbroken horse. Ahead of them, in contrast to the turmoil on the river, all is peace; the early evening light has turned lilac so that the surface of the river, the hillslopes plunging down into the water one after another in succession, the wisps of cloud playing over the hills, and the rushing waters all shimmer pink-purple and violet.

Wang Lung stares transfixed at the thick cord stretching away from the boat and swaying back and forth as the boat heaves to and fro. Their haulers are far ahead of them, tiny figures, sometimes bent so low that their foreheads are almost touching the ground, sometimes disappearing from view altogether behind a thin veil of mist, only the swaying rope evidence that they are making their laborious way along a narrow pathway cut into the rocky hillside. On just this single piece of rattan their lives depend, Wang Lung thinks, for if it snaps, they are done for. In a blink of an eye, they would be whirling madly on the foaming waters and smashed against one of the enormous rocks that lie just beneath the raging surface of the river. Earlier in the day, just after lunch, Wang Lung was leaning over the prow in the very same spot when he saw one of the small, crooked-stern junks specially designed to navigate these waters suddenly appear around a bend in the river and race past, the crew manning the sides with long poles ready to push off from the banks or one of the rocks, the captain and two other sailors struggling to keep the bucking tiller under control, a group of passengers huddled together, clinging to the mast, their eyes bulging with fear.

Now the boy sees that the section of the river ahead is especially turbulent, the waters sloshing back and forth in a white-foam frenzy, hissing and roaring, slapping against a huge rock that protrudes from the midst of the waters, a grim, gleaming black, merciless sentinel, the ruin of many a voyage. Beyond the rock though, he can see that the waters rise up in a foaming white line after which the river is placid and still as a duck pond. The closer they come to that dividing line, the stronger grows the agitation of the water, the boat now buffeted back and forth as though some monstrous creature has seized it between its jaws and is flinging it from side to side. Just as they reach the crest of the weir, the boat's creeping motion comes to a halt. The haulers have come to a standstill, their strength and the power of the river equally matched. For what seems an age, the scene is frozen in balance, the boat suspended in the same spot, held in place by its gossamer thread, the men on the shore bent double under the strain, immobile. Then comes the faint hollow thump of the hand drum, a rhythmic beat repeated once every few seconds, over it a thin voice singing, the words indecipherable but the melody haunting, the voice rising up above the roaring of the waters. And on the beat beginning the second verse, the drum sounds and the men lean forward and raise their legs as one, moving their feet forward a few inches, on the next beat of the drum taking a second, firmer step, then a third, a fourth, and on the fifth the boat heaves over the foaming crest and slips into the still waters beyond.

Wang Lung, who hasn't dared to move, has been rooted in place, lets out a long sigh of relief, feels all his muscles relax as the boat glides easily over toward a small landing, where they are evidently to tie up for the night. The drumbeat stops abruptly and there is a cry of "Down!" at which the ranks of haulers collapse onto the ground, most of them lying there like dead men, utterly exhausted. He looks round to see that Li Po has joined him at the railing.

"Poor wretches," the poet says, "they're no better than beasts of burden. Dead at thirty if they are not killed before then in an accident. No families, far too poor to marry, their whole lives just one day after the next of this kind of work. That ought to make you concentrate on your studies, if nothing else does."

With that rather uncharacteristic admonition, Li Po nods to the table and the scroll Wang Lung had been studying before he got up to watch the boat's passage through the weir. The boy returns to his place and takes up the scroll, the *Tao Te Ching*, which Li Po says contains "all that is of value in the

Tao; the rest is just a waste of paper." The poet meanwhile settles himself in his usual place, saying nothing, just watching the boy. He has made no move this day to take up his story, and Wang Lung knows what kind of an answer he will get if he asks. In fact the poet has been moody and subdued all day. He is, after all, crossing back into the gorges, crossing into his home province of Shu for the first time since he was fifteen. Li Po's life has come full circle, the boy thinks as he struggles to puzzle out a particularly abstruse passage. He is going back to his childhood, back to the womb.

Presently, Li Po says: "Look at that sulky expression on your face. You are like a little child whose kite has been taken away. I know that you want to hear the end of my tale, want to know just how I left Chang An, who said what to whom, how I placated the emperor's wrath (for he was very angry with me, felt personally slighted by my poem). I have told you a hundred times that such things don't matter, that this insistence on a mechanical succession of chronological events is nothing but peevish small-mindedness. Think more broadly! Expand your thoughts to encompass the whole, not just the most recent parts!"

He pauses, contemplating Wang Lung, idly passing a writing brush through his fingers.

"Sometimes," he says after a while, "I think that this insistence on hearing every tedious detail is just a way for you to escape your studies. Aha! I see from your guilty start that the shaft has gone home."

Wang Lung, who hasn't even looked at Li Po, has kept his face studiously impassive, looks up with a smile.

"No. No," Li Po says, waving his hand, "don't say anything. I don't want to hear your excuses or any begging. I *shall* finish the story as you wish. We are very near the end of the tale in any case, and there would be some virtue in having it down complete. But then you will have to devote yourself exclusively to study. After all, I did promise your father that I would make you a scholar, and though you have made some progress in these few months, there is still some way to go before you can hope to wear the cap and gown. So put away Lao-tzu and let us begin:

"The next day I went to the emperor and did what I had to. I groveled to him, said that I was drunk and had spouted the first thing that came into my head, a poem I was composing about the fifth emperor of the Han, had intended no reflection on his glorious conquests, which no one could compare to those of the Han, he taking care to guard the borders against the barbarian hordes, not to overextend his armies. For a while he watched me with that chilling impassivity that had so alarmed me at our first meeting, and I babbled on, saying that I was not suited to the life of court, was too rough, a mere poet, not a polished courtier, had been betrayed by my tongue many times, hated the gossip and intrigue, the gods only knew what was said of me behind my back.

"I talked for a long time, finally falling silent when I realized I was repeating myself. The emperor regarded me wearily, still not speaking, so I repeated my concluding request, begging his permission to leave the court and return to the mountains, there to write poems and pursue my study of Taoism.

"'Li Po,' he said at last with a sigh, 'you have made a fool of me in public. I told you before that I honor you for your talent. I don't expect you to act like one of my courtiers. But I can't allow myself to look foolish or weak. You know that as well as I do. There have been things said about you, it is true, many things, and I have ignored them all until now, but lately I find that the voices have grown very loud indeed.'

"Here my heart sank and I thought of exile to the poisonous south.

"'But,' he continued after a contemplative pause, 'you have been my friend these last few years. I will allow you to do as you say, to return to the mountains and rivers. But you must go immediately, within a few hours, giving no reason for your departure. And you must not return to Chang An until I give you leave to do so.'

"This last, I thought bitterly, I would have no difficulty in fulfilling. Accursed city. Hsuan Tsung, meanwhile, had called over a eunuch and gave orders for a very handsome gift indeed, assigning me the income from taxes on twelve villages in Jiang Nan, a thousand households whose payments totaled four hundred thousand cash a year. He also gave me a little solid silver plaque of a kind I had never seen before but had only heard tell. It was a pass usually given only to imperial messengers and members of the royal family, requiring all officials to lend the bearer aid to the full extent of their resources, including the granting of horses, food and lodging, carriages, servants, guards, and so on. These were necessary if I was to travel comfortably and not allow petty distractions to interfere with my verse-making, Hsuan Tsung had told me with a smile.

"With that, the audience was suddenly over and I was left standing in a hallway in the palace, the tax papers and the plaque clutched in my hands, staring at the great brass-bound double doors, firmly closed, the two statue-still guards posted on either side regarding me from the corners of their eyes. And a few hours later I was riding out through the Tung Hua Gate, the late afternoon sun hot on my back, no farewells, no long explanations or evasions, just a sharp break and out and away, back into the old familiar rhythm of the road.

"I had sent a messenger to seek Hseuh Tao out, but she was nowhere to be found. I left a note in her bedchamber that said only: 'I am leaving. If you wish to join me I shall be in Loyang until the last day of the fifth month.' It was more than her letter left for me those many years ago, much more.

"She didn't come, of course, so I rode on, rode into another life, a life that had nothing to do with her or Chang An and its wiles, refusing all messengers from that vile city, sending them back with their letters unopened, passing only the word by mouth that those who wished to see me were welcome to come. Many of my friends did come, too, and for a time I traveled about with them in twos or threes, visiting ancient sites and famous mountains. Best among these was Tu Fu, sweet young Tu Fu, as contemptuous of the city and its ambitions as I was, fresh from his latest failure, victim of Chief Minister Li Linfu's rigged examinations. We traveled through the old kingdom of Yueh, just the two of us, no servants or hangers on, 'arguing minutely over versification' each night, drinking and singing, sometimes in that long summer 'sleeping under the stars, sharing a single blanket, walking about hand-in-hand during the day,' as he later wrote. But then autumn came and he too was gone, back to his family and a search for some employment, for though from an aristocratic lineage, Tu Fu never had much money of his own, was always seeking a commission or the like, poor fellow. One of his sons died in the terrible first winter of the rebellion, died of malnutrition, Tu Fu arriving from the city to find the household in mourning, the little corpse still unburied for lack of cash. How would we have changed our lives, I wonder, if we had known what was to come?

"After he left I resumed my usual round, my name now so universally known that I had but to knock on the magistrate's door in the smallest of prefectures and a warm welcome was sure to be forthcoming. However, this life soon palled, for I was older, and had nothing like my youthful tolerance for the conversation of generous fools, however much wine they plied me with. So I sought out the Reverend Master Kao Jukuei of the great Lao-tzu temple in Chichou, who had long promised to sponsor me if I wished to take the first step into the mysteries. I stayed at the monastery for four months, living the life of a novice. No wine and endless chanting, a dull business, but I was determined to go through with it and receive my certification and the talisman. On the appointed day the three sacred grounds were prepared, each hidden by the next, and the candidates (there were twelve of us that year) entered with our hands bound, one by one, wearing gray robes of sackcloth. More I cannot say, of course, but I can add that my certificate was written by my friend Kai Huan, who did the job so beautifully—he was the greatest calligrapher of his age, barring only Wang, the monk—that immortals would weep to read it, a great boost to its numinous power.

"Thereafter, armed with the talisman, I returned to the study of alchemy and the search for the elixir. As I have remarked before, there is far, far more to its manufacture than just packing a few ingredients into a brazier. If not, every man in the empire would be an immortal! There was a long period of training and preparation, purification of the flesh through the drinking only of dew and eschewing the consumption of the five grains, which feed the soul-worms. There were also the daily breathing exercises and the disciplines of the bedchamber, retaining sperm with a profusion of partners to increase the power of the pneuma.

"Eventually I succeeded, but at great price, three years of such rigor and a thousand failed attempts, the entire resources of my tax grant each year used up on materials—silver, mercury, realgar, Turkestan salts, sulfur, malachite, lead, and so on—for in addition to all else, the exact processes must be followed, the timing judged just so, the weights, the geographical site, and so on. The slightest slip, a word mispronounced, a sudden occultation of the sun at the wrong moment, and all is lost.

"I came too late to the process, of course. Some men devote their entire lives, and when their coffins are opened only an empty robe and a jade staff are to be found where the corpse had lain. I managed to produce only a ten-year extension cinnabar, not the true elixir of immortality. Perhaps I would have, given more time, but then came the rebellion and all our foolish dreams were snuffed out.

"The rebellion: A great sandstorm, without reason or cause, blowing out of the desert, merciless, all pervasive, mutilating and destroying all in its path. Rohkshan the Bright, the emperor called him in those later years, his chief support, the bulwark of the empire, the delight of his eye. He showered him with gifts worthy of a fellow emperor—gold and silver and jewels by the wagonload, silks and sables, aromatics and perfumes, rare beasts and the swiftest horses, country estates and mansions in Chang An. Nothing was too good for him, each month it seemed bringing a new title or a new command, more and more troops placed under him, his power growing and swelling, but with it, with each new fief, each legion of soldiers, Rohkshan grew more fearful. He was not a stupid man. All those years of playing the buffoon for Gwei-fei, the unctuous companion to the emperor, such deception required much patience and cunning, a sharp understanding of men's natures. And now he recognized that his position was growing ever more precarious, that it drew envy and hatred as surely as the flame draws the moth, perhaps with the same result. Despite his fears, he also grew more arrogant, convinced that the power and titles made him better than other men, that he actually deserved those honors. Then, at last, unable to sleep, haunted by visions of his own execution and dreams of ascending the throne, he could bear it no longer and rebelled.

"Of course, there were other causes, more proximate ones. By then old Li Linfu had finally died (the relatives of his victims had mobbed his funeral cortege and dismembered his corpse; such was the hatred in which he was held that the troops didn't interfere), and a relative of Gwei-fei's had weaseled into the post, Yang Kuo Chung, a man of little distinction besides being a cousin of the emperor's first lady. We should have known that utter ruin was only a step away, but it seemed at the time that this was just another momentary lapse on the emperor's part. No one could believe that Yang would last for long, that Hsuan Tsung could be so blind. But blind he was, blinded by devotion to her; it could no longer have been lust after so many years, I now realize; he must have truly loved her. There was some skulduggery by Yang, the usual corruption running rampant and enemies executed. But the turmoil also held a threat to Rohkshan, who began to hear rumors that his days were numbered. He decided not to await the certain summons back to the capital and the equally certain order to slit his vast belly (by then he was so gross that he had to be lifted onto his horse with a contraption that resembled a crane).

"Thus, out of petty ambition, senile infatuation, and cowardice was disaster unleashed onto us. The storm was stopped for a time by the great Korean general, Ko-shu Han, stopped a hundred miles from Chang An, his forces in the perfect position for an ambush, outnumbered and lacking cavalry, but on the high ground over a narrow defile that could be blocked at both ends, well equipped with arrows and boulders, raging to fight. But tragedy is always preceded by farce. The eunuchs had convinced the emperor they knew best, and orders came from the capital for Ko-shu Han to advance onto the plain and confront Rohkshan there. Four times he refused until, at last, on threat of execution, he advanced, reluctantly, gingerly, the army of a hundred thousand almost to a man to be slaughtered there in the open, overwhelmed by the horses and camels, unable to fire their arrows accurately in the dust. One hundred thousand men dead for the whim of a eunuch. How can the earth respond to such injustice? It should rend itself for the raging grief of mothers and fathers, sisters and wives, brothers and sons and daughters, shake down mountains and tear great rents in the plains. But no, the drunken laughter of the victors recedes, the dust settles, the sun dips, and the vultures and kites slowly swoop in for their feast.

"And so they swept into the capital, those bandy-legged troops from the deep desert, not even speaking our language, butchering and raping and plundering wherever they went, the great marketplace filled with the stench of camels and blood, the sand there soggy and wet with blood, Rohkshan slaughtering every one who had ever given him offense, and there were many, along with their families. He invented new ways of murder as he went along, at last resorting to crowbars to smash the skulls of the last batch of unfortunates, having run through all the traditional methods. And there was more farce amidst this carnage. One of his commanders was sent to the imperial stables to commandeer the best animals for his master. Of course he picked the famous dancing horses, four hundred of the most beautiful animals the emperor's Master of Horse could find, all carefully trained to dance in unison to the music of drums and pipes, the wonder of the court when they performed. But Rohkshan's desert soldier knew nothing of this. To him a horse was for riding, nothing more, and when the animals refused to be mounted (they had never been broken for the saddle) he ordered the alligator-skin war drums sounded, thinking to recall them to their duty. Hearing the beat of the drums, the horses began to prance and sway, dancing as they had been trained, seeking desperately to please but only receiving a whipping for the efforts, for Rohkshan's man thought they must be possessed and sought to drive the spirits out. The harder they were beaten, the faster they danced, knowing nothing else, until at last the soldier cursed the animals, called up his archers, and bade them fire into the corral until every horse was dead, bristling with arrows.

"And so to the fate of Yang Gwei-fei, mistress of the empire for so long. All now know the story: the midnight flight leaving the court behind, just the emperor, Gwei-fei, her sisters, her cousin the chief minister, a few eunuchs, and a troop of the imperial bodyguard. Then after three days, the troops rebelling, slaughtering Yang Kuo Chung and Gwei-fei's sisters as the causes of the disaster, then demanding her life, too, as final propitiation, the emperor at first refusing, raging inside his compound that he would rather die himself, only he and the odious chief eunuch, Kao Li Shih, in the tent, Kao advising him that it would be foolish for him to die uselessly, for the soldiers would surely kill Gwei-fei if he was dead. And at last, Gwei-fei stepping forward and handing the noose to Kao, telling him he would be the one to strangle her (no one would deny that she had courage), the emperor running from the room in horror and Kao doing the deed swiftly, then taking the corpse out to show the soldiers, who, it is reported, were ashamed.

"There is little to add after that. An abdication and a new emperor, the battle swaying this way and that, but over the years imperial forces losing much of the time, Rohkshan's murder by his own son (his belly was slit open with his own sword, appropriately enough), but the storm continuing unabated despite his death, by now having assumed the power of an elemental force so that it mattered not who was nominally commanding the rebel forces or if all of Rohkshan's relatives murdered each other, as indeed they did. It rolled on inexorably, washing over all in its path, a black tide of slaughter, pestilence, and starvation.

"Like everyone else I fled before the storm, trying to find

some safe haven in the south that seemed likely to remain untouched by the fighting, if such a place existed. For awhile I considered returning to Cheng-tu, where the emperor had fled, and offering him my services, pointing out to him that I had predicted everything in my memorial. But then came the abdication and Su Tsung's accession, he based in the far northwest and anyway a man I hardly knew. So I ran south and east, heading back toward the Great River along which I had spent so much of my youth, finally settling on the slopes of Mount Lu above the town of Chiu-chiang on the river's south bank. There I found myself some land on the wooded slope, three hours ride up from the town, my nearest neighbor a Buddhist monastery called Shining Truth. I built myself a small thatched cottage and ringed it about with a fence made of mulberry wood, for there was an abandoned mulberry stand nearby that the monastery had once used in the production of silk. I dug a small garden and planted runner beans, cabbages, and kale. Each day I spent hunting for roebuck in the forest with my crossbow, sometimes walking twenty or thirty miles a day, or idling by the stream that cut across in front of my hut, fishing for trout. Now and then I would ride to town on the donkey and replenish my supply of wine and salt, but otherwise I stayed in that little world through the spring and summer, content to rise at dawn and chop wood or turn the earth or hunt until dark. The hard physical work sloughed off the fat of twenty years, and my body became tough and brown like old mahogany. I wrote little: the getting of sustenance in such a life fills most of the hours of the day and doesn't encourage much reflection.

"After a month had passed, I took my books on war and strategy from the leather trunk, where they had lain since Chang An, and studied once again the battles of Tsao Tsao and Guan Yu, the campaigns of my ancestor The Flying General against the Huns, the maxims of Sun Tzu. But that apart,

I hardly thought of the fighting from one day to the next, hardly thought of anything at all, my mind for once at rest, though my spirit was sorely troubled and my dreams were sometimes very frightening, full of tears and violence, her face often flashing like a beacon through the clouds of sleep.

"And indeed, one day I thought I was dreaming, though it was still daylight, late one afternoon when the shadows of the trees were lengthening and I returned to the hut from the forest where I had been chopping wood to stack and dry against the onset of winter. On the plank bench outside the door sat a woman in a plain blue robe holding an oiled-paper parasol to protect her against the sun. Next to her sat a young boy of five or so, swinging his legs. The parasol dipped up and I saw without surprise that it was Hsueh Tao, those radiant eyes examining me with slightly detached interest, noting that I was carrying an axe over my shoulder, that I wore nothing but a pair of short hempen trousers and a dirty turban. She didn't react as I approached, and I realized that she hadn't recognized me. That made me smile, and at once her face changed, amazement, joy, and wariness passing over in fleeting succession. I felt something heave and burst inside me, the bitterness and anger of all those years washing away at the sight of her, leaving only a residue of regret, regret that I had acted so foolishly, that I had never written to tell her of the anguish our parting had caused, regret as always at my pride and stubbornness.

"'This is your son,' she said, standing up and pulling the child forward. 'His name is Ai-lung and I would have brought him to you much earlier, much, much earlier if you hadn't refused messengers and moved on every time I thought to come.'

"She talked on for awhile, telling of her flight from Chang An, how she had bought a large country estate farther downriver as a refuge. She was headed there when she received word that I had settled on Mount Lu and, inquiring in town, had been sent up to my hut. I listened as she talked, noting that she sometimes spoke a little at random, but my attention was focused on the boy, who was shyly hiding his face in his mother's skirts. Who knew where my other children were. Probably with that Kueichou sow and lost to me forever. This was like a gift from heaven, being granted a son so close to my fifth decade of life. It was like a minor miracle, a shining light that made the seemingly neverending darkness of the rebellion disappear and the coming years of old age glow again with promise.

"I waited impatiently for her to finish talking, nodding and smiling at her words, and at last when she had run dry I said: 'Listen, I am sorry, more sorry than I can ever tell you at what happened. I regret it bitterly, my pride and anger throwing away our chance for happiness. And now, you have come with this little boy. It is a new beginning.'

"But here she interrupted, saying that she had been stubborn and foolish, too, but there could be no new beginning. Too much had happened for us to return to where we had left off. There was too much in the years between, too much risk of another break. She wanted the boy to meet his father before the tide of war swept us apart forever, she said, that was all.

"I began to reply, to persuade her she was wrong, but then I saw she was exhausted, must have been traveling for many weeks, her face printed with the weariness and anxiety of constant worry. All traces of youth were irrevocably gone now, but she was still achingly beautiful, great dignity there, a face I wished to see for the rest of my days, a face I wished to see grow old. So I bade her come into the little hut and cleared away the scrolls from the desk, lit the lamp, and fetched some fruit for the boy, some wine for the two of us, told her she could bathe in the stream if she wished, never asking if she would stay for fear she might say no.

"But this time she did stay, for a few days only, she said at first, and then she must go on to Yangchou. But then there came days of thunder and rain that washed out the roads to the town and she stayed a little longer, walking around now in just a common peasant woman's shift, most of her court gowns still awaiting her in Chiu-chiang along with the rest of her luggage, never a word of complaint, and this from a woman who had spent the last twenty years in Chang An with thirty servants waiting on her every whim. And so the weeks became months, passing into early autumn, a time during which I came to know her again, we knitting together those ties that had bound us so tightly together each time before, finding again the same joy, the same understanding, though there was much to be forgotten and forgiven, and it was many weeks before she finally came to my bed from the other side of the room, where she and the boy were sleeping on a pallet filled with straw, and we felt again the smooth, hot sensation of skin upon skin, our cries muffled for fear of waking Ai-lung, once again like the children we had started out as.

"And there was the boy. He was like a renewal of life for me, his sparkling eyes and silken hair, those red cheeks and happy smile an endless wonder. I taught him how to set a trap for fish in the eddies of the stream, how to cast a line into the swift current, how to tie a bright chicken feather to a piece of buoyant bark from the boab tree to serve as a lure for the trout—all the things a man is supposed to teach his son. He was already studying his simple characters, copying them over and over again, and when we ran out of paper, he wrote with chalk on a piece of slate that the Buddhist monks gave us.

"Often I would wonder that there could be so much happiness in the midst of such horror (for we still heard news of vast battles and much slaughter when we went into town), and it came to me that this was the greatest happiness a man could ask for in life, that all our other striving for title or name were vain shadows to the depth and reality of this joy. Never again would worldly ambitions and desires come between us, I told Hsueh Tao late one night as we sat outside drinking pine wine under the vast canopy of stars, wrapped in wool blankets against the chill. She murmured her agreement, but, strangely, when I looked at her I could see tears sparkling in her eyes.

"And indeed, there was one more page to be turned. A few weeks after her arrival, we began to make plans to move on to Yangchou and thus to her country house. But the tides of war swung down toward the delta and it was months before they receded enough for us to consider traveling. It was a good time to leave my little hut. The nights had turned icy and the boy had contracted a cold. Then a few days before we were to leave, a group of soldiers on horseback came splashing through the stream, three of them riding toward the house, dressed in a livery I did not recognize. I cocked the crossbow and passed it to Hsueh Tao along with the hunting bow, though drawing it probably would have been beyond her strength, then stepped out to meet them, my sword at my side. Surprisingly, they proved docile, obsequious even, reporting that they were from the army of Prince Yung, whose fleet had arrived in town at midnight on its way south to mop up rebel forces in the delta. They passed me a prettily worded invitation from the prince to attend him. I vaguely remembered him, a small, lean man much given to eating and drinking, though he never grew fat. I thanked the soldiers and sent them away, saying I would answer at my leisure.

"You must decline, Hsueh Tao told me earnestly, tell him you are sick. He will be gone within a day or two. But another set of soldiers returned later the same day with another invitation, this one speaking of my fame (my empty name betraying me again!), my renowned knowledge of war and strategy, asking for my advice and promising great rewards in treasure and title. Again Hsueh Tao begged me to refuse, and again I sent them on their way. But the next day, they came for the third time when she was out gathering mulberries, the last of the crop, and this time I went, riding down on a fourth horse they had brought with them, leaving a note to Hsueh Tao saying I would be back in a day or two.

"The town was filled with war banners and mounted soldiers, the shops boarded up, only the taverns doing any business. The fleet crowded the south side of the river, a hundred high-topped junks that could carry three hundred men each, the prince's yellow-and-purple banner streaming from each stern post, a huge multicolored imperial war banner flapping from the tip of the main mast. I was led aboard the biggest vessel, where the prince stood on the great foredeck with his adjutants, all in full armor, gathered round a map table. He waved me over, saying, 'Ah, Li Po, just the man we need. What is this farmer's robe? A peasant's coat for the greatest poet in the empire? Come, we leave in an hour. Report to the armorer and we will have you outfitted in no time, ready to fight at our side. I'll give you command of a brigade and when we have triumphed, you shall sing of our victory in words that will long outlive us.'

"I protested that I could not leave so precipitately; it would mean leaving my family behind, and I had not alerted my wife. At this the prince grew exasperated, saying that he was offering me the chance for glory, the chance to fight for the emperor, and I was talking of my family? He dismissed me with a wave. 'Do as you wish,' he said, 'go home to your wife or stay with us and fight the rebels.'

"And so I sailed with him that day, splendid in a new suit of red-and-gold armor, a quiver of arrows slung to my back, a steel helmet trimmed with sable and kingfisher feathers under my arm. I wrote a note to Hsueh Tao telling her to go to Yangchou, where I would join her in a few months when the work of the expedition was over. I ended with this poem:

Three times, the imperial command came;
On the last, I went. Do not ask
How many days I will be away.
And, when I return with the gold seal of office
Don't be like Su Chin's wife,
At least rise up from your loom
To greet me.

"We sailed out from Chiu-chiang that evening, a bright full moon guiding us downriver, all of us drinking hot rice wine against the cold. When the prince asked me what I had told my wife, I read out that poem—such shame!—and glowed in the roar of approval it drew from the officers assembled on the great foredeck. There was much more wine over the following weeks, and I wrote a great many poems, all much the same:

How easily Prince Yung's galleys calm the
Furious waves; the Great River seems
Like a duck pond!

Give me the prince's white jade marshal's baton;
We'll sweep away the traitors like the south wind
And march into Chang An in bright sunlight!

"I don't know why I began to suspect that something was amiss, though there seemed an inordinate number of troops aboard our fleet for the task we were assigned, pacifying the countryside from which rebel forces had withdrawn, mopping up a few thousand stragglers. Still, each town we entered was swept clean by the recruiting officers, and all our ships were soon bursting with unhappy men carrying shiny new pikes and sabers. Perhaps, too, it was because as each day passed and we drew farther from Chiu-chiang, my heart grew heavier, and even on the most drunken night of revelry I was sore inside as though I had been cut somewhere within me, a cut that wouldn't heal. I wrote a hundred letters, but sent none, for I had no excuse. Nor did I have anywhere to send them, for in my haste I had never sought the exact location of her estate.

"Eventually, however, even I noticed the too loud laughter, the frenzied high spirits of the officers, the hushed conversations that stopped abruptly when I appeared, the knowing smirks. It took several weeks before I was fully convinced that treachery was in the air, and by then their purpose had been revealed, the prince openly proclaiming that the mandate had passed from his brother, that it was to be a time of warring states all over again, like the tales of the Three Kingdoms whose most famous battle sites we passed every day, a fragmented empire in which every man was for himself, the strongest and best prepared taking the prize. I quickly made my prostration as to the emperor—a few years before, even a few months, I might have laughed at him and died happy, but now I found that I had something to live for and was willing to abase myself to survive and return to Hsueh Tao, to make my peace with her and the boy. The prince accepted my obeisance as a right, laughing and saying that I should soon be a duke, *he* would honor the poets in his empire as they deserved. Then he drank more wine and grew expansive. With the rich delta lands, he said, we could feed three armies, could advance upriver at our leisure when our recruits were fully trained. Who controlled the Great River controlled the empire, he said, all knew the truth of that maxim. So how could we be beaten?

"Apparently not many believed him, for once his purpose became known, his soldiers began to slip away in the night, I joining them at the little town of Long An, seeking to make my way to Yangchou. A few days later, however, I saw the prince's head carried past on a pike wearing the usual look of surprise: his own officers had seen the brittleness of his rebellion and butchered him in hope of amnesty. All to no avail, however, for they were executed the same night they brought his head to the commander of the loyal forces. I managed to travel on for a few more days, but again my useless fame betrayed me. I was recognized by a minor customs official checking the cargo in the vessel in which I was traveling. He had once seen me at his master's banquet. I was arrested and jailed, there to rot for nine bitterly long months while my sentence was considered."

Here Li Po jumps up, strides down to the hatchway leading down into the ship, and bawls for wine, a cask to be brought out immediately. He whirls around and faces Wang Lung.

"Now you know everything, how shamefully a man can act, betraying himself and his family, how he can throw away his whole life for an empty illusion. Are you satisfied?"

The boy opens his mouth to protest, but Li Po has turned again to shout for the servants to hurry, the lazy dogs, then begins to pace up and down the short deck.

"When they came to tell me it was to be death, I felt relieved. It was monstrously unjust, an absurd sentence but passed nonetheless, even though I told them that it was an imperial expedition, that I was under orders and had deserted as soon as I learned of the prince's traitorous intent. My enemies at court must have arranged it to get rid of me once and for all. It was commuted, of course, commuted to life in exile at poisonous Yeh-lang. Death might have been better than this slow torture, always drawing away . . . it was she, you know, who procured the commutation of the sentence. Oh, of course, I wrote a thousand letters, wrote to everyone I knew in the capital, pointed out that I had been cleared by the pacification commissioner, the emperor's own appointee. But all to no avail until she sought the help of her old protector, traveling to Chang An herself to seek his aid, or so they tell me, for I have never had a letter from her. Not in nearly two years."

Here the wine is brought at last by a red-faced servant. Li Po aims a kick at his backside as he scurries away but misses, then takes a deep draught of wine and smiles, his mood changing.

"The story is at an end, at last," he says in his shrill voice. "We must celebrate with a night of singing. This evening even you will sing, my boy."

And sing they do, Li Po teaching the boy tavern songs that make him blush, though none would know, for his face is already brick red with the wine Li Po pours him, one cup for every five the poet drinks. Much later Wang Lung is lying on his back, Li Po still singing in the background, a cup in hand, carefully stepping out a complicated dance. The boy looks up at the band of bright stars visible through the roof of the canyon, framed by the blackness of the cliff walls on either side. As he watches, a bank of clouds rolls across from the north, the darkness shot through with flashes of lightning, the mass of clouds blocking out the stars. A gust of rain-filled wind ruffles his robe and then a few fat, cold drops splatter on his face. Behind him, Li Po is singing:

I write to you from
outside the borders of heaven,
Sitting in a pavilion built
to watch the moon.

How little I have heard from you;
spring and the wild geese go north from here,
autumn and they return;
but not one brings
a letter from you.

Now the storm is in full cry, great rumbles of thunder rolling across the skies above the mouth of the canyon like the sounding of iron war drums, a thick curtain of rain lashing down on Li Po as he sings, the sheets of lightning showing that all the while he is dancing a careful round on the open foredeck, streams of water washing through his hair and down his cheeks.

The next day all is unchanged when Wang Lung wakes, the boat creeping upriver, the walls of the gorges towering above, Li Po at his place. But the story is ended, and instead of the scroll, his copy of the *Tao Te Ching* lies at his place.

And so it goes for an immeasurable time, each day so similar it is indistinguishable from the next, merging into a hundred days of numbing similarity. They are becalmed for ten days at the Yellow Ox Gorge after twenty-three of the haulers are swept into the river. Later the rope snaps at another gorge further up and only the relative calmness of that part of the river saves them. Li Po is like a caged tiger, endlessly pacing up and down the foredeck, his mood shifting in seconds from high spirits to gloom, though mostly gloom, every evening drinking and dancing and singing, usually by himself, for the boy has little to say to him and the poet has long since grown bored by the major's conversation.

Then early one morning, the boy is awakened by a shake on his shoulder and he sees Li Po's face, shining even in the flickering light of the galley's night lantern.

"The golden rooster has crowed!" he whispers triumphantly. Wang Lung gapes at him.

"Amnesty, you ignorant boy, general amnesty for all convicted of aiding the rebels! Come at last, at long, long last."

Wang Lung sits up, opens his mouth to ask how and why, but Li Po shushes him, pressing into his lap two scrolls and a heavy leather sack, still speaking in a low voice.

"I am going back downriver as fast as wind and current will carry me. Here are some letters to friends in Chang An, high officials, good men who will help when the time comes for you to take the exams. And there is some gold to help you get there. We can't have poverty distracting you from your studies, now can we?"

Again, Wang Lung opens his mouth to babble his thanks, but the poet places his finger over Wang's lips.

"The thing is, I don't want that fool of a major to know. I heard the word last night in town, but he will require some quibbling official proof and I could be here for another month waiting for it, so I am slipping off now, before the slug awakes."

He squeezes Wang Lung's shoulder hard, then pats him awkwardly on the head.

"You are a good boy. Give your father my regards and remember to wait another year before you take the exams."

With that he turns and slips up the steps. Wang Lung jumps out of bed and follows him. On deck the first light of dawn is breaking over the river, the soaring cliffs on either side of them cloaked in mist, a deep silence hanging over the scene, nothing audible but the muffled thunk of the little river junk alongside banging into the hull. The boy runs to the railing and watches as Li Po scrambles down the side and leaps light as a boy into the boat, which is quivering in the grip of the current, straining to be free. A sailor releases the rope and the crook-backed junk begins to drift out into midriver. Li Po turns to wave, and Wang Lung sees he is carrying nothing but his sword and a bundle of scrolls. He calls down in sudden panic: "But what about your story? What shall I do with it."

"It doesn't matter now," the poet shouts, grinning hugely. "Burn it. Use it to paper the walls of your father's wineshop. It's all nonsense anyway."

He calls out something else, but the captain swings his tiller and the skiff turns its stern full into the current, the words snatched away by the wind as the waters seize hold of the boat and fling it downstream like a pit spat from the mouth of the gods, the ship shooting through the foaming waters and vanishing into the mist, enveloped so swiftly that it is as though the tiny vessel and the poet it carries never existed at all.

epilogue

李白

"THOSE ARE HIS WORDS AND THAT IS HIS STORY. It remains only for me to add the last, sad stone to the pile, to say that halfway down the river he was suddenly gone, no comets blazing through the sky, no earthquake or flood. Some say that he flew away on a giant crane, others that he was carried off to the isles of Penglai on the back of a whale. Most believe that he died of drowning while drunk in a skiff one night, reaching out to catch the moon's reflection in the water. In fact, he contracted a cold after falling asleep late in the evening and allowing the dew to cover his head. This turned to water in the lungs, which finished him. He never saw her again, never had the chance to make his apologies, to fulfill that last promise. Who knows if he would have stayed or if they were destined to come together and be divided over and over again. I am haunted, though, by that last failure to close a chapter in his life, to seal over so deep a wound with a loving kiss.

"It seems that whatever the storytellers may make of a life, there is always this unfinished close. Oh, but how he would laugh hearing that come from me, would shout and say that by telling it thus I am, as always, chasing peevishly after an end to the story. And these days, as you see, I might even agree with him, for after a lifetime climbing the ladder of officialdom, living the life he despised, I turned again to this yellowing scroll, its contents still enough to have me flayed alive a thousand times over. Now, of course, I see much that I didn't when writing it down, much I wish I had taken heed of then, that might have led me on a different path. But mine is another tale, an ordinary story. So let us close with his words once again, his last poem, written on his deathbed. He calls it *The End*:

The great Roc which once
overshadowed the land,
staggers.
Its wings, which once
outpaced the sun's
nine-dragon chariot,
falter.

The stir it has created will last
a thousand generations;
But today, who will weep
tears at its passing,
She being far away in Yangchou
and the news requiring two months
to reach her?

notes 李白

I FIRST ENCOUNTERED LI PO (CIRCA 701–762 AD) when studying Chinese in Taiwan in the early 1980s. Li Po is one of only a handful of truly immortal Chinese poets, so I had of course heard his name and run across a few of his better-known poems. But it wasn't until I read Arthur Cooper's *Li Po and Tu Fu*, still one of the best English-language books about Chinese poetry, that I got a full sense of the genius of his poetry and the flamboyance of his character.

The sole biography of Li Po in English is by the great translator Arthur Waley, who sadly didn't find much to admire in the poet, or even in his poetry. Waley sums up the Li Po who comes across in his poems as "boastful, callous, dissipated, irresponsible, and untruthful."

In writing this novel, I have stuck as closely as I could to the events in Li Po's life about which most historians agree. Happily for fiction writers, Li Po's efforts to mythologize his own life and the legends woven around him after his death by others have made agreement on the details almost imposible.

The character of Peony is pure invention. Li Po did indeed have three wives, perhaps even four, but very little is known of them beyond the few references in his poems, not all of them polite. Hsueh Tao, however, is a real figure, albeit someone Li Po could never have met since she was born around the time that he died. I have taken the liberty of shifting Hsueh Tao's life back in time, and have used the excellent translations of her poems by Jeanne Larsen in *Brocade River Poems: Selected Works of the Tang Dynasty Courtesan Xue Tao*.

Much of the background material about Tang times comes from the extraordinary work of the Berkeley scholar Edward H. Schafer. Books such as *The Golden Peaches of Samarkand*, as well as his numerous scholarly articles, are bursting with glorious and sometimes bizarre details about life during China's "golden age."

As far as the poetry itself is concerned, attempting to reproduce the density of image, allusion, and meaning in some of Li Po's more mystical Taoist effusions has proved an overwhelming challenge even for scholarly translators, and is certainly beyond my meager learning. I have therefore confined myself primarily to the shorter and simpler poems, sometimes using existing translations, sometimes translating pieces myself.

In my own translations, I have, of course, leaned heavily on earlier efforts, particularly those by Shigeyoshi Obata, whose *The Works of Li Po* was published in 1922, but any mistakes are entirely my own. The verses written by Ezra Pound in his *Cathay*, based upon the notes of Ernest Fennelosa, sometimes bear only a family resemblance to the Li Po originals. Still, they are beautiful poetry, and I have used Pound's version of the "Letter from a River Merchant's Wife."

I had several other translations at hand while writing *A Floating Life,* notably *Li Pai 200 Selected Poems* translated by Rewi Alley, *Li Po: A New Translation* translated by Sun Yu, Arthur Cooper's previously mentioned *Li Po and Tu Fu,* and the seminal *The Great Age of Chinese Poetry: The High Tang* by Stephen Owen.

The quotations from the classics are taken from the following works: *Lao Tzu's Tao Te Ching* translated by D. C. Lau, *The Complete Works of Chuang Tzu* translated by Burton Watson, *Confucius, The Analects* translated by D. C. Lau, and the *Book of Songs* translated by Arthur Waley.

I would like to express my particular appreciation to my parents, Robert and Moira Elegant, for their comments, insightful as always. Also, Andrew Sherry and Bob Sherbin, to whom I am warmly grateful for taking the time to read the manuscript. My apologies, too, for what both describe as willfully ignoring their advice. I should also like to thank the staff of Hong Kong University's library, who were unfailingly polite in the face of my sometimes confused queries.

Thanks to Gordon Crovitz, Nayan Chanda, and V. G. Kulkarni, all of the *Far Eastern Economic Review*, who allowed me the time to finish this book. Both Sonia Land and Kathleen Anderson continued to believe in *A Floating Life*, despite considerable evidence that many others didn't, while the editors at The Ecco Press seem to understand better than I do what the novel is really about. Lastly, I'd like to thank my wife, Chee Yoke Ling, for her superhuman patience and consistent good cheer.

SDBE, Hong Kong
April 9, 1997

about the author 李白

Simon Elegant was born in Hong Kong in 1960 and studied Chinese history and language at the Universities of Pennsylvania and Cambridge. He has spent the last eleven years working as a journalist in Asia and is currently arts and society editor of the *Far Eastern Economic Review. A Floating Life* is his second book.